MORE THAN WANT YOU

A MORE THAN WORDS NOVEL

SHAYLA BLACK

more than
WANT
YOU

A MORE THAN WORDS NOVEL

New York Times
Shayla
BLACK
Bestselling Author

SHAYLA BLACK

Steamy. Emotional. Forever.

ONONDAGA FREE

MORE THAN WANT YOU
More Than Words, Book 1
Written by Shayla Black

This book is an original publication by Shayla Black.

Copyright 2017 Shelley Bradley LLC

Cover Design by: Rachel Connolly
Photographer: Sara Eirew Photographer
Edited by: Amy Knupp of Blue Otter
Proofread by: Fedora Chen

Excerpt from *More Than Need You* © 2017 by Shelley Bradley LLC
Excerpt from *Wicked as Sin* © 2020 by Shelley Bradley LLC

ISBN: 978-1-936596-40-9

PRAISE FOR *MORE THAN WANT YOU*

"Amazing! Everything I didn't even know I needed or wanted in a romance novel. Hot. Spicy. Addicting." - Rachel Van Dyken, #1 New York Times Bestselling Author

"Sexy, passionate and oh-so-clever! An intriguing love story!" - Lauren Blakely, #1 New York Times Bestselling Author

"You'll hate him and then you'll love him! A sexy read with a surprising twist." - Carly Phillips, New York Times Bestselling Author

PRAISE FOR *MORE THAN NEED YOU*

5 Stars! "I adore Shayla Black! She masterfully delivers story after story full of passion, love, heartbreak, and redemption." -Chasing Away Reality

5 Stars! "I love this book!!! It has all the elements that takes you on an emotional rollercoaster." -Romance Between The Sheets

PRAISE FOR *MORE THAN LOVE YOU*

5 Stars! "The perfect blend of romance, lust, love and standing in your own way. I love the story." – Alpha Book Club

5 Stars! "One of the best books I've read in months! I love this book!" – Magic Beyond The Covers Book Blog

PRAISE FOR *MORE THAN CRAVE YOU*

5 Stars! "With beautifully written characters and a storyline that I

could not put down this was a fabulous read. It needs more than 5 stars!!" –The Overflowing Bookcase

5 Stars! "…fun, hot and really hard to put down…loved it!"–Sissy's Romance Book Review

PRAISE FOR *MORE THAN TEMPT YOU*

5 Stars! "The More Than Words series is Shayla Black at her best—and this book is absolutely my favorite of the series so far." – USA Today bestselling author Angel Payne

5 Stars! "I nibbled my nails to nubs one minute and had to turn up the A/C the next. I enjoyed the hell out of every step of their journey and was sad to turn the final page. I wasn't ready for the goodness to end…sigh."– iScream Books Blog

ABOUT *MORE THAN WANT YOU*

I hired her to distract my enemy. Now I'm determined to have her for my own.

I'm Maxon Reed—real estate mogul, shark, asshole. If a deal isn't high profile and big money, I pass. Now that I've found the property of a lifetime, I'm jumping. But one tenacious bastard stands between me and success—my brother. I'll need one hell of a devious ploy to distract cynical Griff. Then fate drops a luscious redhead in my lap who's just his type.

Sassy Keeley Kent accepts my challenge to learn how to become Griff's perfect girlfriend. But somewhere between the makeover and the witty conversation, I'm having trouble resisting her. The quirky dreamer is everything I usually don't tolerate. But she's beyond charming. I more than want her; I'm desperate to own her. I'm not even sure how drastic I'm willing to get to make her mine—but I'm about to find out.

FOREWORD

There are infinite ways to tell someone you love them. Some of the most powerful don't require words at all. This was the truth rolling through my head when I first conceived of this series, writing about a love so complete that mere letters strung together to make sentences weren't an adequate communicator of those feelings. For Keeley and Maxon's story, music was my go-to choice.

I *love* music. I'm always immersed in it and spend hours a day with my earbuds plugged in. I write to music. I think to music. I even sleep to music. I was thrilled to incorporate songs into the story I felt were meaningful to the journey. I think of it this way: a movie has a soundtrack. Why shouldn't a book?

So I created one.

Some of the songs I've selected will be familiar. Some are old. Some are newer. Some popular. Some obscure. They all just fit (in my opinion) and came straight from the heart. I listened to many of these songs as I wrote the book.

For maximum understanding (and feels), I seriously recommend becoming familiar with these songs and either playing them or rolling them around in your head as you read. Due to copyright laws, I can't use exact lyrics, but I tried to give you the gist of those most meaningful to Maxon and Keeley's story. So I've made it simple for you to give them a listen by creating a Spotify playlist. Click here for all the enjoyment.

Hugs and happy reading!

I TOUCH MYSELF - The Divinyls
MAKIN' WHOOPEE - Rachel MacFarlane
I PUT A SPELL ON YOU - Annie Lennox
HANDS TO MYSELF - Selena Gomez
I'M A WOMAN - Peggy Lee
WICKED GAME - Chris Isaak
CAN'T FEEL MY FACE - The Weeknd
LOVE THE WAY YOU LIE - Skylar Grey
BIG GIRLS DON'T CRY - Fergie
SOMEONE LIKE YOU - Adele
NEED YOU NOW - Lady Antebellum
WHEN YOU'RE GONE - Avril Lavigne
IT MUST HAVE BEEN LOVE - Roxette
WICHITA LINEMAN - Glen Campbell
I CAN'T MAKE YOU LOVE ME - Bonnie Raitt
COFFEE AND CIGARETTES - Michelle Featherstone
I WANT YOU HERE - Plumb
I GET TO LOVE YOU - Ruelle

Other mentions:
WIDE AWAKE - Katy Perry
LIKE A VIRGIN - Madonna
BUTTONS - Pussycat Dolls
SMOOTH CRIMINAL - Alien Ant Farm

WAITING ON THE WORLD TO CHANGE - John Mayer

DON'T LET THE SUN GO DOWN ON ME - Elton John

TITANIUM - David Guetta w / Sia

BOHEMIAN RHAPSODY – Queen

DEDICATION

This book could not have been possible without the support of some of the dearest people in my life, those who are with me every single day…in one way or another.

Rachel Connolly. My friend, my right hand, my litmus test for tears — not to mention one hell of a cover designer, assistant, and person. Thank you so much for believing we'd finally get to work on this project and embracing it as wholly as you did.

William Black. My husband, my other half, my reason for being able to open up and write this. It goes without saying that you're behind me always, that you listen to me (even when it's after midnight and you're trying to sleep), and that you love me unconditionally. Thanks for being as enthusiastic as I am!

Jenna Jacob. All the late-night phone calls and listening to me go on and on when I was stuck and unsure. Thanks for stopping what you were doing to just hear me. Sometimes that means more than anything.

I must also thank (with big squishy hugs) Baby Black for being not just my daughter but my friend and often my partner in makeup, reality TV, and silly ice cream crimes. Shannon Hunt deserves kudos for expanding her musical horizons so quickly for this story and still speaking to me when I left her in beta-reading, cliffhanging hell. Lexi Blake for insisting that I should. Isabella LaPearl for your excellent vocal skills and critical questions, and reminding me that I could. My late beloved Meow because losing you made me think so hard about communicating love to another being, which is part of when and how I realized that words weren't always possible…or necessary. I hope you're enjoying your life over the rainbow bridge.

Thanks also to Liz Berry and Shayla Freshetian for beta reading, commenting, and giving me your excitement!

You are all wonderful and I feel so blessed!

CHAPTER ONE

Maxon

"*I*'m fucked." I sink into a wooden chair at a high-top inside the dingy sports bar, almost smearing the sleeve of my suit coat through mustard. Britta and Rob, my tireless staff, love this place. For them, I choke down a slab of greasy beef on a soggy bun, surrounded by drunk tourists and neon Bud Light signs, once a week. But not happily.

Then again, Lahaina isn't exactly bursting with five-star dining choices. Maui is a quaint paradise, smaller than you think. Its size works both for and against me at times. This is definitely an against occasion.

"Maybe not, Maxon," Britta counters with a frown. "The call went better than expected."

I'll give her that since Mike Sperry, the attorney representing the filthy-rich Stowe estate, at least listened. Figuratively speaking, I hustled to the "party" late and barged my way through the door without an invitation. But that's real estate. No one ever earns multimillion-dollar years by sitting back and letting the properties come to them.

"I have to agree," Rob cuts in, pushing a feathered wing of his salt-and-pepper hair from his eyes.

I want to tell my marketing manager to ditch the eighties 'do. He looks stuck in a time warp. His somewhat steady girlfriend aside, I'm shocked he'd ever got laid.

"Why?" I challenge.

"At least Sperry agreed to pass your proposal on to the Stowe heirs. You're the number one real estate agent on Maui, and it's ridiculous you didn't get the call to start with. But with you persuading them while Britta and I work the angles...if we get this listing, the social media campaign—and the buzz—will be amazing. Almost easy money."

Despite looking like someone who crawled out of *The Breakfast Club*, Rob is killer with sound bites and live video. He knows how to make buyers desperate to see a house. Sadly, the enthusiasm doesn't always last through escrow.

I scoff at him. "*If*. But I don't just want to list this place. I want both sides of the transaction."

Persuading the seller to list with me *and* finding the perfect buyer will be a challenge. Which is one reason I want to do it.

But not the only reason.

Rob winces. "With all due respect, one step at a time. Focus on convincing Mrs. Stowe's kids to choose you and keep your ego out of this."

"With all due respect, fuck you. This isn't about my ego." Well, not entirely.

Britta rolls her eyes as our waitress greets us by name—a clear sign we come here too often—and takes our orders. While Rob is asking about some new Pan-Asian crap on their limited menu, I mentally sort through our recent meeting. One issue disturbs me. I tried to ignore it on the drive over…but it's not working. My suspicion still tugs and pokes. It has since we ended the call.

I glance at my staff. "Sperry said there's one other agent in competition for this listing. Based on the description he gave, who do you think that is?"

Rob falls silent. Britta suddenly finds the drink menu fascinating. So they've figured it out. Good. I hire smart people for a reason.

"Yeah. It's my brother. *That's* why I want to both list and sell." It's also most likely why I'm fucked.

"You're better than he is," Rob argued.

In some ways, yes. In other ways… Griff has always been brilliant at connecting buyers with the perfect-for-them house. It's an instinct. He creates emotional bonds between people with ready cash and the big-ass mansions with to-die-for views they crave, even half a world away. It's one reason we made a great team. I sniffed out great properties and closed the listing appointments, promising the sellers the fucking world if they simply signed on the dotted line for ninety days. I always market upscale properties with far more than the standard pansy-ass cocktail party of air kisses and champagne. But Griff has a knack for matching buyers with the place they'll fall head over heels for that I lack. Between the two of us, our closing rate was sick.

Then came the debacle with that obscure prince. Then the Tiffanii fuckup. After that…well, we haven't spoken in three years. To say we loathe one another now would be kind.

"I appreciate the vote of confidence"—I nod Rob's way—"but you're biased because I sign your paycheck. The truth is, Griff has gotten shit-tons better at snaring sellers." This part of the deal is still my game to lose, but since I'm not the estate's first choice, I could easily strike out. Or fail to kick the game-winning field goal. Hell, insert the sports metaphor of your choice. "With the Stowe heirs hunkered down with the business they inherited, Griff and I both have four weeks to perfect our pitches. It's essential I lead with something beyond spectacular. Or I have one hell of a plan B. I need ideas. And…go."

Because it isn't every day an oceanfront estate worth nearly thirty million dollars lands on the market. The commission on one side of this deal could reach seven-figure territory, but to get paid by both buyer and seller… I would earn half my usual annual haul in a single transaction, probably well before June. It makes the Realtor in me hard.

But beating Griff would be way more exciting than the cash.

"I think we go in big with a slick video of your endorsements and awards." Rob nods, warming to his subject. "Then show these brats from Vermont everything they don't understand about the Hawaii lifestyle."

Britta shakes her head. "Rubbing a seller's face in what you think they don't grasp is a surefire way to annoy them. The point is to prove why Maxon is the right listing agent." She turns to me. "We have to give them big-picture ideas for how you're going to get quality buyers onto the grounds so they can fall in love. We stress your cache of foreign contacts—China, Russia, UAE—you can bring in the big-money people who won't think much of dropping that kind of cash on the perfect vacation house. We show them the creative ways you've sold before. Your close rate is pretty insane."

"You know Griff's is better. That's what they want. Quick close. All cash." I lean across the table to her. "You're looking at this wrong. Yes, I'm better at listing than my brother, but the seller is already half convinced that Griff is their guy, probably because no one finds the perfect buyer and brings them to the closing table faster."

"So you have to beat the champ at his own game." Rob sighs, sounding like he finally understands my proclamation that I'm fucked.

There's no way to top Griff. He's got a goddamn natural gift.

"Okay, your brother might find a buyer a week or two earlier." Britta shrugs. "But you're the better man."

"They don't give a shit about that."

"You always come through," she argues.

"To the people dying to unload this estate so they can cash out, those seven days make a five-figure difference in their bank account. Besides, they don't know the Maui market. And they don't know me except as the pushy salesman who barged in. They certainly don't know my reputation except through boring statistics and my own claims, which they probably see as bragging. It sounds as if Susan Stowe was fond of Griff, so she picked him. Her heirs would need a damn good reason to cross her wishes."

My brother would have to fuck up badly. And he never does. Well, almost never…unless there's a gorgeous woman involved. Unlike me, he has a bad habit of allowing his dick to distract him. Always has. That's how he started fooling around with Britta at the office once upon a time. Too bad he's not having a torrid fuckfest with someone high maintenance now—at least not according to my spies. A good hourglass-shaped distraction in Griff's bed would sure help my cause.

As the waitress sets down our drinks, the lights dim. Everyone turns to the stage at one end of the cramped sports bar. Ah, the live entertainment. After the tragic act last week, I was hoping we would miss the show.

But then I see her.

Crooked smile. Pink hair. Winged black liner over laughing blue eyes. Vivid red lipstick. Tacky cheetah-print dress. Tiny waist. Sleek legs. Chunky black heels that have seen better days. I don't think I would have looked at her twice normally, but she's got two things going for her: an obvious zest for life and a great rack.

Griff can't resist either.

I turn in my chair to watch as she grabs the microphone with deft confidence. She's comfortable on stage.

"Aloha, Lahaina. I'm Keeley Sunshine. I'm going to sing you

some of my favorite songs, and since I'm a single girl in the middle of a long drought, they'll probably all be about sex. You can buy me drinks after the set if you'd like to change that." She winks.

She's got a certain charm. Griff values that, along with a sense of humor.

"I'd be more than happy to end her drought," Rob whispers in my ear as the small band nods at one another.

Keeley Sunshine—clearly not her real name—closes her eyes as the primal beat of the music rises to a quirky old tune. It's familiar. I know I've heard the song but I'm having trouble placing it, until the chorus. Then, while she sways her hips to the beat, she's belting out that she doesn't want anybody else. She just thinks about me and touches herself.

Oh, yeah.

Less than thirty seconds; that's how long it takes me to have my first boner for her. And I'm a tough customer. At thirty-three, I'm not used to adjusting my dick or embarrassing myself around a girl. That stuff happened, like, fifteen years ago.

As she deftly transitions to the second verse, I picture her naked, pretty tits pointing at the ceiling, legs in the air. In my head, she's got a bare pussy, which I realize may not be accurate, but that's how she looks in fantasy. Griff likes them smooth, too—about the only thing we agree on anymore.

When Keeley assures everyone in the room she would get down on her knees and do anything for whomever she's singing to, she's not looking at anyone in particular.

She ought to be looking at me.

But she seems lost in the song, in her passion for the music. She's got a surprisingly smooth voice with just a hint of rasp. Another check in her plus column.

As the song winds toward the end, her oohs and aahs grow breathier and louder, higher-pitched. Shit, she's having a choral orgasm center stage. And yeah, I squirm, fighting the urge to pry my hard dick off the teeth of my zipper. I can't help it. I'm a guy, and Keeley Sunshine drips sex.

The old Divinyls classic ends to hearty applause. I have to agree that this vixen is a musical savant compared to last week's squeaky screen door on repeat. At a tap of Keeley's toe—I notice her nail polish is black—the band begins the next tune.

Old jazz, the kind you drink to, so easy it makes you smile. But they've modernized it with guitars and drums. Still, I know this tune well because my granddad loved it. Eddie Cantor's 1929 classic "Makin' Whoopee." But she sings it like Rachel MacFarlane, smooth and vampy.

I gotta admit, I'm mesmerized. I can't stop watching her mouth. Her lips are bee-stung and would look great wrapped around a cock. Mine, for instance.

When the jazz standard ends to even more enthusiastic applause, Keeley picks another decades-old tune. I suspect she's got an old soul. It fits her slightly retro vibe.

After a sexy, rhythmic intro, she drags in a deep breath, nearly kissing the mic, and uses her breathy voice to say that she put a spell on me because I'm hers. Right now, I can't argue, especially when her words sparkle brighter than glitter.

Listening to her, I get chills.

Britta leans closer, lips near my ear. "Put your tongue back in your mouth."

I shoot her a quelling glance, but she's right. Under normal circumstances, I'd wait for Keeley Sunshine's set to end, buy her a strong drink, and sweet-talk my way into her panties for the night. But right now the needs of my business outweigh the needs of my dick.

If Griff could see this woman, especially if I cleaned her up a bit, he'd be all over her. In fact, that's a great idea. I need to figure out how to hook the two of them up—fast—so he stops thinking about the Stowe estate with all those beachfront views.

Still, I can't suggest that to Britta without upsetting her.

"Blow me," I murmur instead.

Britta scoffs. "No, thanks. You're an asshole."

"I am." That's something I'm proud of. Best way to get ahead in business.

"It runs in the Reed family."

She's right. My old man is an impeccable textbook example of a puckered anus, too. From him, I learned well. Vaguely, I wonder which pretty young thing he's banging in his office while my mom buries her head in some all-talk/no-action ladies' function, but they've moved to San Diego. It's no longer my problem. I'm only irritated they took my younger sister but didn't persuade Griff to shove off with them. He's a total sphincter.

Keeley hits and holds a growly high note that demands my attention. Her voice sneaks behind my fly and wraps around my cock. Her puffy lips are mobile and soft. Her dress exaggerates the womanly curve of her hips, which she swings as she roars out the last note.

I might have thought I wouldn't look at her twice, but that's bullshit. I could definitely listen to her for hours. And I think I could do her all night long.

As her final note trails off, the applause is even louder, like the audience has realized she's pretty damn amazing.

She blushes as she laughs off our reaction. Her smile quickly proves to be the most beautiful thing about her. White, blinding, real. She's enjoying the crowd and yet seems almost surprised by their enthusiasm.

With a swing of her long pink hair, her curls catch the light, then fall gracefully over her shoulders. She shrugs at her guitar player, an old man who looks impressed.

"This will be our last song for the set. If you have requests, write them down and leave them in the jar." She points to the clear vessel at her feet. "We'll be back to play in thirty. If you have a dirty proposition, I'll entertain them at the bar in five." She says the words like she's kidding.

I, however, am serious. In fact, I'm really pondering this whole situation.

Keeley starts her next song, a more recent pop tune. In a breathy, a cappella murmur she admits that she can't keep her hands to herself no matter how hard she's trying to.

Personally, I'd rather she didn't try at all.

She taps her thigh in a rhythm only she can hear until the band joins during the crescendo to the chorus. Keeley bounces her way through the lyrics with a flirty smile. It's both alluring and fun, a tease of a song.

Though I rarely smile, I find myself grinning along.

As she finishes, I glance around. There's more than one hungry dog with a bone in this damn bar.

I didn't get ahead in business or life by being polite or waiting my turn. She hasn't even wrapped her vocal cords around the last note, but I'm on my feet and charging across the room.

I'm the first one to reach the corner of the bar closest to the stage. I prop my elbow on the slightly sticky wood to claim my territory, then glare back at the three other men who think they should end Keeley's supposed sex drought. They are not watering her garden, and my snarl makes that clear.

One sees my face, stops in his tracks, and immediately backs off. Smart man.

Number Two looks like a smarmy car salesman. He rakes Keeley up and down with his gaze like she's a slab of beef, but she's flirting my way as she tucks her mic on its stand. Our eyes meet. I smile back.

She may not be my usual type, but the attraction is real. Man, I'd love to hit that.

Out of the corner of my eye, I watch the approaching dirtbag finger his porn 'stache. To stake my claim, I reach out to help Keeley off the stage. She looks pleasantly surprised by my gesture as she wraps her fingers around mine.

I can be a gentleman…when it suits me.

Fuck, she's warm and velvety, and her touch makes my cock jolt. Her second would-be one-night stand curses, then slinks back to his seat.

That leaves me to fend off Number Three. He looks like a WWE reject—hulking and hit in the face too many times. If she prefers brawn over brains, I'll have to find another D-cup distraction for Griff.

That would truly suck. My gut tells me that Keeley, with a little sprucing up, will be perfect for the job.

"Get lost," I mutter to the steroid junkie.

"You gonna make me?" he challenges, all but baring his teeth.

"No," Keeley murmurs, her voice husky and assured. "I'm going to tell you I've found someone else I'd like to get to know and ask you nicely to leave us in peace."

"Baby, if you want to end your drought"—he cups his junk—"I've got nine inches of what you need."

She raises an auburn brow at him. "First, no means no, and if you haven't learned that, I don't want anything to do with you. Second, it sounds like you've measured your penis. That kind of guy usually exaggerates, so reality is probably more like five inches. Maybe five and a quarter if I'm being generous. Either way—"

"That's not fucking true. My cock is massive." He sidles closer. "Come with me and I'll show you."

She brushes his hands away and grips the hell out of his balls. His eyes bug out, but she keeps talking with an almost pleasant smile. "I have no interest in seeing it when you're too rude to know that you shouldn't interrupt someone, much less how to bow out gracefully. Also, I'm a grown-ass woman. Don't call me baby."

"Okay," Hulk squeaks.

I manage not to laugh aloud—barely. He's a foot taller and outweighs her by a hundred pounds, but she's got his full attention.

"Now turn your ass around and find your seat."

She pries her fingers off his nuts but leaves them hovering right there in case he decides to get another case of the stalker-creepies. But Hulk Moron finally rubs two brain cells together and backs away, cupping his junk. He's either too cautious or too sore to turn his back on her. When he reaches his table, his buddies are all ribbing him as they rise and laugh their way out the door.

"I'm not sure whether I should be afraid or impressed," I flirt her way. "If you treat all new guys to that patented ball-busting maneuver, your drought isn't really the surprise I imagined when you first mentioned it."

Keeley shakes her head, grinning wide. "I know his type. I grew up in a rough neighborhood with macho guys like him. They only understand a few things. Potentially being a eunuch is one of them." She thrusts out her hand. "Keeley."

"Maxon." I shake her hand, more as an excuse to touch her again. There's still an electric arc between us. A jolt. My blood turns hot. This girl has something. "Can I buy you a drink?"

"Sure. Crown and Coke." She rubs her hands together nervously.

Nice that I get to her. I shouldn't be the only one trying to keep my cool intact.

As I watch her, I spot a tattoo of a musical note on the inside of her wrist. Small and pretty. Feminine but interesting. Does she have more ink? It's not something I usually like on a woman—mostly because I'm not into anything permanent—but this seems to fit Keeley.

"Is that okay?" she asks.

Damn it, my thoughts have been drifting. "Absolutely. I was mentally exploring the ways I might suggest we end your 'drought.' Want to hear my ideas?"

"Not before booze and my next set. After that, if you're still here and interesting...then I just might."

I like the way she banters. And meets my gaze. So many women do that shy, coy thing. I'm not into feeling as if I intimidate lovers.

Rivals? Oh, yeah. All day. That shit's fantastic. Not so much with bedmates. But Keeley meets my stare head on—no flinching—still wearing that hint of a smile that's getting to me.

"I'll be here. I'll make sure you still think I'm interesting. And I won't call you baby." I turn and motion to the bartender, who starts pouring Keeley's Crown and Coke, along with my dirty Grey Goose martini.

"So you're a smart man, then?"

"I try to be."

"You dress well," she observes as she rakes me up and down.

"You dress like a woman who doesn't mind attention." My stare caresses every one of her curves.

No discounting or discarding the truth. I want her.

It's pretty fucking inconvenient when I need her to distract my brother more...but I'm flexible. Maybe there's a way for everyone in this picture to be happy—except Griff.

"I figured if I was finally going to go on stage, I should wear something eye-catching. Good to know I succeeded." The bartender sets our drinks in front of us, and she takes a swig.

Damn, that mouth. Those plush, red lips.

"What do you mean, finally? You've never performed in public?"

"Not really." She smiles and shrugs, her expression saying she may have jumped off the deep end for the hell of it. "I've done a lot of karaoke, which I love. People have said I have a good voice. So I thought...why not try it for real? If people boo me off the stage, then I'll know all my friends are full of it. And then I'll plot revenge, of course."

"Of course," I rush to agree. "But there's no way you would be booed. You're pretty incredible."

"My one practice with the band a few hours ago paid off. Yeah!" She giggles.

I can't help but laugh in kind as I stare at her, cold drink in hand. I can usually figure out the perfect way to proposition a woman. I'm good with charm. But Keeley is different, I think. She's not going to fall for the usual you're-pretty/your-eyes-sparkle BS. But she's easy to talk to, and if my goal was merely to pick her up, I'm sure I could think of something that would persuade her to get naked and horizontal.

Instead, I'm wondering…would it be really awful if I slept with her before I introduced her to my brother? That sounds skeevy, I know. But I'm totally able to separate business from pleasure. Besides, if we have a one-night stand, we'll inevitably part ways in the morning. What's the harm in seeing if we can scratch each other's backs in a different way after the sheets cool?

Actually, the worry nagging at the back of my brain is that she seems so genuine, asking her to deceive and derail my brother will be counter to her nature and earn me one of those unpleasant ball strangulations that might alter my ability to father kids. Hopefully, once I spend some time with her and understand her a bit better, I'll find the words to tell her what I want without totally pissing her off.

"You're really great," I compliment her. "Seriously."

"Thanks. Can you sing?"

"Not a note," I assure her.

"Wow, you didn't hesitate an instant before you answered."

"I know my shortcomings. I mean, I don't have many," I assure with a wink. "But that one is too obvious to overlook."

"So you're tone deaf but otherwise perfect. And obviously humble, too." She raises an auburn brow at me.

"No. In my business, being humble doesn't pay."

The little furrow between her sparkly, purple-shadowed eyes snags my gaze. "You're a doctor?"

"Real estate agent. Number one on Maui."

"So if I scraped some money together and wanted to buy a condo, you're the guy I should call?"

"I could help you find the right agent. I deal exclusively in luxury properties. Normally, I don't touch a place under four

million. Time is money, and unless you treat the first as if it's in
short supply, the second will be, too."

She gives me an assessing gaze as she sips more of her drink.
"Interesting philosophy. I never thought about it like that."

"So what do you do? If you're not making a living from your
voice—and I think you can—what's your occupation?"

"I don't really have one, per se. I have a couple of odd jobs. I
waitress a couple days a week at one of the swanky hotels in
Wailea. I spend about ten hours a week doing admin work for a
psychotherapist down the street. On weekends, I teach some
group exercise classes to seniors and help a zip-line crew with
big groups." She shrugs. "Whatever helps me pay tuition and
makes ends meet. Right now, I don't take anything too
seriously."

Not taking something seriously is foreign to me. I've always
attacked life. Business, workouts, even trivia games. I've been
programed to require winning and given the disposition to do
whatever necessary to make it happen. Though I don't understand
Keeley's attitude, I don't think I'd change it. She's made me smile a
lot in the last five minutes, probably more than I have all week.
That's her laid-back charm.

Griff will love it, too. I try not to think about that just now.

"You're still in college?"

"Yep. At twenty-five, I sometimes feel like the grandma of the
classroom, but I prefer doing school in the mornings after yoga,
when I'm fresh. Night school is for bitter workaholics."

I smile. "You mean like me?"

She cringes. "You went to night school? Sorry…"

I shrug. "No offense taken."

"You're driven, aren't you? You probably finished your degree
in four years."

"Actually, I finished a bachelor's and a master's in four years
while growing a full-time real estate business."

She looks shocked. "Did you ever sleep?"

"It's overrated, and another one of those things I'm not very good at. That's fine. I have more important things to do."

Her expression says she can't imagine what but she politely doesn't say so. "So, Maxon, the workaholic real estate agent who puts me to shame academically, what do you do for fun?"

Interesting question. "Besides close big deals? Well...I like a good game of pool. I read a lot."

"Fiction? It's a good escape. I read tons. And I love self-help. I'm reading this book called *Riding the Wings of Joy* about finding inner peace and—"

"Not what I meant." I laugh. "One of my favorite books is *Master the Close* about killer sales techniques. I also read a lot of trade mags about turning lookers into buyers, that kind of thing. I also need to keep up with the latest in landscaping, staging, marketing... I'm always reading. Any edge I can get over the competition is one I'll take."

I plant that seed. I'll give it time to germinate in her head. Tomorrow, I'll see if I can harvest it.

"So no meditation for you, I guess," she teased.

"How do you keep your mind still that long?" I really can't imagine.

"It's an art. I learn every day new ways to exercise self-control."

It sounds like a crock of shit to me. My base instinct is to crush competitors and seduce beautiful women. I don't see any reason to change that.

"Fantastic," I assure her.

She laughs. "You're a terrible liar."

The owner of the downscale bar trips over a couple of cords as he stumbles his way to the mic and grabs it. "Keeley Sunshine again, everyone."

While the audience applauds, the vivacious beauty beside me chugs down the last of her Crown and Coke. "Gotta go. If you're still here when my last set ends...we'll see."

"I'll be here."

Once Keeley hits the stage, I return to the table to find Britta gathering her purse. "You're leaving?"

She nods. "I can't sit here and watch you pick up yet another woman you'll probably never be serious about. I know you believe in the work-hard-play-hard thing, but when are you going to truly give a relationship even half that much effort? You wasted years pretending with Tiffanii. Invest in your heart for once. Fall in love. Care about someone who can love you back. Worry less about closing the deal and open yourself to someone who can share your life. Or you're going to wind up bitter."

Like my old man. And my brother. I've heard this speech. Britta brings this up more often these days, especially when we're away from the office and she's had a glass of wine or two. "I don't see you till-death-do-us-parting."

"I tried. God knows I did. I couldn't want forever more than Griff."

Instantly, I feel contrite. She's right, and if my bastard of a brother hadn't broken her heart so utterly, she would have loved him until she died. I volunteered to break every bone in his miserable body on her behalf. At the time, it would have made me feel good. She refused to let me. In her words, if he didn't care enough about her to stay, then she didn't want him feeling obligated to hang around.

"You were right to let him go, Britta."

"Damn right I was. And I started dating again within a few months. I'm still open to something serious. I think this thing with Makaio is leading somewhere. He's a good guy." She shrugs. "If it doesn't work out, at least I'll know I'm not alone for lack of trying. I'll see you tomorrow."

Then she's gone, pushing her way out the door and into the night.

Rob tosses down some bills to pay the check. "You owe me, buddy."

I nod absently. "What's with her?"

"You know Britta. She might be younger than us but she's a mother hen. She thinks you're wasting your life alone. If it makes you feel any better, she'd like to see me on the matrimony train, too. In her words, I either love Alania or I don't. So I should move forward or move on. Maybe she's right." He pauses. "About both of us. G'night."

I frown, puzzled. "Night."

Calling for another martini, I toss their words around in my head and focus on Keeley. I'm a man of my word, waiting through two more sets of sensually dipped songs, everything from the Peggy Lee classic "I'm a Woman" to Chris Isaak's "Wicked Game" to "Can't Feel My Face" by The Weeknd. I love that she's both musically eclectic and well-versed. Tunes are something we have in common. I'll do my best to dazzle her later at my place with killer views and my deep playlist. Maybe that will impress her. I'm not sure my…ahem…sparkling personality did that earlier.

Finally, she tucks her mic onto the stand for the final time and gives the enthusiastic crowd a playful little curtsy. The ovation becomes a standing exercise in adulation. She looks thrilled.

"You killed it," I assure her when she heads my way.

"It's really a rush. I wasn't sure if I could do it without the vocal track in the background to keep me on key. But once I stopped worrying about it and just relaxed, everything came together."

"You're a natural."

"I'd love to make a living at this, but who does? I'm hardly going to be the next Adele, so…I'll focus on finishing school. But before the last set started, Gus, the guy who owns this place, asked me if I'd be interested in playing again, so I've got a gig on Saturday night." She shrugs. "It will be fun if nothing else."

"That's great. I'm sure you'll do well. You've got something."

"You're saying that to get in my panties," she challenges with a grin.

"Well…yeah. But I actually mean it."

Her smile becomes a laugh. "Fair enough. So what's next?"

"I thought I'd feed you, then take you back to my evil lair, ply you with good booze, then seduce you."

"It sounds like you really thought through that plan. I'll be way more amenable to seduction after some protein, veggies, and sugar. If you want a sure thing, I'm partial to crème brûlée."

"Aren't you helpful, aiding me in your own downfall?"

"Right?" She nods. "I just need to grab my purse from the back."

"I'll be waiting."

Minutes later, she appears with a slouchy hobo bag that I think is meant to be some shade of brown. The tab to the zipper is missing, so the purse hangs open, but she's offset all that by tying a colorful scarf at the base of the handle and dangling some little charms off the loop of the shoulder strap. I've got to give her style points.

"Japengo sound good? I hear the crème brûlée is killer."

"So this isn't a run through the convenience store for Boone's Farm, followed by the Taco Bell drive-thru? Impressive."

"You describing your last date?"

"Basically. So you really are a gentleman. Or more determined to get laid."

"Probably both." I smile. I'm not sure closing the deal with Keeley is going to be as easy as she makes it sound, but I can be persistent and persuasive.

Tomorrow is soon enough to tell her I want her to distract my brother.

CHAPTER TWO

As we leave the restaurant with full stomachs, I lead her to the valet stand. The night—like so many others in Maui—is balmy, slightly breezy. It's heaven. I might not have loved moving here as a teenager because being pale and green-eyed hardly made me liked by all my native public school peers. But now that adolescence is behind me, I admit that I love the temperate, year-round weather.

Once the valet pulls up in my new vehicle, I edge the teenager out of my way and help Keeley into the passenger's seat. She strokes my Range Rover Evoque convertible in Waitomo Gray. It's almost sexual watching her touch my car, which is great for showing clients the best of Maui, top down, while sporty enough to keep me from feeling like I'm driving my old man's Lincoln.

After tipping the valet, I climb in beside her and take the wheel. As I pull away, I wonder what the night will bring. I feel an urge to ensure she doesn't slip through my fingers, so I rack my brain for some way to impress her—beyond the expensive Japanese food, the hot car, and my stylish suit. She's not a tourist, so I doubt I can wow her with sights around the island. So...I'll have to rely on conversation. Not my first choice. But she looks relaxed, almost happy. I'll go with the presumptive close and see if that will get this deal done.

"That was the best crème brûlée I've ever had." She puts a hand to her stomach. "Good wine. Good company. Good evening."

"It could get even better." I send her a wry grin. "I could ask you if you'd like to come to my place to see my art collection…"

"You don't have any art, do you?" She laughs. "If I'm wrong, I'll be shocked."

I shake my head.

"You're too driven and bottom-line to spend money on old stuff to watch it gather dust."

"Bingo."

"And you'd never stop to simply stare and appreciate it."

That sounds faintly like an admonishment, though I'm not sure she means it that way. Maybe Britta's speech is still lingering in my brain. "You've got me pegged, sunshine. I can think of a lot of things I'd rather spend time on. And people I'd rather spend it with."

As we stop at a light, the trees part. The moon glows on her skin. She looks alabaster and flawless with her soft smile. Her blue eyes seem to shine silver. I can't remember the last time I found a woman so beautiful.

"Come home with me. No pressure. No bullshit. Just you and me and all the pleasure we can stand."

She reaches across the console and drops her hand on my thigh. My whole fucking body lurches, and it takes all my restraint not to pull over, rip off my seat belt—along with her dress—and get as deep inside her as I can.

When did I turn into a caveman?

"Yes." Her one word has me sweating. I can just imagine how perfect she'll feel against me once I have her naked in my bed.

Traffic is thin now. Maybe if I run a light or two, we'll make it to my condo in the next five minutes. Screw that. I'm shooting for three.

"I like you," she elaborates. "I never spend the night with a stranger. Seriously. But I guess there's a first time for everything. You...kind of do it for me, so yeah."

"Kind of?" Okay, I feel myself preening, but come on. This quirky, amazing, funny girl is into me. "You kind of do it for me, too."

She gives me that crooked smile I noticed when I first laid eyes on her. Just like then, my chest beats in some mad rhythm, like John Bonham himself is pounding out a signature Zeppelin drum solo on my heart. I'm a sucker for classic rock. Sue me.

I'm pretty sure my driving is worth a speeding ticket as I head up Highway 30 toward my place. When we reach the complex, Keeley turns to me. "The Ritz? You're bringing me to a hotel?"

I chuckle. "I live here. It's a residence, too. I get all the hotel's amenities as a part of my homeowner's dues."

She still looks confused. "Don't you have tourists underfoot all the time?"

"Not in my building, and some facilities are reserved just for the owners. We always get the first and best service. The food is decent. The housekeeping staff is fantastic. It works for me."

As I drive through the gated entrance, I glance over at her wide eyes. She looks dazzled, and I'm feeling good about giving her an early thrill before the good stuff starts.

"You like it?"

"I totally take back whatever I said. It's beautiful here. The grounds..."

"They're meticulous. And people rave about the views of the water."

"I love the ocean. It's why I came here."

"You moved here just to see the Pacific from Maui?" To me, the view of the ocean is pretty much the same all over Hawaii. L.A.

isn't much different from Honolulu, honestly. Just a few more palm trees and Hawaiian street names.

"Not exactly. I came with an ex-boyfriend because we wanted to see the views around the island. But we could only afford a one-way ticket. We figured we'd work all winter at a resort or something, save a little, then fly back home when we were ready."

"But you loved it so much you decided to stay?"

"No. After work one day, I returned to our little shithole apartment to find that he'd moved out, taken our savings, and flown to Denver."

"Bastard."

She shrugs. "It wasn't going to last. He liked smoking pot more than working, which explains why he headed to Colorado, not home. Besides, the sex was really average."

Keeley doesn't look like she's brokenhearted over this jerk, but I know how crazy someone hung up on the wrong person can behave. Griff was such a dumb ass about Tiffanii.

As I pull up to the front of my building in resident parking, I kill the engine. "How long ago was that?"

"Almost three years go."

She surprises the hell out of me with that answer. "You've stayed here all this time? You must like it. Maui is paradise, right?" I toss over my shoulder as I step out of the car and jog around to her side, then open her door.

"I could never afford the roof over my head and a plane ticket off the island at the same time. In the ages-old tradition of saying 'I told you so,' my mom won't lend me the money to leave. So...here I am." She stands. "Can we talk about something else?"

"Sure." I shut the car door and lock it as I lead her toward my unit.

I want to keep things light between us. If I'm going to ask her tomorrow to tempt my brother into losing his mind, I don't need to get too involved in her life. We're here to have a good time. Yet all these questions run through my head. How long had she and dirtbag been together? Keeley seems to have a soft heart, so how devastated had she been by his betrayal? Has she found it hard to forget this guy? Already I know the sex between the two of us won't be anything but amazing, but I wonder if she still misses the ex. Will she think of him—even accidentally—while I'm inside her?

Okay, I need to stop that train of thought. What the hell is wrong with me? I never ask questions, much less want to know a one-night stand's personal shit. We have a few drinks, a few laughs, a few orgasms, then it's over. I give her a fond memory, and we move on. I don't remember anything more than her name—if that.

Already, I'm pretty sure Keeley will be different.

Worry less about closing the deal and open yourself to someone who can share your life.

Damn it, Britta needs to get out of my head.

Keeley follows me up the stairs with a grateful nod and stands quietly while I unlock the door at the end of the breezeway. It's a pretty standard layout: short hall, closet on the right, kitchen with a bar top overlooking the living room on the left. Hardwoods, granite. It's neutral. I wonder what she thinks.

Keeley barely looks at it. She heads straight for my balcony, which overlooks a portion of the pools and a nice slice of the ocean. It tends to be quieter on this side of the complex. All that will totally help with resale someday.

"Wow, this is amazing." She sinks down into a patio chair, looking mesmerized, and stares at the moonlight beading over the quiet grounds and the waves crashing with a dull thud in the distance. "You must spend all your time out here."

"No." I can't remember the last time I even opened the lanai door. Sure, I look at the view through my window, but to just sit out there? "I'm not home that much."

"Seriously? I'd find reasons to be home. I'd *live* out here. I could clear a spot for meditation. Studying with this view would be fantastic. The sound of waves helps me concentrate. I'd eat out here…" She turns to me. "And you never use it?"

Her words feel like an indictment, and my knee-jerk reaction is to defend myself. "I don't really have time. Drink?"

"Sure. I'll take a glass of wine." She turns to me as I head back to the kitchen. "But when you're home, you don't come out here just to enjoy it?"

"No." I'm getting a little irritated, mostly because I know she's right. Why don't I look at the natural beauty I paid a fortune for? "I don't. Inside is nice, too. All my creature comforts are here. Honestly, I just don't think of it much."

I pour her a glass of red and myself a brandy before heading back outside and sinking into the chair opposite Keeley. As she sips her vino, I watch her. Every move has a quiet female sexuality I don't think I've seen—or noticed before. It's fascinating, her fingers holding the glass with unconscious elegance, the delicate pursing of her lips as she imbibes. Her chest rises and falls, and a pink curl tumbles over one shoulder, then dives between her breasts. They're a nice handful—just right for her body—and obviously natural. I like that she's real. Grabbing fake boobs can be like caressing rocks.

She sets her glass down. "Why would you spend your time inside when the place was clearly the hotel decorating staff's attempt to appeal to the unimaginative? It's not you at all."

I sit back and sip. I've never really thought of all the browns, tans, and creams as being dull, but to Keeley, they would be. "I have some blue throw pillows on the couch."

"They're aqua," she corrects. "And I didn't see a single personal knickknack or photo anywhere in the living room."

"You hardly looked at it."

"There wasn't much to see after the sectional, coffee table, and big-ass TV. Sorry. I'm not criticizing. I'm just surprised. Your car is so…you. This place isn't."

"You think you know me?"

She shrugs. "You have a certain vibe. It's way more bold and masculine than this Tommy Bahama pad. Why haven't you made it your own? Or do you have that male inability-to-decorate gene?"

I don't know how to answer her. I've never tried to decorate. "Probably."

"Describe your first place."

I picture it in my head. Early macho dorm room. Two monster truck tires and a sheet of glass made my first coffee table. Posters of hot chicks straddling hot cars… I frown. Come to think of it, that was all Griff's doing. But I didn't object.

"Okay, you win," I concede with a self-deprecating smile. "I can't decorate."

She laughs. "Take me down to the beach?"

I start to balk. I haven't even kissed her. The conversation has been nice. Okay, it's actually been enjoyable. She's got an interesting perspective. Strange that she's making me look at myself with a critical eye…but not terrible. According to Britta, I need it. I was hoping we'd finish our drinks, then get naked for some mattress tango. But she's looking at me with big blue eyes, and there's a little pout to her lower lip. On anyone else, it would seem childish or petulant, but she looks damn sexy begging.

In fact, I don't hate that idea. But we'll come back to that…

"Sure." It's nearing ten o'clock, so most of the tourists who have kids should be tucking them in their rooms. Honeymooners are done with dinner and drinks and probably boinking the night away. All the grandparents were in bed by nine. We should be alone at the shoreline.

The big smile on her face is worth the twenty minutes it will take me to give her a tour of the Ritz's semi-private beach. She tosses back her wine and leaps to her feet with a wink. "Thanks. If you're not careful, I'll think you're Prince Charming."

"Once you get to know me, you'll know better. Let's go."

As we walk back through my unit, I swap out my loafers for sandals and slip a condom in my pocket because…well, hope springs eternal. I grab the bottle of wine, tuck my keys away, and take her hand. We head for the big, luminous moon hanging over Honokahua Bay. She's quiet beside me, holding tightly to my hand, but the rest of her is fixated by the endless stretch of ocean before us. Absently, she kicks off her heels at the bottom of the stairs. I realize she's more petite than I thought, a couple inches over five feet. Her childlike glee as she darts toward the water and wiggles her toes in the sand makes me smile.

The lazy, back-and-forth breeze makes the trees lining the beach look as if they're doing a sensual hula to the rhythm of the leaves rustling. The inky sky shines brilliant with infinite stars. The white-caps glitter like diamonds. Best of all, we're alone.

It's perfect.

"Wow," she breathes, standing inches from the surge of the water as it breaks along the beach. "Every time I see something this beautiful, I'm in awe. The vastness of the ocean humbles me. I'm one speck of a human, but look at the sleek power of all that water. It hosts life. It balances the planet. It's..." She turns to me, wincing. "I'm babbling."

Kind of, but not the point. "It's interesting to hear your thoughts. I never considered it that way."

"Hmm." She grabs the wine and takes a long swig from the bottle.

There's more in her head than she's sharing with me, but I can be patient. I can coax. I'm not sure why I want to know but I do. "You were being philosophical. Don't let me stop you."

Her flirty glance lightens the moment. "I was just thinking. A sight like this reminds me of Victor Hugo's "The Ocean's Song." I don't remember every word, but part of it goes something like this:

We saw the boundless waters stretch in glory
And heave in power.
O Ocean vast! We heard thy song with wonder,
Whilst waves marked time.
'Appear, O Truth!' thou sang'st with tone of thunder,
'And shine sublime!'"

I mull her words over, then look at the bay again, trying to see it through her eyes. She's right. It's majestic. It's a fucking natural wonder. I'll have to look at it more often.

"This is the perfect place for me to finally kiss you," I murmur, bringing her in closer.

Keeley braces her hand against my chest and looks into my eyes. "I don't have to know everything about you in order to spend the night with you. But I want to understand you. I *need* to. Help me?"

In most instances, I'd mentally roll my eyes. This is a lot of effort for a piece of ass. But I'm studying her face. I don't understand why she feels this way, yet I see clearly that she does. Britta's earlier words ring through my head, and I wonder what I have to lose by getting to know this multi-faceted woman a bit. Besides, if I'm going to convince her to help me with my Griff problem tomorrow, it behooves me to know her in return.

"How can I do that?" I caress her face, startled again by how soft she feels.

"Tell me something about you, something most people don't know." She shrugs. "What's your most prized possession?"

"My professional reputation."

"That's not a possession." The little frown between her brows disturbs me. "The thing you hoard and keep safe above everything else."

No one has ever asked me that. This girl has unexpected depth. She might be wearing a cheetah dress I would have sworn only a refugee from a '90s music video would sport, but Keeley is full of surprises. The first is how much she's making me think.

"My grandfather's watch. He was an amazing man, served in World War II. He was part of the Normandy Invasion." And what kind of guts had it taken to storm the beach that day, knowing he might not live to see the next? I can't imagine. "He rarely talked about it. But Miles Ambrose had grit and honor and..." I got choked up, which is crazy. He died almost ten years ago. But I miss the old guy. "His grandfather gave him a Cartier watch just before he went into the service. Black leather band, white face, roman numerals. Very classic. Growing up, I always thought Granddad preferred my younger brother, despite the fact that my middle name is his first. So I assumed he'd leave the timepiece to Griff. But no. The bastard left it to me, along with a note that said he'd chosen me because I was a man of honor. I just didn't know it yet."

With her free hand, she cups my face, thumb brushing my cheek. I'm having a hard time keeping myself together. I can't even look at her right now. What the hell is going on? It's as if Keeley has found all my weak spots and is determined to poke at them one by one.

"Do you know it now?" she asks softly.

I think—hard. "I'm not sure."

The frown that furrows her brow again upsets me. She takes another pull of the wine. "Are you wearing the watch?"

"Never. I keep it in a safe deposit box."

"Didn't he give it to you to wear?"

It's an obvious but somehow baffling question. Granddad probably had, but I'd always thought it was too valuable and breakable. So I locked it away. "No. He gave it to me to keep safe, so that's what I do. You've asked me a million questions. Tell me more about you. Keeley Sunshine isn't your real name, I'm guessing."

"No. It's Keeley Kent. Not much to tell. I'm an open book. Grew up in Phoenix. Since shortly after high school graduation, I've moved around, looking for a place that fits me. I started in San Diego. It didn't feel right—or maybe I hated the letch who owned the restaurant where I waitressed—so I made my way up the coast. Frisco wasn't for me since all the guys I thought were hot didn't play for my team. Seattle was too rainy. That's where I picked up my ex, who suggested Maui. And here I am."

A part of me wonders if this girl has ever done permanence but I guess I shouldn't care. We're two ships, and she'll probably pass me by after tonight. That's cool. I'll be more than happy to dock in her port once or twice before we sail on.

"What do you want to be, Keeley?"

She frowns as if that's a bizarre question, then avails herself of more wine. "What does anyone want to be? Happy."

I wonder if she intentionally misunderstood my question, then I realize that's exactly what she wants. I barely know her, but I see now that how she reaches happy is irrelevant to her as long as it works out.

That concept has never once crossed my mind in thirty-three years. I've always known I want to be at the top of the food chain, so to speak. I've never stopped to question whether that would make me happy.

I blink, taken aback.

"Did I say something wrong?" she asks.

"No. It's actually…an interesting answer."

And still I realize I would rather be successful than happy. I don't even hesitate. After all, what's happy, really? I'm not sure happy would fulfill me the way wiping the floor with my competitors does.

Keeley cocks her head and her pillowy lips softly part before wrapping around the neck of the bottle again. "I'm not sure 'interesting' is good."

"We're just different. That's all right." I can't stop staring at her mouth.

"I suppose. Tell me about your family."

I'm frustrated. I want to kiss this girl so badly. I have no doubt taking her to bed will be amazing, but I feel an urge to lay my lips over hers—not to silence her but to make sure she feels the chemistry between us. The desire is so strong it nearly chokes me. But she needs to know me to be comfortable. I'm not sure why that matters so much to me, but somehow it does.

"We moved here from L.A. when I was fifteen. My parents

headed back to California a few years ago. They took my little sister with them. Harlow will be twenty-six next month. You'd like her."

"What a pretty name. You two close?" She takes another sip.

I shrug. Probably not as close as we should be. "We talk now and then. She's been busy finishing her master's and planning her wedding, so she's got a lot going on, too."

"Have you met her fiancé?"

"No. They're supposedly getting married on the island in May, so I guess I will then." Which means I'll have to see Griff. "What about you?"

"I'm an only child, and my mom and stepdad have turned into crazy world travelers since retiring. I think they're on a South Pacific cruise right now." She fixes her gaze on me. "Didn't you say you had a brother, too?"

I really don't want to get into this now. Griff will be between us soon enough. I want Keeley all to myself tonight. "Yeah. He's an asshole who lives two miles down the road. We don't speak."

"Why?" The feeling she breathes into that word makes it sound like the biggest tragedy ever.

How much do I tell her? I'd rather not dredge this up. I don't owe her anything. Yet I know she won't stop asking me questions until I give her something. "We used to be in business together until a professional disagreement. Then, just for fun, he decided to start sleeping with my ex-girlfriend three days after we ended a two-year relationship."

"Ouch." She winced. "Did he say why?"

"I don't give a shit why." Every time I think about that period in my life, I get worked up and pissed off. "Look, Keeley. I like you. And I want you. I'm not good at talking or relationships or letting people know me. I'm good in bed. Can that be enough for tonight?"

I find myself holding my breath. If she says no, I have no fucking idea what I'm going to do. After a handful of probing questions, I already feel oddly raw. I rub at a sore spot along my breastbone.

"Yes. Sorry. I have a terrible tendency to be nosy. You're interest-ing…and I really am not a fan of sleeping with strangers. But I think I know who you are, Maxon… Damn it. What's your last name?" She gives an embarrassed little laugh. "Oh, that sounds brilliant."

Her joke totally lightens the mood. I need that. "Reed."

"Well, Maxon Reed, are you going to stand there all night or kiss me in the moonlight?"

The second I get the green light, my tolerance for banter flies out the window. I become a hunter who's just settled on his prey of choice, and I'm looking forward to fully sating my hunger.

I don't bother with words. Instead, I take the bottle from her hands and set it in the sand beside us. Then I fuse my stare to hers and tilt her head where I can most effectively devour her. Her eyes flash with something. Excitement, yes. Apprehension. That surprises me but no denying what I see. And hope… Maybe she's not the only one feeling unexpected things.

Then she parts those bee-stung lips again, and all my thoughts dissolve.

I lower my head and kiss her with a groan.

Fuck if her lips aren't every bit as soft as I imagined. She opens to me, presses against me, wrapping her arms around my neck like she needs to touch me every bit as much as I'm dying to have her bare against me. I'm sizzling, my senses reeling. I'm actually dizzy the longer I kiss her, but I urge her lips apart with my own and plunge inside.

I'm lost.

She's so sweet. Not like a Snickers, which I love. Her flavor is more refined, and the pleasure I get from her is like savoring a good red wine paired with a lush dark chocolate. Then she kisses me back with a sensual sway of her tongue and an indrawn breath that lets me know I'm getting to her, too.

I'm drowning.

My hands are suddenly in her hair, tugging until she gives me full access to every part of her mouth. I go in even deeper as if I'm trying to own her all at once. I haven't had the sort of drought she has, but I can't imagine another five minutes without being inside her, taking full possession of her. It's chemical. It's electric. I don't know how the fuck to describe it because I've never felt anything quite like this.

Suddenly, she breaks away from my kiss, nipping at my lips like a kitten, before tilting her head back completely. Her lips aren't on mine anymore.

I'm dying.

Not kissing her is unacceptable. Then…I see the arch of her delicate throat. She's exposed one of the most vulnerable parts of herself to me. Her ivory flesh glows in the moonlight. Even in the pale gleam, I see the flush staining her skin. I hear the catch of her breathy inhalations. I feel the hard beads of her nipples against my chest. How can I absorb her all at once, experience every facet of her in a single moment? I can't, but I'm damn impatient to try.

"Maxon?" She sounds shaky, uncertain.

I rush to set her at ease. "Why are you so fucking beautiful?"

"If you think I am, I'm glad. Are you going to touch me now?"

She sounds breathless and anxious. Does she imagine for a second that I might say no? *As if.*

"Yeah, sunshine. As much as you'll let me." I dip my head, fists in her pink tresses as I brush my lips up her throat. She's so damn soft all over that I have to groan again.

Then her lips beckon once more, and I'm pulling her against me, back under me. I capture her lips, mold them under my own. Tonight, she shouldn't have her lips anywhere except against mine —unless they're around my cock, of course. But I can't lift my head to tell her because I'm kissing her too thoroughly. My hands drift down her body, imprinting her curves into my memory. My fingers bite into her waist with urgency. It's not enough. I want more of her. I don't care if we come up for air. I hope she feels the same.

She must because she melts into me, her lips opening in teasing welcome. She wants me…but she wants me to work for it. You know what? I'm good with that. I always enjoy something more that I've earned.

So I'm going to be worthy of every scream of her pleasure.

I focus on nothing but Keeley. The moon and the waves and the sand disappear. Right now, only she and I share this space, this moment. I let the aphrodisiac of her flavor intoxicate me again. Like before, she goes straight to my head and I feel a special kind of drunk on her. I taste her lips, take her tongue. My right hand drifts down to cup her ass. I've got to touch her everywhere. She's responding, her breathing heavier. She clutches my shoulders and holds me tight against her. Her left leg curls around my calf, her thigh sliding up mine.

My restraint snaps.

I plunge into her mouth full force. Like a skydiver at fifteen thousand feet, my belly tumbles into free fall. Gravity has nothing on this pull. What's happening between us is a natural phenomenon all its own.

"I want you now." I look at her. God, I can't stop. I scan her eyes. They're dilated, half-dazed, and so fucking soft. "Keeley?"

"What's happening between us?"

"I don't know." Right now, I don't care about anything except feeling her, getting inside her, putting my stamp on her.

"I want you now, too," she admits in a breathy whisper, then kisses me once, twice, grabbing at my neck and pulling me down for a third.

No way I'm resisting.

I meld our mouths together again and cup her ass with both hands. God, she fills my palms, firm and plush and stunning. But I want the rest of her. I can't wait anymore.

I lift her against my body, and she automatically wraps her legs around me, then devours me with a demanding kiss once more. Fuck, yeah. I'm already mentally inside her as I head for the rocks on the west side of the beach that provide the property privacy from the housing development hugging Oneloa Bay on the other side of the inlet.

It's more of a hike than I thought. I'm not winded, just impatient. Keeley is, too. She's climbing my body like she can't get close quickly enough to keep her sanity.

Finally, we reach the rocky edge of the beach. I set her on one of the massive, water-smoothed stones. It's dry now with the tide out, but come early morning, this place will be submerged.

The few seconds it takes me to steady her, Keeley dives into my shirt, unfastening one button after the other until she exposes my chest.

When the last one comes free, she shoves my shirt off my shoulders, grabs me for a frantic kiss, then sits back and stares, mouth gaping. "Oh, my god. You're so perfect it's disgusting."

I shake my head. I'm hardly without flaw, but I won't argue. My shoulders square. I puff my chest out—just a little. I want to keep impressing her, you know? Then I slide my hand up her thigh. Such silky-smooth skin. Firm. Enticing. Can I be inside her in the next thirty seconds?

My other hand follows the first, palming my way clear up to her hip. Holy shit. "You're not wearing underwear?"

She peels her lips off my neck and breathes in my ear. "What? No. The dress showed panty lines. Is being commando a problem?"

"Are you kidding?"

I want to applaud her for making this process faster and easier. This is one efficiency I'll never waste. But as I shove her dress up and bare her legs one alabaster inch at a time, I lose my ability to speak, so it's a good thing she doesn't want me for my verbal skills.

I tell her what I want without words, spreading her legs and looming between them. I tug the dress up higher, eager to see her natural hair color. Obviously, it isn't pink.

But when I expose her pussy, she's utterly bare. "Oh, sunshine…"

She spreads her legs a little wider. "You like me this way?"

I have a feeling I'll enjoy her every way I can have her. But I want to put whatever worries she has to rest. "Oh, yeah. I like everything about you."

Keeley flashes me something that isn't quite a smile. Emotion blooms in her eyes, then makes its way to her wobbling lips. "I like you, too."

Then she reaches for the cheetah-print sash she's tied into a bow with a saucy tilt at her hip and pulls it free. With a tug, the dress unwraps and she's completely naked, except for a black bra that looks strappy, lacy, and strains to contain her breasts. The swells at the top spill above the little garment and make my heart stutter.

"Take it off?" I'm trying not to sound like a demanding prick, but I'm not really asking.

Thankfully, she seems to understand and reaches behind her. A second later, it's falling free onto the nearby rock. Then she leans back on her hands, bathed in moonlight, and blinks up at me with big blue eyes.

I'm never saying no to that.

Under her terrible dress is an absolute treasure. I can't stop staring.

"You're so damn beautiful. I feel like the luckiest bastard in the world right now."

It probably sounds trite, like something a horny guy says to the girl he's hoping to nail. But I'm serious. I've taken gorgeous women to bed, so I'd know. I don't think Keeley would fit into any conventional definition of beauty, but there's something about her. It's as if I can see her soul just by looking into her eyes. I'm sure that sounds stupid. It's new to me, that's for damn sure. Keeley said earlier that she's an open book. I believe her. She looks open to me in every way—eyes raised to my stare, lips parted, posture unguarded, legs spread. She is a woman giving her all to the man standing before her without hesitation or reservation.

I drag in a sharp breath as I watch her, feeling primal, possessive. My blood pounds. There's something inside my chest that's feeling soft like a marshmallow the longer I stare at her. I've never felt anything like this. I don't welcome the sensation.

But I don't have any control over it.

Looking back, that should have been my first clue that she would have the power to destroy me.

"I'm glad," she whispers. "Aren't you going to touch me?"

Definitely. Where the hell do I start? Every part of her demands my attention. She looks soft all over, like she'll be a delight to my fingertips from tousled hair to toes. My mouth waters at the sight of her pert nipples. Peachy-pink and perfectly symmetrical, they're stunning—like the rest of her. Her ivory flesh cascades down to a torso that tells me she's healthy but not a slave to the gym. The night shields the secrets of her pussy. I know she's bare, but I want details I can't see while she's shrouded in shadow. Even more, I smell her.

And I'm speechless. Good thing Keeley wants action, not words.

I manage a jerky nod, then all but tear away my belt buckle. Afterward, I unsnap the button. My zipper falls next. I fish the condom from my pocket. These interminable moments I can't touch her are pure torture, but I finally manage to shove my clothes aside and slide the latex down my cock. It's throbbing in time with the rapid beat of my heart. *Gong, gong, gong.* The sensations are like some euphoric high. I haven't touched drugs since I was a punk-ass kid rebelling against my dad, but this is more potent. Right now, she has me by the balls without laying a hand on me.

This craving for her will go away after the orgasm, right?

"Maxon?"

I give her a rough nod and step closer. "With you."

"No, you're near me." She brushes a hand up my thigh and caresses her way up my ass, pulling me closer. "You're not with me yet."

Jesus.

"Good point." I swallow, holding myself back for another moment so I can warn her. "This may move fast."

"Thank god."

With two words, she seals her fate. Well, stripping naked and begging me to touch her already ensured I would spend the night inside her, but knowing she's as ready as I am to unleash this storm brewing between us is heady.

With one hand, I fist her hair and tug, aligning her lips under mine. With the other, I grip her thigh and lift it above my hip. Our lips brush as the head of my erection nestles against her slick, soft opening. I look down at Keeley. She's breathless, waiting, spellbound. God, I want to give her the world, the stars—whatever she wants…except a plane ticket back to Phoenix.

"Sunshine," I groan before I swoop down and plunge into her mouth while I thrust forward into the tight clasp of her body.

Gliding through her is so smooth, like silicone over glass.

Suddenly, I'm submerged inside her. She fits around me like a perfectly tailored suit. I taste the wine on her breath as I take her tongue. I feel the softness of her body as she rises up to meet me. I see the pleasure rip across her face as I brace myself on the big stone behind her and sink my last inch deep.

I ease back—all the way to the weeping tip of my shaft—then I shove my way inside her again. She undulates beneath me in a sensual ripple of her body and lies back farther, opens herself to me wider.

Desire sucks my sanity clear from my brain. I descend into a haze of arousal, where I'm compelled to meld myself to her. I have no thoughts that aren't of the scent of her blending with me, wrapped in the ocean salt. I have no wants that aren't steeped in delving my way deeper into her body and making sure I've touched every possible part of her.

I shift the angle of my head and fuse our lips together once more. I drink in more of her as I slide into her again. And again.

She breaks the kiss with a gasp and falls back on her elbows, head tossed back. "Maxon..."

Her breasts fill my vision. I lick my way up the side of one. I want to take her nipple in my mouth, roll it on my tongue. They look taut and perfect. They're under-loved, which is definitely a failing on my part I intend to rectify soon. But at the moment, I'm too busy hovering above Keeley and watching her face as I fill her up in a rhythm that picks up speed with every thrust.

"What do you need, sunshine?" I manage to grind the words out. If I'm hurting her, I have to know. Otherwise...I'm not sure much is stopping this pleasure train.

"I'm close." Her words sound strained.

Thank god. I'm on the edge, too.

She peppers kisses up and down my arms. It's the only part of me she can reach in this position. So she drags her lips up the sensitive inside crook of my elbow, nipping at me with her teeth. An electric arc races through me as she plucks at my skin and moans.

Then she thrusts a hand between her legs. I feel her manipulating her clit with her fingers. It's something I'd be more than happy to do to her myself—if I wasn't using my hands to hold my body upright to prevent a full-on face plant into the rocks.

Why did I think sex right here was a good idea?

Next time—and there will be one—I'll make sure I can touch every part of her and hurtle her into ecstasy a few times. After the discomfort of the beachcapade, I owe her a few stellar orgasms.

Despite the fact I can't get a hand free to fondle her where I'd like to, she manages to do a great job on her own. Her moans turn breathy, high-pitched, almost panicked. She clamps down on me. I'm on fire. She's going to make it to the finish line before me...but it's going to be a damn close race.

"Maxon..." She sounds almost distressed.

"Here, sunshine," I growl. "You ready?"

"Yes. Damn it. Oh..." she pants, body heaving and bucking against me. "Yes. Please. Deeper. More. Like that."

I hammer her now—fast, unmerciful, an onslaught of power, desire, and determination to make her come.

Color splashes across her chest, creeps up her neck to stain her cheeks. Rosy. Aroused. So fucking beautiful. Her entire body tenses, and I know she's there.

I brace for my own orgasm. My blood has reached a boil. I've been holding off the tingling brewing in my balls but they feel heavy. I'm close to exploding. The time is now.

As if she can hear my internal monologue, she tenses and looks at me as if only I can save her.

"Keeley." I mouth her name because my voice is too scratchy. "Now. Come!"

We're so perfectly in sync that she lets go the moment I speak her name. Her body stiffens as she thrashes beneath me, all over my cock. I feel her everywhere—under, around, beside—not just my shaft but my whole body. I'm aware of her scream, of her goose bumps, of the gentle sheen of her perspiration.

Then the orgasm I've been trying to hold back runs me over, and all I can do is hold on for dear life and shout her name as I lose my self-control completely.

I'm hoping I haven't lost my sanity, too.

CHAPTER THREE

*A*fter lingering for a few moments, I have to pull away. I'm not ready to break our connection, but the damn rocks are killing my knees. While she rises, I find a trash can beside the nearby towel stand and do away with the condom. When I turn back, I expect to find her dressing.

Instead, she's run stark naked into the water.

I'd ask anyone else if they were crazy, but Keeley flips a laugh at me over her shoulder, like she knows I'm wondering what the fuck she's doing. Instantly, I see a bright happiness beaming from her face. Since that's what she wants out of life, I feel good. Weirdly content.

"Come in the water," she calls to me.

"I'm not skinny dipping in the ocean. What if someone calls the cops to say there's more than one moon shining on this beach?"

Her laugh this time is heartier. "Then we sweet-talk our way out of it or go to jail, but how many times in life will we have the chance to do something like this?"

Probably not very many. She has a point.

I shuck my shoes and pants. "I must be crazy. I blame you."

"Good." Keeley turns to me, flashing me a full frontal of her glorious nudity. "You should."

I just had a monster climax less than five minutes ago, but I'm already hoping my recovery time is short. I'd love to get her back to the condo, into my bed, and do every crazy, dirty, wonderful thing to her I can think of.

"I will," I promise as I head into the brisk Hawaiian water.

Her smile—whether she means it or not—looks sultry. "I love being a dangerous woman."

Though she sometimes seems so sweet I could get a cavity, I sense her wild side just under the surface. The male animal in me wants to feel her again. Tame her—at least for an hour or two.

I take her hand. With the other, she bends to splash me.

"You want a fight?" I challenge.

"Maybe…"

She's flirting. I love it. I'm never playful after sex. Most of my partners get their clothes on and leave, which is a relief. Tiffanii always showered the smell of sex—of me—off her body before she rolled over and went to sleep. In fairness, as a flight attendant, she often had to be up by four to work the 6:30 a.m. flight to Honolulu. Still, it pissed me off.

But Keeley wants to…frolic. I can't think of a better word. She's splashing and giggling and enjoying life.

It's contagious. I smile and splatter her with water in return.

With a sigh, she falls against me, still grinning, then steals a kiss. She's gone before I can pull her in closer, staring out at the vast ocean again.

I sidle up behind her and wrap my arms around her. My lips fall to her shoulder. She's the perfect height for me to press kisses there. She shivers in my arms.

"If you don't stop making me happy, how are you ever going to get rid of me?"

"Who says I want to?"

She scoffs. "Oh, I know your type. If you're too busy to come home and take advantage of this view, you're too busy for a relationship. It's okay. I get that you want satisfying, not meaningful."

A few hours ago, I would have agreed with her. Now I don't know what the hell is going on. An impulsive side of me I would have sworn didn't exist is telling me that I should try to make something of my connection with this girl. Keeley is interesting. She holds my attention. She's not into herself—her life, her parties, or her looks. She's into the people around her. She's into living. She makes me look at my life differently. Come to think of it, she's everything I've never had in a woman before.

If Britta truly knew this woman, my assistant would approve.

But Griff, the thirty-million-dollar listing, and the task I need to ask of Keeley tomorrow loom. I want to keep her with me longer... but my brother will lose his shit when he meets her. He'll fall all over himself to win her. He'll half-ass the Stowe estate to be with her. Doesn't that sound stupid? But trust me, it's true. And once the Stowe heirs see he's too busy chasing tail to chase leads, they will cut him loose. Then *bam*, I'm in. It's gold. I'll celebrate.

But I'll be celebrating alone.

Well, not exactly. I'll have Rob and Britta. They'll make a pretty penny from this deal, too. And I'll find another woman to make me feel good again, right? Now that I know how important personality and a carefree spirit are, I'll look for those qualities.

"I may surprise you yet," I tell her.

Not with the meaningful relationship stuff. Although...I wonder if there's any chance she'll agree to distract Griff and continue to sleep with me.

That sounds bad, I know. I probably shouldn't even consider the possibility. I'm worried about asking, too. I've seen what she can do to a man's gnads. It makes me shudder.

"Really?" She turns in my arms and smiles. "I think I'd like that. Now take me back to your place. It's getting cold."

Judging from the position of the moon and the incoming tide, midnight is fast approaching. She's small, and the wind begins blowing. Her nipples turn hard, and I have to remind myself her reaction isn't because she wants me again.

I'll work on that.

I pull another round of gentleman out of my ass, scoop up her clothes, and hand them over. "You got it."

She wraps her dress around her damp body. It clings everywhere. I stop in the middle of shaking sand out of my pants to stare. She simply sparkles.

"Hurry." She curls her arms around herself.

I can almost hear her teeth chattering as she shoves her bra in her dress pocket and fetches the bottle of wine.

I'm looking around for my damn boxer briefs when sand pelts my back. It sticks to my skin, and I know it's going to be impossible to get every grain off before I have to slip my clothes back on.

I whirl around to find Keeley holding in a laugh. "You threw sand at me?"

Her eyes dance. "Oops. My hand must have slipped. My bad."

"You're a shitty liar."

That makes her laugh more.

I raise a brow at her. "Don't worry. I'll get you back."

"Oh, big man with big words."

"No. Big man with big promises." I fumble around in my clothes until I finally find my underwear, then do my best to brush off what sand I can before thrusting them on.

"I'll look forward to that," she taunts.

I finish dressing and we make our way back toward my unit. She tosses the wine bottle in the nearest bin, and I grab her hand. It feels automatic. By her own admission, she likes me and doesn't seem to mind that I'm the kind of guy who puts business first. Maybe that will work in my favor tomorrow.

When we reach the condo, I direct her to the guest suite, which has a private bath attached to the separate bedroom. Moments later, the water turns on, and after some rustling, I hear a grateful sigh. I would rather have showered with her, but I have so much sand stuck to my body, I'm not sure I can get clean without getting her dirty again. Okay, that's not the only issue. I'm also out of condoms in my bathroom.

Once we're both showered and in the bedroom, though? Yeah. I smile and melt under the spray of water.

As I'm stepping out, my phone rings. I look at the clock. Eleven fifty-two p.m. It's either an emergency or an international buyer, but either way, there's no question I'll answer.

"Maxon Reed." I wrap the towel around my waist.

Twenty minutes later, I hang up with the client from London who conveniently forgets about the time difference a lot and leave a quick e-mail for Britta about follow-ups from the conversation. I also tell her I'll be in late tomorrow. I don't say why, but I know talking to Keeley about Project Griff isn't likely to be a five-minute process.

Once finished, I pause. I'm not hearing rustling around the rest of the condo. I get the feeling that quiet from her can be dangerous. I frown. Has she gone back to the lanai? Or fucking left me?

After throwing on some shorts and a T-shirt, I charge into the living room—and stop short at the sight of Keeley asleep on my sofa. Her damp hair is wound on top of her head in a haphazard knot. Her face is completely devoid of makeup. Without all the color and sparkle and vampy lipstick, she looks young. And really lovely. I've been with women who wear their cynicism all over their faces, even when they sleep. Keeley lies in repose with her hands pressed together under her cheek, every muscle in her body perfectly relaxed.

Do I ever allow my guard down this much and just let go?

I stare a moment more. Should I wake her up and move her to a bed? That strategy holds the most potential for another round of sex. I don't want to pass up that opportunity, especially if she stops talking to me tomorrow.

"Keeley?" I shake her shoulder.

She doesn't even open her eyes, merely swats at me with a half-hearted backhand. "Go away."

I can barely understand her mumble. "Don't you want a bed?" I fondle my way up her stomach to cradle a breast, and the second I get her flesh against my palm I get hard. "How about round two? C'mon, sunshine. Let me make you feel good again."

Her little grunt is cute. "No. Happy."

She rolls over and turns her back to me. I stand, stare, blink. Then I have to hold in a laugh. Apparently, she doesn't like to have her sleep interrupted. Message received, loud and clear, even if I don't like the content.

I sigh and fish a blanket out of the closet near the door, then spread it over her supine form. She lets out a contented little sigh. Her rhythmic breathing tells me she's fallen into deep slumber.

So…I guess that's it for tonight. I should go to bed and try to grab a few hours of sleep myself. I need to hit tomorrow hard. I have a Griff problem to solve and Keeley is key. I hope she'll be open to remaining lovers. But from everything I learned about her, I don't expect it. And if it's a choice between keeping the woman or crushing my adversary…Griff is going down.

Sunlight burns through my lids as I swim to consciousness. It's already after sunrise?

Stunned that I've overslept—I can't remember the last time that happened—I open my eyes. The clock in front of me shows three glaring red numbers—9:18?

I've normally fielded a dozen calls by now. The damn device starts ringing in earnest at just after six most mornings, but a glance at my nightstand tells me my phone isn't there.

Gaping, I sit up, raking a hand through my hair. I might have been disoriented a few moments ago, but I'm wide awake now.

"Good morning," a soft female voice says beside me.

I turn to find Keeley. The previous evening rushes back to me. So does the task before me today.

God, she looks gorgeous, face freshly scrubbed, hair falling in soft waves around her as she reads my morning paper with a glass of orange-mango juice in hand.

"Morning." When did she get in bed beside me? "Um…"

"I hope you don't mind. When I woke up about three, your bed looked more comfortable than the sofa, and I wanted to be with you."

I've been curled up beside her for hours and I didn't know it? I'm slipping. I wish I had a do-over so I could do her again. At the very least, enjoy that the sheets beside me are warm and smell like her. I've had my fun, though. I hate it, but the time has come to shift focus from pleasure to business—at least for now. "Do you know where my phone is?"

She gives me an uncertain smile. "Your text messages started dinging at ten after six this morning. When you didn't move at all, I figured you could use the rest. So I silenced the phone and moved it to the kitchen."

She's let me sleep through critical business communications for the last three hours?

I leap out of bed. This is terrible. Fuck, it's catastrophic. If there's an issue, my chance at the Stowe listing could slip through my fingers and right into Griff's hands so fast.

"About an hour ago, someone named Britta called and wanted you to know the world hasn't collapsed."

The driven Realtor in me who knows I didn't get to number one on the island by sleeping the day away? That part of me wants to chew Keeley a new one. I don't. She meant well. Still, I can't quite keep my voice softer than a dull roar as I hover over her. "You silenced my phone and then answered it? What if it had been a client?"

"Relax," she insists. "Geez, you're so tightly wound. One of the body's most natural healing mechanisms is sleep. You said you hadn't had any in a long time, so when you kept snoozing through the dinging, I thought I was being considerate to let you rest. And I wouldn't have answered, except the caller ID popped up as 'office,' and she rang you three times in five minutes. Is she a colleague?"

"Britta is my assistant."

"She didn't sound happy that I'm still here. You two have a thing?"

I shake my head. "No. I think of her like a sister. A few years ago, she was involved with…" Why am I opening this can of shit? It's not important right now. "I need my phone."

Keeley gestures to the bedroom door, which leads out to the kitchen.

I stomp my way across the hardwoods and pick up the device. Twelve texts, five missed calls, two voice mails, and seventeen urgent e-mails. I groan aloud as I attack everything I missed.

Surprisingly, one of the voice mails is from Britta saying that she's handled most of the e-mails and half the phone calls. I realize the majority of the texts are follow-ups from the other missed communications.

The sky isn't falling—yet.

The only e-mail that disturbs me is from a buddy who owns a drone used for snapping panoramic real estate photographs. He says that Griff left him a message last night, asking him to assemble a video of shots he's taken of other oceanfront, multimillion-dollar estates around the islands. And could he have that done in under four weeks? Griff is bringing out all the fun, new weapons to seal the deal with the Stowes.

Fuck. Playtime is definitely over.

I start a cup of coffee for myself, drag in a deep breath, and shuttle my temper for two reasons: One, Keeley is hard to stay mad at. Two, if I'm going to persuade her to distract my brother, yelling won't help. Granddad might have been a poor Nebraska farmer, but Miles Ambrose was also a damn smart man. I remember him telling me that a body would catch more flies with honey than vinegar.

As the Keurig fills the last of my mug and sends steam upward, I splash in some creamer and head back to the bedroom. I stare at her, looking so relaxed, leg bent and thigh exposed. Is she wearing one of my dress shirts? Yeah, and she looks sexy.

"Please don't be mad," she says softly.

"I'm not mad. I'm simply meticulous about the way I treat clients."

"Of course. I know business is everything to you, Maxon, but there's more to life."

Obviously, she believes that. That's her choice. I like the fact that she's passionate about her point of view. I simply disagree.

I drop the argument. Annoying her doesn't serve my purpose. It's far more important to decide how I can bring her on to my team. Do I sweet-talk her into doing me a favor? If I give her an emotional plea, I stand a better chance of keeping my balls when I tell her what I want. She's the kind of girl who will always help a friend. I just don't know if she considers me one.

If that doesn't work, I'll move on to plan B.

"Now is an incredibly busy time, and I'm working on a deal that could make or break my future. After Griff splintered away, I could have lost my business. I already felt as if he'd stolen my girl and half my sanity. All deals are important, but if I land this one, it will cement everything I've worked my ass off for my whole adult life."

"You already said you're the most successful guy on the island. Don't you have enough money?"

"It's not just that." And she should understand. She speaks fluent emotion, right? "This is about confidence, too. It's about believing in yourself, knowing you've done everything to be your best. When you make moves you really feel are best for the client, the market, and your future and they're completely rejected by your own brother, someone you loved and you swore would always love you back…" I have to take in a bracing breath to finish this sentence. Something about being near Keeley dredges up all the hurt I thought I'd shoved down. "It's tough to recover. This deal is critical for a lot of reasons."

That's admitting way more than I want to.

"Oh." She sets the paper down. "I know I don't have a head for business, but I didn't think of all that. Sorry."

If she doesn't have a head for business, I wonder what she's studying in college. She must have *some* plan. "What are you majoring in?"

"Hospitality and tourism, with a minor in culinary arts. It's taken me a few years and a lot of dropped classes to figure out what fits me. So…I've still got three semesters left before I graduate."

And probably a mountain of student loan debt. That might give me some leverage—if it comes to that. "What will you do with your degree?"

She hesitates. "I have an idea. I'm excited about it…but you'll probably laugh."

Why the hell would she believe that? "I won't."

"It won't make sense to you. You'll think it's silly."

"Try me."

She pauses. "Okay. You should love what you do, right? Be happy and all that. So…I have this dream to incorporate a bunch of the stuff I love by opening a bed and breakfast on the water some-day. It would be a paradise for foodies who also like yoga and the outdoors. I want to source as many of the ingredients for my meals as possible from locals. Everything I cook would be healthy but delicious. I'd have yoga in the morning, great outdoor activities like hiking and snorkeling all day, top-notch spa facilities, then guided meditation at night."

I can see Keeley doing that. If she could get the paperwork, taxes, P & L statements and all the other stuff she'd consider boring but practical, that would be a fantastic fit.

But something about the scenario bugs me. I realize she wants to share her happy life and favorite hobbies with someone, but has seemingly subtracted a steady boyfriend or husband who will cherish her in favor of a revolving door of preppy, earnest millennial guests. Not that I'm volunteering for the role, but I wonder why. I have a feeling this answer is important if I want to understand her.

"I like it." I sip my coffee. "Add some of your live entertainment to the mix and you might be onto something good."

She blinks. "You think?"

"Yeah. There's a market for resorts like that. Good online promotion could drive word of mouth, and you might create a real destination." In fact, this concept may be the most practical idea she's had. I wouldn't go to a place like that—the meditation and the yoga make me roll my eyes—but I can't deny they're both popular activities. Add in a pretty Hawaiian beach, along with awesome food, and it could be sought-after and trendy. A moneymaker.

"Really? That's a relief." Keeley sighs. "You're the first person I've ever told."

She chose *me* to bare her dream to? I feel humbled…and guilty. I was a bit curious, sure. But mostly I wanted ammunition I might use to convince her to help me sink Griff. That probably makes me sound like a terrible human being. At least I'm honest.

I have to press forward. What else can I do? I would be stupid to put a girl I haven't even known twenty-four hours before the business I've worked a lifetime to build simply because the sex was fantastic and I like her as a person. Time to put on my big boy britches. I need to compartmentalize my wants into a mental slot below my responsibilities and do my job.

"How many classes are you taking a semester? A full load?"

She shakes her head. "One or two. It's all I can afford. And time is usually tight since I still have to earn multiple paychecks to keep a roof over my head."

"So you're a handful of classes short of graduation?"

"Four, yeah." She sighs. "So close but so far away, just like my goal. Even if I get out of school soon, I'll be stuck working for someone else while I build up enough savings to buy a place. Oceanfront won't be cheap, and I'll probably have to do renovations. But I'll figure it all out eventually."

She has dreams but lacks capital and knowledge. Now I've got real leverage...

Why am I feeling suddenly squeamish about using it?

Fuck that. I have to forge ahead or Griff wins. "What if we could help each other?"

"How? Do you know someone willing to be an investor?"

"Not someone. Me. I need a favor. And I could help you in return. You have goals and are lacking some resources to meet them, right?"

"Yeah."

"I'm in the same position, actually. Remember I told you I was working a big deal? I'm actually in competition to list one of the premier estates on the island." I hesitate. After Keeley bared her soul to me, this conversation is uncomfortable. Since all's fair in business, I shove the feeling away. "I have one competitor. He's good, but I'll do a better job. The heirs of this estate lost their mother and want to be rid of the house quickly. I can get them top dollar. Landing this listing would give them everything they want monetarily during their time of grief while helping cement my recovery from the past. A win for everyone."

"Where do I come in?"

I have to tread carefully. "The person I'm competing against is Griff. After romancing my ex-girlfriend so shortly after our separation, he walked away from our business and left me in a lurch. I had to start over entirely. I'm still building back. Now he's trying to elbow me out of this critical deal." Well, it's sort of the other way around but... "He'll do his best to stab me in the back again. I can't lose."

"I see why you two don't talk. He doesn't sound like a great guy."

Actually, he can be. We were not only brothers but best friends once. One terrible week changed everything.

"He's not the same man he used to be." He stopped listening to me, stopped trusting. He turned even more cynical and ruthless than me.

"I'm sorry. It must have been hard. I don't have siblings so I don't completely understand, but..."

After losing Griff as both a business partner and a confidant all at once, I grieved as if he had died. "Damn hard, yes. So I was hoping you could help me move on. Would you be willing to lend me a hand to land this deal?"

"I won't be much help." She chuckles at herself. "Remember, I've got no head for business."

"Don't worry." I flash her a smile. "I have that part down."

Keeley shifts in the bed, sips her juice again, and pauses. "What do you want me to do?"

I brace myself with another sip of strong brew, then set the mug on my nightstand. This deserves my undivided attention.

"I know my brother well, both professionally and personally. I know his strengths and weaknesses. I know this isn't the right listing for him...and I know how to ensure he doesn't get it." I clear my throat because it feels incredibly tight. I'm nervous. Damn it, this never happens to me. "He's not good with multitasking. If you'd be willing to...distract him for a couple of weeks, he'll lose focus and the heirs will choose me as their Realtor."

She frowns, clearly thinking. I sit back and let her. Rushing her won't help my cause. Suddenly, realization dawns across her face. "I'm confused. Do you want this listing...or do you want revenge?"

"I'm not trying to stab him in the back." Much. Just enough for him to feel the sting. I don't wish him actual harm. "It's just business. It's survival, in fact. I would compete hard against any other agent who wants the same seller." And that's true. "It's just a coincidence that Griff and I are related. The heirs of this estate will absolutely come out on top if I list their property. But I need your help to make that happen."

"So…this is nothing underhanded?"

"He'd do the same to me."

"That doesn't make it right. And you didn't answer the question. Tell me what you mean by 'distracting' your brother."

I shrug like it's no big deal. "Talk. Be friends. Invent a few small problems he can help with. He can't resist a damsel in distress. If you disrupt his focus for a while, I'll give you a hundred thousand dollars—cash—the minute I get the listing. Think of the student loans you can pay off or the down payment for a B and B you can start accruing interest on. That money could solve a lot of your problems."

"Money isn't everything."

"Sure." I say the words to humor her, though it's pretty damn important in my book. "But this could turn your life around. All you have to do is say yes, and you could be starting your future."

"What about integrity? Six figures is a lot of money simply to 'spend time' with your brother. In order to earn this small fortune, do I have to sleep with him, too?"

What are the odds that he won't try to seduce her? Big, fat zero. I try not to wince. The idea that Griff might put even a finger on Keeley makes me want to punch his teeth down his throat. But I want this listing more than I want anything. Not for the money. Not even for the prestige. But I can't let the chance to beat Griff and return the big "fuck you" slip past me because I've got a soft spot for this woman I barely know.

Hopefully, I can make her see that my business maneuvers have nothing to do with how much I like her.

"I'd rather you didn't sleep with him, obviously. I had a great time last night. I usually don't have much interest in seeing a woman beyond the morning after, but I want to see you again."

That's as honest as I can be. If she digs much deeper into my motives, I'll be coughing up the details of my life tragedy and showing her all my battle scars. I never share that with anyone.

"Seriously?" She sounds incredulous—but not in a good way.

"Look, I'm in no way trying to offend you. I would never ask you to sleep with someone else, especially a guy you don't want."

"Well, that's good to hear," she replies tartly.

"On the other hand, after one night, I don't have the right to ask you to be exclusive. You don't strike me as a girl who's looking for permanence right now, anyway."

"I'm not, but what if flirting and acting a little helpless isn't getting the job done? What if the only way I can pull his attention from this listing is to drop my dress and climb between his sheets?"

I shy away from that visual because if it scrolls across my brain again, I might lose my composure. Damn it, this is unlike me. I try to focus on what to say instead. Normally, I'd mumble some platitude about everyone sacrificing to get what they want in life. But I doubt Keeley would ever give up her scruples to get ahead. The realization makes me feel a little guilty. No, kind of like a shithead.

I'm unfamiliar with those feelings. Being with Keeley Kent is exhilarating—but confusing.

"Um..."

"What you're really saying is that if your brother likes me and I'm motivated to screw him, you won't be thrilled but it's all for a good cause, and you'll pay me handsomely for my efforts." She tsks. "You know, having sex with people for money is usually called prostitution. And the people who make the hookups happen are usually called pimps."

I didn't think of it that way. Keeley has a point I'd rather not see.

"If your charm alone isn't stealing his attention, then we'll talk about it. Come up with a strategy."

"That may include whoring myself," she asserts. "You're not denying it."

She's taking the worst possible spin on this. "I'm also not enjoying it! For the record, that's not what I think of you at all. And

I didn't mean to upset you. We can get creative, so all you have to do is make him *think* you might have a thing with him someday. Maybe after you clear up your aggravated case of herpes with a gonorrhea chaser."

"What? I'm not lying to him about something like that!"

"It would be a good reason for him not to have sex with you." Actually, about the only reason I can think of.

I'm botching this totally. I know it. Every time I open my mouth, I shove my foot even deeper.

"Here's a better reason: I'm not saying yes." She tosses her hand in the air. "I can't believe you're offering to pay me a hundred grand to most likely sleep with your brother *after* we've spent the night together." She slams her juice down and launches herself out of bed. "I thought I liked you. And now I feel like a total impulsive idiot. I don't know who the hell you think you are, but you're clearly not someone I want to spend another minute with. I don't want any part of this low, demeaning scheme." She stomps out of the room.

I follow. "Keeley. I'm sorry, sunshine. I'm not trying to insult you. This is all coming out wrong. You're amazing. Fantastic."

"Do *not* try to sweet-talk me. There's no positive spin you can put on this that will make me want to help you screw your brother over by letting him screw me." She jerks her dress and heels off the arm of the sofa and marches for the guest room. "That's not who I am. And just because I was easy for you doesn't mean I'm cheap." She slams her way into the bathroom.

Shit. That did not go well.

I lean against the door. "I don't think you're cheap. I think you're beautiful. You make me laugh. I can't tell you the last time a woman—hell, anyone—has done that. And you even make me look at myself critically. Those are just a few reasons I don't want to stop seeing you. Those are the qualities I know will intrigue Griff, too. I wasn't trying to insult you. It's a compliment…just poorly worded. Will you come out so we can sit down and talk about this?"

Keeley doesn't say anything until she yanks the door open, now fully dressed in last night's clothes. "No. Even putting aside the whole *Pretty Woman* aspect of this scheme, it sucks. You can phrase it however you want, but this is about revenge. That's bad karma. It will come back to bite you in the ass. I don't want anything to do with it. He's your *brother*. Don't do something you'll regret later."

She grabs her purse and stomps to the front door.

I grab her arm, feeling more than a little panicked. "Where are you going? I drove you here."

She jerks free and reaches for the knob. "It's a hotel. I'm sure I can get a taxi."

Yes, the bellmen are very helpful that way. Damn it... "Don't leave like this, Keeley. The last thing in the world I ever want to do is upset you."

That part is so true it almost hurts.

She pauses, stills. "I really wanted to like you. Hell, I really wanted to keep you. But not after this. Good-bye."

Her sniffle tears at my heart. Before I can call her back, she's out the door.

CHAPTER FOUR

ome Saturday evening, I'm back at the crappy sports bar, hidden in the corner, waiting for Keeley to take the stage. For the last few days, I've been miserable and spent at least half my time trying to track her down. My place has felt empty. My sheets still carry a hint of her scent. It not only makes me hard, it makes me miss her. Britta says I've turned into a short-tempered prick.

"What are you going to do?" Rob asks beside me. "Grovel?"

I told my marketing manager about my grand scheme. He agreed that Griff would fall all over himself to pursue a woman like Keeley. He's all for whatever puts us in the win column.

"It's crossed my mind."

The truth is, I'm not sure what to do. I can't give up on Keeley. I need her help to undermine Griff...but I want her for myself. It doesn't make sense. I only spent a handful of hours with this woman. I'm surprised by how thoroughly she's stuck in my head.

"You'll need a more robust strategy than that. What did she object to most?"

"Everything. But if I had to pick one issue, I'd say the hooker/pimp thing. And the karma." I look for a way to help Rob—

who's every bit the bastard I am—understand Keeley. "She's got a soft heart."

"The sort who roots for the underdog against all odds?"

"Yeah."

In the past, I would have dismissed her attitude as unrealistic. I like coming from a position of power. I don't believe in fighting wars from the bottom, just annihilating enemies from the top. That strategy won't work with Keeley.

"Try some reverse psychology on her. Be contrite. Tell her that you've seen the error of your ways or some shit like that. Tell her you realize screwing Griff over isn't really in your best interest but in *his*. Frame it as a life lesson for your brother. Maybe that will work."

I shake my head. "I've already thought of it. Too thin. Instead of helping me improve Griff's moral character or giving me a hand to remove him as an obstacle, she would suggest I talk to my brother. Share my feelings."

"What good would that do?" He recoils. "I'm thinking you need to find another woman to do your dirty work. While you do, Britta and I will have your back at the office. You need that. I've got to tell you, so far the distraction you found for Griff has only succeeded in screwing up your A game."

He's right, and I know it. But there's a problem. "I've looked for someone else to occupy my brother. Name one person we know will appeal to him whom he hasn't already slept with or that he won't see coming a mile away? Hell, I'd turn Britta lose on him, but..."

"Bad idea. I don't know whether she'd break down in tears or fry his balls for breakfast. If we're lucky, she'd kill him." Rob taps the side of his beer glass. "Since it sounds as if Keeley Sunshine won't help you get revenge without a damn good reason, I'm not sure what to tell you, man."

"And I don't have a better idea. I've tried to think of one, too. Griff seems laser focused on this listing. Just about every hour, I hear of some other tool he's throwing into his arsenal to wow the Stowe heirs. I'm falling behind." Because all I can think about is Keeley.

"We're running out of time."

I turn to Rob. Does he think I don't know that? That I'm not aware every day—every hour—that all the minutes and seconds are ticking by and I can never get them back? That each grain of sand through the hourglass is taking me closer to losing out to my asshole brother for good?

"Aloha, Lahaina. I'm Keeley Sunshine."

Tonight she's wearing a top that's soft white and lacy with barely there sleeves that brush her shoulders. It almost looks demure, except for the deep V-neck that shows off the swells of her cleavage and her delicate collarbones. Her pink hair is in a messy bun. Everything about her tonight is more sedate, even the sheer nude pink of her lipstick.

"I hope you'll indulge me while I sing some of my favorite songs," she continues. "Since I just had my heart bruised recently, they might be a little melancholy. But I figure if you're here and dateless on a Saturday night, you might be feeling lonely, too."

Her words dig at my chest. She can't possibly see me with the bright lights in her face. I'm sitting in a shadowy corner. But I can feel her across the room.

She turns to the old man who plays guitar and nods his way. The music begins. I find myself sitting at the edge of my chair.

She starts with a familiar tune, "Love the Way You Lie." As a kid, my sister used to play the Eminem and Rihanna version over and over, but Keeley chooses Skylar Grey's simple, stripped-down rendition. When she sings about me standing there and watching her both burn and cry, I can't help but twinge with an itsy-bitsy heap of guilt.

"Oh, buddy. Those are some heartrending songs." Rob shakes his head. "You pissed her off."

I hear it, too. And I hurt along with her. How can that be? We had one night. Okay, one great night. One magical night. But still just one fucking night.

My obsession should wear off soon, right?

I hope. I haven't really slept since she left. I definitely can't be in my bed without thinking of her.

At the conclusion of the song, the audience applauds. The ovation is muted because the mood in the room is, too.

Keeley smiles. I can tell it's forced. "Thanks. This next song will be familiar to a lot of you."

When she breaks out with Fergie's "Big Girls Don't Cry," I can't stand it. Her nose is red, her eyes a bit swollen. Contrary to the song, she *has* been crying.

Keeley follows that up with Adele's "Someone Like You." A good-bye and a kiss-off. Everything logical in my head tells me not to wait around until after the show to see if I can speak to her, maybe get her on board—or get her back to my place so I can touch her again—but logic isn't winning the argument tonight.

After a brief break, when she disappears in the back of the joint instead of inviting someone to flirt with her at the bar, she returns for another tear-my-heart-out set, starting with Lady Antebellum's "Need You Now." The only thing that's good about it is how beautiful her voice sounds and the fact that she obviously hasn't forgotten me. I'm sure of that when she shifts her vocals to Avril Lavigne's "When You're Gone."

The way she grips the mic, the emotion on her face, the pleading note in her voice... Yeah, I'm totally convinced this woman walked away from me because I was a bumbling idiot that morning—but she's not over me. We're nowhere near done. Still, I can't give up on orchestrating Griff's downfall.

Where the hell does that leave me?

When she completes her final set with Roxette's "It Must Have Been Love," the nod to *Pretty Woman* seals the deal. I have to stay. I have to try again.

No fucking clue what I'm going to say.

As the audience applauds, she takes her last bow, looking so solemn I want to wrap my arms around her. I don't know if I'll scrape together the right words to ask if she'll come back to me and agree to my plan. But...no guts, no glory.

Beside me, Rob slaps me on the back. "Good luck, man. Don't do anything stupid."

I grab his sleeve. "What is that? What would be not stupid in this scenario?"

I really don't know anymore.

"You're serious?" Rob rears back with a frown. "Wow, I've never seen you less than totally confident. If you want this girl more than anything, you have to apologize, offer to start over, and drop this scheme of yours."

Give up my long-term ambitions for a woman I barely know? "I can't."

Rob looks like he both understands and agrees. "I know you can't. Repaying Griff for his assholery is much more important. Don't worry about the girl. Play her. Get what you need out of her. Then toss her back in the sea like every other fish. She's no big deal."

Then he's gone. I do a quick search of my soul—it doesn't take long—and I realize I want both revenge and Keeley. Absolutely. Probably more than I should, but that doesn't stop me from staring at her like she'll disappear if I blink.

Am I so hung up on this woman because it's been years since anyone walked out on me? My ego isn't fragile. Am I making some subconscious attempt to rewrite my history with Tiffanii and succeed this time with Keeley? No. That mumbo jumbo doesn't ring true.

Then what is my problem? I need to screw my head on straight.

After I toss some bills on the table, I scrub a hand down my face. Keeley stashes the mic, then smiles at the crowd one last time before heading to the employees' area of the bar.

"Keeley..." I charge after her.

Fuck it. I'll dream up something to say. I don't really have too many impulsive bones in my body, but I think fast on my feet. I'm in sales, so something will come to me. I can sew this deal up. I hope.

Except I don't want to sell her right now. I just want to see her.

"Keeley!" I call again, louder this time.

She whirls and catches sight of me. She stops dead in her tracks. "What are you doing here?"

"I want to talk. I never meant to insult or upset you. I've felt terrible about the way things ended, our misunderstanding."

"Misunderstanding? So you didn't tell me to spend time with your brother and if my dazzling wit didn't charm him, it was okay to use my bedroom skills?"

"I know it sounds terrible. Just…give me an hour. Let me explain. I'll feed you more crème brûlée…"

"I'm not a potential client you can reel in with a free dessert coupon, Maxon."

That hurts, especially because I know she's right. "You're not. I never thought that."

"So what *did* you think? That I'd crawl from your bed, put on my slutty dress so I can cloud your brother's head with lust, and never think there was anything wrong with it?"

Pretty much, and when she puts it like that, I wince. "An hour. Please. Will you hear me out?"

She hesitates, and tears tremble on her lower lashes. "I shouldn't."

I'm a bastard but I use her soft heart against her because I want this too much to let it go. "Don't you believe in second chances?"

"You know I do." She sighs. "All right. Don't make me regret this. Where can I meet you? I'm driving myself."

"We can go wherever you want. Name it."

"Sale Pepe. I'm in the mood for Italian."

"I know where that is. I don't mind driving."

She shakes her head. "That didn't work out so well last time. I want a way home, just in case."

My sister would say that Keeley is playing it smart. But the little spitfire with pink hair is usually impulsive and funny and a little bit wild. She's showing me none of that tonight. If I want her to give an inch, I have to stop trying to take a mile.

"All right. I'll follow you to the lot."

Fifteen minutes later, we sit at a two-top in the corner together. The place isn't very crowded this late at night. The waiter is fast, greeting us before I have more than a chance to thank her for agreeing to talk to me.

She orders a veggie panini and a Pellegrino. Now that I'm with her, my appetite finally makes an appearance for the first time in days. I order rigatoni quattro formaggio and a glass of house red. The waiter seems to take forever recounting everything back to us, but finally the kid—who can't stop staring at Keeley—scrams.

We're alone. Well, mostly. A handful of people lounge around the restaurant, but none are seated close to us. Our little corner is as private as anyplace public is going to get.

"What do you want, Maxon?"

Direct. No hint of teasing or flirtation. No smile. I feel slightly panicked and I'm not sure why. Something about her never talking to me again, maybe?

I clear my throat, still grasping for the right words. "I realize everything I said to you the other morning was an insult. I never meant it that way."

"Maybe you believe that. But it wasn't just about the way you treated me. I understood clearly in that moment how you see me."

"No, you don't. You're not cheap. You assumed that. I certainly never said it."

"Maybe you don't think I'm cheap in the hooker sense, but you view me as disposable. I hadn't had sex with anyone in about a year. I only share bodies with someone I think I can share souls with, too. You were a mistake. I can't be with someone who wants revenge more than they want me."

Her words make me feel like a douchebag. "That's not how it is."

Well, not entirely.

She doesn't respond as the waiter sets her sparkling water in front of her. Instead, she merely raises a skeptical brow at me.

I sip my wine. I need to regroup. Come up with something. Appeal to her heart. Simply being near me isn't getting the job done.

I stare into my glass. I need to explain somehow, give her a damn good reason for her to both like me again and help me. The only rationale I can think of is the truth. "Remember I told you that my brother slept with my ex-girlfriend? That my assistant, Britta, is like a sister to me?"

"Yeah."

"That's because she should have been. My sister, that is." I tap the table nervously. "I really thought she and Griff were going to make it…"

"Get married?"

I nod. "He'd started talking about it. He loved her—or I thought he did. They seemed perfect together, but the fucking bastard crushed us all and never looked back."

Her face softens. I'm not looking for sympathy but it feels good to know she's listening. "What happened?"

I blow out a breath. Now it gets hard. "Three years ago, I picked up an overseas client. Royalty. He bound me to absolute secrecy because he wanted someplace lavish to stash his favorite mistress, and the truth would be a terrible scandal. Legally, I couldn't tell anyone, not even my own brother. Despite the fact Griff hadn't assisted with this client, I had every intention of closing the deal and depositing the money in our joint account, like I always did. We shared everything we earned fifty-fifty."

"Makes sense. Why would he get angry about that?"

"Just before signing, Griff found out I was working this side deal and assumed I was trying to screw him out of both the glory and half the commission on the twenty-million-dollar property. He accused me of trying to undercut him and the business we'd spent six years building together. No matter how much I swore it wasn't true, he didn't believe me. He said that because Tiffanii and I were in the throes of splitting up that I'd let her screw with my head."

"So he left the business. You told me," she says. "That upset you, so you want revenge, right?"

"Sure, I'd love to repay that bastard, but if all I wanted was revenge, having you 'distract' him isn't personal enough. If I merely wanted to make him suffer, I'd punch him in the face and hustle all his business out from under him. But it's not that simple. There's more."

"I'm listening."

"By the time the estate closed, Griff had already taken his half of the money from our joint account and moved out of our office—all without saying a word to me. In less than twenty-four hours, he hung out his own shingle and started taking listings. Britta was crushed he didn't take her with him—or even let her know. They'd been dating for a year. But her nightmare got so much worse when Griff e-mailed me to say that he wanted me to know how being stabbed in the back felt, so he fucked my ex. Repeatedly. He even sent pictures. Wasn't that thoughtful? Of course, he knew my assistant would read the message first..." I frown. "Britta had just learned she was pregnant."

I watch Keeley's soft lips fall open. She covers her heart with her palm. "Oh, my gosh... She must have been devastated."

"Utterly. But she's a fighter. She's come back and has been raising my nephew alone. I make sure she and Jamie have everything they need financially. I visit the little guy and play with him when I can." But I'm keenly aware that I'm not daddy material. I'm too much like my own father for that. "To this day, Griff has never acknowledged his son and has never given any indication that he cares."

The waiter comes by with hot plates and sets them down. He tries to break the tension by engaging in small talk that makes me gnash my teeth. Finally, I growl at him until he gets the message.

When he slinks away, Keeley blows out a breath. "I don't blame you for feeling as if your brother has behaved like an absolute bastard. That's a lot to overcome. I'm sorry for you, for Britta, for your nephew. I hope karma gives Griff exactly what he deserves. But, Maxon, if you repay anger with vengeance—no matter how good the reason—what do you think happens next? It becomes hate. Hate is awfully hard to come back from. He's your *family*. This festering fury isn't helping either of you. Maybe you should just call him, clear the air, and—"

"Fuck that. *He* walked out on *me*." I realize I yelled at her and I feel like an asshole. "Sorry. I know you're trying to help. If Griff had shown one iota of remorse, if he'd given us any indication that he missed Britta, wanted his son, or gave a damn about his only brother, I might be willing to let this go. Sometimes I miss him and the closeness we used to share like hell. But he left. He has to be the one to come back."

"Is pride more important than family?"

I curl my fingers around the arms of the chair. If I don't, I'm pretty sure I'll hop to my feet like a fidiot and say something I'll regret. "You have a knack for asking the one question designed to crawl under my skin."

"No, Maxon. I ask you the question designed to make you think."

It's working. And I'm annoyed. Though I shut my mouth before I say anything else. She has a point, and I need to consider it. I take a bite of pasta. It's decent. The wine is better, and it's way more likely to improve my temper.

"He hurt everyone who cared about him," I finally say.

"I get that. And I grant you that I'm removed from the situation, so I don't exactly understand the betrayal you felt. What I am sure of? If you try to make him feel the hurt you've suffered, you'll be no better. Take the moral high ground. I don't know you well, but I believe your grandfather. You're a man of honor, even if you don't know it yet."

She did not just say that. Yes, damn it, she did. "It's not that simple. This shit eats at me every day."

"Stop letting it."

I grab my wineglass and lean in, teeth clenched. "What would you do to get back at the pot-smoking ex who ran out on you? How far would you—"

"I wouldn't. I refuse to give him that much of my energy. But losing the deadbeat dragging me down didn't have the same impact as your brother. I didn't love Tim."

And I'd loved Griff. I sigh. "I can't just let it go."

"Then...I'm not sure we have a reason to see each other anymore." She looks sad at that prospect.

I feel fucking wiped. "Not even to date?"

"Do you really date? You don't make time for the ocean that's literally in your backyard. You're preoccupied with business and one-upmanship. I can't imagine you actually have time for me."

When she stands, I feel my guts drop to my toes. I hop to my feet. "Don't go, Keeley. What about the money I offered you? That's got to mean something."

She shakes her head. "I would never sacrifice my conscience to line my wallet."

Without meaning to, I've insulted her again. "I can't say the right thing here..."

"You can. You just don't want to. You're not ready yet. I'd offer to listen if you wanted to purge your feelings or guide you through some meditation meant to reduce anger—"

I snort. I don't mean to. It just slips out.

A sad smile lifts her lips. "That's what I thought, so I didn't offer."

"I want to see you again, Keeley. I like you." I swallow. "A lot."

That's a pretty big admission for me. I can usually say I like a hookup's tits. I might even say I like her laugh or her eyes or whatever. But I feel like I know Keeley in a way I probably shouldn't after so little time together. And what I do know, I'm enamored with.

"Somehow…I really like you, too. I wish things could have been different." Her blue eyes fill with regret as she tries to sidle past me for the door.

Of their own free will, my fingers wrap around her wrist. "Don't walk out on me, too."

I can't say precisely why I'm… What's the word I'm looking for? I search my mental thesaurus and can only come up with one: begging. Sadly, that's accurate. I have a sneaking suspicion my urge to have her near has less to do with repaying Griff and more to do with my desire.

"I need to go," she murmurs. "Give me your number. I'll…think about it."

With most anyone else, I'd call bullshit. But Keeley has never been less than mindful and ethical and wonderful.

I hand her a business card. My cell is listed on the front. She takes it without a word. Instead, she kisses my cheek, gives me one last look of regret, then shoulders her way past me and out the door.

My head tells me that, Griff aside, it's for the best. As Keeley pointed out, I don't have time for romance. I don't need someone so sentimental they overlook the practical. The chemistry between us would probably fizzle out in another night or two anyway.

So why do I feel as if letting her go might be the biggest mistake of my life?

CHAPTER FIVE

*T*hree long days drag by. I feel like I'm standing in slow motion while everyone is running in fast-forward around me. Rob and Britta are putting together amazing materials to wow the Stowe heirs. Dazzling marketing videos, brokerage tour concepts, and high-dollar-buyer party suggestions. Even a fucking slogan. They are brilliant, thank God.

My brain is stuck.

I'm going through the motions, wishing I could force myself to get my head in the game. I look at my phone again for the umpteenth time today. Not that I expect anything different, but Keeley still hasn't called.

She's gone.

I could track her down…but she has my number. If she wants me to find her, she'd tell me where to look. I feel antsy because I haven't talked to her since the weekend. I even called Gus, the guy who owns the lousy sports bar. He couldn't say if or when Keeley would be singing again. When we spoke, he sounded disappointed, too.

"You okay, buddy?" Rob asks, briefcase in hand.

I glance at the clock. Is it really six fifteen? "Yeah. Have a good one."

"Will do." He hesitates, then looks over at Britta, still huddled over her desk in the far corner. "She all right?"

Britta grilled me about why Keeley was answering my phone the other morning. I couldn't tell Griff's ex that I'd hatched a grand plan to make sure my brother caught a giant case of lust for the woman I put in his path. Britta would see that as a betrayal, whether she wanted to admit it or not. Instead, I told her that Keeley and I had been triaging my old family wounds. Not surprisingly, Britta seemed skeptical of a lounge singer in a cheetah dress giving me life coaching.

"I think. You know Britta."

"Still touchy sometimes. What about you?"

Have I been acting weepy or something? "Me? Sure."

Rob rolls his eyes. "Listen, I know I'm the last person who should give you romantic advice…"

"Um, yeah."

My marketing manager is pushing forty and has never come close to marriage. Until recently, he's always loved them and left them, then somehow convinced them to come back again so he can screw them once last time before casting them off for good. He makes me look like the poster boy for consideration and sensitivity.

"Ha!" Rob rolls his eyes. "I'm going to give you advice. Get laid. You've let this chick mess with your head. Move on. Find another pussy you like." He shrugs. "It usually works for me."

It would be a waste of my breath to point out that he's practically living with Alania, a mortgage broker he met four months ago. I don't expect it will take him much longer to realize that in terms of prowling like a bad boy, she's moved him into the "former" column.

I also don't want to admit that I'm one step ahead of him. On Sunday night, I hung out at the hotel bar near my unit and hit the jackpot with a bachelorette party. Eight single ladies, all eager, all looking to make dreamy memories in paradise. Instead of zeroing in on one from the group and sharing a great night with her, I drank a scotch, nodded their way politely, and left alone.

"Thanks," I say, despite knowing he's full of hot air.

"Have a good one, man. Night, Britta," Rob calls. With that, he leaves.

My assistant stands and stretches, glancing at the time on her computer. "Oh, it's later than I thought. I need to go get Jamie. You going to be okay here?"

"Yeah. Do you need my help with anything?"

"No. I think we'll just have soup and watch a few cartoons before bed. You're welcome to join us for dinner. He likes when Uncle Maxon drops by."

It's been a while since I've seen the little guy, and I'll bet he's grown. I'm certainly not accomplishing much here. I open my mouth to say I'd love to. I'll even bring dinner. But the door to the suite opens.

My heart fucking stops when Keeley walks in. Then it begins to chug triple time. Damn, she looks good dressed in a black tank top, sexy cutoff shorts, and a pair of blingy flip-flops. Her pale skin stands out amidst all the Hawaiian tans. She looks like a pearl, all luminous and gorgeous. It's no surprise I want her. Then again, I probably would have drooled even if she'd been wearing a sack.

"Hi." She gives me an uncertain smile. "Can I talk to you?"

Does she really think there's any way I'm going to say no? "Of course."

She glances at my assistant, hand outstretched. "You must be Britta. I'm Keeley."

I'm floored when my dependable, always friendly assistant fills her hands with work-related stuff and sniffs Keeley's way. "I gathered. Stop messing with his head. He refused to track you down so he could set you straight about my ex because he's a good guy. But I have no such qualms. Griff ripped us both apart. Stop being an AFAOE and actually listen to his side of the story."

"AFAOE?" Keeley frowns.

"Don't worry about it, sunshine." I give Keeley a gentle push toward my office. "Britta is just tired. Cranky. Don't you have PMS, too?"

My assistant utterly ignores my heavy-handed hint to shut up. "It means a fucking authority on everything. That's how you're behaving. You waltz into Maxon's life and want him to give up the biggest deal of his career—his lifelong ambition—over some high-minded ideal about being kind to the man who stabbed us in the back, then left us bleeding to die without a second thought. Grow up."

The room is utterly silent as she slams out the door. I have to close my eyes and shake my head. Could this visit start off any more awkwardly?

"Sorry about that." I show Keeley to a chair in my office, then loop around the desk to sit. Damn, she's a sight for sore eyes. "Coffee?"

"No, thanks. What did you tell her about our conversation?"

I had to tell Britta something. I couldn't think of another quick excuse to explain my moping and lack of focus. Besides, we don't keep many secrets from each other. "I told you a bit about her life to help you understand my situation with Griff. Since I divulged some of her painful past, I felt as if she deserved to know a little about our conversation and…" I need to stop digging myself a verbal hole and shut up. "I told her the advice you'd given me."

"Clearly, she didn't agree." Keeley presses her lips into a grim line, then sighs. "Britta isn't the reason I've come. Can we talk?"

"Of course. I was hoping to hear from you."

Understatement of the century.

"I've given a lot of thought to your request over the past few days."

To my request. Not to me. This isn't exactly what I want to hear. Still, my palms get sweaty. My cock stands straight up. It's all I can do not to drag her into my lap to see if I can work off those Daisy

Dukes and get her in a compromising position. Maybe with her legs straddling my chair and her bobbing on my cock?

"I'm listening." Or I'm trying. My eager dick is making it really tough to hear.

She clasps her hands in her lap and blows out a breath as if she's come to a major decision and is simply working up the nerve to tell me. "I'm willing to take you up on your offer if it still stands."

"What?" I can't have heard that right. Hadn't she all but lectured me that my horrible, unscrupulous plan was an affront to her golden moral compass? "What made you change your mind?"

While it would be most logical, everything inside me hopes she's not merely here for the money.

"A lot of meditation. I'm a big believer that things happen for a reason. When we first met, I admit I hoped you were the soul mate I'm meant to share my life with. But clearly that's not the case. So I asked myself why our paths crossed. The only answer that made sense is that I'm meant to help you see you're a bigger man than this—call it whatever you want—scheme. Maybe I'm supposed to show you that your plan won't work and that you should just talk to your brother."

I stare at her, trying to absorb everything she's said. But it's like pops and buzzers. Nothing makes much sense. "So...after listening to terrible music and closing your eyes to focus on your breathing, you came to the conclusion your soul wasn't born for mine"—I scoff. Who dreams this shit up?—"And that your cosmic purpose is to make me hate my backstabbing brother less?"

She shakes her head. I can tell that, despite herself, she's amused. "That's not exactly how I would characterize it. What I meant was, I think my purpose in your life is to help you resolve the issues with your brother."

Before I can do something stupid, like question her sanity—because she obviously really believes this—I plaster on a smile. "So what's my purpose in your life?"

Keeley won't have a comeback for this. Watch. She's obviously thought about what she knows, what I don't, and all the reasons I'm a dumb ass. Or... "Is this about the money? You want me to finance your future?"

The cynic in me is sure of that, but the rest would rather not hear that I'm right.

"Of course not. I told you I wouldn't accept the money. I meant it." She shrugs. "I think I'm meant to expand my understanding of business so I can succeed with my B and B in the future." She raises a brow at me. "Then again, maybe you're in my life merely to teach me patience."

I can't tell if she's kidding until she sticks her little pink tongue out at me.

I don't want to, but I find myself laughing. "Maybe. So you're actually agreeing to help me distract Griff?"

She nods but holds up a finger. "With conditions."

Of course. I sit back in my chair and cross my arms over my chest. If she's ever negotiated a deal in her life, I'll be shocked. I, however, have been doing this for damn near a decade. "Lay them on me."

"I'm not sleeping with Griff for you, not even if I'm failing. I'll be friends. I'll flirt. I'll lead him on, even. But I won't go to bed with your brother unless it's something I want."

I'm good with that. I intend to make sure Keeley never wants to sleep with my brother. Ever. I don't think I could stand it. "Agreed."

"Good." She nods as if that little win has given her the courage to give me her next condition. "At a time and place of my choosing, you and your brother will sit down, face to face, and have a conversation of no less than one hour."

I lean in, brace my arms on the desk, and I laugh. "How are you going to make him agree to that, sunshine? Griff hasn't talked to anyone from his former life except Harlow in three years. There's no way you'll force him into the same room with me."

"If I can't, that's on me." She shrugs. "But if I'm able to persuade him to listen to reason, you have to sit down and talk. Agreed?"

It'll never happen. "Sure."

"Great. While I'm doing your dirty work, you'll be mentoring me on how I can succeed with my business plan. You'll teach me how to buy the property, how to find reputable contractors, how to advertise on the Internet, and whatever else I need to know. We'll be exchanging...services. As such, we should mutually agree that we're working together so we won't be sleeping together."

She's better at negotiating than I thought, but I only have one answer to that. "No."

"No to what? You won't help me?"

"I'll teach you anything you want to know, sunshine. I'll write up your bid. I'll hand-walk your paperwork. I'll do whatever I can to help you open the inn of your dreams. I will never agree to not having sex with you."

Keeley frowns at me. I see her reddish-brown brows draw together and a little vertical line work in between. "Fine. Because I won't agree to have sex with you. So unless you're going to force me..."

I sit back, cursing under my breath. I won't, and she's probably ninety-nine percent sure of that, so she'll take the tiny gamble. "Tell you what? I won't stop trying to seduce you. Of course, you're always free to say no. I'll never push you to do something you don't want...but I won't give up trying to get you back into bed."

"Why? Because you like an easy lay?"

"Damn it, that is *not* how I see you. I won't stop because I want you."

"Whatever. Don't touch me when I haven't consented, and we'll be just fine."

"All right."

It will be my mission in life to make her burn for me. In fact, I wonder if I can bend her in the next twenty-four hours. How can I stack the deck in my favor? Then I realize I have an ace up my sleeve. "Learning to distract Griff is a full-time job. If you're going to do that, you need to give up everything but school."

"Then I can't afford my rent. Are you going to pay it?"

"No. You're going to move in with me. I've got a spare room."

"I can't break my lease."

I smile. "You can't. But I can." It's been a while since I've looked through a lease for a loophole, but I'm sure I can find one. I scoot closer, move in for the kill. "Think of this as a money-saving opportunity. Free rent. Free food. Free clothes. Free business advice."

Keeley hesitates. "For how long?"

"A month." That covers the three weeks before the Stowe heirs lift their nose from their business, plus another one to make sure the job is good and done. "After that, I'll help you find a place and negotiate a better rental agreement if you want. You're going to come out ahead."

"You're only offering me this option because you want to have sex with me again."

I choose my words carefully. "*And* because I want to divert my brother's attention away from this mega listing. Until today, those two desires have been mutually exclusive. You're giving me a way to have my cake and eat it, too. I'm merely agreeing."

"I don't want to live with you, even in a separate bedroom."

I could tell her that's the deal. Take it or leave it. The words are on the tip of my tongue. But I swallow them. "The ocean in your backyard every day. Meditating to the sound of the waves. I'll even clear a space on the lanai for your yoga."

She bites her lip. I've tempted her. I tamp down a smile.

"That's ruthless."

"That's what I'm good at. Yes or no?"

Her lids slide shut. Her blue eyes are so readable, so being closed off from her is a disadvantage. But if I had to guess, she's really considering my proposal. "I have a couple of events scheduled I can't miss. I have two tests next week. I have to study."

Not a problem. "I have to work. You'll prep for your exams while I'm chained to my desk. When I come home, you're mine."

I'm really hoping we spend most of our time horizontal.

"Since you work a lot, that should be fine. I also committed to teach a yoga class at a senior center near my place every Sunday at nine a.m. It only takes an hour. That's a hundred bucks I could use."

"I'll pay you for your time."

"I can't let them down. I've been doing this for months. They really look forward to it. So do I."

What kind of curmudgeon would I be if I took exercising and socializing away from some old folks? I'm an asshole…but not that much of an asshole. "All right. An hour once a week."

"Next Wednesday night, I'm supposed to see my friend Cami. She's a hairdresser. We trade out. She does my hair, and I help her with guided meditation."

I shake my head. "You won't be needing her, so she'll have to find someone else to guide her thoughts into nothingness."

"But my roots." She points to the top of her head. "My hair doesn't grow in pink, you know."

"It won't be pink for long. Griff has a type. It's very specific. Even if you only flirt with him, you have to turn his head. That color will not do it. The lovely ladies at the Ritz-Carlton spa will transform you under my direction into my brother's wet dream. Since that's the reason for this venture, that point is nonnegotiable."

Keeley doesn't like it. I can tell she's absolutely pissed off. But I'm right. I know exactly what Griff wants, and I'm going to dangle the most beautiful, charming, big-hearted woman in his face…then make sure he can't have her. Screwing Griff out of the Stowe deal will be sweet. But screwing him out of the woman he's dying to have will be every bit as delicious. And if I can be screwing her myself, that will be the sublime cherry on top.

"You're paying to put my hair back exactly the way I'm wearing it now at the end of a month."

"Done." I like it pink, actually. It's darker than an Easter egg, lighter than a raspberry. It suits her. If we haven't boinked our brains out and gotten tired of one another after four weeks, then I'm good with this style.

Hell, as much as I want her now, I'm not sure I'd care if she went bald.

"One more thing. I called Gus this morning. He's doing some remodeling at the bar, expanding the stage. He says the gigs have gone over well. He'd like to have me back on the nineteenth next month."

Two days before the end of our bargain. I weigh carefully my mission versus how much I enjoy hearing her sing. "I'll compromise with you. A week prior, we'll look at our progress. If I think it's sufficient, you can go. If not, you cancel. That gives him a week to find a replacement."

"You're pushing me," she warns. ·

"Look, in different ways, we each hold parts of the other's future in our hands. You're helping me with now, and I'll teach you how to succeed later. I've given where I know I can, but I want evenings dedicated to me." *To us.* "We have a lot to accomplish and not much time to do it. I drive a hard bargain because that's who I am. For the next month, I think you know you should worry more about keeping me happy and worry less about Gus. If, to your point, you won't be making your living off your vocal cords, all you'll have at that crappy sports bar is a good time." *And, sunshine, I'll give you a better one.* "If you want to make your living as an innkeeper, I'm your man."

She sighs. "I feel as if I've conceded a lot to you."

"I've compromised, too." But I know I have Keeley mostly where I want her. I just have to not screw up my good thing.

She gives me a wry smile. "You trying to convince me of that doesn't actually make it true." When she shakes her head as if she's questioning her sanity, I know I've won. "All right. You've got a deal. When do we start?"

"Now. I'll take you back to your apartment. While you pack up, I'll make some arrangements. Text me your class schedule. I'll do my best to be back at the condo by seven every night. You're mine until midnight. No interruptions. I'll see how many hours I can cut out of my weekends." I sit back in my massive chair, feeling a supremely satisfied smile streak across my face.

I'm going to do this so right Griff will never know what hit him.

CHAPTER SIX

*B*y the time we reach my condo, it's nearly nine. Keeley looks pale and a little shell-shocked. Everything has moved fast tonight for a couple of reasons. I didn't want to give her too much time to rethink our deal…and I'm impatient to get her back onto my turf, into my bed.

We wait for the bellman to bring up her belongings. Thank god she rented the apartment furnished, so we only have to move her personal items. That frees up my hands. I can't not touch her, so I tangle fingers with Keeley, pressing our palms together.

She wriggles away from me. "Don't. This is a business relationship now."

I could argue that it doesn't have to be, but now isn't the time to pick that fight. Later. When she's comfortable and happy, when she's feeling less overwhelmed.

"All right. It's late. I'll call for dinner. There's a menu in the kitchen near the microwave. It's propped against the wall."

Keeley picks up the well-loved page and scans it with a wrinkle of her nose. "You clearly eat someone else's food too often. So much sodium and fat and preservatives. Um…I'll cook. Do you have any staples in your pantry and fridge?"

"Booze. Popcorn. Maybe a can of soup. I don't cook here." In fact, I'm wondering if, other than an occasional egg or sandwich, I've ever made a meal in my own kitchen.

"Oh, my gosh. You're such a man."

The way she rolls her eyes tells me that's not a good thing.

"Hey, I get by."

"Clogging your arteries every day, sure." Suddenly, she points at me, determination all over her pixie features. "I'm going to addict you to good-for-you food in the next month. You're going to crave meals that didn't come out of a damn freezer. And I intend to make sure you can feed yourself properly after I'm gone."

"As long as I get five hours of your time every day, why not?"

I have to eat. Sure, I could be healthier. Since I turned thirty a few years back, I notice that weight creeps up if I don't maintain my strict gym habits. I'm sure less crappy food would make it easier to stay healthy. And I'll get to spend more time with Keeley.

After she prowls through my kitchen, she turns to me with a shake of her head. "It's empty."

"I'm not—"

"Here that much. You've told me. As far as dinner goes, that's going to change."

For tonight, we call room service. While we wait, she moves into the spare bedroom. I linger in the doorway, try to talk to her. I attempt to be charming. I really want to remind her that half of my big bed is empty. I wonder if she would buy my argument that we could help the environment if we only needed to wash one set of sheets each week?

"How have you been the last few days?" I venture that line of questioning to see where the conversation goes.

"Perplexed," she says honestly.

I understand what she means. "Me, too, I didn't get a chance to tell you the other night, but you sang great."

"Thanks."

That's all she has to say? Since she simply continues to pluck garments from her suitcase and hang them in the closet, I guess so.

I search for another conversation starter. "So you'll just call your other jobs in the morning and quit?"

"Yes."

And? "If they require two-week's notice, you can't give it to them."

"Understood." She sounds a bit down about that.

I want to comfort Keeley, but she has an invisible force field around her that warns me to keep out. Instead, I promise her something more practical. "Since you'll be out of work, the offer of a hundred grand is still there. Just say the word."

She gives me a noncommittal hum. I'm back at proverbial square one. If I touch her...well, I saw what happened to Hulk Moron's balls the night we met. I promised I wouldn't lay a hand on her against her will. Actually, I didn't think she'd have much will to resist me. But I suspect this woman is far more stubborn than I gave her credit for. What if we spend the whole month without sex?

At the thought, I want to hang myself with barbed wire.

"This arrangement is going to work out." I'm more hopeful than convinced, but I'm doing my best to be persuasive and upbeat for her.

"Sure."

Her one-word responses are killing me. I grit my teeth. "You know, we'll be together for a month. We have to speak to each other."

Keeley finally pauses, looks away from her suitcase. "We have to speak about Griff and whatever I need to learn about the man in order to wow him. We have to speak about business stuff and how I can run the best inn ever." She gives me a tight smile. "We don't have to speak about anything else. Call me when the food is here."

With that, she shuts the door between us, right in my face.

Screw being at square one. I'm less than zero.

I'm beginning to think that, despite negotiating this agreement to my advantage, I got thoroughly screwed.

I CAN'T SLEEP. Knowing that only one teeny-tiny closed door separates me from Keeley frustrates the fuck out of me. On the other hand, she's so much closer than she was the night before. I'm getting the sense that I need to accept the small victories with her while plotting the larger ones in the future.

It's already after midnight. I can't sit still. The heavy doorknob that opens Keeley's portal is like a magnet, urging me toward her with a gravitational pull I can hardly resist.

But I have to—for now.

As promised, I clear a spot on the lanai and stow her yoga mat out there so she'll have it in ready position after sunrise. I also find a local grocery store that takes online orders. Grabbing the list Keeley made earlier, I take my laptop to bed and arrange for everything to be delivered by four o'clock tomorrow afternoon. I'll ask her to be here. That way she can sign for it all and start cooking. We'll eat as soon as I walk in the door. Maybe domestic bliss will ensue...which might include hugging and kissing and reintroducing her to my bed.

I'm fantasizing about tomorrow evening. She doesn't mind spending a little time on her knees, right? But I'm equal opportunity. If she wants to lie back, spread her legs, and let me do my worst, I'm all in. Hell, I'm fucking excited. In fact, if I get any more excited, I'll have to take myself in hand. This raging erection poking at the fly of my pajama pants is pissing me off.

Why is Keeley the only woman who makes me lose my self-restraint?

I'm trying to solve that conundrum when my phone rings. The name on the display provokes a smile. "Hey, Harlow."

"Hey, big brother. What's up?"

"Work. You know. Not much new." Well, that's not exactly true, and if Keeley could hear me, she'd raise that brow and look at me like my ethics suck. "Well, maybe a little new. I might have met someone."

"Yeah? I was going to talk to you about Mom and Dad's latest drama, but this sounds way more interesting. Tell me more."

"Her name is Keeley. I met her in a bar."

"Oh, dear god. So it's a meaningful relationship, then?" Harlow snorts.

"I'm kind of hoping it is." I like her. That's more than I can say for most of my hookups.

"Exactly how did you two meet?"

I debate whether to tell her about my scheme to sidetrack Griff because A) since Harlow still speaks to both of us, she asked me not to put her in the middle of our feud a long time ago. And B) even if she didn't call me twenty kinds of dumb ass and agree to keep my secret, I don't want anything—even unwittingly—to slip loose.

On the other hand, Harlow would make a hell of an ally...and a spy.

It's a calculated gamble, but after some mental debate, I decide it's worth the risk.

I give her the abbreviated version of events, minus the sex. "Want to help me make sure Keeley succeeds?"

"Maybe. Tell me the truth first. You nailed her, didn't you?"

Harlow has always been smart and good at reading between the lines.

"I couldn't help it. I'm really into this girl. I'm not sure yet what we have in common. But she's a good person. You'd like her. She only agreed to my plan because she's convinced she can help Griff and me patch up our spat." I scoff. "Like that's ever going to happen."

"If you keep being a douchebag, it won't. Isn't three years long enough to hold this grudge? You didn't love Tiffanii, thank god. Don't be so bitter."

We've had this argument before. "It's not about Tiffanii." Although when he moved her in with him, it sucked knowing my brother was shacking up with the woman I'd thought I might marry someday. In retrospect, it didn't actually hurt. "What burned me was the way he handled everything."

"If it helps, I think he regrets it."

On the tip of my tongue sits my usual acerbic answer: *Isn't it too late for that now?* I hold the words in. The sentiment is old, and I'm tired of feeling it. Besides, she knows my outlook on this. "If that's true, he could start by apologizing."

"You could help him along by not trying to dangle a woman in his face designed solely to trip him up. You know he gets terribly distracted."

I do. His business almost didn't make it the first four months because he was too wrapped up in Tiffanii to pay attention to much else. I heard a rumor that he'd planned a surprise getaway for two to Bora Bora. When he came home to pack a suitcase, he instead found some other guy packing his cock into Tiff's pussy.

Can't say I was surprised… She cheated on me, too. It's why we broke up.

"He's getting what he deserves," I argue.

"Maxon, stop. I know he hurt you."

So fucking much. I really still don't know how to reconcile the kid brother who did everything *with* me with the man who did his utmost to take everything *from* me.

"Did you ever stop to think that maybe you hurt him, too?"

"Bullshit."

"Ugh, you and Griff both have way too much fight and pride for your own good." Harlow sighs on the other end of the line. "You know, I've never met this Keeley woman, but maybe she's onto something. If one of her conditions to this hare-brained scheme is for you to sit down with Griff for an hour and just talk, I can get behind that. I'll even spy on him for you if it helps to end this."

"Excellent." I smile.

"That remains to be seen. I just hope I don't regret my decision."

Somewhere in the back of my head, I wonder if both Keeley and Harlow are right. Will my plan do anything more than ratchet up this ugly family feud?

Who cares? a voice in my head asks. It's unlikely we're going to be pals again tomorrow. Or ever.

"You won't." I give her an empty assurance because I know it could become a shit storm. But I have to try. "So what's the Mom and Dad drama?"

I'm not sure I actually want to know. It's always horrendous. Frankly, I wonder how they ever got along enough to conceive three children. They only stay married now because it would cost Dad too much money to divorce Mom. She puts up with his crap because she's never worked outside the home a day in her life and wouldn't know how to start now. So they have a sick, co-dependent union. Mom shakes him down to "maintain her lifestyle," and Dad puts up with it because he can't afford to do anything else. Besides, she's the grand hostess for glitzy community events that make her giddy and the stuffy business parties that further his career.

"I don't know if they're going to make it out of this, Maxon. Something's up. Something more serious."

I frown. "If they're not speaking, that's nothing new."

"Of course it's not," Harlow agrees. "This is more than the normal resentment, silence, or accusations and yelling. This is ugly. It's…cold."

Harlow isn't the sort of woman to be dramatic. Mom and Dad took care of all that for us kids, so we had to stay pretty grounded or lose our minds. "You think they might actually split up for good this time?"

"I think it's really possible."

Her words sink in. Not that they've been married in spirit for at least the last two decades, but the thought of them being legally divorced is chilling in a way I don't understand. "See if you can find out what's going on and keep me posted, okay?"

"Sure. Britta and Jamie doing good?"

"Yeah." I think. I haven't actually seen the little guy in a while. Other than Harlow, they're really the only family I have left. I should make time for them. I'll need them when I'm old and gray, I guess. And I care. That's pretty rare for me.

"She still hasn't changed her mind about making Griff live up to his responsibilities with Jamie?"

"No." And she's not likely to.

When Griff didn't acknowledge Britta's pregnancy, we both figured he just didn't care. She pleaded with Harlow, who still talks to the asswipe, to leave it alone. If Griff didn't want his own son, she didn't want anyone trying to make him give a shit. My sister didn't love it but she agreed to respect Britta's choice, mostly because she was pissed at Griff, too. And we all agreed that Jamie needed to be kept a secret from my parents. My mother would have turned that into a custody battle worthy of a made-for-TV movie. We know all too well how my father would treat the boy.

"He's going on three..."

I get the emotional argument for Jamie meeting his father. I do. I would have loved a father who gave a damn about something besides business. "I think Jamie is better off. Britta gives him unconditional love."

Barclay Reed never gave that to his sons. Neither of his apples have fallen far from the tree, either. I worry Griff would only use his son to manipulate Britta, and because she would move heaven and earth to protect the little guy, she'd let Griff run all over her. Keeley would probably find my low opinion of him shocking, but what good does lying to myself do?

"I know she does," Harlow agrees. "And she's been through a lot, but I think Griff has changed. He's... I don't know. Less angry."

Or better at hiding his problems. "Maybe you caught him in a good mood. Griff is never going to change. I don't think he wants to."

"Do you?" she asks softly.

I grit my teeth in irritation. "Haven't you done enough probing, Freud? Why don't you bug your fiancé for a while?"

"He's in London on business, so I decided to call you instead. Aren't you lucky?"

I have to smile. "Honestly?"

"No," she teases back. "Keep your opinion to yourself. I should get back to studying. Big exams coming up. Tell me when Keeley is ready to go in. I'll call Griff, see if I can figure out where he's at mentally and what his schedule is like. After they've officially met, I'll be nosy, find out what he thinks of her, then report back."

"Perfect." Having a co-conspirator should feel good—a sign that I'm not fucking up everything with this plan. But ultimately, Harlow is on Keeley's side. I can't lose sight of that.

So...I'm alone. What else is new? And why does that suddenly bother me?

CHAPTER SEVEN

*K*eeley is still asleep when I leave for the office. I know it would piss her off, but I sneak into the spare room. I have to make sure she's all right, don't I?

She takes my breath away. Lying on her back with her arm cocked up and knuckles brushing her smooth, pale cheek, she looks angelic. She also appears as if she's sleeping naked. I want to peek under the blankets to be sure, but I can't risk waking her up and inciting her wrath. I'm smart enough to pick my battles. Still, I don't see any sleeves or spaghetti straps. If she's in the buff, maybe that's a silent sex invite.

Or not, dumb ass.

When my phone starts buzzing in my pocket, I slip out so I don't wake Keeley. All through my workout, I speak to a client in Vienna. After a quick shower at the hotel's fitness facility, I head to the office. There, the pace doesn't change all day. It's one phone call after another from clients buying or selling amazing properties on Maui. They have multiple demands. This sort of thing has beaten me down over the last few days. But right now I'm energized. I'm making it happen. Tonight, I'll go home to Keeley. She'll fix me food. Hopefully, we'll talk, preferably in more than monosyllables. Then…who knows?

I smile.

As afternoon slips toward quitting time, Britta drops a hand on my shoulder. "I'm sorry about yesterday. I lost my temper."

It's unlike her, so I know Keeley's ideas about healing the rift between me and my brother upset Britta on some level, probably the one where she'd be forced to see Griff—and maybe share their son—if we mend fences. "Don't apologize. You have a right to your thoughts and feelings."

"And she has a right to hers." Britta looks down, peeling a bit of old turquoise polish from her thumbnail. "I think I was a bit jealous, too. If Griff meets Keeley, even to negotiate peace, I'm sure he'll be attracted to her."

Britta sees that, too. Nice validation of my plan…not so nice reality for my assistant's feelings. She knows precisely what kind of woman attracts Griff since she's paid attention to the wide swath of females my bonehead brother has "dated" since their split. That tears her up, probably more than usual because she couldn't really date in the same way. She gave birth to a much bigger responsibility that doesn't allow for random sating of her sex drive. I'm glad for her that she has a seemingly steady someone now, even if it still seems weird to see her with someone else.

"Hey, why don't you take off early? Go spend more time with your little man. Jamie would like that."

"I can't. He had a field trip today. They won't be back at daycare until five."

"Do you miss him?"

"Jamie? Every day but—"

"Griff."

Britta falls dead silent. She presses her lips together. A furrow takes up residence between her brows.

She's not the same woman she used to be. Before everything went to hell, Griff and I decided that Britta would become my assistant so the two of them didn't keep mixing business with plea-sure. He hired an empty nester looking for something to occupy her time since the last of her kids had gone to college. Sheila still works for him, I hear. But three years ago, Britta always wore bright colors and a smile every day, along with heels and short skirts and a cocky attitude.

Today, she's got on a navy pencil skirt that almost covers her knees, a plain white starched blouse, and a beige cardigan that does nothing to liven her up. She's scraped her blond hair into a tight bun. If she wore makeup this morning, it's gone now. Britta dresses like a librarian. She acts like an old maid. She looks as if she has the weight of the world on her shoulders.

"No," she answers hesitantly. "I don't miss him."

She sounds as if she's trying to convince herself.

"Be honest."

We haven't talked about this in well over two years. At first, when the anger was still fresh for us both, we ranted and railed and trashed her apartment together. We grieved. We grew close. I wonder why I've never wanted to have sex with her. Under her current frump garb, she really is gorgeous. I guess in my head she always belonged to Griff.

In so many ways, she still does.

Britta swallows and won't quite meet my gaze. "I tell myself I shouldn't. He obviously hasn't looked back."

"But you do?" My heart softens. It's been doing that a lot lately.

I'm not a fan.

She sighs in defeat. "Sometimes. More than I want to."

"Me, too," I tell her. After all, I don't want her to feel alone.

Besides, Griff is a ghost in the room all too often. I kept meaning to move my offices elsewhere after he left. I just…didn't. Never enough time, never high on my priority list. I never got around to it.

"But it's over and it doesn't matter anymore." She forces a

chipper expression. "Tell me, what's the deal with you and Keeley? I thought she'd be temporary."

I frown. "Why would you think that?"

"Not that many people meet the love of their life in a bar, Maxon. And I admit, that tight animal-print dress just said 'bimbo' to me...which I realize is judging a book by its cover and that's unfair. She's nice?"

I nod. "And interesting. Smart. She makes me laugh. She even makes me think."

"You, think? That's a feat." Britta gives me a teasing grin. "Oh, my gosh, you like her."

"Yeah." I won't deny the obvious. But I also can't tell my assistant more. "We'll see what happens. Maybe nothing."

"Or maybe she's the someone you can finally invest your heart in. That would be great. I'd be really happy for you." She turns quiet. "You deserve better than Tiffanii."

Can't argue there. "What about you? You deserve to be happy, too. Are you still seeing Makaio?"

"Yes." Her smile turns muted.

"He seems like an okay guy. How's that going?"

"He's a good man. Kind. Patient. Funny. He seems to love spending time with Jamie. I'm lucky."

The words she uses to describe this guy suggest he's top-notch boyfriend material. She might say she's lucky, but she doesn't sound happy. She's not in love, though I suspect she wants to convince herself she is. "You guys have been dating for...six months?"

"Eight." Her voice has gone quieter.

"Getting serious?" I ask.

I don't think she's ready for that.

"He's spending a couple of nights a week at my place." Britta hesitates. "I have this feeling—intuition?—he's thinking about proposing."

I sit back in surprise. "Really? That's...fast."

"A little," she concedes.

"How do you feel?"

"He says he loves me."

I analyze her expression, her body language. She's closed off, her movements small, her voice gone soft. She didn't actually answer my question. "You don't love him back."

I see a crack in her outer shell. "I care a lot. And if he asks me to be his wife, I can't think of a single reason to say no. He's loving and steady. He has a good job, a great family. He treats Jamie like his own. He helps with everything when he's around the house. His heart is open…"

In other words, he's perfect—for someone else.

"You can't help it if you're not ready to move on."

"I need to be! I loved your brother. But he's gone, and I can't stay stuck here."

She's got a point…but one point isn't the whole picture. "If Makaio wants to marry you, don't you owe him your whole heart? Is it fair to make him settle for only the parts of you that you've wrested free from Griff?"

Now she looks agitated. "Maybe knowing I'm committed will make a difference. Maybe that will free up my heart. All I know is that Griff has taken years of my past, and I refuse to give him more of my future."

That's wishful thinking. "I get it, but—"

"Why are you grilling me like this? In the old days, you would have just asked if he made me laugh and if he was good in bed. What's with the probing questions about the state of my soul?"

I can't refute her. Normally, I would ask those very questions. I might claim I want details just to watch her blush. But I fear the reason I'm different now has something to do with Keeley's bad influence.

"You're right. It's none of my business. I'll shut up."

She sighs with regret and shakes her head. "Sorry. You asked fair questions. I just don't have any answers."

"I'm always here if you need help figuring it out."

"Thanks. You're one of my best friends." She gives me a sisterly pat on the shoulder. "I mean this in the most loving way but, at least for now, I need you to butt out."

If she was grilling me hard-core about my love life, I'd probably be touchy, too. "All right. I'm butting out. Just don't rush into anything, okay?"

"It's been three years. I'd hardly call that doing a ten-yard dash to the altar." She picks up the last of her stuff. "I think I'll go ahead and leave. I can run a few errands before I pick Jamie up. Good night."

"Night."

I've got two hours before I can go home. I return a few phone calls, answer a few e-mails I've been putting off. Rob and Britta have assembled a "war room" in Griff's former office and filled it with ideas for the Stowe estate. I poke around, see their progress, make a few mental notes. Something is bugging me about everything they've laid out so far. I was loving it yesterday but today it feels like too much hoopla. Like we're planning a rockin' New Year's Eve party in March. The strategy seems overdone and outdated. The visuals look like overkill. Everything feels…wrong.

What would be right?

No damn idea. What do I know about the Stowe kids or their preferences? I don't usually research clients. What's there to say? They have a house to sell and I know how to list well and find a buyer. End of story.

Except my gut tells me not this time.

When I plop behind my desk again, my eyes go immediately to the clock on my laptop screen. Seventy minutes until I can close up shop.

Could this day drag on any more?

I can fill it by staring at a wall and thinking about all the fantastic things I'd like to do in bed with Keeley. With the sleek line of her shoulders and back, along with the feminine flare of her hips, she'd look great if I fucked her from behind, filling my hands with her tits. Mentally, I throw in a few of her gasps and cries because of course I'm going to make her come. On the other hand, she'd look great on top, too. That bright hair thrown back, exposing the delicate, pale curve of her throat, breasts bouncing with every thrust as she grabs my shoulders and cries out my name.

Yeah, I can picture it now.

Unfortunately, it also makes my cock so hard my pants are damn uncomfortable. And I still have sixty minutes before I can leave. Even when I get there, no matter how much I want to touch Keeley, she's not going to say yes simply because I want her to. If I press her, she'll remind me that she's not fair game.

Maybe I should pull my brains out of my dick and focus on work.

Google tells me that the Stowe descendants are George, twenty-seven, and Vivienne, twenty-three. Their father died a decade back after a lingering bout with cancer. The elder of the Stowe kids finished an MBA from Yale three years ago and has been running the family business day to day since. Shortly thereafter, their mother moved to Maui and remained until she died of an unexpected heart attack ten days ago. Vivienne graduated from Vassar last year and, though planning to be married soon, is making the Stowes' legacy, their syrup company, her number one priority. The *Burlington Free Press* even included a picture of the siblings clutching hands and sharing a moment of grief on the snowy day of their mother's funeral.

I sit back, ponder. By all accounts, these heirs value family, tradition, and their New England roots. George was quoted as saying that he had never stepped foot in his mother's Maui home and never planned to. He sounds proud of that fact. It seems a bit like sour grapes to me, but I imagine that if I'd come from a normal family—which I didn't—if my father had died and my mother took off to someplace seemingly exotic seven time zones away, I might be bitter, too. Confused at the very least.

It also makes me realize that George and Vivienne probably aren't attached to the idea of having Griff list their place, as their mother had been. They simply don't have a good reason not to. If I give a better pitch than my brother, I might have a real shot at this listing.

With a curse, I tear everything pinned up on the war room's walls down, tuck all the ideas away in a drawer, find a marker at the white board, and write two words: THINK SIMPLE.

I return to my laptop and pound out an e-mail to Rob and Britta, linking them to the articles I've read about the Stowe siblings. I close with assurances that we'll regroup and discuss tomorrow. We can get this done.

I'm onto something. I feel it. Griff is going big, bold, loud—and he's in deep with that strategy. Somehow, I know that's so wrong and I'm completely right. I'm going to find a way to win. I just need one more advantage to get it done.

Keeley. I look at the clock and I smile.

Now it's time to go.

Game on.

WHEN I ENTER THE CONDO, I find all the doors and windows open. Ocean salt mixes in the air with ginger and sizzling sesame oil that smells like one of my favorite restaurants.

Keeley is cooking. More than my stomach jumps with excitement.

"Hi." I set my keys and laptop on the bar and peer at her behind the stove. "What are you making?" *And what are you wearing under that little sundress?*

She turns with a distracted glance. "Asian."

I peer closer. "I had a wok?"

"No." She huffs out a breath that says she doesn't want to speak to me but knows she has to. "When I finished school, I came back here to start homework. The groceries arrived on time, but you have almost no pots, pans, utensils… How did you think I would cook the food?"

That might be a fair question. "I had, um…a couple of saucepans, didn't I? A skillet, a cookie sheet, and some other stuff."

She rolls her eyes. "And how long have you lived here? Never mind. I already know your excuse. You're not home much."

"Right. So, the wok came from where? Did you have one in your boxes?"

"No, I used my homework time to run to the Target in Kahului to buy a few things I'll need if we're going to eat reasonably in this place for the next month." She reaches into her pocket, pulls out a strip of paper, and slaps it on the bar. "Here's the receipt."

I glance at it. She managed to fill my kitchen with stuff for less than a hundred and fifty dollars. Frugal. I would have ordered a bunch of crap from Williams Sonoma and paid the exorbitant shipping fee for the convenience. But the fact that she stopped what she was doing to take care of me…

Well, probably not *all* for me. She's feeding herself, too. But she's including me, so that counts. And it smells spectacular.

"I'll give you cash," I promise her. "I didn't consider that my kitchen wouldn't be stocked. Sorry."

She softens and shrugs. "I know. But you're on dish patrol. I'll finish my homework then, so we can get started on…whatever."

"Sure."

"Thanks for laying out my yoga mat, by the way. I really enjoyed my morning workout. What time did you leave?"

"Six thirty. The usual."

"You put in a twelve-hour day?" She frowns like she's worried.

Does that mean she cares a little?

"Eleven. I worked out first. Actually, I cut today a little short, but coming home to these smells makes it worthwhile. What's in there?" I try to peer across the space between us and into the wok.

"Not telling. You have to try it first and let me know whether you like it. I set some placemats and silverware out on the lanai. And some wine. This will be ready in two. Go change."

"You're bossy."

"You need it," she tosses back without missing a beat.

I laugh, relieved that she's giving me more than clipped, one-word answers today.

After a quick change into shorts, I come out of my bedroom to find her carrying two plates outside. The evening is warm, pleasant. Sunset beckons over the glittering blue water, filling the sky with shades of pink, orange, and yellow. I pour wine as the sultry breeze grazes my skin. It's nice out here. Why didn't I ever spend time outside before? I can't really remember a reason. Just…busy.

But I'll change that to savor every moment I can with Keeley.

She sits beside me, staring out at the water and sipping her wine. "Good day?"

"Interesting. Britta sends her apologies for yelling at you. She's got a lot going on." Vaguely, I worry about whether Makaio will propose to Britta and how she might answer. The idea of my parents divorcing niggles at me, too. But I can't borrow any more trouble now. I need to focus on prepping Keeley to become the distraction Griff can't afford…while figuring out how to bend her no-sex rule—a lot. "I might be making some progress on the big deal I was telling you about."

"Yeah?"

I shovel the first bite into my mouth. My taste buds are ready to declare undying love. This is probably more vegetables than I've eaten in the last month, but everything is so crisp and fresh. I'm devouring it with my eyes and my mouth—and I'm loving it. Maybe she's right about dining out too much. Nothing at a restaurant ever tastes like this. "Hmm. This is amazing."

She smiles proudly. "Now you can say you like tofu."

I choke and try not to spit it out. "What the fuck?"

"Don't think about it. Keep chewing. Tell me about your deal."

We talk a bit. As long as I don't think about the fact that I'm eating soy milk that's coagulated into curds, I enjoy the flavor. I show her some pictures of the estate and walk her through what I've learned about the sellers.

"I think panoramic pictures and big parties and streaming a live YouTube event is the wrong plan," I muse aloud. "On paper, it should be right. This is a really unique, breathtaking estate. But to convince these sellers, I think less is more."

She looks at the pictures on my phone, then takes another sip of wine. "Absolutely. Flaunting this estate and celebrating it for these two syrup heirs who may never understand their mother's decision to leave them even before she died will be a losing strategy."

There. Keeley put into words exactly what my instinct was telling me.

"So it stands to reason that the approach I use for sheiks, European business moguls, Asian dignitaries, and assorted royalty around the world isn't the one I should take now."

She shakes her head. "Not for two grieving, salt-of-the-earth siblings."

I send her a challenging stare. "I thought you didn't know anything about business."

"I don't. But I know people. And from everything you've said, those two want this over and they want top dollar for their mom's place. I'll bet they want to put the funds back into the business and honor their family's legacy."

What she says makes a lot of sense. I should have thought of that sooner. I know business…but I never thought people mattered that much. I'm marketing houses. I'm making money. None of that is about individuals.

But maybe that's why Griff is more successful at selling. He's good at reading folks. He watches, listens, pays attention. Which is why I could never understand how he completely misunderstood my intentions when he walked off without saying a fucking word. How did he not get that I loved him and I would never have betrayed him? Why did he think I was capable of such deceit? Not that I'm not a bastard. I am. But if I wanted to mess with a loved one, I'm not the kind of coward to stab them in the back. I'd punch them in the face.

"You're right. That makes so much sense. I need to tell Rob and Britta." I reach for my phone.

"Finish your dinner first. Nothing worse than cold snow peas."

"And tofu," I grouse.

She laughs at me. The sound sparkles. The waning light of the day makes her fair skin shimmer with a warm glow. I'm drawn to her as if I'm the dark daring to peer into the light.

"All right." I take another bite. "Thanks for listening, by the way."

She nods. "So...I guess if I'm going to tempt your brother into losing his mind, I need to know about him."

I nod. Down to business. I can respect that, even if I'd rather keep things between us personal. "Griff—Griffin, which he hates— is three years younger than me. He's almost my doppelgänger. But of course I'm way more awesome." I flash her a cheesy grin.

"I had no doubt." She rolls her eyes. "What is *he* like?"

The fact that I'm not good at reading people does not help me with this question. "Um..."

"What does he like to do? What are his hobbies? What does he value? What are his goals?"

I frown. Three years is a long time, and I don't know how much his interests might have changed. After he left, I tried to close my memories of him away into a little box and nail that sucker shut. The knowledge feels rusty.

"He likes to succeed as much as I do. He's better at socializing, so he'll put on a gregarious face and act like your best fucking friend. But under the facade, he's a ruthless bastard, too. Like me, he'll crush anyone in his way. He values hard work and everything that comes with it—money, success, beauty... If I had to guess, his number one goal is to beat me."

"So how is he different than you?"

Good question. We had roughly the same upbringing, with a mother who didn't know how to control two rambunctious boys, so she gave up trying, and the same asshole of a father, who didn't mind doing whatever it took to squeeze the most out of us.

"Up until he walked out, I would have told you Griff was the most loyal bastard imaginable. The one time I saw him love, he went full throttle—hard and open. He didn't care what anyone thought." Well, except our dad.

"And that bothered you?"

I shrug as I finish the last of my dinner. "I didn't think about it. I didn't love. Too much of a weakness, so I overcame it. I don't know if Griff ever did."

Keeley looks totally horrified by my answer. "Who told you love was a weakness?"

"Dear old Dad. If you think I'm a raving son of a bitch, you ought to meet him."

She frowns as if she would rather not. "So you think Griff loved Britta?"

"I would have sworn he did, but it didn't matter in the end. I'm sure he thought that, as my assistant, Britta was in on the secret deal I was working at the time, the one he thought I took to undercut him. But she didn't know about it, either. I gave her some tasks associated with the purchase, but I never told her the client's name or the address of the residence. She was totally in the dark."

"You're right. He should have asked questions, but if your father only taught you disdain for love…"

"That might be an understatement. He told us both from the time we were kids to learn from his mistake and to marry only if a woman upped our stock. If she brought cash or a pedigree to the marriage, that was logical. But love did nothing except give a man an Achilles' heel enemies could use against us."

At her look of horror, I'm almost embarrassed by my upbringing. Most people would be jealous. Big house, gated community,

the best schools, all the new toys and gadgets, trips, money, oppor-
tunities. I was full of first-world problems.

"It wasn't that bad."

"It doesn't sound good," she contradicts. "So his marriage to
your mom isn't...happy."

I scoff, then snag a swig of wine. "No. Dad has had more
mistresses than new ties over the years."

"Do you resent him for it?"

Interesting question. "I don't know. It just is. I don't like him for
it. I think..." I sigh, grappling for a way to explain my family. "I
first found out about his extracurricular sex life when I was eight.
I'd done really well on a math test he had warned me not to fail.
After school, instead of going home, I convinced a friend's mom we
carpooled with that I had to go to my dad's office. I pleaded some
emergency. When I got there, I barged in and found his secretary on
her knees in front of his massive office chair, her head bobbing in
his lap. They jumped apart guiltily." I close my eyes, still remembering how much that day shattered the boy I once was. "He wore
a ring of her lipstick around his dick."

Keeley holds her breath. "What did you do?"

"My friend's mom dropped me off in front of my house, but I
ran to the nearby park instead and hid. I didn't make it home until
almost midnight."

She braces a hand over her heart, and I can almost feel her
worry. "Your parents must have been worried sick."

"I was too pissed to care. A neighbor finally found me." I'd been
hiding between two bushes, dry eyed and hungry and confused as
hell. At that age, I wasn't precisely sure what my father was doing
with that other woman, but I knew it was wrong. "When I got
home, my mother screamed out her anger that I worried her for
nothing before she retreated to bed. Once we were alone, my father
sat me down and told me not to be a righteous little pussy about
what I'd seen that afternoon. Then he took a conference call with
someone in China. We never spoke about it again."

"Did you ever tell your mom what you saw?"

I shake my head. "You have to understand... I was a kid who wanted to please the father who never seemed to have time for me. I thought keeping his secret—and a lot of the others I learned about over the years—might make him care more. Besides, I think my mom knew and tattling would have been merely rubbing her face in all her misery."

"Does Griff know what kind of man your father is?"

"Of course," I assure her. "He figured it out a few years later when he discovered Dad banging his third-grade teacher."

Keeley pushes her bowl away, shaken. "I can't imagine... My father loved us with all his heart. The day he passed away, he squeezed my mother's hand in his hospital bed, kissed my forehead, and promised her that his love for us was deathless, even if he wasn't. He was a good man. Despite having remarried a few years ago, my mom still wears a locket with his picture around her neck. I miss him."

Tears shimmer in her eyes. The memory is one she holds close to her heart. She's proud to wear the emotion on her face.

I'm not the enemy, but if I was, she just exposed a big chink in her armor. Does she know that? Or does she trust me enough not to use her feelings against her?

I like that idea.

"And mine is a selfish, womanizing pig. Griff and I saw a thousand instances of that as teenagers. When we were little kids, he seemed to take delight in watching us twist and contort, trying to please him. But when we interned with him a few summers, we bonded over our dislike of the way he treated us. We swore we'd never be anything like him."

Yet I fear he's exactly who we've both become.

Our shared boyhood crap held us together until three years ago, when that goddamn deal with the freaking Middle Eastern prince splintered our pact into a thousand pieces. If I'm being really honest, I've been somewhat lost since.

"I'm getting the picture," she murmured. "Did you try to talk to your brother after he left?"

"Sure. I thought someone had stolen money from our bank and broken into our office at first. I called him that morning he didn't show up for work. He answered with 'Fuck off, you backstabbing shitbag' and hung up. So I went to his place. He lives in a guarded complex. He told the guard there to advise me that I was no longer welcome."

That's one memory I would rather forget, driving over to Griff's building and trying to reason with security as the pounding rain soaked my freshly starched shirt thirty minutes before I was supposed to FaceTime this royal prick every square inch of the property he was signing for later that day. Security wouldn't budge, and I drove away soaked and confused and fucking sad.

"That's it?"

"What else did you want me to do? He wouldn't see me. He wouldn't see Britta, even when she sent a letter to his house to tell him that he would be a father in seven months. He just cut us cold."

Keeley pauses, and I see the wheels in her head turning. "Then came his nasty e-mail with the pictures of him and Tiffanii naked?"

"Yeah, and there was nothing to say after that."

She nods. It's a lot to absorb, and it sounds as if she had a really awesome childhood with parents who loved her. No wonder she's not really grasping all the baggage from mine.

"It's safe to say that your dad's behavior affected Griff, too?"

I never thought about it quite like that. I mean, we were both warped. That's a fact. Emotion never entered into our decisions. Showing weakness was the worst thing we could do. I thought I had feelings for Tiffanii, but lifelong commitment to one woman was something I shied away from because, of course, why pluck a single flower when I would always want to plow the whole field? I really thought that until recently. Griff's departure had me examining the past. Keeley's perspective makes me reevaluate my attitude. No doubt about it...filtered through her lens, my life looks fucked up.

"It must have. I've wondered for years if he left Britta and Jamie without blinking because the responsibility scared him or, like Dad, he was just incapable of caring. I don't know."

"What do you think he saw in Britta? I mean, you said he has a 'type'?"

"And she's the epitome of what trips Griff's trigger."

"Blonde?"

I shake my head. I can accuse Griff of a lot of shallow shit because I know he's screwed hordes of willing women. Hell, in college he used to love the tourist hangouts because the ladies were drunk and easy and looking for a good time. Britta seemed to change all that. Or I'd thought so until the day he left.

"Smart. Sharp. Someone with attitude and verve. Good tits help."

Keeley swats my arm. "Seriously?"

"What?"

"Tits?" she challenges with a cock of her head.

"Do you like *breastsss* better?" I intentionally stumble over the word because, really, it's not the easiest word to say.

"Yes, especially when you're not being an ass about it."

I try not to roll my eyes. "Don't make me call your girl parts a vagina," I warn. "That's a pussy. Yours is a really pretty one."

Her expression turns tart. "Mine is off-limits to you. We're talking about your brother."

"But not in the same sentence as your pussy."

In all honesty, I'm poking at her. I don't know why exactly. To lighten the mood? So she stops feeling sorry for me? So things seem less heavy? Probably all that. When I'm with her, I have so many thoughts. But they're more than thoughts when they make my chest squishy. They're feelings.

Jesus, I'm allergic to those. I need to stop.

"All right," she sighs in exasperation. "So your brother likes smart women with personality?"

"Yeah. He has this…thing about dating a woman who's his intellectual equal, who is also good with banter. Arguing—sorry, debate, as he calls it—is his foreplay. He needs someone who can keep up. It's no fun to verbally beat someone who didn't have a prayer of winning in the first place."

"For real?"

I can't tell whether she's intrigued or horrified. "When he met Britta at a caravan—that's the term for a bunch of Realtors spending a morning hopping from property to property en masse to preview new listings for their clients—she was filling in for her sick boss. She looked impeccably beautiful. Crisp white shirt that hugged her body. The open collar revealed just a hint of cleavage… The black skirt flirted with her knees and wrapped to a slit up the back that showed most of her legs. She wore these ridiculous heels with wraparound strap thingies. She had great legs. Don't get me wrong. She looked professional as hell. Put together, low-key makeup, understated jewelry. But she looked like a woman. And she put him in his place with a sentence. That's definitely Griff's thing. He likes to conquer the strong and dirty up the pretty."

Keeley looks at me as if I've lost my mind. "Then you picked the wrong woman for this task. I've never been understated or professional in my life."

"I can make you those things."

"You want to *change* me?" She raises a brow in warning.

"No, *I* like you as is. But for the purposes of derailing Griff… Think of it as a—what do you women call it?—yeah, a makeover. If you really decide to be an innkeeper, it could help you."

The accusation on her face relaxes, and I'm damn glad I think fast on my feet.

"Maybe," she concedes.

"Besides, I'm only altering the way you appear temporarily. It's *you* he'll want. Your humor and wit. Your charm. Your intelligence.

Your quick comebacks." And her compassion. He'll like that, too. "Once my brother has conquered and dirtied, he wants someone he can relate to. I don't know if he'd ever admit it, but that's what he once liked most about Britta. She understood and accepted him."

Keeley nods as if she grasps all that. "That makes sense."

"Right. To stay with someone long term, you have to talk after you boink, I guess. I've never experienced that, but I'm sure it would be nice. Tiffanii wasn't a conversationalist—unless she was the subject. Every time I tried to talk to her about my past, she'd tell me to see a therapist, then shove her earbuds in her iPad and watch another YouTube video about makeup."

Keeley rolls her eyes as if she has a strong opinion about Tiff that isn't good. "You think I'm smart, huh? That my personality is slightly dazzling?"

When she smiles, I'm captivated by this little dimple in her cheek. I never noticed it before, but it's a spot of cute on an otherwise beautiful face.

"Fishing for compliments?" I tease back.

I like this happy Keeley way better than the serious, digging-in-my-psyche version.

She looks like she has a quick, playful reply right on the tip of her tongue, then reconsiders it. "Mostly I just want to know why you chose me."

It's a fair question. I can't put it into words except to say, "It's a gut feeling. I looked at you beyond the makeup and the dress and I heard you. The way you sang. I could hear...your heart, I guess. That probably sounds stupid because you were totally singing about thinking of me and touching yourself."

"Well, not you specifically."

"Of course it was me," I refute with a wink. "Everyone in the room knew it."

"You mean, except the three other guys who wanted to pick me up?"

"They were dense. You could look at them and tell their IQs were in the neighborhood of their shoe size."

"Maxon..." She laughs at me as if she can't do anything else.

At least it clears up the last of the tense air between us. But I'm not dumb. She'll go about her business tomorrow, then come back with more questions. She'll dig deeper and want to understand. Really, I've never dissected my life like this, and it's funny how much I'm realizing just by saying it out loud. At this rate, why would I ever need therapy when I have Keeley?

"To be honest, after you teased the audience and put that one wrestler wannabe in his place, I knew Griff would be intrigued. Then I pictured you in something tailored and classic yet feminine and put it together with your sweetly assertive personality. I knew my brother would go insane."

She takes a sip of her wine. "If you wanted me for your brother, why did you sleep with me first?"

How much do I tell her? Anything I say makes me sound like a dirtbag. Then again, I've never apologized for who I am. Why start now? "I couldn't help myself."

Her face softens. She has to be thinking that she couldn't help herself, either. Some gentle sentiment I can't quite decipher pours from those blue eyes. Despite all the sparkly shadow and heavy black liner, I see it. Hell, I feel it.

But Keeley doesn't speak it. She merely nods.

"I understand wanting what you want when you want it. The truth is, we can't always have that."

A veiled warning not to come on to her again. I don't know how the hell I'm going to heed that. We're sitting close. During the conversation, night has fallen and the moon makes her glimmer under its soft silvery beams. She's chewed her bottom lip so much it's swollen and red. Our forearms are so close I can feel the body heat rising from hers. If I lift my hand, I could tangle our fingers together. I think about it. I think hard. One little move and I could be touching her...

But that would make me an even bigger asshole, wouldn't it?

Having this sudden conscience is annoying.

I pull back. I try to be all suave about it, lean back in my chair like I didn't want to jump on her all along.

Not sure she's buying it when she leans back and crosses her arms over her chest pensively.

"Yeah. Whatever," I flip back at her.

Keeley sends me a skeptical glance but lets it go. "So what's next? How do you make me into Griff's fantasy girl?"

I'm happy to be back on conversationally easier ground. "I've made you some appointments next week. My brother can be an SOB pig but he loves a lady. Polished in public, slutastic in private. I also called a former client of mine. Clarisse has trained pageant contestants. Don't give me that face."

That only makes Keeley's expression stormier. "I am not going to look like a mannequin in sequins."

"You're not," I rush to agree. "But she's also a body language coach. She'll teach you to sit, stand, walk, and talk all while flirting in the subtlest way. Griff eats that shit up. After that, you've got a full two days at the spa. In the meantime, my sister is learning his schedule. We'll figure out a time, a place, and a look that's just right for the occasion. Then we'll go in."

"And when do you start teaching me about business and what to do so that I can eventually buy my own B and B?"

I pause. It's a fair question. Besides, keeping my end of the bargain will enable me to spend more time with Keeley.

"Saturday. I'm dropping by to preview a place in Kahakuloa for another client. After that, I should be free for the rest of the day. I know some houses for sale not far from there that might be good properties for your purpose. Why don't we walk some of them, talk about the pros and cons, what to look for and what to run away from, how you'd utilize them to your maximum benefit…that kind of thing."

"That would be great." Her warm smile returns.

Every time I see that expression, I relax and simply enjoy her beauty. And of course, I have to smile back.

"It's a date, then."

Her smile falls. "It's not. We're business partners. We're giving each other something we want so we can get ahead. Once Griff trusts me, I'm going to do my best to help you repair your relationship with your brother. But you and I are not dating. We're not having sex. We're not anything."

My immediate reaction is to be pissed off. My head knows that's the deal we struck. The rest of me isn't accepting it.

"Figure of speech." I shrug by way of apology.

But deep down...yeah, put me in the stupid column. I'm still determined to have my cake and eat it, too. I *will* have this woman again. I'll spend day and night working for it until I earn her.

CHAPTER EIGHT

*S*aturday morning rolls around. After a contentious staff meeting with Rob and Britta the day before where they finally admit I'm right—well, that Keeley is right—about the Stowe heirs and their emotional detachment from their late mother's estate, I'm happy to avoid the office for a couple of days.

Following a light breakfast my luscious houseguest insists on cooking, she contorts herself on the lanai in a way that makes me scratch my head. Then we leave. She walks beside me, toward my car. Her small denim shorts cup her ass, and I can't stop myself from glancing down at her behind. *Damn...* She doesn't seem to notice my ogling since she's focused on our day.

As we walk, her fingers brush mine, and I clench my fists to stop myself from reaching over. Rob asked me yesterday what I wanted more, to keep Griff from landing the Stowe estate or dance the horizontal mambo with Keeley again. He wouldn't take both for an answer. If I *had* to choose? A few days ago, the answer was simple. The moment my marketing assistant confronted me I felt less certain.

That confuses the shit out of me.

I sidestep Keeley and press the fob to unlock the car and open her door. I stand close. She has to brush past me to ease in. As I feel her breasts on my chest, she looks up at me, steadies herself with a hand on my shoulder. I get hard in an instant. I can't look away.

"Excuse me," she murmurs, sliding her fingertips down my arm as she sinks into her seat. Then looks up at me with big blue eyes.

I start to sweat.

After blowing out a breath as I round the back of the car and adjust my straining fly, I fold myself into the driver's seat and we head out.

"Are you making any progress at the office about how best to approach the Stowes?"

I'm grateful for something else to think about besides her exposed thigh and the hint of cleavage framed by the buttons of her black blouse. I jerk my eyes back to the open road. "Some. We keep trying to come up with ideas that will respect their feelings about the estate while still showcasing its features. I guess Susan Stowe didn't throw parties, but it would be a great place for gatherings since it's on four acres and a lot of that land is a wide greenbelt overlooking the ocean. There are multiple pools, a massive kitchen, eight bedrooms. There's even a detached ohana, so it would be great for honeymooners or spa stuff."

"A what?"

"Ohana. On the mainland, it's usually called a cabana or mother-in-law suite."

"Oh… In Arizona, we call it a casita. But I get it. How do you tell these two siblings that their mom had an amazing house that will net them a fortune without making them feel stupid for not glorifying a place they resent? That's the question."

"Yeah, and if we don't make a big deal out of the property, how do we get them top dollar for it? If they give me the listing, that will be my responsibility." I feel like I've wrapped my brain around this delicate dance for days and I've still got no moves. "I just need to keep working on that. How did your meeting with Clarisse go the last couple of days? You learn about the body language of flirting?"

She crosses her right leg over her left, sleek thighs rubbing together. I notice she's wearing some killer heels. High. Black. Slender. One tiny strap wraps around her ankle, emphasizing how delicate she is. Absently, she swishes her foot back and forth to the rhythm of the song playing on the radio in the background. Then she takes a deep breath. It thrusts her breasts out.

I must be hard up if her merely breathing is flipping my switch.

With a toss of her long, bright hair, she turns to me. Her lips are slightly parted. She's wearing a shimmery, sheer gloss that makes it impossible not to look at her mouth. When her tongue peeks out nervously, it's all I can do not to groan.

"I don't know." She flips a coy glance over to me, then glances down at my crotch. "It seemed like a bunch of BS to me, but I think it's working on you."

Wait. She's been giving me some act?

"I'm horny in general," I protest.

"Hmm." She pauses thoughtfully over my words. "Maybe I didn't learn as well as I thought, then. I'll try harder."

She leans in, elbows braced on the console as she lifts her fingertips to brush a soft line over her exposed skin, tracing the line of her collarbones then down, so freaking close to her shadowed, sugary cleavage. I want my hands there. My mouth pressed to her skin. My tongue laving that same path.

Why didn't I drink her in the night I had her on the beach? She was open. She wanted me. But I was stupid and chose the quick fuck. I missed out on all the details that are driving me insane now. I really want a do-over. Or a do-again-and-again.

I bite back a curse and try to focus on the traffic as we make our way east along the coast. She drags the toe of her strappy sandal up the side of her calf, jerking my attention back to her killer legs. I imagine my hands sliding between her thighs to touch her wet folds, then my head between them so I can taste her. After she's screamed her throat raw and is convinced she's sated, *then* I'll slide my hips between her legs and fill her pussy with every inch—

"Maxon?" she murmurs. It's breathy, like she's beginning to feel aroused.

I glance at her face. She purses her lips just slightly, as if she's deep in thought. But her cheeks are flushed. When she lifts her gaze to mine, I can't look away. Are her pupils dilated?

"Yeah," I choke out, gripping the steering wheel in a fight for control.

Suddenly, she tosses her head back and laughs. "Gotcha! My body language is totally turning you on. You ought to see your face. If I encouraged you, I think you might actually pull over, come across the console, and try to strip me naked."

My cock thinks that's a great idea. I don't want to give her the satisfaction of admitting she's right. And giving her that kind of power over me isn't smart.

"All right. You learned well," I concede.

I should probably shut my mouth, but she has to know she's capable if she's going to use these maneuvers on Griff. God, I don't want to think about that. At least I don't have to look at it.

Keeley gives me a giddy clap. "I had you going."

She still does.

"Don't do that again unless you mean it."

As we roll to a red light, I zip a hot stare across the space between us. My eye fuck must have some impact on her because her breath catches.

"What do you mean?"

"Tease me again, and I'll have you in my bed, stripped down, and taking the pleasure I give you so fast you'll be dizzy, sunshine."

Neither of us moves or speaks for a long minute. Is she reconsidering her no-sex policy? I'm praying to any god I think may help me get laid when I hear an impatient honking behind me.

I jolt. The light has turned green. Keeley is now leaning away, arms crossed over her chest and staring out the windshield.

The moment is gone.

I curse under my breath as I step on the gas. The car lurches forward. The rest of the ride is silent.

After another strained ten minutes, we reach the house I'm previewing for an overseas client. He's a Chinese banker looking for a place to entertain clients supposedly. I don't really care if he uses this as a party hotspot or a love shack. He wants a luxury waterfront showplace, so I'll find him one.

When we reach the house, I stop the car in front of a plantation-style estate. On the first level, a lush lawn leads to a huge stone patio, which gives way to wide wooden stairs. At the top, benches line the lanai, along with lush plants and a couple of cozy rockers. A beautiful dining room table sits squarely under the shade of the patio roof with a swaying ceiling fan providing an extra nudge for the gentle trade winds licking across my skin. The view of the ocean is full frontal and 180 degrees.

I don't see doors at the threshold of the house. Instead, the opening has been widened to accommodate a floor-to-ceiling accordion glass door. The effect brings the outdoors inside, right into the adjacent, open-concept living room.

In keeping with custom, we kick off our shoes before we head inside. Two huge bamboo sofas with thick tropical-print cushions sit perpendicular to the entrance. A matching block table separates them. At the apex, a wide chair designed for reading the day away while overlooking the palm-tree-and-Pacific heaven has been positioned like a throne. Every wall is white, except one covered in well-stocked bookshelves. Skylights abound. Ceiling fans turn in lazy circles, dangling on downrods from the soaring ceilings above.

A simple wooden guitar hangs on the wall beside a hall tree on our way to the adjacent bar area. The little space is kitschy. The cabinets are bamboo. Someone hung a grass skirt as a border with old forty-fives of Elvis tracks as decor. But somehow it doesn't look old or dated. Surprisingly, it's neutral and functional.

On the far wall, the kitchen gleams white with a few rustic exceptions. There's a wooden island, a giant eat-in kitchen with an old-fashioned oval table, but a sleekly modern hooded stove, double ovens, and clean white subway tile lining the walls.

The place oozes charm.

"It's...amazing." Keeley looks around, completely wide-eyed, blinking, oohing and aahing, brushing her hands along every surface.

She's in love.

I don't blame her. Besides being beautiful, the house is cozy. A person could live here, relax here, while away their days in sheer bliss.

"If your client doesn't buy this, he's crazy. If I had the money, I absolutely would."

I shrug. "I think he's looking for something more modern. Something he can show off, rather than a place where he can hide away."

I snap off a few pictures of the view, the dining, entertaining, and kitchen spaces.

"You done in here?" she asks.

"Yeah." Is she suddenly in a hurry?

"Good." She grabs my hands. "Let's go see the rest."

I laugh as she tugs me back into the entertainment space, then through wide double doors and into an airy bedroom. More white. More plantation-cottage vibe. Flowing white drapes flap in the breeze as they frame the open French doors. Other than flowered prints on the bed in neutrals, the room is soft and simple and comfortable. Multiple windows overlook the green expanse of grass and the ocean beyond.

A door at the back of the room leads to a bathroom with double sinks framed in marble and open shelving in the cabinets beneath, punctuated with bamboo baskets instead of drawers. Double mirrors, hanging pendant lights, and a bright atmosphere add the perfect touches. I like it.

Around a corner, I find a softly shadowed hallway, a huge closet, a king-size soaker tub, then another doorway. When I push it open, I find a giant walk-in indoor/outdoor shower made of gray lava rock. The walls on three sides protect anyone from seeing in, but whoever built this place was smart enough to cut an open window with a direct view of the palms and the ocean. There's even a pedestal for bath items. Five shower heads line one wall that must be six feet long. A whole football team could probably shower in here at once and never touch.

"Oh, my gosh…" Keeley's bare feet patter along the stone floor as she drinks it all in. "Can I just die here? This is…"

"Stunning," I finish for her.

"Yeah. But not stuffy. Why would anyone sell this place?"

I shrug. "Hawaii is more of a destination than a residence for some people. They buy a house, thinking they'll come here more often than they do. A few years slide by. They realize they're paying taxes, maintenance, whatever…and just not finding the time or energy to come here enough to justify the money."

"That's crazy. If this place was mine, I'd forget ever going back to Phoenix. I'd live here and never leave."

I see what she means. It's secluded. Quiet. A stroll in gives me a sense that I should relax more, worry less, share this world with someone important. I glance Keeley's way.

Dangerous train of thought…

"Well, we can't stay," I remind her as I grab snapshots of this bedroom and bathroom area. "Let's see about the rest."

On the other side of the main living area is another bedroom, similar in size and color to the first. This one is set up as a children's room with two double beds, a big TV, and a pair of comfy chairs with a library of books and DVDs. The bathroom is smaller but stylish. More than adequate for a guest or two.

"So cute," she remarks. "If I'd had this bedroom growing up…"

With a shake of her head, she glances out over the expanse of the ocean. "I would never have sneaked out and found trouble."

"You were a bad girl?" That surprises me.

"Terrible," she assures. "When I was thirteen, my best friend, Betsy, and I toilet-papered the house of the cute boy down the street, then we took his bike, which he'd left on his front porch, for a joyride all the way to the end of the block."

"Did you return it?"

"We did," she concedes with a teasing grin. "But it was almost midnight."

"Scandalous." I shake my head as if I'm very disappointed.

"Totally. I followed that up at fifteen by sneaking out to study with some kids in my biology class at the all-night pancake house down the road."

"You were worried about your grade?"

"No. There was another cute boy. He dared me to sneak out my window."

I pause. If I dare her to lose those shorts and muss up one of these beds with me…

"Whatever you're thinking, the answer is no." She shakes her head.

"What?" I go for innocent. "I was just thinking that we should look upstairs."

"Sure you did, perv. Let's go."

She follows me up, onto the landing. I walk beyond the delicate chair and small table with the glowing lamp, then push open the double doors. A humongous bed on a raised wooden dais sits majestically under a teak ceiling. Just like the floor below, the usual doors have been removed in favor of a sliding glass wall that's been shoved off to one side, allowing open skies and the Pacific breeze to stream in.

"Holy ocean view…" Keeley whispers beside me.

"Yeah." Nothing but blue water, white sand, green grass, and swaying palms. It really is perfect.

Through the opening, a deck jets out onto the rooftop covering the lanai directly below. A round table, chairs for two, and a chaise take up the space. The vistas go on forever. I've lived on Maui for so long that I often think I'm immune to the sights of beautiful tropical beaches. I joke sometimes that I'm going to vacation in Alaska for a change of pace. Then a place like this comes along and reminds me why I didn't move back to the mainland when I had the chance.

You just can't beat Maui. It's not perfect, but it's damn well become home.

In fact, if I had my own family, I wouldn't mind calling *this* particular place my home.

Keeley seems to float to the edge of the railing and stare out at the unobstructed views. I know in my head that there are neighbors nearby, but they're far out of sight. Someone planted palms years ago along the property line so the illusion of being utterly alone with nature is completely maintained.

"Just…wow."

I couldn't agree more. I see beautiful places every day. I deal in them. I never look at anything that isn't gorgeous. But this is special. Homey. "I know."

"Not to depress myself, but what does a place like this cost?"

"About five and a half million. It would be more, except it's only three bedrooms and three thousand square feet."

"Only?" She snorts. "I could put four of my last apartment in here and still have room leftover."

She isn't exaggerating. I saw it as we moved her out and wondered how the hell she didn't trip over her own two feet in there.

"I can see this as a bed and breakfast. It would be cozy and quaint. Exactly what I wanted…" Her face looks wistful, but her posture is completely defeated. "There's no way I can come up with that kind of money."

"There are less expensive places on the water. If you find something with good bones, you can fix it up and give it the kind of charm you want, especially if you're handy or an out-of-the-box thinker."

Keeley bobs her head. "Yeah...but I don't know if I can ever accomplish this."

"Don't give up before you start," I murmur as I step behind her at the railing.

It's all I can do to keep my hands off her. I want to touch her— that's a given. But I'd like to comfort her, too. Tell her I'll help her and that it's going to be all right.

I refuse to make a promise I can't keep.

"Did you say this place has a detached ohana?" she asks.

"It does, but it needs work from what I read."

"Can we see it?"

I shrug. "Sure. Follow me."

On our way out of the room, we spot a private dining room on the far side of the space with those fold-back windows and killer views. A kitchenette sits tucked in one functional corner. On the other side of the bedroom is a luxurious bathroom that's all sleek and teak and glass. Spa-like and lush. Like something out of a magazine.

After snapping photos, I pull Keeley out of the room reluctantly. We wend our way through the house, retrieve our shoes, then head around back. A stunning infinity-edge pool is situated between the main structure and the ohana, seeming to drop off right into the ocean. It's an optical illusion I don't think I'd ever get tired of if I lived here. The deck has a tropical feel with waterfalls, palm trees, and native stones. It looks almost like this man-made oasis grew organically out of the ground.

After grabbing more images on my phone, we stroll to the ohana. On one side of the structure, we climb its stairs, then open the door. Cans of paint and boxes of tile await. The ceilings obviously need repair since I see daylight, and the owners have a tarp thrown over a computer workstation against one wall, probably in case of rain. But it's a wide space with double French doors and more of that amazing view.

"Morning yoga here would be so inspiring. It always centers me, but this would be beyond."

I don't downward dog, but I can imagine that any period of time up here in silence trying to commune with your body and thoughts would be a hell of a lot less trying if the view was this fantastic.

"So when you're looking for a place of your own in the next few years, keep some sort of ohana in mind. With a little spit and polish, this would be a great asset to your inn."

"Sure," she says quietly. "That makes sense."

But there's no enthusiasm in her voice. Reality has set in.

A place like this is way beyond her reach.

After capturing the last of my snapshots, I lead her toward the car.

"Wait." She looks back at the place as if she's drawn to it against her will. "Can I go back inside? Just one more minute."

I'm at her disposal for the rest of the day. If that's what she wants to do, it doesn't bother me. I'm weirdly fond of the house myself. "Sure."

Keeley gravitates back to the family room, sits on the sofa, and stares out at the ocean. Before I can settle in beside her, she's up and headed for the kitchen, touching the sleek, pale quartz counters. She visits each of the bedrooms and stares as if she's trying to imprint herself with their memories.

This place has actually been vacant for the better part of six months. The owner moved back to Australia and paid a management company for its upkeep until it sells. If a house had feelings, this one would be lonely. And Keeley looks more than eager to keep it company. If I could simply give it to her, she would be its most ardent caretaker, I'm sure.

"Let's go," she suggests finally. She sounds more disheartened than ever.

After checking my phone, I take her to a few other properties around the island with ocean views. The first is another plantation-style house in white, so I'm thinking she'll like it. It's about half the size and acreage. It needs work, and the price reflects that. But it's got nice bones and a good view of Molokai.

We tour the house in silence. Like the last one, it has three bedrooms and three baths. I admit, the kitchen needs an overhaul, the bedrooms are cramped, and the bathrooms are crappy. But the beach is awesome, very private. She could do worse.

"Well?"

She shrugs. "I'm just not feeling it."

"I know. But I'm trying to teach you two valuable lessons."

Keeley raises an annoyed brow at me. "You're kicking a girl when she's down, huh?"

"No, sunshine." It hurts me to see her dejected, so I take her hand. I'm so thrilled when she doesn't pull away. "Helping you see this through a business eye. First, when you start shopping for property for real, don't look outside of your budget. It's way too easy to get attached to something you can't afford."

"Yeah, I'm learning that lesson fast. You should have warned me to stay in the car on our last stop."

"You would have ignored me," I point out.

Her noisy sigh tells me I'm right. "You could take some of the blame."

Her grousy attitude is kind of adorable. "All right. I will. It's so my fault."

"Thanks. I don't feel better. What's my second lesson?"

"Don't look at what it is. Consider what it could be." I lead her out the door from the family room onto the lanai. "This place could benefit from a fresh coat of paint. They're selling it furnished, so that saves money."

"A lot of this furniture is really beat up."

"Smoke and mirrors. Buy some slipcovers, learn to reupholster. Add bright accents. You'd get the most out of this view by taking half the crap out of the crowded space, anyway. Spend the money to replace some of the old windows with an accordion glass door and maximize the view. That's why vacationers come here, not for the sofa. That other stuff can wait."

We walk the place one more time, and I give Keeley the more logical breakdown of how this property could be a moneymaker. She's not having it. In all fairness, when she points out that none of the bedrooms have a view of the water, I can't refute that. That's something else customers want. Her realizing that enormous flaw is a bonus.

We hit the next place, this one about three hundred thousand more expensive than the last. It's got five bedrooms...but only two baths—awkward for guests who don't know one another. It's smaller than the last place. Nicer views, sure. But the house is a turquoise-colored cracker box in need of repair with a giant satellite dish in the front yard.

"No." Keeley doesn't even want to go inside.

"The house has redeeming qualities," I argue.

"I don't care. The dirt road up here was so jarring I don't even know how many teeth I have left."

"You're being stubborn," I point out.

"You're being ridiculous. Who puts this giant hunk directly between the house and the beach?" She points to the dish. The existing owners have tried to cover it by planting a bird of paradise...but there's really no disguising something this ugly. "And it's so far away from civilization. Is this place even connected to the island's sewer system?"

"It's completely off the grid, but you've got solar panels and a fresh water well that's certified. If you're looking to appeal to green-minded guests—"

"But I have to live here, too, and that's a lot of hassle. Let's go."

With a sigh, I escort her to the car and drive her to the last location on our tour. It's in Haiku, perched on the side of a cliff. When we pull up, the views are absolutely majestic but...

"How do you get down to the—" Keeley frowns as she looks over the edge. "There is no beach."

No, just black rocks below, which guests would undoubtedly kill themselves trying to reach. "You'd have to see about building a great pool."

"I doubt the ground is level enough since this place is built into the side of a mountain. Besides if I'm on vacation, I've come to the islands to feel the sand on my feet, to splash the ocean salt on my skin."

I can't argue with that. "At your price point, you have to compromise. This house has more than 180 degree views of the ocean."

We head through the front door. The layout is immediately freaky because we've just walked into a disaster.

"Someone call the 1980s. I'm sure they want their kitchen back." She's getting tart now. Feisty.

"I'm just the messenger. This place is already close to one point four million. Three bedrooms, two baths, two thousand square feet. And hey, water, electrical, and sewer are part of the bargain. Besides, the kitchen isn't that bad. Lots of windows. Good view. The marble floor is classic. Gut or paint what you don't like."

"Why is the refrigerator on the far side of the room, next to the breakfast table?"

I shrug. "You're nitpicking because you're still attached to the first place."

Keeley doesn't say anything for a long time. "All right. I am. I'm not sure how to get past that."

"Time. Perspective. Thinking about what's really important to you in a property."

"But it was as if I could see my whole life at that first place, entertaining guests, walking in the sunlight, teaching yoga, raising children…"

Normally, I would pfft that and tell her to get practical. But if Keeley was more practical…she wouldn't be the woman I know.

And want. And oddly I can picture being in that big house. I can imagine living there with her.

Crap, I need to get my head screwed back on straight.

"Lunch?" I ask. "There's a great fish place not far from here."

She shakes her head. "I need to get back and study before we start working on…whatever we're going to work on tonight. Tests begin Monday."

"Sure."

I take her home. She's absolutely silent. I see the pensive thoughts roll across her face. Instead of reminding her of her own sage words—*I understand wanting what you want when you want it*—I reach across the car to squeeze her hand. She doesn't stop me. In fact, she squeezes back.

I'm silently celebrating my small victory when we hit my front door. But the moment we enter my condo, she runs into the spare bedroom and shuts herself in. I hear the lock engage. I'm not sure, but I think I hear sobbing ensue, too. I want to comfort her, but I think she needs time to reconcile her dreams with the reality of property value on Maui. Besides, I'm pretty sure she'd tell me to fuck off.

When seven o'clock comes and goes, I still haven't heard from her. This time is supposed to be mine. We still have so much about Griff to discuss…but I don't want to be a bastard and add to her burden right now. I order some pizzas from room service in case she gets hungry, then take my laptop out to the lanai.

The view really is spectacular. Being out here clears my head. Even if I don't have Keeley beside me, I can thank her for the appreciation of my outdoor space. That's something.

But I'd rather be holding her right now.

CHAPTER NINE

The next morning, Keeley teaches her seniors' yoga class, then returns. About the time she pops in the door, I receive a frantic call from a client whose neighbor advised them that their investment property sprung a leak and there's water everywhere. By the time I arrive at the house, located on the other side of the island, it's flooded. I know the exotic hardwoods are toast, and this will be a major remodel before we can market the property again. I get the emergency cleaning crews out there and deal with the mess the owner can't manage because he's half a world away, then I look up. The sun has already set.

I haven't eaten since seven a.m. and I'm exhausted.

When I open the door to my condo, the smells of Italian greet me. I inhale, so damn glad I don't have to call someone for mediocre food that takes an hour to arrive.

"Lasagna?" she asks.

"Please." I grab a beer from the fridge, then notice an apple on the counter. I rarely have produce around the house, and I need to eat something *now* before I fall over. I bite into the fruit and hold in a moan. When did apples start tasting that good?

"Rough day?" she asks.

"Terrible. You?"

"It was all right. I got in a lot of studying. I feel ready for my tests."

My logic tells me that's good. We can spend time this evening discussing my brother and exactly how to trip him up. But I'm so wiped out. It's unusual for me—I don't normally like TV—but all I want to do is curl up with Keeley on the sofa and feel her soft body beside me while we watch something mindless.

"That's good." I take another bite of the apple as I open my beer and wash it down.

"You okay?" she asks.

"I will be once you feed me. How about you?"

Keeley pauses as if she's gathering her thoughts. "Yes. I apologize if it seems like I threw a hissy yesterday. I was overwhelmed by how far apart my dream and my pocketbook are. It's not your fault, and you were trying to show me alternatives, the bright side, other ways to look at this. I was being a brat. I'm sorry."

"Not a brat, sunshine. It's my fault. Realtor 101—never show someone a property they can't afford. They'll always fall in love. I didn't put viewing the property for my client together with your pro-and-con list until it was too late."

She purses her lips together. "There really were major flaws in all the other properties you showed me."

"Absolutely. But this is when the business side of your brain needs to kick in. If you have to make hard choices, figure out what you value most. What can you live with? What won't you accept? You'll find your answers."

"Will I ever succeed or is this just a pie-in-the-sky dream?"

She's looking at me with such troubled eyes that I can't stand it anymore. I reach out, pull her against me. She stiffens for a moment but doesn't protest. When I settle her against my chest and kiss the top of her head, she lets out a long breath and relaxes, curling her arms around me.

This is the most satisfying moment I've felt in nearly a week, since the last time I held her.

"You'll make it," I murmur. "You're too stubborn not to. It won't be easy. It will require sacrifice. But you're helping me with Griff. I promised I would help you with your inn. We'll get there."

At the reminder of our deal, she backs away, swiping at a teary eye. She gives me a brave nod, and I wish I'd kept my damn mouth shut.

"Of course. If you want to shower or change clothes, we've got about twenty minutes before dinner."

"Both." I risk pressing a kiss onto her cheek. Her body goes rigid but I'm already dashing into the bedroom before she can protest my embrace. "Back then."

As I stand under the spray, I'm tempted to take my aching cock in hand. I'm hard and I have soap. I've had plenty of orgasms here, especially in times, like now, when I've been too busy to give my sex drive the relief it craves.

I lather up and give my erection a few strokes. I'm having trouble concentrating with Keeley in the next room. I feel like a stupid teenage kid, jacking off instead of simply telling her I want her. She knows and she might turn me down, but I refuse to admit defeat that easily. Maybe a little wine, a little conversation, and a little charm will work wonders.

I give up on the self-pleasure concept and finish my shower. Some shorts and a tank top later, I'm waltzing into the kitchen as she's dishing up steaming plates and handing one to me over the bar.

"Lanai?" I ask.

"Why would we eat inside?" Her voice tells me that concept is absurd.

I smile as I swipe a bottle of wine and a corkscrew and take them outside. She's following with her own plate and a salad bowl a few minutes later. She's barely dressed the tossed greens and taken three bites of food before I've cleared my plate.

At the empty carnage of red sauce all over the white china, she blinks. "That was fast."

"I was starved. And that was amazing."

To the sound of her laughter, I head in for seconds. When I emerge and start eating again, the pace is still brisk but at least I'm not imitating a Dyson.

"After last night, I'm at your disposal," she says between bites. "What should we do?"

I'm about to suggest something that requires her to straddle me. Or maybe a reverse cowgirl would be awesome, if athletic, after the crappy day I've had. But I have to get serious about my goals, too. Griff didn't lose a whole damn weekend to other clients, I'll bet. No matter how tired I am—or how much I don't want to think of Keeley with my brother—I have to start taking advantage of the time I have with her now.

"I've been giving this some thought. In order for you two to 'meet' and spend time together, you'll need a cover story. The easiest would be for you to come to him as a client, but he refuses to romance where he sells. He's got an assistant he won't part with. Sheila is ruthlessly efficient, and she'll have to quit if she ever wants to be rid of him. Besides, after Britta, he'll never touch someone in his office again. His social circle is like mine—small and closed. Who has time, anyway? The one thing I know he does is hit the gym." We have that in common, too. "He ran cross country and played basketball in high school. He does some of his best thinking when he's in an aerobic zone." And thankfully, one of his neighbors is an older and very nosy woman who is more than happy to tell me everything if I call to chat with her. "I know where he works out. I also know they're looking for a morning yoga instructor."

"I'm not certified."

"I had Britta call the gym. All you have to do is audition. They're having trouble keeping anyone decent over there. She, um…introduced herself as you. They're very excited you'll be coming in on Friday to discuss a job. It pays decent money."

"You said you didn't want me working while I was helping you."

"I'll make an exception for this."

"So I'll be in the same gym as Griff. How am I supposed to meet him? Does he do yoga?"

I scoff. "I doubt that."

"All right. Then I'm supposed to, what? Come on to him while he's working out?"

Yeah, that's sounding less likely. "Or, hell, just strike up a conversation. Get him to talk about himself. He likes to do that. Smile. Be his friend. You already look pretty, so you don't have to try there. Dazzle him with your charm."

"If he's attracted to a sharp, professional woman, how am I supposed to dress smartly in yoga pants?"

She has a point. Not that he'd never look at a woman in spandex. But he's like iron to a magnet when it comes to a babe in business garb who has a sharp brain to match. If I want to snag his attention and distract him quickly, I need a different tactic. I really don't want Griff seeing Keeley dressed in the way designed to slay him. I certainly don't want my brother thinking about her sexually. But how else will he ever let her in his life? Since my brother won't touch a client, pursue a colleague, or let a new friend close, that leaves me one option. Keeley will have to sweep him off his feet, the way she did me.

Shit.

"Never mind." I sigh, completely annoyed. "I'll check with Harlow, find out what bar he's frequenting these days when he's feeling lonely and wants a hookup. I'll see if she knows when he'll be swimming the pool of other single professionals looking for a watering hole and a meaningless fuck."

"I'm still not sleeping with him."

Please don't. "Totally understand. I just need you to tempt him a little."

She nods nervously. "I hope this mission doesn't require more."

ON MONDAY AFTERNOON, I cut the workday short. Rob and Britta finally camped onto my way of thinking about the Stowe estate, so they're plunging headfirst into what my assistant likes to call a more elegant strategy. A nice way of saying we're going to strip this bitch down and focus on showcasing her tits. Sorry, her *breastsss*.

They're brainstorming so hard I'm half expecting a tornado to take out the office before I leave and head back to the condo. Sure enough, when I arrive, Keeley is there with an iPad hooked up to a portable speaker. It takes me a minute to realize she's YouTubing karaoke music and singing the hell out of a Katy Perry ballad.

I watch her and let that sweet, velvet voice caress my eardrums. Every note resonates with something that feels a lot like heartbreak. I want to touch her.

When she cries out for the final time that she's "Wide Awake," she turns off the tablet, then spins around for her bottle of water and spots me in the entry. She presses a hand to her chest with a gasp.

I swallow my tongue because she's wearing a bikini top that barely holds her in and some of the tightest yoga pants I've ever seen. A glance at her ass tells me she's undoubtedly commando.

"I didn't hear you come in." She looks away in embarrassment. "I didn't expect you for a few hours."

"We've got an appointment tonight. Makeover phase one is about to begin."

"Oh." She doesn't look thrilled. "What about dinner?"

"We'll get it while we're out." I grab her hand, glad when she doesn't resist. "It's regrettable that you need to throw on a bra and panties, but you'd start a public riot wearing what you've got on. Oh, and choose clothes easy to slip off."

"You are not seducing me, Maxon Reed." She wags a finger at me.

Maybe not in the next five minutes, but soon. At the very least, I need to remind her which brother she met first before I send her off to derail Griff.

"It's nothing like that," I tell her innocently.

She doesn't look as if she really believes me, but she disappears into her room. A few minutes later, she emerges in a pair of khaki shorts, a pretty crisscross blouse in some blue-green color that does amazing things for her eyes, and a pair of beige heels with studded straps around her ankles that attach to a matching band across her toes via a slinky gold chain. If shoes ever said "fuck me," it was these.

I almost swallow my tongue.

The trip down to my car is an exercise in restraint. I want to adjust my dick in my ever-tightening pants so badly it's driving me mad.

When I get Keeley settled, I manage to move my zipper so it feels less like a tourniquet for my cock, and we drive down the road to an outdoor shopping center to grab a nice steak. It's so awesome to spend time with a girl who likes her meat. (Yeah, I went there.) Afterward, I take her hand and we stroll a few doors down.

"You going to tell me where we're going?"

"And end your curious squirming?" I give her a mock frown. "Why would I do that?"

She pulls free. "You're mean."

I just grin. "It's one of my better qualities."

"Says you." She scowls.

"Well, yeah. My opinion is the only one that counts," I tease. "At least tonight."

I expect Keeley to have strong thoughts about what we do in the next hour or two, but I know my brother, so this is my show. She needs to listen when I tell her something will drive Griff crazy with lust.

I shove aside the reality that he will check her out like a slab of meat. But he will. It pisses me off, too. Keeley is way more than that. Will he love her singing? Will he care that she's a damn good cook? Will he even bother to notice how funny she is? If he's going to treat her like a pig—

I stop the thought cold. Maybe that's better for me. Maybe… after this stupid pissing match with my brother is at an end, Keeley and I can try something more than being each other's one-night stand or partner in crime. Maybe we could actually date. Or try a relationship. Yeah. I feel safe with her. Okay, that sounds fairly stupid because obviously she's not the sort who will take a tire iron to my face. But I mean I feel as if I can be myself with her and she accepts me. That's pretty epic. Certainly not the way my sentence— sorry, commitment—with Tiffanii worked.

"Stop with the hints and spill it. What are we doing tonight?"

She can't stand not knowing. It's kind of nice having the upper hand for two seconds. As clever as Keeley is, I don't expect it to last.

"You can't worm it out of me," I vow. "Unless you want to make me lewd sexual promises you'll absolutely fulfill later."

"Nope. You know the rules."

"*Your* rules," I point out. "And they suck."

Beside me, she shakes her head like I'm an idiot. "You can't have it both ways. I'm either with you or with your brother. This is your call."

"Can't you be with me while pretending to be with my brother?" I'm actually serious now. "I don't understand."

She gives me a sad smile. "The fact that you don't reminds me of all the reasons I have to say no. So I guess we're at a standoff. Neither of us is giving in."

"Ugh. I miss girls who act stupid."

She turns to me, her expression a warning that she better not have heard me right. "What?"

"You know what I mean. You're twisting my balls until they're fucking blue. At least other girls pretended to be dumb so I could talk them into raunchy acts that would make everyone but a porn star blush. Well, maybe a few of them, too. But you…" I sigh.

"All brains and ethics and doing things right. I'm not used to that."

Keeley laughs at me like she can't do anything else. "Poor baby. And now I'm making your life miserable."

"Yeah."

"Because I won't be your quick, conscienceless lay."

"Something like that." But there's more.

"You know, I'm not the only woman on this island."

I narrow my eyes at her. "You're telling me to go fuck someone else?"

"We're not committed."

That answer absolutely pisses me off. "I've zeroed in on who I want."

She cocks her head at me, chin slightly tilted, hair brushing her arm. "We've talked about this. Just because you want me doesn't mean you can have me."

The teasing has turned serious, and I need to make myself clear. "You should rethink that. When I want something, I will pursue it to the ends of the earth. If necessary, I will still be reaching for it when I take my dying breath. I will obsess day and night until I have what I want."

She tries to look unmoved, but I see a little shiver run through her as I stop in front of the door that's our destination.

"I believe you," Keeley assures. "This crazy plan to sabotage your brother that you've dragged me into proves you're persistent. But you're forgetting something: you don't own me. Just like you're free to fuck someone else, I'm free to do the same." After tossing out that zinger, she tries to peek through the glass door. "Why are we here...wherever here is? This place closed ten minutes ago according to their sign."

Before I point out that she is *not* free to fuck anyone but me for the next three weeks—and maybe never—the door opens. A woman in her mid-forties greets us with a wide smile. "Hi. Maxon Reed?"

I hold in a curse. This is a terrible time for the sales associate to be helpful. But she's bending the rules for me. We have two hours to accomplish a shitload. I can't afford to waste a minute. I'll table this discussion with Keeley…for now.

"Yeah." I shake the woman's hand. "Thanks for seeing us after hours, Jennifer. You have what I asked for?"

"Absolutely. Come on in." She steps back to admit us, then locks the door.

Keeley peers around curiously at the tasteful, upscale boutique of ladies' clothes. Most of it is resort casual with a few evening-out pieces. I see shoes, belts, bags, hats—all kinds of stuff artfully placed on the walls surrounding the racks of clothes.

What I don't see are the sorts of garments I requested. "Where?"

"In the back. Have a seat," she invites with a smile, gesturing to a stuffed chair she's dragged near a fitting room. Once I comply, she smiles. "You must be Keeley."

My pretty accomplice nods cautiously. "I am."

"Excellent." She scans Keeley up and down. "Size eight?"

"Mostly. Sometimes a ten, depending." She shrugs. "I like food."

"I do, too." Jennifer pats her slightly rounded stomach, but really, for a woman at least a decade older than me, she's definitely fuckable. The me of a couple of weeks ago would totally have done her. "You look great, and I have plenty of things that should fit perfectly. Size medium underwear?"

"Yes, but—"

"And you're a…" Jennifer cuts in and dissects Keeley. "I'm guessing a 34C?"

"In the neighborhood. Sometimes a D," she says, turning a bit red.

I don't know why she's blushing. She sounds hot. Hell, she *is* hot. I've handled all the goods. Not as much as I'd like to. Not as much as I plan to. But Keeley has absolutely no reason to be embarrassed.

"Good. Sit tight. I'll be back in two minutes."

When Jennifer disappears into the employee-only area, Keeley whips her gaze around to me. "You're dressing me from the skin out, including lingerie?"

"Yes," I growl just loud enough for her to hear me. "And let's get one thing clear: you are not free to fuck anyone else when you're with me."

She holds up her left hand, wiggling the finger beside her pinky. "Until someone puts a ring on this, I am. And I know that someone will never be you, so…I am free. Choose your battles, Maxon. You're not winning this one. If you want me to wear this button-up Betty garb, I suggest you focus on that fight."

Before I can reply, Jennifer emerges with a rolling rack filled with garments zipped up into dark, protective bags. The shelf at the bottom between the wheels holds something like thirty pairs of shoes. "I meant to ask your shoe size. Most of my samples are a six or seven."

Keeley puts on a smile. "I'm usually a six and a half."

Jennifer lights up. "Perfect. Then most of these should fit. Let's get started."

After she unzips all the bags and hangs the clothes meticulously on the rack, I see the caliber of the garments she's brought and I smile. Tailored. Designer. Impeccable. The muted colors aren't typical. Yeah, there are navys and grays, but I see pale peach and a powerful orange. A soft green suit with a leopard print trim at pockets and cuffs catches my eye. I spot a really sexy dress in black with cream-colored cut-outs at cleavage and waist, giving the illusion of skin that's actually covered. A pretty salmon-colored skirt snags my gaze next. On the hanger, it's been paired with a silky white blouse and a taupe cardigan sporting just a hint of texture. This is a visual feast, and imagining how it will all look on Keeley is making my aching cock press into my zipper again.

I point to a classic pinstripe suit that looks designed to hug the body. The one deviation from tradition is that the lapels drape softly to ruffle down the torso. "Let's start there. What goes beneath?"

"It's actually designed to be worn alone. You can pair it with a shell but it's not necessary."

"So...cleavage?"

Jennifer nods. "Quite a bit."

"Perfect."

"Do you want my opinion?" Keeley asks me.

I try to keep it diplomatic. She warned me to pick my battles. I intend to win the war. "I want to see how everything looks, then we'll compare notes afterward."

"Fine," she huffs.

Jennifer hustles her into the dressing room with several boxes of shoes and some lacy stuff that will no doubt make my heart race dangling from her palms. "We'll be back in a few minutes."

I hear the ladies talking. Fabric rustles. The ever-helpful associate darts out from the little room to dash for her jewelry case. After a cock of her head, she reaches for several pieces, then hustles back to the dressing room. Another two long minutes pass before the door opens.

Keeley emerges looking a tad less than comfortable and confident in that pinstripe suit. I don't know why. She should be thrilled. It hugs every curve, exaggerating the flare of her hips and the slender shape of her calves. Her feet look almost Cinderella dainty in the sexy black wedges with straps wrapped around her ankles a time or ten. I almost see the swells of her breasts. The chunky silver locket high on her throat is a distraction, but I'm sure if I look hard enough I'm going to see tits. Only I don't. It's classy yet sexy. Jennifer has even wound Keeley's pink hair into a French twist behind her head.

Overall, she looks stunning. I always preferred babes in bikinis or tight dresses, but now I see exactly what Griff responds to by lusting after women in suits. Oh, my god, the thought of stripping away her power and getting her under me, hearing her cry out my name while I'm—

"Do you like it?" Jennifer butts into my thoughts.

"Yeah. Everything. Just like that. What else do you have?"

"Let me show you."

She proceeds to change Keeley into the pale green suit. It's classic but reminds me of springtime. It's paired with a black shell that highlights the animal print trim. She's even found matching cheetah shoes that should seem hookerish, but with such an elegant ensemble, it's perfect. Delicate jewelry. A thin headband to hold Keeley's hair away from her face. Feminine and prim with a hint of vixen.

I want to dirty her up bad. "Yes. Love all that. Next?"

By the time we're done, we've chosen four suits, three dresses, ten pairs of shoes, four purses, and a handful of accessories. I can't help but notice the seven bras and matching panties she's sliding into a soft pink box all wrapped in tissue paper. I wish to fuck Keeley had modeled those for me. I'm hard just imagining what she'll look like in those transparent confections of silk.

I pay Jennifer handsomely for everything she selected and assure her that I'll call if I need anything else. Keeley is quiet and looking a little shell-shocked as I loop the packages over my wrist and drape all the hanging bags over that same shoulder. With my free hand, I take hers as we leave.

"You okay?" I ask.

She takes a few minutes to answer. "It's…realer now. We're really going to do this." She looks up at me with concern. "Maxon, I'm not very good at deceit."

I can picture that. Keeley is so open and kind. She would help puppies and old people across the street. She'd stand between a bulldozer and a historic building. She would hate lying to anyone.

"That's a crappy trait in business"—I squeeze her hand—"but I like you that way. Just remember, you're doing this to help me repair my relationship with my brother."

"I am. But you're not."

"My motives don't have to be yours, sunshine. Look, my soul is black. I'm perfectly happy with subterfuge and revenge. But you didn't get into this to hurt anyone, just help. You don't have to get down on my level. Just…do what you do."

Slowly, she nods. "I have to be honest, if the opportunity to bring you guys together presents itself, I'll probably ditch the whole flirtation thing and just 'fess up."

It won't but I love the fact that she's not in a hurry to have sex with my brother. It's up to me to make sure she doesn't want to have sex with him—or anyone else. I'm not precisely sure why I'm feeling so possessive, but there it is. I'm not dissecting it now.

"I know," I murmur as we reach the car. I doubt Griff will ever let her into his soul enough to talk about family rifts, so it's a nonissue. "I'm okay with you being you."

More than okay.

She lets out a relieved breath as I help her into the car. When I slide in beside her and we speed out of the nearly empty lot, she reaches across and grabs my hand. "For what it's worth, I don't think your soul is black. I hope you see that someday."

CHAPTER TEN

*B*y the end of the week, January has rushed into February. I feel my days with Keeley slipping away. In fact, my time with her is almost half gone. She's the first person I talk to in the morning and the last person I think about before I go to sleep. I want her, yeah. But it's more. I want to be with her all the time. I look forward to coming home to her at night.

What will I do when the month is up and she moves out? Maybe I should convince her to stay. That sounds great…but how?

The worry makes me tense as I shower and get ready for a long day of showing an overseas client who's flown in some properties around Maui and Oahu. I would rather spend my day with Keeley…but I've made other plans for her. Important ones. Now that we've managed to have all her clothes altered with the proper nip and tuck to suit her petite frame, today's endeavors represent the last of our preparations. Keeley has practiced the body language on me so much now I'm perpetually hard. She knows enough about Griff not to step in shit but not so much that she'll have to feign surprise as they're talking. I'm so close to implementing my plan. I should be thrilled, excited—ready to bring a bastard down.

All I can think about is that beating Griff might mean losing Keeley.

Trying not to ponder that thought too hard, I don my suit and tie, then grab some of the sprouted bread with almond butter that Keeley keeps around for breakfast. Different...but not bad. When she's gone, I'll miss the food, too. I'll miss her laughter. I'll miss the way she loves my lanai.

I have to stop sounding like a maudlin limpdick and buck the fuck up. Our arrangement is temporary, and I was doing all right on my own. Kinda. Sorta. If I want something more with her after this is over, maybe we can renegotiate.

After I wolf down my last bite of toast and toss my plate in the sink, I tap on Keeley's door. "Sunshine?"

Nothing. It's a quarter after seven. I'm surprised she's not up.

Slowly, I ease her door open. I don't want to wake her, but I need to let her know about her appointment this morning.

As my eyes adjust to the shadows in the room, I spot her. My body tenses. My heart starts thumping uncontrollably.

She's sprawled across the bed, face down, stark naked. A sheet covers her luscious ass and shapely legs, but it's thin. In this light, I almost swear I can see through it. Probably wishful thinking, but I want to believe I can discern the outline of her hips, the soft line bisecting her backside, the slight spread of her legs that almost reveals her bare sex beneath.

I must be fixated on her because I've been two and a half excruciating weeks without sex. I could have ended my torture last night with someone else...and I chose not to. What's wrong with me?

At midnight, I got a call from Milan, a not-quite friend who wanted benefits. I turned her down flat. We've exchanged favors not so infrequently over the last two years. The phone call wasn't unexpected, really. We're busy professionals with needs. Neither of us has time for a relationship and we both like dirty sex. I've never minded scratching her itch in the past. I just didn't have any enthusiasm for the concept last night.

Keeley shifts, absently brushing her pink strands from her face before settling back into slumber. A foot peeks out from beneath the sheet. Her black toenail polish is chipping. I suspect I'm staring at the reason I had no interest in Milan.

Fuck.

"Sunshine…" I call in hushed tones so I don't startle her.

"Hmm." She barely manages to crack her eyes open for a moment before they slide shut again.

Normally, she's a morning person, but after the long week of exams and the bottle of wine we drank on the lanai last night, I think she's wiped out. Actually, watching her sleep is kind of cute…up until the point where I want to rip the sheet away from her body and fuck her until she can't think.

"Time to get up," I murmur.

"Sleeping in."

"You're not. The Ritz spa is expecting you at eight. You've got two full days of pampering."

She cracks one eye open. "Seriously? Why so early?"

I tsk at her. "Poor thing. How dreadful all that massage and therapeutic aromatherapy must be. I know manicures and pedicures are a terrible chore, and who the hell wants a relaxing facial or a seaweed body wrap? I'm totally glad I'll be with some dude in a suit with whom I share a language barrier all day. That sounds like way more fun than being rubbed on and coddled. So glad I don't have to endure your torture…"

Keeley grabs the sheet and pulls it up, covering all her goodies before she rolls onto her side and sends me a quelling glare. "I see the early hour hasn't dimmed your sarcasm."

"Nothing dims that," I assure her with a wink. "Now up with you." I can't resist smacking her ass.

She shrieks and jumps to her feet, clutching the sheet. "Don't do that. Get out. I'm naked."

"Are you?" I act surprised. "I'm not sure I believe you. Maybe you should drop the sheet and prove it."

Gritting her teeth at me, Keeley gives me a shove. "Go. If I have to be downstairs soon, I need to rush through my yoga and put myself together."

As much as I'd rather stay and bait her, a glance at my watch tells me I have to go. "I'm meeting a client at a chopper hangar by the airport. We're touring property all day. I don't know what time I'll be back. Probably late, if at all."

And I hate that so much.

"Oh." Her disappointment gives me hope. Whether she wants to admit it or not, she likes spending time with me, too. "Okay."

"It's the banker we checked out that plantation-style house for last weekend. He just flew in from Hong Kong and only has two days to find a place. I have to stay until that's done."

"Sure." But she doesn't sound any more thrilled than before. "Just...I guess keep me posted. Let me know whether I should cook for two tonight."

"I will." I risk coming closer. The reality that I won't see Keeley all day—and maybe all night—isn't making me a happy camper. "I'd rather be with you. You know that, right?"

She gives me that stunning crooked smile. "I would hope I have more appeal than a stuffy banker or I need this spa appointment way more than I thought."

I smile back. "Have a good day, sunshine."

"You, too."

She doesn't back away. As I stare at her, breathing isn't as easy as usual. Sleep has softened her face even more. She looks like a goddess rising from that white sheet, and knowing she's not wearing anything else... It's taking everything I have not to call the banker and tell him to screw himself so I can fuck her.

Next thing I know, I'm raising my hand and brushing a stray curl from her face. Her cheek is smooth and warm and delicate. On my next pass, I can't resist dragging my thumb over her bottom lip. I swallow.

"Maxon?" she breathes.

"Yeah?" Does she want me half as much as I want her?

She doesn't speak. I see the thoughts turning in her head. Tumult shines in her eyes. She's questioning something—everything?—but doesn't make a sound.

"Sunshine, you okay?"

"Do you ever wonder if you're making the right choice? I mean, in your situation, you could probably just pick up a phone and call Griff's office and ask him if he wants to end this feud. It might be a huge relief to have your brother back and—" She sighs in exasperation. "Don't shake your head. It's possible."

"It's not. I'm stubborn, I admit. But Griff is a fucking immovable object. Once he's made up his mind to cut someone or something from his life, it's absolute."

Harlow says he's changed, but I think she wants to believe that more than it's actually true. I wish like fuck she was right. Not having my own flesh and blood as a mortal enemy would sure be easier. It would probably make me happier, too. Being friends with him again… Nothing would thrill me more—if it could be like the good old days. But it can't. I've accepted that. Once Keeley knows Griff, she'll understand, too.

"But that was three years ago," she argues.

"Three minutes. Three hours. Three centuries. Griff's resolve will be the same. I know you want to believe the best of people, and it's one of the things about you I find most attractive. But the man has refused to acknowledge his own son. Jamie is a little boy who did nothing to Griff except be born. My brother has chosen to live without the little guy because he thinks the boy's mother is a liar. If he can handle every single day without caring about his own kid, I'm pretty sure his brother means even less."

"But you don't know that. You could try." There's a whine in her voice that surprises me, like she really wants me to see her perspective.

To help her understand, I'm going to have to admit something so real to her. It's one reason I don't like talking about Griff. This fact just slaps me in the face over and over. "I did. If I put myself out for him like that and he pushes me away again, I don't know if I could take it."

"It's just your pride, Maxon. It will heal."

Damn it, will this woman not understand? "It's my heart! He fucking broke it and he doesn't give two shits. So now we're enemies, and that's it. Will you drop it?" I step back, rake my hand through my hair. "Jesus, has no one ever broken your heart? Is that why you don't understand?"

"Yeah. Someone has. I chose to get over it. Repair the damage. Forgive and forget. Be happy again."

Even delivered in the softest tones, I hear the rebuke in her words. They're like a blade slicing open my chest and jimmying around my heart, creating utter carnage. I know she doesn't mean them that way. I'm probably overreacting.

I can't seem to stop.

"Well, you're a better person than me. We both know that." In my pocket, my phone buzzes, and I yank it free. Mr. Zhang is waiting at the hangar, and I'm twenty minutes away. "I have to go."

I want to touch Keeley again but I don't. Instead, I turn and leave, pretty sure I'm going to have a miserable fucking day.

SOMETIMES, I hate it when I'm right. Mr. Zhang didn't like any of the properties I showed him on Maui. Too remote. Too relaxed. He's looking for a party palace. Why else would he have agreed to drop four million this afternoon on an oceanfront penthouse with decor that makes a French bordello look sedate? But after island-hopping to Oahu yesterday, my pal from China finally fell in real estate love in Honolulu. I submitted the offer earlier today. For hours, we waited for the seller's response in a bar, during which the banker got utterly shitfaced and loud. I nearly kissed the bartender when the seller accepted our terms. Afterward, we took the chopper back to Maui, and I put Zhang in a taxi back to his hotel.

I'm finally heading home.

Now that I've got some quiet, I wonder if Keeley missed me last night. I tried to call her, but it was late and she didn't pick up. She texted about eight this morning to say she'd slept through my call because the spa exhausted her, and if they plucked one more thing on her body, she might punch someone. With a laugh, I told her if she was going to get into a girl fight to roll video for me because that turns me on. Keeley replied by snapping a pic of herself performing an obscene finger gesture. We may not have much in common, but I love her sense of humor.

By the time I pull up in front of my condo, I feel as if I haven't seen her in two weeks. Anxiously, I call the spa. When the receptionist answers, I cut the engine. "Hi, this is Maxon Reed. Is Keeley Kent finished with her appointments?"

"Almost, sir. She should be ready to check out in the next ten minutes."

Which will give me just enough time to walk over there and pay her bill. Convenient. But my cynical smirk dims. Truth is, I'm really eager to see exactly what they've done to Keeley. She's a gorgeous girl in my eyes. I hope if they've transformed her, they've merely enhanced her beauty, not changed her entirely.

"I'll be right there."

The afternoon is quickly becoming evening as I walk the winding garden path past the main pool, then between a few buildings on the far side of the property. Behind buildings three and five, I spot the spa.

As I push my way past the front door, I enter a cool oasis of calm music, tropical tranquility, and dim lighting. The receptionist behind the counter smiles. I wonder how she sits there all day and listens to the waterfall without having to pee constantly. Not my issue, thankfully. She wears the usual severe bun that signals her efficiency and kills all hint of sexiness. As she rises in greeting, I see she's wearing head-to-toe black, like everyone else in this place. I've seen livelier outfits at a funeral. Is management intending to send a message to patrons with their color scheme?

"Hello, Mr. Reed."

What's her name? Ashley? Annie? Avery? Something like that. I make small talk with her when I come here for the occasional massage, so I should probably know. She often flirts. I suspect she'd do me if I asked, but I'm not interested today. I'm beginning to wonder if I ever will be again. "Hi. If you've got the bill ready, I'll settle it and wait for Keeley."

"Of course." Whatever her name is clicks around her computer. The nearby printer spits out a long list of treatments. She glances it over, then hands it to me with a grin I'm sure she intends to be professional but looks slightly manic.

Uh oh. Two full days of spa services is going to cost me a fortune.

I glance down at the total and try not to choke. Yep, expensive, as usual. I could feed an entire village in a third-world country for a year on this amount. At least the Ritz is consistent.

Grabbing a pen, I add gratuity and sign, then sink into a nearby chair to wait. They need to hurry this show up. I'm eager to clap eyes on Keeley. I'm sure she's going to look great. But right now, I just want to be with her.

I missed her more than I thought I could.

I'm glancing at my phone and scrolling through Facebook. One of Griff's ads comes up in my feed. I tamp down my annoyance and look through analytical eyes. Griff obviously wrote the text because the verbiage sounds exactly like him. Overall, it's good. I've already toured the property he's pushing and the post makes even me want to see this place. I wish again that I had his knack for making the emotional connection with buyers and sellers. Keeley was onto something when she helped me to better understand the Stowe heirs. I need to think more like that, about people. With emotion.

Even if the concept usually gives me hives.

"Maxon?"

Keeley. I recognize her voice. I jump to my feet, pocketing my phone, then turn to face her. And I freeze.

Oh. My. God.

The woman has haunted me since I last saw her. But this version of her is fucking glamorous. Polished. Poised. Perfect. I recognize the pale green suit that hugs her body perfectly, along with the cheetah pumps she's wearing. Yeah, it's definitely Keeley. So much about her now is lovely and familiar, but the trappings are all different and mind blowing.

Her hair is shorter than when she sported pink tresses. The loose, beachy curls now hang just over the tops of her shoulders. But the current color is what has my eyes popping out most. "Red?"

Not just any red. A dark, rich russet. The color looks absolutely stunning on her. It sets off her pearlescent skin. It frames eyes that now look so intensely blue I wonder if I could drown in them. The words running through my head are awfully fucking poetic, especially since my tongue is utterly tied over this woman.

She. Is. Beyond. Beautiful.

"It's actually my natural color. Do you hate it?"

"No," I breathe. I feel a lot of things, especially below my belt buckle, but hate isn't on the list.

"Good." She smiles uncomfortably as she shifts her weight from one foot to the other and bites her lip. "So…"

"You look amazing." I'm finally able to pull my head out of my ass long enough to set her at ease.

She gives me a blinding smile. "Whew! If you didn't like it, my spa adventure would be a huge waste of time and money."

"Not at all." I hold out my hand to her. A jolt that feels a lot like the first time we touched—but stronger—races through my body. "Not even a little. Wow. I can't stop staring at you."

A flush crawls up her skin. She looks away, but not before I can see how much my compliments have pleased her.

The spa has done an amazing job of bringing out her natural beauty. The best part is that she looks put together without looking made-up. I believe she could be a corporate powerhouse, but no one would ever mistake her for anything less than a woman. Even the way the technicians applied her cosmetics is subtle and perfectly suited to her skin.

The receptionist barges into our moment by handing Keeley a sizable, sturdy bag. "Here are your purchases, Ms. Kent."

"Thanks." Keeley looks grateful for something to focus on beside me eating her up with my stare. Then she risks a glance my way. "If I have to recreate this look, I need the things in this bag. A shampoo that will keep my color vibrant. A moisturizer…" She pulls it out and holds it up. "This will help my new foundation lay flawlessly on my skin." She withdraws the little bottle of liquid pigment, too. "And I don't have any eye shadows or blushes like this in my makeup case, so—"

"Whatever you need," I assure her to stop the explanation she seems awkwardly compelled to give.

She relaxes. "Good. Thanks."

I nod. "How do *you* feel? Do you like it?"

"I'm not used to the clothes yet, but the hair, the makeup? Yeah. I feel like…me. I've only been pink for the last three months. I was platinum before that. I like to try different looks, but I always come back to red."

It's still impossible for me to take my eyes off her as I hold out my hand again. Something weird happens when she slips her palm in mine. It's as if her grip has squeezed around my heart, which is now beating like a tribal drum at a luau. I can barely breathe as I pull her close. My ability to speak evaporates once more.

"Are we going?" She blinks in question.

Yeah. Leaving now. "Dinner out?"

"Please. Believe it or not, being poked, plucked, prodded, and primped is really exhausting, so if I don't have to cook—"

"Not a problem." In fact, I love the idea of going out and showing Keeley off and keeping her close so that every other guy fucks off because it's obvious she's mine.

Except she isn't. Soon, I'll have to dangle her in Griff's face like a tasty treat.

I'm not thinking about that tonight. Nope. Not happening. Right now, I'm just going to enjoy my time with Keeley after the nearly thirty-six hours we spent apart. Yeah, I was counting.

After a little discussion, we wind up at Pacific'O, a romantic spot for seafood and sunsets. Dinner and wine are nice. Watching her turn every male head is gratifying. Her company is the best part of it all, though. She looks vivacious, like she's very comfortable in this skin. She has a renewed sense of self.

Or maybe I'm finally seeing her as she actually is.

I ponder that thought as the waiter sets down our check.

"Hey," she murmurs. "Do you have an early morning tomorrow?"

"Not any more than any other day. What do you have in mind?" I feel the smirk cross my face. I can't help it. I have a whole lot of ideas filling my head. I wonder if she'd say yes to any of them...

She glances at her phone. "I know it's already after nine, but I was wondering if we could do one more thing before heading home."

"Like?" Keeley already turned down dessert, so I can't imagine what she wants.

"There's this little pub around the corner that has karaoke on Wednesdays and Sundays. I've missed singing. It's soothing."

My knee-jerk reaction is a big hell no. I pause as I realize that she didn't ask *me* to sing. That's key. I don't understand her assertion that warbling in front of a bunch of strangers is anything but an exercise in trying not to nervous puke. But she seems really excited. How am I supposed to say no?

"As long as you promise not to drag me on stage…"

"Totally. I just need to belt out a song or two."

I'd love to hear her sing again. "Do I get to pick the songs?"

"When we get there, you can look at the choices and make suggestions. I'll see if I can manage any of them. Deal?"

"Deal." This could be fun.

When we get there, it's dark and loud and a little crowded. We spot a couple leaving in the back and grab their high-top table and chairs. As soon as we're situated, someone passes us the big binder full of songs. I hope Keeley gets to sing soon because some drunk tourist in platforms trying to be Beyoncé is already giving me a headache.

Keeley passes the thick tome of song selections my way. I riffle through absently as the waitress takes our drink order.

"Anything catch your eye?"

I grin. "'Like a Virgin'?"

She gives me an adamant shake of her head. "Absolutely not."

"What's wrong with that?"

"First, it's really one of the dumbest songs ever, in my opinion. Second, I'm not in the habit of lying. But most of all, c'mon. How about a challenge?"

Point taken. "How about…'Buttons.' Who doesn't like the Pussycat Dolls?"

Mostly I just want to hear her sing suggestive lyrics to me.

Keeley shakes her head. "I like the song, but Nicole Scherzinger isn't hard to sing, either. How about something with teeth?"

"Britney Spears?"

She rolls her eyes. "Stop insulting me. Harder."

"You want it harder, baby?" I flash her a leering grin. I know I'm about to get smacked but it's too fun to stop.

"Vocally, not sexually. Give me the book."

Oh, I'm still making it too easy on her? Fine. "No. I said I'd pick something. I will."

I whip out my phone and after a little Google, I choose three songs and dart up to the deejay. Despite having a bad-hair decade, the guy is really easy to talk to, and we soon settle on a great song I can't wait to hear. He has me jot her name and info on the sheet attached to his clipboard. Then it's done. All I have to do is wait.

When I head back to the table, Keeley looks beyond annoyed.

"We were supposed to discuss this," she grits out as I slide onto my stool beside her.

"We did. But since you're such a pro, and my selection wasn't difficult enough, Google helped me go for the gusto."

"What did you sign me up for?" Now she sounds almost nervous.

I just smile. "Not telling…"

It's hard to find patience until Keeley is called, especially when I have to sit through a terrible rendition of "Smooth Criminal" and an even worse stab at "Waiting on the World to Change." The bar finally starts to clear out. A version of "Don't Let the Sun Go Down on Me" that's only slightly awful follows.

Finally, the deejay, who really does the comb-over proud, grabs the mic. "Time for Keeley on the stage. Keeley, everyone."

"What am I singing?" she asks as she gets to her feet.

"You'll see." I'm stubborn like that when I want to be.

"I'm totally getting you back for this."

"You're welcome to try…"

She sends me something like a snarl before she heads to the front. After a verbal interaction with the deejay that includes a little arguing and a lot of nodding, she finally grabs the mic off the stand and takes a deep breath. God, she really looks stunning, especially when the first note hits and she lifts her head to meet the song head on.

Three minutes later, I'm absolutely floored. She's nailed "Titani-um," including every one of those high notes the deejay swore to me tripped up most. I didn't give her this song to watch her fail, though. In my head, I could hear her singing it. I knew she could do it. I wanted her to know that she could, too.

But messing with her in the meantime was too much fun.

The crowd cheers. She smiles back. On her way off the stage, she speaks to the deejay. He looks over at me. Oh, that's how she intends to get me back, make me embarrass the hell out of myself in public. No way. No how.

As soon as Keeley reaches the table, I grab her hand. "Let's go."

"Nope." She plants herself firmly on the floor and raises a brow at me. "Your turn."

"You promised I didn't have to sing."

"If I don't get to have a say in my own song, I don't have to keep my word," she points out. "Suck it up, buttercup."

"Not happening. I'm leaving."

The waitress finally comes with our cocktails and hustles away before I can pay. I don't even know how much the drinks cost. *Shit.*

"You were saying?" Keeley smiles and flutters her lashes innocently.

"This sucks."

She laughs. "You'll live."

I'm nervous. It's stupid because I know I'll never see these people ever again. Hell, half of the patrons in this dive are so sauced I doubt they'll remember being here at all tomorrow, much less some tone-deaf chump butchering a tune. That still doesn't stop me from looking for the waitress, cash in hand, so we can find the exit.

"Maxon," the deejay calls. "Where is..." He spots me and motions me over. "Come on down, buddy."

With a groan, I get to my feet. I shoot Keeley a glare that promises retribution. When I reach the stage and grab the mic, I try really hard not to realize that about fifty people are staring at me like they expect awesome.

I will sorely disappoint them.

"Keeley says you're a karaoke virgin," the deejay begins.

I nod. "I haven't been called a virgin in a long time."

The crowd laughs. At least I've got a little comedic goodwill going before I burst their eardrums.

"Your fine lady picked an oldie for you. She said you'd want a challenge."

Oh, that's it. Despite paying a small fortune for her makeover, I'm going to kill Keeley the moment we get home. I stare across the bar at her. She's smiling and looking so damn happy. I put that expression on her face. My stupidity and sheer lack of talent are making her downright gleeful.

Okay, I'll suck it up this once.

I'm worried she's assigned me a song that requires fast thinking, like Eminem. Or worse, chosen something damn near impossible, in the neighborhood of "Bohemian Rhapsody."

Instead, when the monitor lights up, I see a song title scroll across my screen. "Wichita Lineman" by Glen Campbell. Wasn't this was one of my Granddad's favorites? I think…yeah. It reminds me of summer, of sneaking ice cream past Grandma and into the barn for an afternoon treat, of good times with a good man. Maybe if I focus on my fond memories of tinkering with the old guy, I can get through this.

After the whiny opening notes, the words on the screen flash and it's clear I'm supposed to start singing. I don't really remember the melody or cadence. Hell, I barely remember the song at all. Somehow I make it through the first couple of lines, but I can't disguise how badly I suck. Not a single note is on pitch. I look to Keeley for help. I know I should be a good sport and all, but I'm really not equipped to make an ass of myself in public. Say what you want about the male ego, but this kind of torment is making my insides curdle and my balls shrivel.

I'm so focused on how tragic my singing must be on everyone's eardrums that I miss the next line altogether. She makes a hand gesture at me, and I look at the monitor. I'm behind. Damn it. The words flashing are blurry. I'm sweating. My fingers are tingling as I try to hold the mic. Why can't I breathe?

As the tune fills my ears, my brain kicks in. It seems kinda familiar, so I pick up again and sing something about the whine before managing most of the next line. But when I gear up to belt out the last word in the verse, I vaguely recall the note is much higher than my limited range can handle. If I even try this, my voice will crack like a thirteen-year-old boy's.

I fall silent. More panic grips me. The sweat is coming faster. My heart chugs uncontrollably. I'm getting dizzy now and brace myself on the deejay's table. I look to Keeley for help.

She grabs her stuff and runs up to save me. But by the time she makes it to the stage, I'm blinking at the audience like an idiot. I'm trying to get it together but the words seem to be scrolling even faster across the screen. I swear to fuck my knees have locked and I'm about to pass out.

Suddenly, she's beside me, purse dangling from one shoulder, her other arm around my waist. She takes the mic from my hand and starts singing about needing and wanting me for all time.

I always thought this song was nonsensical. But hearing it for the first time in easily two decades—with Keeley's voice dripping emotion—I'm experiencing these lyrics through a whole new filter. When did this seemingly stupid cowboy song get so damn yearning and full of devotion? So poignant?

Keeley manages to salvage this musical train wreck, though singing an octave higher than I've ever heard the song. After another verse, I can finally breathe again. My vision is righting itself. She's solid beside me—a rock. I'm good. I even chime in a word here or there. Then the chorus comes around to rip my chest open again. The gut-churning lyrics roll through my head.

Suddenly, the lights come up. I hear applause. The crowd is lauding Keeley, but I feel enormously better that it's over.

She grabs my hand and leads me back to the table, takes care of the drinks, and guides me to the car. "Keys?"

"I got it."

"You don't." Keeley shakes her head. "You look white as a polar bear."

I open my mouth to argue but stumble over my own two feet trying to reach the car door. "Fuck."

"You were saying?"

With a huff, I hand over my keys. "Do you know where you're going?"

"Of course. Sit back."

She escorts me to the passenger's side and helps me sit. A moment later, she's next to me, starting the engine. I've never been a passenger in my own car. It's not a feeling I like.

As she pulls away, I'm glad the top to the SUV is down. The wind whipping across my face is both helpful and sobering. "I don't know what happened back there."

"I think you had something between stage fright and a panic attack."

That's ridiculous. "I don't have panic attacks."

"It's nothing to be embarrassed about. My mom had them for the first few years after my dad died. You're just wound up...and emotionally closed off. When you try to tamp your emotions down, sometimes the body can't adjust and this happens."

I want to call bullshit. I don't have emotions.

On the other hand, this has happened before. One time, a few years back, I even woke out of a deep sleep feeling like I couldn't breathe or must be having a heart attack. I called 911, and the paramedics took me to the hospital. I was shocked when they told me nothing was wrong with me. I'd had an "episode," whatever that means. They prescribed me a few tablets of something I couldn't pronounce. I was supposed to take one if it happened again and call if the symptoms persisted. I didn't need another pill for months, then one night I was on the couch watching a horror flick... I got wound up. It had to be the movie, right? I thought so, and I took a pill, but it made me so sleepy I was conked out for twelve hours. The hangover the next day made me feel like a zombie. I flushed the rest of the prescription down the toilet.

"I don't want to talk about it."

Her face softens as she grabs my hand. "It's not abnormal. There's nothing wrong with you. You just need to be aware of yourself. And I hate to sound like a broken record, but meditation would help. Really."

I shake my head. "I'll be fine."

Keeley doesn't seem thrilled by my pronouncement but lets it go. "I give you a lot of props for getting on stage and trying at all. The first time I sang in public, I was so nervous my voice shook. I thought I was going to throw up."

Despite the awful night, having Keeley beside me is soothing me. Her story lightens my mood. "I relate."

"Sorry I put you in a position to be uncomfortable. You poked. I teased back. I didn't think it would upset you."

I hear her sincerity. I squeeze her hand in return. "Thanks. I… um, missed you last night."

The admission comes out of nowhere, and before I can cover it up with a joke or try to change the meaning, she glances my way. "I missed you, too."

Hell, I think she's serious. Suddenly, the employer-employee barrier that she put in place a couple of weeks ago isn't so impenetrable. I sense her breathless thoughts, almost as if they're a tangible thing between us.

Silence stretches across the next two minutes as she pulls into the lot and drives toward my unit. Some invisible tug is pulling us closer together. I'm fantasizing about the moment I have her upstairs, alone, behind my closed door. I'm so ready to be with her in every way I can.

Keeley presses the button to lift the top on the SUV, then rushes out of the cab. I do the same, and she locks the car door. We meet again at the front of the vehicle and stop. Stare. Breathe. Does she feel this weird rush, too? Like she can't wait until we're alone? Like she's impatient for me to hold and touch her? Like she's eager for me to strip her down and make love to her all night?

I could swear she does, and I can't take the wait anymore. I tug on her hand and dash for the stairs. She's right behind me, heels clacking as she runs up the flight and sprints down the hall with me, all the way to the front door.

With trembling hands, I shove the key in the lock. It takes a few tries, but the door finally opens. I fling it against the wall and nudge her inside. As I follow, Keeley tosses her stuff on the bar. I secure the door behind us. Then I turn to her.

Her back is against the wall. Her breaths are heavy between us. She's staring at me with hunger, eating me up with her eyes.

Fuck yeah.

I come closer, one deliberate pace at a time. I feel this moment in every nerve of my body. I've been waiting to touch her for what feels like an eternity. I've fallen asleep to memories of her taste on my tongue, her cries in my ears, her naked body filling my head. My chest tightens. My gut clenches. I'm so focused on Keeley that nothing else registers. I don't give a fuck if this building burns down around me.

I want this woman more than I've wanted just about anything or anyone in my life.

There's a gravity in the air, tense and sharp, as I press against her, brace my forearm on the wall above her head, and cup her hip with my free hand. Her head falls back as she meets my gaze. I hear her panting breaths.

She wants me, too.

Thank God.

"You going to stop me?" I ask.

"This isn't smart."

Probably not. "That doesn't answer my question."

She licks her lips nervously. Everything in my body clenches at the sight.

"Try me. See what I do."

I don't even know what she's conveying, just that she's all but dared me to kiss her. I can't let that pass. I refuse to stop trying to take her for my own.

I tug on her hip. I lean my entire body against her. She holds her breath, waiting. Her lids slide shut. Her lips part.

I'm toast.

As I finally lay my mouth over hers, a groan slips out.

Fuck me, she's every bit as soft and sweet as I remember. I crush my lips against hers. But that's not enough Keeley for me. I need more. I need deeper. I need everything.

So I nudge her mouth open, slip inside. And I lose myself utterly. This woman is going to be my downfall. Right now, I just don't care.

No one has ever felt this perfect to me.

She tilts her head to offer more of herself and grabs my shirt. As she clings to my shoulders, Keeley yanks me closer until her every curve is plastered against my body. She sucks in a breath, and I feel her heart racing in time with mine. The sound is gonging in my ears. She's potent, and I'm high on her. I don't ever want to come down.

Her tongue slides against mine, a dance, a tease, a caress. I hear her little catch of breath, followed by a desperate moan in her throat.

I want to hear more of that sound. As I'm sliding inside her and telling her how beautiful she is. Yeah. I want that now.

Screw all pretense of being cool and in control. I slide her skirt up her thighs, then hoist her up, bracing her against the wall. I spread her legs and fit my body between them. Heat radiates from her pussy. Her panties are damp. I want to tear them off so badly I'm about to lose my mind.

She clutches at my hair and grips me tightly with her thighs as the kiss goes on. I feel as dizzy as I was on stage, but it's all good now. The sensation is totally swarming my head. Sweating, blood jetting, heart chugging—the works. But no anxiety, just full-throttle, unstoppable arousal.

I lift my head long enough to catch my breath and make sure she's with me. "Keeley, sunshine... Tell me you want this. That you want me."

She has to confess. I need to hear her say it.

Slowly, her lids open. She focuses on me, her blue eyes so dilated and hypnotizing and searching. No idea what she's looking for, but it's all I can do to stand still and hope she finds what she's seeking in me.

Suddenly, the emergency chime on my phone dings. I'd ignore it, but only two people know how to ring that roof-is-on-fire peal. They both work for me and they know not to freak me out unless the situation is critical.

"What is that?" she asks.

"The worst possible fucking timing ever," I snarl as I back away and wrench the phone out of my pocket. With a press of a button, I answer. "What?"

"Um...Maxon?"

It's Britta. She sounds unsure, but I hear a note of excitement in her voice.

"Yes." I'm trying not to tear her head off in case it's really important, but Keeley is watching me intently, her thumb caressing my jaw and neck, then sliding into my shirt.

I close my eyes. Shit. I can't concentrate with her hands on me.

"Sorry it's late. I had to run back to the office to pick up some photocopies I need for the Barnes closing first thing tomorrow. We had a voice mail."

We have them just about every day. I wish she'd get to the point. "And?"

"I tried to text you but... Are you sitting? If you're not, you should. George Stowe called. He wants to hear your pitch this coming Friday at noon."

That shocking pronouncement whacks my short attention span into shape. "Really? Did he say anything else?"

"Just that he'd looked you up and realized that he should at least give you a listen. Of course, he's also hearing Griff. The afternoon before you. He was upfront about that. But…we have a decent chance."

"Absolutely." I know the next words out of her mouth, though: our strategy isn't ready. "Get to the office as soon as you can tomorrow. We need to get this bitch nailed down."

"I've already planned ahead. Makaio is going to take Jamie to daycare on his way to work, so I don't have to worry about doing it after I get the Barnes escrow wrapped. I'll call Rob and let him know, too." She pauses. "Do you think we can get this done right? I doubt a bunch of words and a solid preso will be enough."

My assistant is a damn smart woman. Of course it won't be. I'll have to out-Griff my competition.

I glance at Keeley. I'm glad I've already got a plan in place. I just have to find the balls to tempt my brother with her.

Shit.

"We'll figure it out," I assure Britta, hoping that's true. "What the fuck time is it in Vermont now?"

"Six thirty in the morning. But his voice mail says he's an early riser, so you can call after seven his time."

"I'll ring him up in thirty minutes, let him know we're in."

"Thanks. I know that means staying up late." Britta hesitates. "But I'm hoping the payoff is worth sacrificing a little sleep."

Absolutely. "Landing this listing is worth sacrificing everything."

A little gasp draws my attention to Keeley. She overheard my exchange with Britta. And obviously she's taking it the wrong way.

Or is she?

The gorgeous redhead in my arms is the key to this plot. The bait. *My* sacrifice. I've had the passing thought once or twice that going down this path will mostly likely mean giving her up, but there's no avoiding that ugly reality now. She's made it clear that she won't pretend to have the hots for my brother while having a fling with me.

She rips out of my embrace and sends me a stare I can only describe as crestfallen. God, it's like a stab in the gut.

"Keeley…sunshine."

She doesn't heed me. Instead, she whirls around to storm out of the kitchen. My heart drops.

"I have to go." I rush to hang up the phone, but Keeley has already marched into the living room. I follow. "Come back. Let's talk."

She flips me off. "Not much more to say than that."

I groan. "Sunshine, don't do this."

"Do what, be angry that you'd rather put business above whatever we could have?" She tosses her hands in the air. "This is my fault. I really let myself believe you weren't the mercenary asshole I thought you were when we met."

"I'm not." Well, not completely.

Keeley goes on as if I didn't say a word. "I should have known better."

"You shouldn't. I mean, I want to be with you," I insist, but she's still stomping away from me.

"No, you want to bang me," she calls over her shoulder.

I can't tell her that's not true. But it's also not the whole truth.

"Damn it, will you sit down and listen to me?

"Oh, I've heard enough. Go work on your big listing. You don't need me."

"I never said that. Let's forget business until tomorrow, enjoy our time together and—"

"It's over. I told you when we agreed to this deal that if I was going to be your accomplice, I wouldn't be your convenient lay, too. My small lapse of judgment a few minutes ago aside, I meant it."

I grab her arm. "Why does it have to be one or the other? We're two adults who can share a good time while we do our jobs."

"That may be business as usual for you, but this hired whore doesn't work that way. I'm going to bed. Alone."

Keeley slams her bedroom door shut between us. I can't miss her silent message. I don't know what to say, but my choice is obvious.

Am I really prepared to use the woman I want more than anything to tempt my brother into losing the deal of a lifetime?

CHAPTER ELEVEN

"...*D*o you hear what I'm saying?" Rob's voice breaks into my thoughts.

It's noon on Monday, and I've put literally everything else aside to work on the Stowe presentation. Britta ran in an hour ago, after the Barnes closing, carrying bagel sandwiches and coffee. Now that we've all chowed down and caffeined up, we should be set to brainstorm for hours.

Why am I having trouble keeping my thoughts on business?

The answer is easy. Keeley keeps crashing into my head. Last night, I didn't have a clue what to do. Despite a restless night's sleep and focusing on this dilemma way more than I should, I still don't.

Keeley is important—more important than she once was. More important than my head wants her to be. I can't seem to control how often I think about her or how much I ache to touch her or how completely I want to make her happy. I have no idea what the fuck is wrong with me, because when I talked to George Stowe last night, he made it clear that I'm the underdog and my presentation better blow him away. Otherwise, he'll be choosing Griff.

But no pressure.

I need to get my head in the game.

Sure, it would be easier to walk away. Let my brother have this one. I hate to admit that he's probably earned it. But if he closes this deal, he becomes the number one agent on the island. And I lose. At that realization, I hear my dad's voice in my head, the same stern taunting he's been barking out since my brother and I were old enough to talk. He's asking me for the umpteenth time if I'm a pussy or a fighter.

So...yeah. I can't let Griff win.

There. I've admitted the problem. And I kind of loathe myself for it. What kind of full-grown man is still looking for Daddy's approval?

On the other hand, is it so wrong to want your father to be proud of you, just once?

What if I have to give up Keeley forever to earn it?

Invest in your heart. I hear Britta in my head again.

Second place is first loser. Are you going to let your younger brother be the winner in this family? And there's my shining male role model, right on cue.

Fuck, I'm so confused.

"Maxon?" Rob barks into my thoughts, snapping his fingers. "Where are you, man? We've got to start making some decisions."

I jerk my thoughts to the present. Or I try. What's really rolling through my head is the way Keeley shut me out last night. I tried to talk to her through the door, but she merely started the shower so she couldn't hear me. After my dutiful half-hour call with George, I thought she might have cooled down a bit. But when I checked her door again, it was locked.

I went to bed last night wanting to hit something, to scream, yell...even cry. None of that is adult or manly, so I refrained. But seriously. I'm tied up in knots. When did this woman I never intended to want for more than a night begin to mean as much to me as a career-making deal? Am I really thinking of chucking my ambition, pride, and future for her?

Maybe I'm looking at this wrong. Is it possible to land this listing the old-fashioned way? Good idea, good pitch, good schmooze. Maybe. If I go home to Keeley tonight and admit I've been an asshole, she might listen. If I apologize and explain that my bad personality is really a family predisposition I'm struggling to overcome, she may not feel so betrayed. If I explain that I intend to persuade George Stowe to give me a chance without using her to distract Griff, it could possibly make a difference.

Maybe. But if I do that, I'm almost guaranteed to lose almost everything else, even my self-respect.

What the fuck am I going to do?

"Right. Decisions." At least I've got a clear head about the pitch. "I'm thinking we take a total departure from the norm. Like I've been saying, the Stowe estate doesn't have to be billed as flashy or splashy. I think we understand that Susan Stowe came here for solace. Her children may not have understood her need to grieve alone. They might not still. But we can make this property about the calm and serenity, about returning to nature. We focus on the grounds and the atmosphere, not the over ten thousand square feet, the eight bedrooms, and the multi-level infinity pools. We make our presentation a tribute to a woman who loved her husband so much that she couldn't bear to live the life she'd once led without him."

Britta and Rob both look at me as if I've sprouted another head. Yeah, that insight is pretty damn sensitive for me.

"But throw in the ohana, and you're talking about really posh party space for twenty," Rob points out.

Britta frowns. "Think of the weddings someone could host here."

"You're both right. What I'm suggesting is that we also look at this from the perspective of someone who might want more than a fiesta pad or a place to stash a harem. I'm saying we tell the Stowes that we want to honor their mother's memory and see if someone wants to buy it as a private treatment center or a secluded getaway from the real world. This place doesn't have to be just about the big shindig or showing off wealth. It can be about recovery. Rebirth."

My team sits back for a quiet moment, digests what I've said.

"And you think the Stowe heirs will hear that more than crap like Internet TV commercials, skywriting above a sporting event, or whatever the hell Griff has planned?" Rob muses.

"Exactly."

"You know… I think you're onto something." Britta nods. "I like it."

"Me, too," Rob adds. "What's our next step?"

After an afternoon of hammering out our most specific approach yet, making a few phone calls, and beginning to flesh out the presentation, I'm surprised when I look up to find dusk fast approaching.

I glance at my phone. I've tried to call Keeley a few times today. She hasn't answered. I've left texts. She hasn't replied. In a voice mail, I even gave groveling my best shot. Nothing.

No doubt, she's pissed.

On the one hand, it's good. She must feel something for me or she wouldn't care that I might want to use her to divert my brother's brain from work. On the other hand, she was pretty clear that she feels used. I hate that. Not only is she smokin'-hot and sex with her is beyond phenomenal, she's like…a friend. I've told her some of my darkest secrets, and she listened, just squeezing my hand. No judgment, no platitudes, no bullshit. She gets me. That's rare.

So why is she having trouble understanding that what I want and what I need are diametrically opposed? If she'll try to understand me just a bit more, she'll get that wanting her and wanting to screw my brother over don't have to be mutually exclusive. After all, I'm not plotting to hurt *her*.

Damn it, why won't she call me back?

After Britta flies out the door to try to reach the daycare in the next fifteen minutes before they close, Rob grabs his stuff and heads for the exit. "So…hey. What about your little side plan with Keeley? I didn't ask in front of Britta, but how's that going?"

Subtext: *You're not wussing out, are you?* I don't know what to say. The logical, success-ladder-climbing side of me knows that if I don't give every angle my all, I might as well concede to Griff now. But everything from shoulder to shoulder, between my neck and my navel, seizes up. That part of me is already doing a million-emotion march against the concept of letting Keeley anywhere near my brother.

"I'm rethinking."

"Why? You know your brother will go mental when he meets her. She can charm him right out of his sanity. Is she backing out? You found the leverage to bend her into this agreement, right? If so, you need to remind her—"

"No. That's not the problem." I'd rather not tell Rob my personal situation. He'll only roll his eyes anyway.

"Then what is it? Do *not* tell me your conscience has decided to get uptight."

Okay, that's annoying. "Don't you think it's a shitty thing to do to a woman? Imagine how she feels."

"Who cares? She'll be gone in two weeks." He curses. "Christ, when did you grow morals?"

Rob's tone makes it clear he thinks I'm a fidiot. Maybe I am. I just… Last night, after I kissed her with a wholly new passion that stemmed from somewhere other than my dick, then all but blurted that I'd give her up to beat my brother, the devastation on Keeley's soft features nearly took me out at the knees.

"Don't be an asshole," I snap at Rob. "I have to think about this. She means something to me."

"Since when? Have you even fucked this girl again?"

I remember all the times Rob and I swapped morning-after stories. At one point, I knew every sexual partner he had in the last three years. I also knew whether they were a screamer or if they liked their sex kinky. I was pretty good about reciprocating, even with Tiffanii. But Rob's question now infuriates me.

"That's none of your business."

"In other words, no. Grow up and get laid. I mean this as a friend and a business associate. Don't fuck this up. You asked Stowe for a shot."

"And we're going to pitch to him."

"Yeah, blindfolded with one hand tied behind your back. Why would you do this halfway?"

"Why throw Keeley under the bus for ambition?"

"For fuck's sake. Your *feelings* are going to cost us a lot of money, like six figures each. I need that money. Britta does, too. Why don't you tell Keeley you like her and give her a cut of the payoff to play along?"

"I tried." More or less. "She won't."

Rob rakes a hand through his hair like he can't believe what I've said. "Persuade her. You fucking sell things for a living. You have this whole plan in place. You've been working it for two weeks. Now five feet short of the goal line, you're going to pack up your gear and quit? Who are you?"

That's a good question. I'm not even sure I know the answer anymore. I don't feel happy without Keeley nearby teasing or scolding me. I don't run right when I don't know where she is, if she's happy, or whether she'll be home when I get there.

I'm so fucked.

"Get off my back."

"Give me a reason to. I came to work for you because you never failed to go for the kill. I would have sworn you'd stab your own mother to get ahead. And now you're giving up your chance to catch the biggest deal of your career for some fucking broad you met in a bar two weeks ago." He shakes his head at me. "When did you become the guy willing to fuck me out of a paycheck so you can get laid? Get your shit together, or I don't think I can work for you anymore."

Before I can say anything else, Rob is gone.

I honestly don't know if he'll be back. He's an essential part of my team. He knows how to make sales faster…and he knows where all the bodies are buried, so to speak. This sucks.

I curse and grab my gear. Rob's tirade aside, I know I have a hard decision to make. I have to talk to Keeley—somehow. We need to work this out. No matter what happens with Griff, in my head she's mine and she's going to stay that way.

I can't say I'm in a great mood when I climb into the car and tear out of the parking lot for home. Yes, I've known for a long time that Rob is a complete bastard. Frankly, it's one of the reasons I hired him and why we worked well together. Birds of a feather and all. Sometimes I have to be charming for clients, but I could always count on my marketing manager to be ruthless.

His shit tonight was way over the line.

I get that my indecision has thrown him for a loop. Since he gets paid when I get paid, I realize that if I don't reel in the Stowe estate, I'm costing him a lot of money. He should also know I'm going to do my best to succeed and make things right for him. If he's calmed down tomorrow, we can try to work it out. If he continues to be an asswipe, I may be hiring a new staff member.

My phone rings, butting into my thoughts. There's just enough glare left in this sunset that stabs my eyes through the windshield, I can't see the display on my Range Rover. But my insides torque up at the hope that Keeley is finally not pissed enough to talk to me.

I grope for the button on the dash and stab it. "Hello? Keeley?"

"Sorry. It's Harlow."

"Hey, sis." I try not to sound disappointed.

She laughs at me. "Tell me how you really feel?"

"Give it a rest."

"You got it bad for this woman, don't you?"

Yeah. I'm not sure what that means yet or how it's going to play out in the future. The not knowing is making me antsy. "Did you want something?"

"Well, I called to tell you a few things, but since you're so ribbable now, I think I'll keep the good stuff to myself until I've had my fun."

I sigh. "Why aren't you taking your frustrations out on your fiancé? Is he still in London?"

"No. He's flown on to Athens. He's very important," Harlow says in a voice that makes me worry she's questioning her own importance to him.

"You okay?"

"Are you?" she counters. "How is it going with Keeley?"

I'm a smart guy...usually. I am definitely intelligent enough to realize that I will never understand the female mind. Harlow isn't much like Keeley—but she's closer than I'll ever be.

"I'm not even sure. Good one minute, not so good the next." I fill her in on last night's un-hilarious comedy of errors.

"What are you going to do?"

"I don't know. What do you think I should do?"

"You have never once asked my advice with a woman. By the way, if you had, I could have told you Tiffanii was a selfish whore."

"Thanks for the FYI. I figured that out."

"Finally. Look, you're obviously tied up in knots over this girl. Are you in love with her?"

I've never been in love. How the hell should I know? "Maybe."

Harlow laughs without humor. "You sound so clueless. It would be funny if it wasn't so sad."

Gritting my teeth in frustration, I bite back a curse. "Are you going to make fun of me or help?"

She hesitates, and I wonder how much she's enjoying my torment. She's not usually cutthroat like the males in our family, but she's also no slouch. My little sister learned from some of the most ruthless assholes ever and she can keep up. I'm actually worried about her answer.

"Neither," she says finally. "Look, there's no redeeming Dad, so I gave up on him a long time ago. You and Griff... It's been a toss-up which side of the fence you two would fall on. But I'm starting to have hope for you. You seem like a better man with Keeley."

I want to be a better man. I even feel like a better man. I don't want to let that—or her—go. But I don't want to give up the Stowe estate, either. It's not just a property or a payday. It cements my future.

"What are you saying?"

"That you need to figure it out. I could tell you how to play this, but if I do, whatever move you make won't be authentic. Keeley sounds like a smart cookie. I'm guessing she'll see right through any choice that doesn't come from your heart."

Most likely. "I don't know how to choose with my heart. I have three chromosomes—X, Y, and asshole. How do I change that?"

"Stop making excuses and decide what you want most. I only called to drop a little knowledge on you. First, tonight Griff is going to someplace called Lelani's Beachside Grotto. He should be there about…now. So if you want to proceed with your original plan to introduce Keeley to him, here's your chance."

My breath seizes up. My heart pounds so hard I swear it's going to bruise my rib cage. I have to decide now? Right this minute?

There's still a little part of my brain screaming that I'm an idiot if I don't follow through, but all the function in my body seems to be coming from my chest these days. It's telling me that my head needs a fucking vacation.

"Thanks," I manage to mutter. "And he's still not seeing anyone?"

"Nope. But something is going on. I talked to him today. He sounds really wound up."

"He's probably on edge about the Stowe estate." The end of the week is going to creep up on both of us.

"Maybe."

"What's the other reason you called? I mean, besides the chance to talk to your amazing elder brother," I try to joke.

It falls flat.

Harlow gets quiet, sober. My gut starts screaming.

"Mom picked up and left yesterday."

"What? What happened?"

"I don't know exactly. Dad called me in a huff this morning. Mom didn't come home last night. She didn't call. She didn't say she was going anywhere, she just…left. She also took her Mercedes, a suitcase…and half their checking account."

"Damn it. That move sounds as if Griff, that fucker, has been giving her pointers. You think she's gearing up for a divorce?"

"Apparently, she called a lawyer."

"She's done that before," I rationalize aloud. "She usually backs down."

"True." Harlow lets out a troubled breath. "But something tells me this time will be different."

As soon as I hang up with my sister, I call Keeley again. Still no answer. I leave her another voice mail with some assorted groveling and a casual question about the bar Harlow mentioned. Has she heard of it? Damn it, why won't Keeley even talk to me? I can't seem to go on without this woman.

How can I soothe her anger so we can have a… What do shrinks call it? Yeah, a dialogue. I start racking my brain for ideas. I'm pretty sure she would find flowers lame. In the larger scope of things, they're easy and cheap. But if I try to buy her something expensive or substantial, she'll tell me she can't be bought.

Where does that leave me?

I reach my condo and dash through my door, hoping that Keeley will be here, waiting. Maybe she's just too pissed at me to answer the phone. Maybe she wants to yell at me before we talk. I'm okay with that. I'd probably feel like I wasn't important if someone tried to persuade me to flash a little leg or whatever to make them a buck.

My hands tremble as I shove the key in the lock and push the door open. "Keeley?"

Nothing. The place is painfully quiet.

As I glance inside, the kitchen looks completely spotless, so I have no idea whether she even stayed for breakfast. Nor has she set anything out for dinner. That worries me.

I toss my keys on the bar and scan the family room. Nothing of Keeley's is lying around. No book. No glass of half-imbibed water. No rumpled pillows on the sofa.

My guts starts to clench with dread.

"Keeley?" I call again.

I can't stand that she's not here, not responding to me. I swallow as I dash to her bedroom.

Please tell me she's not gone for good.

The minute I hit the threshold, her absence is palpable. But the bedroom smells so much like her it nearly drops me to my knees. A pang for her obliterates my composure. I imagine her skin. I see her smile. I can almost feel her heart.

Keeley Kent would never use or sell me. She would never put her job first. If she loved someone, she would never betray them, hurt them, or leave them.

I have fucked up so badly. Every cell in my body aches with that truth.

The worst part is, I don't know if the damage I've done is reparable.

Taking four giant steps across the room, I rip open the closet door. And I breathe an audible sigh of relief. Her clothes are still hanging. Her shoes are still lined up along the bottom of the closet.

I work a lot of long hours, so I don't always think about the fact that my condo could be tidier. But Keeley not only tucks everything away, she has this knack for arranging items around the room so they're both clever and functional. I've noticed recently that she's completely turned my kitchen upside down—in a good way. Same is true of this bedroom. It used to be a spare space for guests to crash. Now she's brought in pictures, throw pillows, and knick-knacks. The space actually looks homey.

What the hell do I do if she decides not to come back? Will she send me a Dear John letter asking me to return her stuff while telling me to fuck off?

Those thoughts pelt my brain over and over as I change into pajama pants and head for the sofa. Absently, I turn on the TV to wait. I text her to say I'm home. No reply.

With a sigh, I tune out the news. Politics—don't care now. Economic data—whatever. I usually listen to the housing info, but I can't even pretend to give a damn tonight. The program drones through the local news and special interest stories.

Still no Keeley.

I call once more—just in case. She ignores me utterly.

My stomach goes from tight to nauseous. The clock tells me it's past time to eat dinner. For maybe the first time in my life, I'm way more worried about someone else and how they feel than what the fuck is going on in my life. Food will come later. Once I know what's up with Keeley.

Eight o'clock rolls past. Stupid sitcoms with bad laugh tracks can't hold my interest. Nine o'clock comes and goes. I don't even know what Keeley is doing, where she's gone. If she's trying to teach me a lesson, I think I've learned.

Finally, my phone rings. I pounce on it, fumbling with the answer button. But the display tells me it isn't Keeley.

"Britta?"

"Yeah. I just wanted to check on you. I finally got Jamie in bed and thought I'd call. As I backed out of the parking lot at the office, I thought I saw through the window that you and Rob were arguing. Everything all right?"

I need to get control of myself. Stop this man-period I'm having. I have to not freak out.

Deep breaths.

It doesn't help.

"I'm good."

"You don't sound like it," Britta chides gently.

She's not stupid, and I shouldn't treat her that way. "He threatened to quit."

"He *what*?" I hear the shock in her voice and grimace. "That man has devoted years to you. What the… Everything seemed all right when I left."

It was. And now that I've opened my big mouth and started talking, I don't have any other way to explain our fight except the truth. "Keeley isn't just the woman I'm hooked up with right now. I was grooming her to distract Griff so we would get the Stowe listing."

I explain everything, including the fact that I have no idea at all what to do next.

When I'm done, Britta says nothing for an unnervingly long time.

"You still there?" I ask. My voice croaks with nerves.

"How dare you."

My assistant doesn't yell or scream. I wish she would. Then we could get into a knock-down-drag-out and purge her anger. But no. She says the words so softly I have to strain to hear them. I know Britta's temper well. Silence is bad.

"Um…because I'm stupid?" I'm hoping that's the right answer. When I explained my scheme aloud again, that's how it sounded.

"Maxon, you are thirty-three years old. You need to learn that you don't always get your way."

Actually, I feel as if I'm figuring that out damn fast. "Yeah."

"I'm only going to admit this once, and if you ever tell anyone, I will deny it until my dying day." She pauses. I hear her swallow. "I love Griff. I will always love him. I think about your brother every single day. I see him every time I look at our son. I think you know that."

"I do."

"So how could you betray me like this? It's one thing for Griff to troll bars and pick up tourists and bimbos. I can tell myself they don't matter to him. But Keeley is different. You're *teaching* her to be everything Griff could ever want and shoving her in his face. You're giving him a woman to fixate on. You're guaranteeing he never looks at me again. I thought we were family and that you would never hurt me."

Something that feels a lot like shame liquefies my guts. "I didn't mean to hurt you."

"Maybe, but you didn't tell me earlier because you knew the truth would cut me deep."

She's right, and if I refute her or attempt to soft-shoe this, Britta will know. And she will only distrust me more.

"I'm sorry."

A stifled sob sounds over the line. I tense against her cry because it almost causes physical pain. "Maybe you are, deep down. But you're also your father's son, just like Griff. You're all selfish bastards to the end."

"I know. I'm sorry. I swear." I don't know what else to say. "I screwed myself up, if it's any consolation. I'm really into Keeley, and the thought of her with anyone else…"

I can't finish that sentence.

"How about with your own brother?"

I grip the phone and close my eyes. At her words, I'm both sick and want to commit murder. "She said she wouldn't sleep with him."

Unless she wanted to.

"Oh, grow up. You've seen your brother in action. He can be very charming… If you don't want her to become another notch on his bedpost, then stop all this. Do the right thing for once, Maxon. Be the bigger man. Think about the people around you. Care about someone more than yourself."

She's right. I know that deep in my heart. There's just one problem… "I'm not sure I know how to."

And there goes my voice again, broken and coming from some-place deep in my gut.

"Figure it out because if you do this, if you go ahead with your plan to make her Griff's latest lover—"

"Don't say that," I growl, teeth all but bared.

"Lover. His lover. Keeley would be Griff's lover," she spits the words at me. "Call it what it is. Now that you've started this ball rolling, you can't run away from it. You groomed her to warm his bed and you didn't give a damn who you upset in the process. He hurt you, so you wanted to beat him—and fuck everyone else. But if you continue with this, fair warning, Maxon. I quit."

I groan aloud with the actual pain twisting my insides up. "Don't."

"You're not leaving me many choices. I'll never try to stop you from seeing Jamie. You're his uncle, and he loves you. He was just asking for you this morning." Her voice is clipped, as if she hates to admit that. "But you and I can't work together if you're going to intentionally do things to keep breaking my already broken heart."

"Rob threatened to quit if I didn't go through with my plan."

"Then you have a choice to make. This is all on you." She sniffles.

Why doesn't she just take an ax to my chest? It would hurt less.

"You know what's at stake." I realize I'm wheedling and quit.

"Money. Your pride."

"My career. My future." As much as that's inconvenient, those are indisputable facts. "I'm incredibly fond of you and I love Jamie, but—"

"Don't rationalize this!" She finally starts yelling at me. "There will be other big-dollar properties. You will still have a career and a future without the Stowe listing. Your biggest problem is that you can't stand to let your brother win. You have an insane need to be better than Griff at everything. You know I'm right. And he's no different. You two are both egotistical, and I'm tired of trying to be the water always flowing around your immovable rock. If you want me to stay, you're going to have to change direction for once."

I'm digesting her speech. It's raw. Starkly honest. She's stripped me down to the ugliest place in my soul. I'd rather look away, but just like a train wreck, I can't stop staring.

"Britta…"

"Don't call me again unless it's to tell me that you're not going forward with this stupid scheme. And by the way, I know I need to accept that your brother and I are never getting back together. Makaio asked me to marry him yesterday afternoon. I'm going to say yes."

Then she's gone.

I scrub a hand down my face. Holy shit. Britta married to someone other than Griff. I guess it's time. I mean, they've been apart for three years. I shouldn't be shocked. Somehow, I am. My brother used to be the most protective, possessive boyfriend ever. I can't imagine that he'll take seeing Britta wearing another man's ring well.

Then again, I never imagined he'd let her go at all.

I know *I* don't want to, professionally speaking. She knows me well. We work together seamlessly. She fills in the blanks when I'm too busy or disorganized. She's so knowledgeable. I would be lost around the office without her.

I look at the clock. It's after ten now. I can't sit here. I have to pace.

Thirty seconds later, I realize that wearing a path in the floor from one side of the condo to the other isn't doing me a damn bit of good. I feel so fucking wound up and turned inside out. I need more space. I need air.

What I really need is Keeley.

I wrench open the door to the lanai and step outside. The sultry Hawaiian breeze immediately sweeps across my skin, ruffling my hair. I look out at the inky water shimmering under the golden moon hanging low and lazy. But there's no peace. I seize the railing in a crushing grip, as if I can funnel everything I'm feeling out of my body through my hands.

Impossible.

Along the beach, I see the rocks where I stripped away Keeley's reservations and clothes before I took her body. At the moment, I'd give anything to take that night back and start over. Get to know her just for her. Because she's interesting. Unique. I sigh. Because it feels like she belongs with me. To me.

I'm fucking doomed now. What if she never speaks to me again? What if… *Oh, shit.* What if I fell in love and I realized it too late?

Behind me, I hear the slam of the front door. I spin around and see Keeley entering the living room, staring at me through the glass door. She's decked out from head to toe in the pinstripe suit that hugs her body so well it's impossible not to see that she's made for sin.

I wrench open the patio door. "Keeley?" *Thank God you're here.* "I called. I texted. Where have you been?"

"Doing my 'job.' I met your brother tonight." She lifts her chin. "We should talk."

CHAPTER TWELVE

*M*y heart comes to a screeching, skidding halt. She met Griff?

Why do I have the sinking feeling that I'm even more fucked? Because my brother goes out for drinks about seven. Keeley is breezing in about ten thirty. A lot could happen in three and a half hours. I try not to imagine what.

My feet feel like blocks of lead as I enter the condo, shutting the lanai door behind me.

"You went outside?" She sounds surprised.

"Yeah." I nod nervously as my heart decides to wage an all-out war with my chest. The battle is so loud I hear it in my ears. "You were right. It's nice out there."

I'm babbling. I wipe my sweaty palms on the soft cotton of my pajama pants. I want to touch her so badly, but her face is unreadable. I don't know what to say.

She nods and kicks off her pumps. "Do you want to know about my evening with Griff?"

Yes and no. Mostly no. I wish like hell I had any idea what was rolling through her head. I stand there mutely, a boiling pot of emotion melting my brain. I blink. She looks beautiful. There's really no way my brother didn't see her, zero in on her, want to know everything about her before he saw every inch of her.

The thought is killing me.

"I'm not sure."

She softens a little. "Sit."

Keeley chooses the corner of the L-shaped sectional. I sit one cushion over, going through the motions of breathing so I don't freak out.

This makes no fucking sense. Twenty days ago, I didn't even know this woman. I would have passed her on the street and stared...before I shrugged and walked on. Now I'm seriously thinking of surrendering my future to her. Giving up the only sense of self I've ever known for her.

"Did you talk to him?" I finally ask into the protracted silence.

"Yes. He's...like you. And not. He's smart and ambitious and interesting. You've got that in common. But he's more serious. More intense."

Griff is. He always has been. I wonder if it's because he has a chip on his shoulder about being the younger brother, if he always feels like he needs to dig deeper to keep up.

"What happened? What did you talk about?"

"I got your message with the name of that bar that Harlow passed on. I thought I'd go over there and see if I could figure him out just by observing. I was on my stool about two minutes when he came over to me, drink in hand and swagger in full swing."

Knowing he studied her and sized her up as a potential nightly fuck makes me want to both curl into the fetal position and beat him senseless. Breathing is hard again. I'm wishing I had booze or a punching bag—something to bleed off my growing fury. Griff looked at her, damn it.

The worst part is, I have no one to blame but myself.

"What did he say?"

"Not much. We made small talk, exchanged names and a little

info. We joked about our favorite drinks, then made a pointless bet about whether the new waitress would drop a huge tray of drinks. He won, by the way. She wasn't practiced enough to handle all that. We mentioned where we were from, where we'd gone to college, and the fact that we're both single."

Technically, Keeley is single. I know it in my head. The rest of me is shouting a big "fuck no."

"That took three hours?"

She raises a brow at me. It's a subtle warning that I don't own her.

"We took our time. We ended up finding a booth and sharing appetizers. We talked about business. I gave him a cover story. He thinks I work retail but am thinking about going into real estate. That opened him up to talk about business. He spoke in veiled terms about the Stowe deal."

As much as I hate the cozy picture her words paint, it doesn't sound as intimate as I feared.

I let out a pent-up breath. "Okay. So that's it?"

"No." She folds her hands in her lap and looks at her entwined fingers.

Is she trying to collect her words? Or hide her guilt?

"And?" I demand, hearing an edgy note creep into my voice.

I can't stand being on tenterhooks anymore. The not being able to draw in a deep breath, along with the sharp, perpetual tensing of my gut, is killing me. The pain bolts down my sternum.

"We talked about family. He mentioned you." She taps her thumbs together and pauses again.

"Spit it out."

"He hates you."

I guessed that. The feeling has been unspoken for something just north of a thousand days. But Keeley's soft words makes every-thing inside me crater.

Not knowing the truth for certain was easier.

Fuck, one deal tore up my family. This one is going to rip up my heart.

Goddamn it.

"Yeah."

"And he loves you. He didn't say that, but I know it."

My heart nearly implodes. I love him, too.

I shut my eyes and feel tears sting like acid. I miss that stupid motherfucker so much.

"Maxon?" she prods at me.

I refuse to cry. It's been an absolutely terrible day. Not the first. It won't be the last. I clench my teeth together. I will not lose my composure. I am fucking going to hold it together so I can hear the rest of this.

"Yeah." I drag in a shuddering breath. "So where did you leave things?"

"He asked me to dinner tomorrow night."

Jesus. Motherfucking son of a bitch. My stomach tightens so much it's one giant ball of ache.

"What did you say?"

She looks past me, out to the lanai, biting her lip. The tension is killing me.

Finally, she nods. "I, um…told him this week was hell on my schedule and I'd have to juggle my schedule to make it work. He gave me his number. I'm supposed to call him tomorrow afternoon."

"Where does he want to take you?" That will tell me a lot about how interested Griff is.

"Nowhere. He wants to cook for me."

That's a lie. He wants to fuck her.

I can't take that sitting down.

Lurching to my feet, I lunge across the room, raking my hand through my hair. "It's a ploy. He only invites a woman over when—"

"He wants to sleep with her. I've been around the block, Maxon. I know."

"What the hell? I…"

She can't go. I can't let her. On the other hand, will she even listen to me? Does she want Griff?

"So you had drinks and appetizers and came home."

"I came back to your place," she corrects me.

It's not home to her. *Right.*

I swallow as I turn to face her. "Did he walk you to your car?"

"Yes."

"Did he kiss you?"

"Yes."

I stagger. That one word feels like the sharpest blade buried right in my heart.

Before I can wrap my brain around her reply and insist that she's never seeing him again, she cocks her head and speaks. "When do you want me to go out with him? I have a feeling I can undo him in a night."

I gape at her like she's lost her fucking mind. "Less than a week ago, you were preaching Kumbaya bullshit about repairing the relationship between me and Griff, and now you're smacking lips with him and willing to help me tear him down."

"Once I realized that you were never going to care about more than business, that didn't leave me with many options. I can either keep forcing a peace on you that you don't give a flip about or I can live up to my word. You want to destroy your own family? You're the one who will have to live with the consequences. Why am I standing in your way? You've painted Griff as a man who abandons his loved ones and doesn't care about the son he's never met. As far as I can tell, you're both getting what you deserve. When you approached me with your plan, I naively believed that everyone has good qualities. That, deep down, all people are capable of love. Yes, even you. I was sure you wanted happiness. I just had to show you the way. But most every choice you've made since I've known you has been selfish."

I wince. She's right. "Keeley—"

"No. You brought us to this place so now you're going to listen. You don't know what love is. And it's clear to me that you don't have the first clue how to be happy. So if you want to know why I'm all in with your stupid plan suddenly, it's because I want to get this over with and move on to a less toxic situation. Griff's pitch is Thursday. Isn't that what Britta said last night?"

"Yeah, but—"

"There's no 'but' here. That doesn't give me a lot of time to work, but since you're willing to sacrifice *everything* to win, I won't feel bad about being really fucking charming to your brother over the next two days. It's not like Griff is hard on the eyes. By the time you pitch to George Stowe on Friday, he'll have a muddled head. And you should have a clear path."

I tear across the room, torn between violently pounding the wall and clutching Keeley to me like a sobbing boy until she swears she won't let me go. "No. No! Fuck no! You swore that you didn't intend to sleep with him, that I couldn't make you. You didn't want to be a whore, and I respected that."

"You accepted it because I forced you to. But it's my body and my life. It's just sex." She shrugs. "No big deal."

I grab her shoulders and lunge in her face. "It is a big deal. Huge fucking deal. You can't date him. You can't touch him."

She tilts her head, raises a brow. Somewhere in the back of my brain, I know those are warning signals. I try to slow down my outrage and fear. Somewhere under that, I feel logic lurking, trying to reassert itself. But at my head's insistence that maybe she's right, my emotions shove those thoughts down.

"Why?" she asks softly.

I'm used to animated Keeley, the one who teases and cajoles while she tries to get me to see the best in every situation. That woman lightens me, soothes me, balances me. I've grown so attached to her that I'm thinking…yeah, maybe the whole love thing isn't a crazy hoax. But the Keeley in front of me now is cool, almost calculating. She's willing to blow up everything between us.

Fuck. This is exactly how she felt when she seemingly over-heard me giving her up for my ambition last night. Unimportant. Confused. Destroyed.

"Why, Maxon?" she prods. "Why shouldn't I go distract your brother?"

Because I love you. The realization rolls through my head. It jets blood through my veins. It envelops my beating heart. She thinks I don't know what love means, but suddenly I understand. Abso-lutely. Totally. I would kill for this woman. Die for her. Do anything to make her smile. I cannot live without her. I cannot release her from my life.

I cannot give her to Griff.

"I-I…" Do I tell her? Will she believe me? Do I give her that kind of power over me? Will she even care?

Too many questions pelt my brain. As I'm sorting through the tangle—tough to do when I'm dizzy, shocked, and grappling with how much Keeley Kent has changed me—someone starts pounding on my door. This isn't a polite knock but a nonverbal demand that I open up now.

Damn it, talk about the worst possible timing.

"Who the fuck is that?" I snarl under my breath.

No one ever comes to my place except Britta and Rob. I don't have any other friends. Come to think of it, I don't have anyone I can really talk to.

Except Keeley.

I'm going to ignore this unwelcome visitor. If I don't answer, my staff will assume I'm not here or that I'm busy. If it's a solicitor or religion peddler, they'll go away soon enough. Everyone else, I don't give two fucks about.

This beautiful redhead in front of me is definitely at the top of my give-a-fuck list—in all ways.

But whoever is outside is clearly a persistent ass, as the beating on my door resumes, even harder than before.

"Whoever you are, go the hell away," I shout.

I'm focused on the most important person in my world.

"Open up, you stupid snot. I brought you into this world and paid for your overpriced education. I've come a long way. Show me a little fucking courtesy and let me in."

I'd know that voice anywhere.

Keeley gapes at the door. Dread fills my belly before it drops to my toes in a sickening rush.

"Is that…" She frowns as if she can't quite believe what her ears are telling her.

She's about to see me at my very worst. No way she'll ever love me after this. And there's not a fucking thing I can do but watch my demise happen.

"Yeah." Fucking son of a bitch. "That's my dad."

WITH A CURSE, I pull away from Keeley. "This will probably be ugly. Go to the guest room and shut the door. If Dad has come all the way from San Diego unexpectedly, this won't be good."

She pauses, and I expect her to run to the safety of the bedroom. After all, he's already shown his usual charming stripes. To my surprise, she shakes her head. "I may be mad as hell at you right now, but from the sound of things, you'll need a friend."

She's right, and that something soft lurches in my chest again, as if it can get closer to her. I would love to have her hold my hand while my dad, just by being himself, drives me crazy. But my need to protect Keeley is stronger. I can already guess how her interaction with my father will go, and I want to spare her. "I would feel better if you didn't get in his path. Please."

A million reasons crowd my head but Dad starts pounding again. I don't really have time to relay all the terrible crap between me and this man. It's impossible for her to understand the decades of our complicated relationship, even if she saw each moment in real time, much less to blurb it in ten seconds.

Keeley looks as if she's going to resist, and I grab her hands. "Please. I promise I'll get through it. After a lifetime with him, I'm a pro. If he pisses me off, I'll come talk to you afterward. He'll want privacy. If he doesn't get it, he'll be an even bigger asshole. Go."

When I nudge her toward the guest bedroom, she drags her feet a bit but finally nods. "I'll be here if you need me."

I nod her way, then when she's safely ensconced in her room, I slump toward the front door. Dread is digging a hole in my stomach as I turn the lock. I haven't clapped eyes on my father in over three years. Hell, I've barely talked to him. But he's come from San Diego on the spur of the moment and insists on seeing me. Every moment I keep him outside is just another moment for him to get more irritated.

Knowing I can't put it off anymore, I wrench the door open and step back to admit him. Damn, he's aged. Before he left Maui, his hair was still salt and peppery. Now he's completely silver, even his beard. He sporting a summer tan in early February, which tells me he hasn't stopped being a regular at a tanning booth. He's fit, as always. But his shoulders are slightly slumped. His jawline isn't as firm as it once was. He's wearing glasses now—a weakness I never thought he'd bow to. He'll turn sixty-two this year, so maybe I shouldn't be surprised that time has changed him. He no longer appears invincible. When I was a kid, my dad was always larger than life to me, and seeing him look more like an old man is a shock.

"Hey, Dad," I finally manage to say.

He scowls at me—nothing new—as he barges inside, dragging a huge suitcase on wheels behind him. His overstuffed briefcase dangles from one big hand. "Took you long enough. What are you doing, jacking off?"

"No. Nothing you'd care about. Welcome to Maui. This is unexpected. Does your sudden visit have something to do with Mom leaving?"

"Your mother, that ungrateful bitch," he huffs, then plops himself on the couch. "I fed, clothed, and supported her for thirty-five years. I bought her a lavish house, took her on extravagant vacations all over the world, gave her designer everything. She had two responsibilities. *Two.* Throw good parties—something she's never managed without a caterer—and to give me a good-looking family for corporate Christmas cards. You and Griff were exactly what I had in mind, but she had to get knocked up a third time."

I want to butt in that it takes two to conceive, but clearly he thinks the responsibility for not getting pregnant rested solely on my mother, never mind that he's both the aggressor and the one with the sperm. What a dick.

He hasn't changed a bit.

"But fine. Whatever." Dad tosses a hand in the air. "Harlow was a cute kid. Her fucking wedding is going to cost me a fortune. But Linda couldn't even manage to raise you kids while I worked my ass off without constantly wanting my input or for me to straighten you boys out. How fucking hard is it to change a few diapers and drive someone to soccer practice?"

My father gives me a disgusted sneer. I can't imagine why I'm stunned. He's never hidden the fact that he wants nothing to do with his kids. Playing the family man gave him good corporate optics at a time that shit mattered. He's good at his job. Great, even. He should be since he's a workaholic. He has no friends and doesn't value his family. With every passing year, he's grown more cynical and bitter.

I can't stand him.

Even as I'm staring at him, thinking what a grade-A asshole he is and that I shouldn't let him upset me, the fact that I was nothing more to him than a clean-cut face on a card sent to his associates once a year cuts me deep. Maybe it bothers me so much now because I'm already agitated by the kiss Keeley shared with Griff.

I'm fucking bleeding inside at the thought. I don't need my father's attitude right now.

"Have you gone mute?" my father hisses, then rakes a hand through his hair. "Jesus, I gave you good genes to work with. You mother was a beauty queen with half a brain. I'm a self-made billionaire. What's your problem?"

"It's just been a long day and I wasn't expecting you," I bite out. "So Mom has never been all you want her to be and…what else?"

"She left me. *Me*. Are you fucking kidding? What did I not give that bitch? My thirty-five best years, a fortune—"

"You didn't give her love," I cut in, vaguely aware that I'm sounding like Keeley. Then I swallow because I know Dad won't understand a word I've just said. The shit is about to hit the fan.

"Oh, boo hoo. I knew I shouldn't have left you here when I moved back to San Diego. Apparently, you've grown a vagina since then. You know love is all greeting-card crap."

Yes, I've known how he felt my whole life.

"Linda knows that, too. Love was never part of our deal."

That throws me for a loop. I guess I shouldn't be surprised that he approached marriage like a business agreement. Somehow it kinda does.

"So Mom has finally decided to leave you? Why do you care?"

I don't know why I'm trying to understand. Dad will cut off her access to all other funds, and within a few weeks she'll most likely come home. This drama played out when I was four, again when I was eight, and for a final time at fifteen. Since then, their marriage has seemed steadier, though not necessarily happier. But after they came through three incidents in roughly ten years, I'd hoped the last eighteen years without separation meant something.

Obviously not.

"I care because it looks bad! She claims that she's fallen in love with Marco, some asswipe she met on a dating site for the over-fifty crowd. He likes old movies, antiquing, and wine weekends." My father rolls his eyes. "What kind of pussy does that sound like?"

The explanation that all people are different and each have various likes and dislikes will only be lost on him. I know from experience, so I don't waste my breath. But Dad's explanation still manages to shock me.

"Mom is *dating* someone else?"

"Yeah. She says she's moving in with him. Apparently she's been seeing this bastard for almost a year. And fucking him that long, too."

Good for her, finally getting some on the side. "Did her decision have anything to do with you finding another new mistress?"

"I suppose." He slumps down on the sofa, almost pouting like an overgrown kid. "I never hid them. Your mother and I had an understanding. I pulled her out of her dirt-poor farming town in Nebraska, and she performed the two wifely duties I outlined. She never liked sex much, so our arrangement worked. She lost her mind when I told her that Amanda was pregnant."

"Amanda?"

"My most recent mistress." He sighs. "She's due in April. I'm too fucking old to be a father again."

My world has just tilted on its axis. Now I have to sit down, too. "How old is this woman?"

He doesn't meet my gaze. "Twenty-five."

I hate to be judgmental…but I'm grossed out. I never imagined that my old man gave up his mistresses, but I'd hoped that they had somewhat aged with him. "She's Harlow's age."

"I don't think about it like that. Amanda looks fucking hot in Victoria's Secret. Or she did."

Now I'm even more grossed out. "How did you not take precautions to ensure that Amanda didn't get pregnant?"

"She said she was on the pill. Hell, I've seen her prescription since I spent half my nights at her apartment in the city."

"You could have gotten a vasectomy years ago. You should have if you didn't want more kids."

He rears back and stares at me like I'm stupid. I know that look well since I've seen it all my life. I actually know what he's going to say before he even opens his mouth.

"No one is cutting off my balls. Besides, Amanda conceiving was a fluke. She seemed equally mortified when the doctor confirmed that she was knocked up. But she refused to have a damn abortion, even when I offered to pay for it." He waves his hands at me. "Before you unleash whatever blah blah bullshit I see all over your face, she and I are over now." He shudders. "Never could stand fucking a pregnant woman. Big bellies and leaking tits... Ugh."

I try not to roll my eyes. The universe has always revolved around him—at least in his mind. Why shouldn't a woman growing another human being in her womb keep her pre-pregnancy shape for dear old Dad?

"So, you two broke up. Has she asked you for child support?"

"You know she has." He sounds cynical and pissed off. "I'll be DNA testing that kid the minute he pops out—it's another boy. If he's not mine, I'm going to rip Amanda a new asshole."

Because that's what every new mother needs. Why can't he just thank his lucky stars and move on since he doesn't want the baby, anyway?

I shake my head at him because I really don't know what to say. "And if it is yours, now you'll have four kids."

"Six," he grumbles.

"What?" I stare at him like I don't even know who he is. Honestly, I probably shouldn't be shocked but I can't seem to help it. "I have two other half-siblings?"

Dad hems and haws and does his best impression of a bobble-head while stalling. Finally, he sighs. "I have a daughter named Bethany who's six months younger than Griff. Evan, my other son, was born three days before Harlow. Both kids have different mothers. But I've paid for everything—"

"So what? They grew up without a father. God, you're a selfish bastard. Forking over some cash doesn't excuse you from being an absent parent. You had a responsibility to those kids." And to the ones my mother gave him.

When I stare at him, he's wearing his I-don't-give-a-fuck expression. "A father's responsibility is to provide. I think I've done that handsomely. What good would I have done by being a more involved father?"

Actually, he's right. He would only have warped us kids more. Mom was unhappy and worn down by life, but she at least tried to be kind and occasionally affectionate. Dad made her too brittle to love us, I think. She tried her best, but he mentally belittled her and beat her down, just like he has everyone else in his life.

I, too, know exactly what it's like to feel small and inconsequential after a chat with him. In fact, I feel like that after virtually every conversation we share.

"So what's your next move?" I ask. "Are you actually getting divorced this time?"

He raises a brow. "I hear she's trying to serve me with papers. I am not giving that bitch fifty percent of everything I've broken my back to earn. She took half the money in our checking account. Fine. It's a pittance. But my portfolio is substantial. I'm not giving her a penny of that."

Mom deserves it. Hazard pay for putting up with him for so many years—the mental abuse, the infidelity, the single parenting and corporate bullshit. But I'm keeping my opinion to myself. It's not worth the argument. *He's* not worth it. I can't change the fact that this small-minded, bitter man is my father. He's right that he gave me life and one hell of an expensive education. But I learned by his example, and I'm not proud of it. He also gave me anger and baggage and years of misplaced indifference toward most everyone around me.

"How are you going to avoid that? You can't sidestep being served until Mom can claim abandonment. You're talking years. You've never been able to stay away from the office for more than seven days."

"I'm still working on that. Right now, I'm taking a vacation while I sort out all the legal stuff. I'm talking to a cutthroat lawyer who can ream your mother a new asshole before we ever make it to court."

"What leg do you have to stand on?" I ask before I can think better of it. I'm outraged on Mom's behalf.

But as soon as I've spoken the words, I know the dragon I've tried to slay for years is going to turn all his fire on me.

"Oh, because I'm the philandering prick? Because I wasn't 'sensitive' and didn't let her carry my balls in her purse? I provided for her, gave her identity and community. She was someone because she was married to *me*. I bought her diamonds in Paris. I made sure she became PTA president when she wanted to run. I never missed a birthday, holiday, or special occasion. You think the courts are going to punish me because I don't believe in love?" He scoffed as if he found that laughable. "Your mother knew exactly who she was marrying when she said, 'I do.' She told me she would do anything to ensure she didn't have to go back to Halsey, Nebraska, population 144, the day I met her. She was Miss Blaine County and had earned a scholarship because of it, so she'd managed to get as far as the university in Lincoln, but that wasn't far enough from home for her. She wanted to move somewhere warm and never worry about money again. I gave that to her. She swore she'd never care who I fucked and vowed never to divorce me. In the last few months, she's gone back on her word in every way, while I've lived up to every promise I ever made her. And you think I'm the bad guy here? Fuck, you've turned into a whiny little bitch, like I always said you would." He stands and reaches for his suitcase. "I'm going to your brother's. He's got more steel in his spine. That's why you always played first loser to his winner." He claps me on the shoulder. "Until you pull your head out of your ass and be a man, you always will."

I want to scream at him that I'm not a loser, but I bite the knee-jerk defense back. Instead, I hit him with something he'll understand and respect. "Fuck you. I'm the number one real estate agent on Maui, thank you very much. I've earned that. Griff has been chasing my tail for the last three years."

My dad shrugs. "Call me when you've made your first hundred million. Then I might be impressed. But I know you, Maxon. You lose to him every fucking time because you lack the killer instinct. Your mother coddled you too much as a kid, until I told her to stop ruining you. By then, it was too late. I even tried pitting you two boys against each other in the hopes that you'd grow some real balls. But only Griff's got bigger because you didn't accept that even your brother can be your enemy. Instead, you rolled over and showed him your vulnerable belly and tried to make him your friend." He shakes his head like he's utterly disgusted at me. "Dumb ass. What a waste. I'm going to go stay with the winner. Does Griff still live in the same place?"

I can barely digest all the ugliness in his speech. Worse, I know this is Dad's version of truth. He really believes everything he's saying. Mom is ungrateful because he did her one decent favor when she was nineteen. Never mind the ensuing thirty-five years of terrible. He really doesn't understand why she's no longer kissing his loafers. Just like he doesn't understand that Griff and I never wanted to be at each other's throats. My brother was simply better at hiding it, and half the time I let him win so that Dad wouldn't berate him and tear him down. I could tell my father that, but he'd only respect me less, and he's settled on a reality that works in his head. I'll never change it.

"I don't know, Dad. Griff and I haven't spoken since a few months after you moved away."

"Did you argue about a deal or a girl?"

Does it even matter? "Both."

"It's too late to tell you to wrestle that deal to the ground and hump it into submission, I'm sure. But fighting over a woman… Tiffanii?"

I have no idea why he wants to know. "Yeah."

My father shrugs. "She might have been good in bed but she wasn't worth losing a deal. Get your fucking priorities straight."

I feel as if an elephant stepped on my chest. I can't breathe. "You slept with her?"

"It was easy." He says the words as if any idiot would have logically made the same choice. "Girls like it when you flash cash and give them attention. She was more than happy to put out in return. Don't look at me like I just took away your toy. I didn't think you'd care. After all, I was willing to share my mistress with you when you turned sixteen."

God, I'd blocked that out. When Dad summoned me to his office right after I'd gotten my driver's license, I'd hoped it was because he wanted to congratulate me, maybe finally tell me he was proud. No, he just wanted to introduce me to Danielle, his latest assistant/fuck doll. He told me that she was going to make me a man. The whole thing was both tempting and skeevy. I tore out of there, heading straight home.

"You were a pussy even then," he barks. "When Danielle dropped her dress, you nearly pissed your pants, then ran home to Mommy. My father got me laid at fourteen, and I was damn grateful. So was your brother when I gave him your same opportunity with AnnaBeth a few years later. He was far smarter than you. I think he even came back for seconds when he thought I wasn't looking. He's always had the killer instinct. I don't know how the fuck I went wrong with you."

I can't take any more. This whole day has been too much. Rob and Britta both threatening to quit. Then Keeley disappearing for hours…only to find out she's kissed Griff. Hearing that it's not a big deal to her if she has sex with my brother. And now my father dropping all his shit in my lap and making me feel like an inadequate boy all over again. Worst of all, Keeley is just on the other side of her bedroom door, no doubt hearing one of the most terrible, demeaning conversations of my life. Seen through the filter of my father's eyes, he's still trying to man me up. But through

Keeley's lens, she knows just how tainted my soul is and why. She probably has no problem understanding the reason I was all business and bravado when she met me. And now she knows for certain that I'm not redeemable.

It's killing me to know that she'll never look at me again the same way.

At the thought, every joint aches and every bone feels as if it's about to break. But I can't look at this hateful bastard for another second.

I pick up his suitcase and walk it to the door. "Get the fuck out."

He stands slowly, laughing. "Look at you, suddenly all defiant. It only took you thirty-three years, Maxon. But that doesn't change anything." He hoists his briefcase onto his shoulder and meanders to the door, gripping his suitcase as I open the portal. "You're still a loser, and you're always going to be one, especially where your brother is concerned."

"And you're always going to be an asshole, you miserable bastard. You're going to die alone, old and bitter, knowing that no one cares about you. And I'm going to cheer because we'll all finally be free from your toxic cloud. I hope to fuck you've learned something by then. But you're so stupidly self-important I'm not counting on it."

I slam the door in his face and throw the latch. Finally, he's out of my life, and I should be happy. Right now, I just feel exhausted and turned inside out.

I lean my forehead against the door and drag in labored breaths. I know I have to turn and face Keeley, who will be emerging from the bedroom any second... But I can't catch my breath. My heart races. My fingers are tingling again. I can't hold myself together.

I'm so fucking angry he unloaded on me, that I still feel like a kid again after being verbally whipped by the old bastard and his slurs, that Keeley will know me at my absolute weakest and worst.

No. No! Fucking no!

I can't take it. I stomp to the kitchen and swipe all the loose papers there onto the floor. It's wholly unsatisfying. There's no crash. No destruction. If I'm coming apart, everything around me should be, too. Goddamn it.

I look for a better target. The coffeemaker stands squarely in my crosshairs. *Yeah.*

Yanking the cord from the socket, I jerk it from the counter and hurl it against the closet door on the other side of the foyer. It falls to the ground in a twisted heap. The water in the reservoir splats all over the walls and floor. After a belch, the guts hang out. The unit lies there without fight, totally dead.

Unfortunately, I still have a raging ocean of fury flowing inside me. It's boiling, brewing, bubbling. I look around for my next victim. The microwave looks promising. That son of a bitch has never worked right, and it would be so satisfying to teach it a fucking lesson.

But as I pull the cord free and wrap my arms around it to hoist it up, I feel a soft hand on my shoulder. And I freeze.

Keeley.

I drop the appliance on the counter. If I didn't want her to see me beat down by my old man, I didn't want her to see me enraged, either. Shame slithers through me. I close my eyes, wishing the world would swallow me up whole.

"Go away. Let me do this alone. I don't want to talk about it."

With a gentle hand, she curls her fingers around my arm. I know I should resist, but how can I refuse something I want so badly? Someone I love so much?

I let her pull me around to face her. I still can't look at her, but I feel her all around me. Her empathy. Her tenderness. Her adoration.

"Maxon. I'm here." She pulls my stiff form closer, toward her embrace.

I try not to go. I try not to cry. I try not to be the loser my father accuses me of being. "You should go."

"I won't leave you like this."

"I don't want you feeling sorry for me. Don't do it." I stab the heels of my palms into the sockets of my eyes and retreat from her until my back hits the counter. "Don't you fucking dare!"

"That's not what I feel at all. Maxon, look at me. Please."

I'm huffing. I can't get myself under control. I can't find my center. The fury rages with a sadness I can't get out from under or push away or process out. It's just sitting in the middle of my chest, suffocating me.

But her voice is pulling me away from the darkness, beckoning me with hope and kindness and promise.

Finally, I open my eyes. Blink. Stare. "Jesus. Oh, sunshine…"

CHAPTER THIRTEEN

*K*eeley is naked. Every inch of her skin is pale and glowing and exposed. She's looking at me with blue eyes full of not pity but concern. A desire to help and comfort. An open kinship that says she understands and she'll be with me.

My guts knot. My eyes sting. Water. What the hell is she doing to me?

"It's all right," she promises in a voice so soft it almost hurts me.

I shake my head, slowly at first, then the motion picks up steam and I think over and over how wrong and terrible tonight's scene was. "I *never* wanted you to hear that."

All of a sudden, she wraps her fingers around my fists and kisses her way up my clenched jaw. I feel her gentle touch clear down to the living, breathing anger inside me.

"I know," she assures. "And I know everything he said hurts. I'm sorry. Truly. But I understand so much better."

"What, that I'm fucking broken?" A tear slides down my cheek even as rage keeps my heart pumping in a stomping rhythm. "You knew that. Why the hell is it good that you've seen the gory details?"

As I mentally replay every word she overheard, mortification curdles my blood. My father's beatdown is a brand blackening my soul. He couldn't have found a more complete way to humiliate me.

"No, *he's* broken. You…" I hear a shaking in her voice and risk a glance her way. Tears pour openly from her eyes as she cups my cheek. "You've survived. I'm so proud of you."

At those five words, my knees buckle. I've been waiting to hear them from someone my whole life.

I choke back more tears and try to modulate my voice. "He's left me with a lot of scars."

"Of course he has," she says earnestly, right into my eyes with no shame for the emotion she's spending on me. "But you're stronger for them. Better. And softer in here." She places her hand on my chest.

My whole body lurches. I grit my teeth. "I don't want to be softer!"

"It's not a bad thing." Her fingers graze my cheek. "It's what separates you from him. He will never be capable of caring about the people around him, not even his own children. You're right that he'll die alone and unloved. He's reaping what he's sown. You have a chance to be different."

When she reframes the situation like that, I see she's right. I absolutely can't rail about the fact that he doesn't give a rat's ass about anyone, then be afraid to care about people myself.

I take a deep breath, hang my head. I'm still wound up and turned inside out. And I'm doing my best to apply familiar logic to emotion, like if A plus B equals C, then A plus C must equal B. I know that isn't accurate, but when I fill in the blanks with feelings and opinions, it works. If hurt plus resentment equals egotistical bastard, then hurt plus egotistical bastard must equal resentment. Yeah, that makes total sense.

"You have a chance to purge everything he dumped on you and be whole, Maxon. Let it go and be happy."

The words come out so softly. Every syllable grips my heart and squeezes. But her meaning kicks me in the teeth. Forget everything the old bastard has ever said or done to me? Carry on as if the demeaning way he's treated me for thirty-three fucking years doesn't matter? I can't bend my brain around how to pretend all that away. How would that make me happy?

I gape at Keeley. A cynical comeback streaks through my head, perches on my tongue.

Then I stop. Think.

What good does it do me to expend so much energy and hate on an asshole I rarely see if I neglect to live?

I've come to a fork in the road. I can be a motherfucker, like my old man. It would certainly be easy. I've learned from the master, after all.

Or I can be my own man.

I can't believe how much courage it takes to simply open my eyes and look at Keeley. No way I can hide the tumultuous confusion churning my insides like a blender. For once, I don't even try. I just lift my head and meet her stare.

She's blurry because my eyes won't stop watering. I grind my teeth together. I'm not sure I've ever openly cried in my entire adult life. It's ugly, I'm sure.

It's also like a runaway train I can't stop, especially when I see the empathy waiting for me in her blue eyes. It nearly fells me.

I grab her shoulders to hold on. She closes the distance between us and wraps her arms around me. God, how fucking badly I need her touch…though it's unraveling me even more.

My chest heaves. My breath is a sob. Another tear falls. The part of me that's resistant to change doesn't want this, yet I know I need it.

"I'm here," she vows. "I'll catch you. Just…fall."

If anyone else were standing in front of me, I would scoff and insist they fuck off. But I believe Keeley. This woman is everything to me. In this moment, I'm pretty sure that, despite everything, she must love me, too. Why else would she put up with my crying-baby routine? Yeah, compassion and whatever. I have to believe she isn't comforting random people on the street. The fact that I'm special to her fills me with peace and warmth that smooth over so many of the wounds my father gouged out in his wake. I want more of her comfort. I need more of her caring.

As I seize her in my arms, I crush her against my chest. I feel complete when her heart beats in time with mine. But it also turns me inside out. The shield around my soul is splintering apart with every quiet moment we're locked together. All I can do is hold on tight and let myself feel.

I splay my fingers across her back until there isn't a single breath between us. I can smell her, feel her, inhale her. I fucking sob into her hair. A part of me is waiting for her to laugh, call me a pussy, and bark at me to man up. But that old tape belongs to my dad. Keeley will never say those things. She simply soothes me with slow strokes of her palms up and down my back, comforts me with kisses up my neck and across my cheek. I feel her tenderness like a blanket wrapping me in safety, care.

Love.

The idea of this woman giving her heart to me is both reassuring and terrifying. I would never mean to, but what if I'm a thoughtless jackass and I break it? She's giving me something precious. I have to figure out how to not fuck it up. The fact that I have no clue terrifies me all over again.

I shake as I try to rein in more sobs. But stopping them seems pointless now, so I'm rolling with it. Not like I have a choice...

Her lips press against my temple. She breathes over to my forehead. I have to bend down so she can reach me, but the effort is worth the payoff, especially when she eases back to look into my eyes. "Better?"

Yes and no. It's confusing. "I don't know."

She sends me a smile of soft understanding. "That's honest."

"Why are you here for me? Why do you give a shit what

happens to me? I've been an inconsiderate asshole. I've tried to make you do things that go against your grain."

"Don't forget that you've consistently tried to get me into bed, too. But under all that, I see *you*. Not the cocky but likable douchebag you project to everyone else. I see the boy who was neglected and hurt, so he never learned to trust his heart. I see the man dying for someone to not only care for him but give him undying devotion. And love. He's strong…but he's so afraid to ask for what he needs most."

I choke out a groan and drop my forehead to hers. "I sound pathetic."

"I could call you a lot of things. That's not one of them." She brushes her hand through my hair. "Maxon?"

I hear the shift in her voice. It beckons me to search her face again. I see not just tenderness there. I see invitation.

"Yeah."

"In case it's escaped your notice, I'm naked. I want to be with you." She caresses her way down my nape. "Make love to me."

My heart stops. *Is she serious right now?* I've waited and ached for Keeley for interminable days and endless nights. And she wants me when I'm sniffling, red-eyed, and too raw to have a filter?

It's official: I will never understand women. But I'm grateful for this one.

"You sure?" I croak out.

Keeley smiles at me, nothing but assurance in her big blues. "You've been trying to hustle me into bed for nearly three weeks, and now you're hesitating?"

"I want you to be sure."

"I don't have a single doubt."

That's all I need to hear.

Keeley believes in the concept of soul mates. I never have…but I'm wondering if they're real and if she's mine.

I bend and lift her against my body, cradling her in my arms.

She wraps herself around me, curling her legs about my hips. The glance we share steals my breath.

I can't stay away from her for another second, so I plunge into her mouth. Tonight, she's mine, and I want her to feel it. I'm thrilled when she melts against me with a moan.

Though I'm drowning in her taste, I somehow manage to stumble through the maze of the kitchen and foyer. I'm thankful I keep my living room uncluttered. When I hit the threshold to my room, I have a clear path to the bed.

With one hand, I tear the duvet down. Pillows topple and scatter. Pristine white sheets beckon. I lay Keeley in the center of the bed.

She looks perfect because she belongs here. I've fantasized about having her in my bed so many times, rolling to me in the night for pleasure, cuddled up to me in the morning for warmth. But she's looking at me now as if she wants all that and more. She wants the things I've never been willing to give anyone—my heart, my soul, my promises of tomorrow.

A week ago, I doubted I'd ever be capable of giving anyone all that. Now I'm seriously considering whether I could share every moment with her and—maybe for the first time ever—be happy.

I brace above her, drinking in her beauty. I have no idea how she saw past my inner asshole and decided she likes me, anyway. The only explanation is that I got lucky.

Her fingers climbing up my arms and curling around my shoulders distract me from thinking. When she winds her hands around my neck and tugs me down, I don't fight the urge to plaster myself over her bare body and sink into her mouth again. As my naked chest settles against hers, I groan.

In the past, women have felt good. Women have felt dirty. Women have never simply felt right.

Keeley does.

I lose myself in her. She's sweet and soft and open beneath me. Her thighs part, and I slide between them, deeply resenting my pajama bottoms. I could shove them aside, reach into my night-stand for a condom, and be inside her in less than sixty seconds if I want. Which I do…but I don't.

Over the last couple of weeks, I've had time to think about all the ways I wish I'd touched and taken Keeley that first night. I'm not letting this opportunity pass me by. Yes, I want what I want when I want it—and I'm determined to get it this time. But I also want her to be dizzy and dazzled. I want to give her everything she could ever yearn for in a lover. That means I can't go about this like an impatient shithead again.

I tangle my tongue with hers, losing myself in the sway of our rhythm. Then I ease back, press a kiss to her mouth, brushing my lips over hers before I lean away. She groans and tries to pull me down again.

"One second, sunshine. Trust me. I'm not going anywhere."

It's too dark, so I flip on the light. I want to see her. Once I do, I blow out an amazed breath at the soft glow beaming across her bare skin. Then I reach into the nightstand with one hand while shucking my pants with the other.

Keeley smiles at me and crooks her finger my way with a come-hither glance.

She won't get an argument from me.

I knee my way between her legs again. She welcomes me without hesitation, and I set the foil packet aside. It's within reach when I'm ready…but that won't be for a while.

Because for the first time in my sexual life, the goal of tonight isn't pleasure, it's connection.

Shit. Do I even know how to do that? I'm good at sex, but I don't know the first fucking thing about joining more than bodies.

"What's wrong?" she whispers.

I can't tell her that I'm lost. I'll sound stupid and dickless. Inept.

"Sunshine, tell me how to give you what you want. I want to do this right for you."

Her face softens. Then she curls her fingers around my hand

and brings it to her breast. She caresses my chest in return. "Just touch me. Be with me. Let it flow from here."

Keeley makes it sound so simple, like all I have to do is close my eyes and breathe.

Does it have to be more complicated than that?

I'm certainly willing to give it a try. The alternative is to hang around with my dick in my hand, staring at her like I'm stupid. Um…no. Not happening.

Instead, I cradle her flesh, thumb her nipple, and bend to take her rosy lips under mine. They're already slightly swollen and so fucking soft. She meets me halfway, eyes half-dazed, arms winding around me. As we join mouths, I delve deep. We share breaths. She arches into my palm. Her legs wrap around me. I feel her heat, sense the excitement skidding through her.

"Maxon…" she moans.

I press my forehead to hers to catch my breath. Normally, after a few kisses, I'd be impatient to get on with it. Not now. Not with Keeley. "I don't want to rush this, sunshine. I didn't savor you last time and I've regretted it like hell."

She nips at my lobe with a dainty bite, then whispers in my ear. "I don't regret anything. In fact, I think it happened for a reason. It brought us here."

Good point. Damn, this woman is smart.

I need to keep up, make sure that, after all the waiting for tonight, it's worthwhile, give her something she'll never forget.

After a passionate crush of my lips on hers, I kiss a path to her chin, over her collarbones, down her sternum. Her breasts beckon. No, they're not just tits. Keeley's are special, at least to me. I nuzzle the side of one, dragging my tongue up the so-soft skin while my thumb teases the hard tip. The little sounds in the back of her throat urge me on. Her body has a language all its own. The way she's flushing and arching speaks volumes.

I wrap my lips around her nipple, suckling, laving. Even her skin is slightly downy and sweet. I bring her closer, move in for seconds, lose myself in everything that makes her special.

She glides one hand over my short hair and tries to pull me in tighter. She pants. She sighs. She writhes.

I move to the other breast. I don't even want to open my eyes and deal with any reality except Keeley right now. So I suck harder on her nipple while I press my fingers around the other, giving it a squeeze. Satisfaction jolts me when she cries out my name.

Risking a glance up her pale body, I watch in fascination as she tosses her head back, throat arched, lips parted. God, she's so beautiful. So…what's the word? Unabashed.

Keeley isn't afraid of anything, least of all what she feels.

My father would call me a loser and a pussy for even imagining she matters as anything but a fuckhole, but he can eat shit. This woman excites me. Inspires me.

Completes me.

Clutching her waist, I travel farther down her body, my hips sliding out of the cradle of hers. As my knees hit the floor, I drag her to the edge of the mattress. Her legs part even more as she plants her feet on either side of my head.

She braces on her elbows and stares down her body at me. "You don't have to—"

"I want every part of you I can get my hands—and mouth—on. Pleasure seems like a small gift after all you've given me. But I can give you so much of it, sunshine. Let me."

As I kiss the inside of her thigh, she melts back to the mattress with an aroused sigh. "Please."

Keeley doesn't have to ask me twice. I rake my tongue through her slit. She's wet, plump. Ready. So fucking sweet. I swipe at her hard button and focus there, suckling, teasing, mixing the touch point and pressure. It doesn't take long before she's curling her toes around the edge of the bed, grasping for the fitted sheet, and panting out in passion. I love watching her unwind and give herself over to me, even as her body tenses in anticipation of the climax I'll give her.

I slide a pair of fingers inside her, almost groaning when her flesh closes around them and clamps down tightly. Once I thrust inside this hot heaven, I won't last long…but she's going to get a thrill first. And I can always give her oral seconds, right? Yeah. I'm digging that idea.

Her body jerks, bringing me back to the now. She's flushing. She's close. And she's a stunning sight to behold.

"That's it. Give it to me, sunshine," I murmur as I stroke my thumb over her clit, only to replace it with my tongue again.

Her knees fall even farther apart, and Keeley opens herself utterly to me. She keens out her surrender as her hips buck in need.

Almost there…

I give her one last nudge with my tongue, then suck her clit deep—and she's gone. Screaming in a long, hoarse cry, she seems to soar up in pleasure and sail in weightless ecstasy before she shudders her way back to earth and into my arms.

Keeley in climax has to be one of the most beautiful sights I've ever seen.

"Maxon," she sighs in satisfaction, then holds out her arms to me.

I'm Johnny-on-the-spot, vaulting up the bed to scoop her into my embrace, taking her deeper into the soft cocoon of sheets with me. I can't wait to get my hands on her again, especially when I look into her eyes. They're dazed and dilated. Her cheeks are red, her breathing rapid. And that crooked smile of hers is epic.

"Hi, sunshine." I can't help but grin at her. "Happy?"

I hope so because I know that's what she wants out of life.

"Yeah." Her smile widens. "You're awfully proud of yourself."

I glance off as if I really have to think about this. But she's right. "I'm thinking I just gave you some of the best minutes of your sex life."

"It's always about you…" She laughs with a roll of her eyes.

I pause. "No. That was all about *you*. That statement was just my asshole way of making sure you really liked it."

Her smile morphs into a laugh. "You know I did. I'm pretty sure your neighbors know it, too."

"Fuck them." I settle over her and stroke her hair away from her damp forehead. I love the spill of loose red curls across my sheet. I'm glad my bed will smell like her again. I'm thrilled that I'll have a memory of her here with me I can play over and over.

Before we make more together.

"I'd be happy to reciprocate, you know." She brushes her fingers across my jaw, caresses my shoulder.

I'm excited about the idea of Keeley on her knees in front of me, moaning as she takes my cock between her sweet, bowed lips, into the sweltering heat of her mouth, while I wrap my fingers in her hair and let her have at me. Just imagining it, more blood jets south.

I'm not going to lie. Of course I want that. But right now I want to feel her beneath me, against me, around me way more.

"That sounds great." I reach for the condom. "Later."

Her breath catches. "All right. Can I ask for a favor?"

This ought to be interesting. Keeley never fails to surprise me.

"Shoot." I'm poised to rip the foil wrapper, depending on what she says.

She nods at the little square. "Can you hurry that along?"

"Impatient for me, are you?"

Her eyes soften as she seems to open the windows to her soul wide for me. "I'm impatient to be *with* you. I want you to feel as good as you made me feel."

God, the woman just keeps giving to me with her big heart. How am I worthy of her for even a second?

"I have no doubt it will be my pleasure, sunshine." I tear into the condom, roll it down my length, then align my erection against her opening.

Keeley is already welcoming me, curling her arms and legs

around me, tilting her head as I nudge forward and plunge inside her, taking both her sex and her mouth at once.

I groan into her. Now I understand the difference between mere pleasure and connection. I feel the contrast between sex and love. I'm drowning in something that feels so much like devotion.

Fuck, I really do love this woman.

We're rocking together, breathing together, surging through pleasure together. I break the kiss. I have to look into her eyes, see if Keeley is feeling the way I am. She's right there with me, lids heavy, lips parted, skin rosy. To a man who didn't know her, they might see the quirky, carefree, emotionally in-tune woman. If he wasn't looking carefully, he'd fail to see the sensual grace just under her surface that blooms when given attention and passion. When she trusts.

Weeks ago she told me that when she gives her body, she gives her soul. I feel both now.

Tonight, she's all mine.

I lay my face over hers, foreheads and noses touching, as I thrust deep again. I'm looking right into her eyes, so blue and available. Everything about her reaches inside and rips me wide open—guts, chest, feelings—and spills them out between us.

My personal "number" is probably embarrassing. I've nailed too many chicks to count. None have felt anywhere as amazing as Keeley.

Her fingers curling around my shoulders suddenly begin digging into my back. I feel the prick of her fingernails, the tightening of her walls around me. Her breathing picks up pace. Those pretty blues flare with sensual tension.

"Maxon, I need to come."

"Do it, sunshine. I'm right here. I'll make sure it's so good. I won't let you down."

If I have to bite the shit out of my tongue and think of something boring, like the fine print on escrow documents, in order to keep my self-control together, I'll do it. For her.

"Come with me." A high, keening note fills her voice.

It's so tempting…

I ease back and rock into her again. And again. Jesus, I'm going cross-eyed. It's that good. I know I have something precious right now and I don't want it to be over. But holy crap, I don't know how long I can hold off.

"I want it to last," I pant out before I take her lips again.

Kissing her is an addiction. There's always something new about her mouth to explore. She's sweet…but then she's tart. She's teasing and sly…before she turns eager and draws me in like a siren. I'm waxing on and on—mostly because I never knew I could feel this way about a woman.

Keeley eases away, and her lips drift up my neck until I shudder with a whole new ripple of excitement. My blood boils; my head is hazy. I don't even have words to describe how hard I'm working to ignore the ache in my balls.

"We have all night…" she murmurs in my ear. "We could do this again, you know."

We could. We will.

"I'm planning on it. It's so good, sunshine. I don't know how you'll ever keep me away from you. I'm always going to want more."

"Hmm, know what I thought about the first time I saw your lanai?"

From her tone, I'm guessing it's not about the pretty ocean and that my dick is going to like it. "No."

"I wanted you to touch me out there. I wanted to lean on the rail wearing one of your shirts—and nothing else—while you sauntered up behind me in just your pants and filled me. No one else would know. It would be our secret. But we could move like the waves of the ocean while we watch the sea crash…"

Oh, fuck. That sounds good. That sounds amazing. "Next time around, I'll make that come true."

I nuzzle her neck, breathe against her skin, squeeze one of her nipples. Her entire body tenses around me.

"Can't wait," she breathes.

Neither can I. She's so close…and I'm right behind her. At first, I resist but I see the future. I can make her come now *and* later. I can make her come tomorrow and the next day. I can make her come for the rest of our lives.

I slam deeper into her, grinding against her to put pressure where she's most sensitive. She gasps, reaches out to me like she needs me to steady her. Her eyes go wider. Yeah, that got to her. I do it again. Her pussy clenches on me so tight I can barely move.

With a grin, I roll to my back and take her with me, until she's straddling my hips, hands braced on my shoulders, swaying over my body. Her hair grazes her arms as her breasts bounce and I surge up beneath her, deep into her, hitting the one spot that should coalesce all the tingles and aches into an eruption she can't deny.

But leave it to my Keeley to change things up on me. She doesn't sit passively above and wait for me to make her come. Of course not. She surges with me, gliding, sliding, slamming until there's really no stopping the runaway ecstasy from taking over.

Her cry of unrestrained pleasure fills my bedroom. The sound sends me over the edge. I lose all hint of composure. Some grunt that's low and dark and shocked by the force of my climax spills from my chest in a guttural roar. I empty out my balls, my energy—my fucking heart—until I'm lying beside her spent and gasping and wondering what the hell hit me.

Is that what love does?

"Wow," she sighs.

I gasp. "Yeah."

"We should do that again soon."

I look over, watch her chest rise and fall rapidly as she tries to catch her breath. She looks sated and happy, just like I feel.

"Very soon. That was amazing." I prop my head on my elbow.

"You may laugh or not believe me but…it's never been like that for me."

She smiles like my words please her as much as my touch does, then she gives me a wry grin. "So I'm better than your usual good time?"

I lift her hand, press a kiss to her palm. "You're the best."

I want to tell her I love her. I think she'd be happy to hear it. I hope. I think she loves me, too. But what if I'm wrong? What if she says it's too soon? What if she laughs?

This should be simple, right? Why does it now feel so complicated?

"You okay? Your face got serious all of a sudden."

I swallow. I have to grow a pair. It's not as if she's going to put up with me for the rest of my life if I can't tell her I love her. I mean, I want to hear it from her, too.

I suddenly realize that Dad didn't believe in love because he didn't want to deal with emotion—too inconvenient—and didn't care enough about anyone else's feelings enough to try—too much effort. Fuck him. I *am* different. What's the point of living and working your whole life if you don't share it with anyone? Granddad used to say that. I wonder why my mom couldn't be more like her father. Maybe Barclay Reed shut her up over and over so she just shut down.

I can't imagine ever smothering Keeley that way. I don't want to stifle her or make her feel less than worthy. I don't want her to wonder if I love her. I just have to work up the courage to tell her everything I'm thinking.

"Yeah. No. Good. I'm—"

Suddenly, my phone rings. How many times can a guy get interrupted in one evening?

Then I realize I haven't heard this chime in three years. My ears aren't deceiving me. But I don't know how that's possible. After Griff stopped answering this number, I figured he'd changed it. I didn't even remember that I'd set up a special ringtone for him. I certainly never thought to change or delete it.

Holy shit.

Keeley groans. "Who is that?"

I rise from the bed and snatch up my boxers. The chime sounds again. I drag in a bracing breath. "That's Griff."

CHAPTER FOURTEEN

"*G*riff?" Keeley sounds as confused as I feel. "Now?"

Exactly. The only reason I can think of for my brother's sudden call is Dad.

I've already put up with as much shit from that man tonight as I plan to. And I can't imagine why the fuck Griff would bother to call me about him. It's not as if my brother will want to compare notes about what a son of a bitch Barclay Reed is. We both know that well. There's no way in hell Griff simply wants to talk to me.

Something must be wrong.

Heart pounding, I fumble through my pockets until I find the phone.

I glance at the display. Sure enough, it's Griff.

With a trembling finger, I press the button. I'm not sure what to say. There's no etiquette for greeting the brother you haven't spoken to since he splintered your business, called you a shitbag, and fucked your ex-girlfriend all in the same week.

"What?" I say cautiously.

"God, you're still a selfish prick, sending Dad to my place while I'm working my ass off to finish my pitch. These are the two most critical days of my career! Harlow swore you'd changed. But nope. You're still putting yourself first and not even bothering to tell the people around you to fuck off. You just behave like an absolute bastard until they do."

"Hey! He came here first, behaving like the same ugly sphincter as always, bitching about Mom…and whatever the fuck else he rants about. After he laid into me about his shitty life and tried to make me feel as welcome on this planet as a turd, he decided he'd rather be with you. No idea why. Maybe he feels more comfortable with you since you two are so fucking much alike. But I didn't *send* him your way."

"Even if I believed you—or gave a shit—you can't deny you're trying to steal the Stowe business out from under me. I know you wheedled a chance to pitch to them."

"I don't deny it at all. George and Vivienne are going to list that house, like any other owner. I'm just giving them a presentation from the number one agent on the island so they can see what I plan to do for them. They deserve to hear more than one thought on how to sell their mother's estate. That doesn't make me a bad guy."

Griff scoffs. "You tell yourself that lie if it helps you sleep at night. But I'm going to get this listing. I'm planning to make a major splash and it will blow everyone away, especially you. I'm going to crush you into the ground, big brother. Then I'll be number one on the island, and you can go eat shit once and for all."

Then three impersonal beeps tell me he hung up. Our first conversation in three years, and it's as brief and ugly as the one that wedged the chasm between us.

I stare at the phone, numb. I wanted something different out of that. I'd hoped…

Like Keeley says, you can't always get what you want when you want it.

"What did he say?" She climbs from bed and makes her way to my side, arms open. "That didn't sound good."

I don't think about the fact that some would see me as weaker for needing her embrace now when I know it will make me stronger. "That Dad is cramping his style. Whatever. Griff apparently has a plan for the Stowe estate. He says he's going to win and I'm going down in flames."

"You know it's talk. He feels threatened."

"Yeah." I nod. "I know. But…what if he's right?"

"That he's going to 'win'? First, your careers aren't really a race that ends unless one of you gets out of the business entirely. If he pulls ahead for a year…there's always next year. You two push one another to make the other work harder. That's not necessarily bad."

No. In fact, that's probably true. But… "What I mean is, what if he's right about strategy? He's going in big, like it's the real estate equivalent of a Super Bowl halftime show. I don't know if he's got dancers and marching bands or what. But he sounds so…smug. Like he knows something I don't." I drop the phone on the mattress and begin to pace. "What if my simple strategy looks like I've been slacking in Loserville to the Stowes? Maybe I did this all wrong."

"We talked about your pitch." Her touch is so gentle and earnest.

"We did," I concede as I plop my ass back on the bed.

I don't want Keeley to think I don't value her contribution or see her point of view. She opened up my eyes, gave me a whole new way to view this listing. Hell, my business and my life. But I can't not wonder if the touchy-feely approach won't work with these two syrup heirs who just want to unload a property. Maybe they don't want to be understood; maybe they just want top dollar.

"Now you're not sure it's the right approach?"

I shake my head. Griff's words scorch through my brain. My dad's aren't far behind. What if I've fucked up because I'm always going to be first loser in this family?

"No." I look at her. "I'm worried and I don't know what to do."

"Is he done with his pitch?"

I shake my head. "Still working."

Keeley is quiet for a long minute. She meanders to the kitchen and fetches a water bottle from the fridge. Absently, she unscrews the top and sips.

I have an idea…and I hate myself for it.

"What are you thinking?" I ask.

She shrugs. "He asked me to dinner tomorrow night."

"I know." At his place, where he could be alone with her and try to sweet-talk her into bed.

We're both silent for a long time. I know we're thinking the same thing.

I could ask her to finish the task I lured her in to start.

I cringe at the thought. My guts shrivel. It was easy to think about her spending time with Griff when I barely knew her. Now… everything is different.

But it's also not. I'm still stuck in the same years-long feud with my own goddamn brother. My dad still thinks I'm a pansy-ass failure. I'm still struggling to feel good enough for both of them and searching for the life I want to have.

With a sigh, she settles beside me and takes my hand. "Tell me what you want me to do. I'll do it."

I know she will, even though she doesn't have a hateful, spiteful, or mean bone in her body. She would do something that goes against her own moral code because I need the outcome only she can provide. Yeah, she hasn't said that she loves me, but why would anyone do that for someone they aren't emotionally devoted to? My heart does a little dance at the thought…until I realize she's looking at me intently, waiting for an answer now.

Do I keep her here where Griff can't touch her or ask her to finish this one critical task for me?

I chew the inside of my lip. I don't want Keeley to think I don't value her. After tonight, she knows everything is different, right? She must. I'm an emotional dolt, so if I feel our connection, a smart girl like her will totally know. We're a unit. We're in love. We have a future.

As soon as I can put the past and this stupid rivalry behind me once and for all.

I close my eyes. Hesitate. Once I open my mouth, it's final. I can't take it back.

But I don't see another choice.

"Can you have dinner with him?" I croak. "You don't have to do anything but be a smiling, slightly flirty friend."

She gives me a vague smile as she stands suddenly. "Sure. I'll make sure you get what you want most, Maxon."

Her words give me pause. I don't like the way she's phrased them. They're careful. They could have more than one meaning.

"I want you, too." I assure her. "I need you to know that."

"I do."

But something about her demeanor still feels off. "You okay?"

Keeley breezes past me, strolling out to the lanai wearing nothing but my shirt. She situates herself at the rail, letting the breeze ruffle the cotton swinging around her thighs, and tosses me a gaze over her shoulder. "Of course. Maybe you'll come over here and give me what I want most?"

For me to make love to her on the lanai.

Yeah, she loves me. She gets me. Everything is going to be great, if I can stop being paranoid.

I grab a condom from my nightstand drawer, then saunter up behind her. I cup her thigh, then lift my hand up to her bare pussy, urging her legs apart. As I kiss her neck, I shift my cock out of my boxers and roll down the condom. Keeley arches back to me, and I smile against her skin, breathing her in.

"You want to fuck out here but you don't want anyone to know?"

"Yes." The word is a whisper, uttered on a catch of her breath.

"You're a screamer, sunshine. And I'm not going to go easy on you. You'll have to figure out how to keep this our secret…"

Because I don't give a crap what my neighbors think, I don't pause even a second so she can decide how she's going to manage that before I slam deep inside her. I'm so damn grateful and blessed that we'll have the chance do this every night for the rest of our lives. We just have to get past the next forty-eight hours.

Despite that thought, something is bugging me. And when Keeley turns to me over her shoulder, lips pursed in silent pleading for mine, it's crazy but I find myself wondering if I'm kissing her for the last time.

MY DAY DRAGS ON. Keeley texted me this morning to tell me that she got in touch with Griff, who invited her over at seven. No emojis. No hearts and kisses or LOLs. I frown. It's possible she's nervous. It's also possible she's pissed. But when I ask again if she's all right, she sends back a vague `Fine.` `I'm headed into an afternoon study group.`

"You okay?" Britta comes up behind me with a gentle hand on my shoulder.

I just guiltily shove the phone in my pocket. I hate that she's going to be angry with me. I hate that she's probably going to quit. I search for something to say, some persuasion I can give her to make her understand that my decision to use Keeley to eliminate the competition is in no way a reflection of how I feel about her. Britta really is like a sister to me.

Damn it.

"I'm all right. Just a lot on my mind. Friday is coming up fast."

"Yeah." She blows out a breath. "My nervous stomach feels that. So does my mouse hand."

As she shakes the appendage, I smile. "The graphics you've created are great so far. Thanks for making the phone calls to those nonprofit organizations you heard about."

She nods. "I'm glad I remembered reading that article last night about how some of them keep their portfolios solid by buying real estate. I'm excited that United Way, Catholic Charities USA, and

Goodwill all said they'd be willing to look more closely at the property next week."

"I think it's a strategy that could both keep the Stowes happy and make sure the place benefits others in the future." At least I hope I'm not wrong. I don't mention my doubts now.

It's really too late to change direction. I have to hope Keeley comes through.

"Exactly. One of the organizations talked about using it for corporate retreats and donor gatherings, which isn't my favorite but a necessary evil, I guess. Another charity talked about it as a recovery center for people dealing with depression and suicidal tendencies—that kind of stuff. I've only seen pictures, but I think this estate would be perfect."

I agree.

"Anyway, great job."

She looks around the office and sees Rob ducking into the bathroom. "Did you decide what you're going to do about Keeley and…"

"Griff?" My gut tightens.

She nods as if she'd rather not say his name. "Any thoughts?"

I hate to lie to her. I really do. But Keeley isn't going to have sex with Griff. She probably won't even kiss him again. Right?

"Nothing is final," I finally mutter. "I'm just…"

I let that trail off so she can draw her own conclusion. I don't want to hurt her—and part of that is not freaking her out unnecessarily.

She gives me a stiff nod. "How are things going between you two?"

I blink at Britta. I might be steering into a gray area about my business plan but no reason not to come clean here. "I'm in love with her. I realized that for sure last night when my dad suddenly appeared on my doorstep and infuriated the hell out of me." I fill her in about my parents' divorce and what a fuckbag my dad is. "Keeley was there to make sure I didn't commit murder. Or fall apart. She's really great. You guys will get along, I'm sure."

As soon as she's done "distracting" Griff. Then we just won't talk about that. It will all end well, so what's the point of hurting Britta?

"You, in love? She and I got off to a bad start, which was my fault, but I want to shake her hand." She smiles softly. "Can you two come to dinner tonight?"

I nearly stumble on my tongue.

"She can't. She's got plans," I say vaguely.

I'm uncomfortable that I'm lying like a motherfucker. I'm even aware that in the last twelve hours my morals have been...iffy. But I'm going to get business managed, then I'm going to be the most devoted husband for the rest of my life.

If Keeley will still have me.

"Why don't I take you and Jamie to dinner somewhere? Coconut's?"

"Sure." She smiles. "Fish tacos sound great. Makaio had to hop over to Oahu for a meeting until Thursday, so it will just be the three of us."

"Fantastic." I'm relieved actually. He's a decent guy and all... but I feel weird seeing her with someone other than my brother. Stupid, I know. But they just seemed so meant to be. "Did you... um, accept his proposal?"

"Not yet," she says with a shake of her head. "Jamie slammed his finger in a door last night. He's okay, but we had to make a trip to the ER. His finger needs a splint for the next two weeks, but you can't tell a toddler to leave something like that alone, so we had to wait to see the orthopedic surgeon on call and get his advice. We got home late. So Makaio and I didn't get to talk about anything before he left and I collapsed into bed."

Then this dinner is perfect timing. I can spend time with Jamie and make sure Britta doesn't find out where Keeley is tonight... while I talk her out of marrying a guy she doesn't love.

Rob emerges from the bathroom, checking his long, floppy bang in the mirror one last time before he flips off the light. He frowns. "You two all right?"

"Fine." Britta checks her watch. "Actually, if you're happy with our progress on the presentation, I'm going to scoot out a few minutes early to pick Jamie up. I told his pediatrician that I'd swing by so she could look at his finger, too. She'll probably set his entire hand and forearm in a cast until it heals."

"Seven o'clock okay?"

"Perfect." She shuts off her computer and retrieves her purse.

"I'll pick you up."

Seconds later, she dashes out of the office. Rob watches her go. The second the door swings shut behind her, he turns to me with an expectant stare.

I know what he wants. Goddamn, he's always been a pushy bastard. I more than slightly resent his interference.

"Keeley is having dinner with Griff tonight. I lied to Britta and I feel like a heel. Back off."

Suddenly, he's all smiles as he claps me on the back. "I knew you'd come to your senses. You're not the kind of man to put pussy before profit."

I snap. I don't know why. He's made similar statements in the past, and his point of view made sense to me back then.

Now it just pisses me off.

Without any conscious decision, I find myself picking Rob up by his shirt and shoving him against the wall. "Shut the fuck up. Keeley is not just a pussy. She's a woman. She's smart. She has a big heart. And she deserves respect. You know, maybe you're not married because you treat women like interchangeable whores."

"What the hell is up your ass? 'Cause let me remind you, you're no better, chief. I don't know what kind of special magic this woman's cunt has, but it's addled your brain. You're being an asshole. Get your hands off me."

I let go—but I don't step back. "I'm opening my eyes. I'm seeing the value of women as people and I feel like a prick that I didn't do it sooner. But I had my old man as a role model, so it took me extra time to pull my head out of my ass. What's your excuse for being a miserable misogynist?"

"Fuck you." He pushes me away. "I respect women. I'm great with clients. I've never treated Britta as anything other than my peer and my equal."

I actually can't fault him there. He's golden to clients. He's been pleasant, kind, deferential, even fatherly at times with Britta. He's helped her assemble a swing set for Jamie, rescued her when her car got a flat in the rain, and helped look after her when she sprained her ankle. I know he's not in love with her or anything. To him, women are either Madonnas or whores, no in between.

That used to be me. I see that now. I feel like an asshole all over again.

I'm thankful once more that Keeley came into my life.

"See if you can extend that to the other women around you. You threatened to quit yesterday if I didn't all but whore out my..." Girlfriend? Love? I can't say fiancée...yet. "Well, Keeley. But let's get one thing clear: I will fire your ass if your attitude doesn't improve."

I stare Rob down. Regardless of the bluster, we've been friends. He knows when I mean business. Plus, he's got a bit of short man's disease. He talks bigger than he actually is or feels. Once he knows this chauvinist shit bugs me, he'll back off. I can't change his heart and mind, but I can sure as hell adjust how he behaves around the office.

"Okay." He frowns as if he doesn't understand why I'm making a big deal out of this, then straightens his tie. "You don't have to get cranky."

"I didn't appreciate you threatening me yesterday. Keeley is going to try to get the job done, but she's not spreading her legs for anyone. Don't expect her to. And I can't guarantee that she'll succeed in throwing Griff off his A game. If you have a problem with that—"

"I don't," he rushes to tell me. "It was never a guarantee. I just wanted to make sure you were giving it effort."

"I am. Leave it there."

With a nod, I shut down my computer, grab my keys, and get the hell out of the office. As I head to my car, I text Keeley to tell her I'm taking Britta and Jamie to dinner. She tells me to enjoy and says she's leaving my condo now.

`Call me when you've left his place. And don't do anything that makes you uncomfortable or unhappy.`

`Fine.`

There's that word again. I hope she's okay…but I remember some bit on YouTube where a guy said that when a woman says she's "fine," she's pretty much mad enough to cut your balls off. Before I can call her to check on her again, a client rings about an upcoming closing. I slide into my car and assure him that everything is going smoothly while I walk him through the process and paperwork. Thirty minutes later, I'm sure she's already close to Griff's. I guess I'll have to wait to talk to her until later tonight, so I pick up my dry cleaning. By then it's too late for me to swing home before going to Britta's. It's fine. A few extra minutes with Jamie will be nice.

When I arrive, my assistant has changed into a casual sundress. Jamie comes running to give me a big hug. I don't see the little man as often as I should. Wow, he's growing so fast. I'm painfully aware he needs a father figure—now and in the future. Since Griff is still ignoring his own son, I realize that someone in Jamie's life can either be Makaio…or me.

Nothing against the banker Britta plans to marry, but Jamie doesn't have the Reed surname. He needs to have some of the Reed swagger—though only the good parts.

I picture myself trying to semi-parent and wonder if I'm crazy.

But at least it doesn't scare the shit out of me. I've actually learned something since I met Keeley, enough to know I'd like it even more if she and I were raising our own son—or daughter—together.

Now I sound like a sap, but what the hell? For the first time in my life, I think I finally understand what it means to be happy and why Keeley would want that above all else.

I'm going for it, too.

"Hey, Jamie. How you been, big boy?"

He tugs me toward his toy trucks. With a few grunts and small words, I get the gist that he's setting up his own racetrack. As we play together, he bangs his new blue cast on the nearby hearth. Obviously, he's not digging the constraint. I ruffle his hair and take a few snapshots on my phone. He really is a cute kid.

My obstinate brother has cut away the best part of himself. If I wasn't so attached to Keeley, I'd tell her to dive into his head and make him acknowledge his son by any means possible. But she's mine, and Keeley being super close to Griff will only lead to sex. That isn't what either Britta or I want. I hope Keeley doesn't, either.

Still, in a weird way I wish things could be different.

After a quick plate of fish tacos, we head south down the coast to Lappert's for some Hawaiian ice cream. Jamie's evening is complete, and by the time I take him and his mother home, the tyke is half-asleep.

After an abbreviated bath and a bedtime story, Britta tucks him in. All the while, I'm checking my phone. It's getting close to nine o'clock. I guess I shouldn't be too worried yet.

Still, I am.

I'm just about to shout down the hall that I'll leave them to their evening. Of course, I'll just go home and pace. That sounds terrible. But hanging around here, where there's no hint or trace of Keeley, is unsettling me. I can't say why exactly. I keep remembering my last face-to-face with her, and the notion that I've really fucked up again keeps plaguing me.

"Sorry that took awhile," Britta says as she emerges from the hallway that leads to the bedrooms. "He's having a hard time settling in with his cast. Since he couldn't play in the tub as usual, he wanted an extra bedtime story."

I nod. "Poor little guy."

"Coffee?"

"Nah. I should head out."

"Can you spare me ten minutes?"

Britta and I talked pretty in-depth earlier. She's not any sort of shallow party girl, but it's also unlike her to drag me into multiple serious conversations in one month, much less in one day.

"Sure."

She gestures me to the sofa, then sits in the chair beside me. "Why did you lie to me?"

I freeze. "What do you mean?"

Britta has always been soft and sweet and a little quiet. Very feminine. But right now, she's giving me a mean-bitch glare that's making me shudder. "Don't act like you have no idea what I'm talking about. I believed you this afternoon when you hinted that you'd given up your idea to flash Keeley in Griff's face. I even bought that she had a prior commitment. But all night you've been checking your phone every two minutes."

It's not like I can tell her that I'm expecting a call from a client. She'd ask which one...and know I'm lying. Frankly, I'm tired of deceiving Britta anyway. I probably need to tell her the truth and let the chips fall. Keeley would want me to.

"All right. I admit it." I blow out a breath. "The thing is, Griff called me last night."

At that, Britta sits up straight, looking beyond shocked. I don't blame her. "And?"

"He just wanted to yell at me about Dad. He said some ugly things and I reacted badly. I'm really beginning to regret asking Keeley to go tonight. I have this gnawing worry..."

"You should. You know your brother."

I do. A devoted man-whore—except when he'd made Britta the center of his world.

"Fuck. I haven't heard from her." I drag my phone into my palm again. Still nothing.

Britta stands, wraps her arms around herself. "I can't believe you went through with this. And that you lied to me."

I say the first thing that pops into my head. "Don't quit."

She whirls on me, betrayal in the tears pooling in her eyes. "Why shouldn't I?"

Valid question. I have very few persuasive answers. "I'm sorry and I'll make it right."

"You can't." She sighs. "Besides, I have to stop caring what Griff does. He and I are over."

Suddenly, I realize I played a huge role in that. My falling out with my brother was largely his fault because the stubborn fucker wouldn't even hear what I had to say about my secret royal client. But his split from Britta was at least partially my doing. I kept her in the dark and didn't give her even enough information to convince Griff that she wasn't involved. I also didn't do anything to force him to acknowledge his son. I told myself it wasn't my responsibility, that my brother didn't deserve to know Jamie if he was going to behave like an asshole. Harlow even agreed. But now I'm rethinking everything.

I don't want to make promises to Britta that I can't keep, but I also think it's time I try to right some of my wrongs.

"Do you want Griff to be involved in his son's life?"

She ponders that for a long moment. "Yes…and no. Jamie needs a father. For a long time, I've wished Jamie could have *his* father. But I worry that, deep down, he's too much like his own. You, too."

"I'm trying to change."

"I think you actually mean that." She sends me a sad smile. "But I also don't think you're there. What you did today proves that."

I'm not going to lie. That's a knife in the heart. But I've earned it. "I'm sorry."

She shrugs. "Sometimes, sorry isn't enough."

Britta is right. Unfortunately, I don't know what will be enough to right the stupid-ass wrong I've done.

I need to hear from Keeley.

"Are you going to quit?"

She looks past me, out the window. "I don't know. I have to give it serious consideration."

If she marries Makaio, she'll have the luxury of leaving her job. He can more than support them all.

We fall silent for a long minute. I can't help it. I check my phone again. Twenty minutes after nine. Nothing.

On the one hand, imagining that Keeley can exchange small talk and have dinner, then unravel all Griff's focus about the deal of a lifetime in under three hours is crazy. On the other hand, I've seen my brother get a woman from hello to horizontal in under ten minutes.

"Are you so jumpy because you're worried Keeley will fail?" Britta asks.

My business brain tells me that should be my main concern. If she doesn't find a way to make sure that Griff's presentation goes poorly on Thursday, I'm probably screwed. But that's not what's on my mind at all. "I'm worried because she wasn't acting like herself after we agreed she would have dinner with Griff."

"Was she mad?"

I shake my head. "She just seemed off. She said she was 'fine.'"

Britta winces. "You know that's bad, right?"

"Yeah, but I think I heard that in a comedy routine, so I wondered…"

"It's terrible. Fine really means 'you've pissed me off and I'm not going to give you the satisfaction of explaining—because you should know—or let you defend yourself because I'm both too angry and I don't want to hear your lousy excuses.'"

That's been my fear. "Bitchin'. So what do I do now?"

Because there's no way Keeley can not talk to me. That can't happen.

Britta shrugs. "I don't know. All I can say for sure is that you telling her to even go flirt with another man really told her that you value your career and your ego more than you value her."

Those words shoot a cannonball of dread into the pit of my stomach. She says what's been dancing around the edge of my consciousness, that thing I suspected but didn't want to acknowledge. It was an inconvenient truth.

I'm worried I'm going to pay the ultimate price for ignoring it in favor of my own version.

"I swear, that's not how I feel," I argue. "Nowhere near, actually."

"Uh-huh," she drawls cynically. "I'm telling you, your words might be saying that, but your actions are giving her an entirely different message."

I plop my head into my hands. "Fuck."

"*If* she's still speaking to you and you actually do love her, I suggest you find some way to let her know that, from now on, she's first and always will be. That you value the relationship you two have more than business or money or this insane need you have to be better than your brother. By the way, it's the same problem he has."

She's right, one hundred percent. From grade school on, Dad made us compete against each other. For too long, we didn't stop to question why or whether we should. When we began the business together, I thought we were solid and determined to throw off the old man's yoke. But in a blink, childhood programming overwrote our goodwill. Maybe...Griff acted before he thought. Maybe I wasn't much better. Not to excuse what either of us did. But isn't the first step to solving a problem admitting it?

The real question is, how do I fix it from here?

"Do you want Griff back?" I ask Britta.

"What?" She says the word as if I'm speaking a foreign language she doesn't understand.

I know she heard me perfectly well.

"If we're both going to get the truth out and be totally honest, then let's cut the shit entirely. Do you want him back?"

Britta purses her lips together and glances down at her bare ring finger. "I think Makaio has already picked out a ring. It's really just…too late."

And as she utters the words, she looks as if she's going to cry.

She wants Griff back; she's too afraid to admit it.

I reach across the space between us and take her hand. "Help me out of this mess and I'll get him back for you."

Tears are swimming in her eyes as she looks up at me as if I've lost my mind. "You can't make that promise."

Actually, I think I can. Griff loved her once. Until her, he'd never loved anyone in his life. Not his parents. Maybe not even me. He hasn't loved anyone since her, from everything I've heard. I think there's a damn good chance I can succeed. "Then I'll sure as hell try. Just help me figure out how to tell Keeley that I'm sorry and I'll be putting her first for the rest of our lives."

Britta pauses a long time. Sadness, agony, and regret haunt her face. It's so naked I almost flinch. "Don't do anything to bring Griff back into my life. I've moved on. Jamie will have a new stepfather. It's basically done. But if you want Keeley back, do the one thing your brother never did for me: find out what she values most and do your damnedest to give it to her. Not monetary things." She shakes her head. "Meaningful things. What does she want out of life?"

"I asked her that the night we met." More to make small talk and figure out how to coax her into bed. "Her answer was so simple yet so surprising I didn't know how to interpret it at the time. She wants to be happy."

"What do you think would make her happy?"

Suddenly, I know. In fact, I know everything I need to do. It's obvious. I just didn't want to see it because it's going to be hard. I'll have to sacrifice—something I've admittedly never been good at.

But finally, I think I'm ready. No, I know I am.

Keeley comes first. Somehow, I'm going to convince that woman to admit she loves me. Then, if she'll let me, I'm going to spend the rest of my life making her happy.

I glance at my phone. I just need her to call me and tell me she's coming home.

CHAPTER FIFTEEN

*K*eeley never came home Tuesday night. No note. No return phone call. Nothing but silence. When I arrived at my condo, I found the guest room empty. Every one of her things was gone.

So was she.

And clearly, she had no intention of coming back. I don't think I've ever felt such a gut punch in my life. When Griff and I first had our falling out, I didn't freak, because he's family. I thought it was temporary.

Keeley's departure feels permanent.

That night, I texted. I called. I left apologies galore. No reply... until five hours after her date with Griff began. At midnight, she sent one curt message. `I'm making every effort to give you exactly what you want. Don't call anymore.`

My heart collapsed. As I suspected, "fine" didn't mean she was fine at all.

With shaking hands, I messaged back and apologized like hell. Nothing. She hasn't spoken to me in any way since. It's been nearly forty-eight hours since she left. I still can't breathe. I'm a fucking wreck.

When she left for Griff's house before their date, she knew she was leaving me for good. Is she living with my brother now? I don't know. Since she doesn't have her own apartment anymore, where else would she be? That possibility cuts me up. I can't even think about the woman I love in bed with him. I mean, I know Griff slept with Tiff. Honestly, I didn't care. Keeley is totally different. Losing her is gut-wrenchingly terrible. Even worse, she's free to do whatever—and whomever—she wants.

Why doesn't someone just stab me now? I'm miserable. I'm contrite. I'm nauseous at the thought of ever seeing her with my brother.

I utterly and completely fucked up. And I'm definitely getting what I deserve.

Since Tuesday night, I've practically been living at the office. I hate going home because I see Keeley everywhere—in the kitchen cooking, on my bed looking up at me with welcoming eyes, on the lanai as she waits for me to pleasure her. The place smells like her. I can't sleep. I'm a goddamn disaster.

What am I going to do with the rest of my life?

As I enter my condo and toss my keys on the bar, I try not to let memories haunt me. I'm only here because tonight is the cleaning staff's designated evening to scour the office. When they walked in, they looked a little bit like they pitied me. And they avoided me as if I needed a shower. I probably do.

With a sigh, I head to the bathroom and take care of that chore. I put on pajama pants and contemplate what I'm going to choke down for dinner and how I'm going to sleep in the bed still rumpled from the last time I rolled Keeley on those sheets.

As I meander through the living room, I grab the room service menu off the counter. It all sounds like shit. I can hear her in my head talking about sodium and saturated fat and all the stuff I didn't give much thought to before her. Instead, I grab an apple from the bowl on the counter. She's already washed it. This is the last one.

I bite down into it and remember the last time I ate one, talking to Keeley after work. In some ways, I can still taste her. Her kiss, her caring, her heart.

Jesus, I'm becoming a weeper. I choke down the succulent bite but all the while I'm fighting actual tears. I almost want to know when this feeling will go away. On the other hand I don't. Once this heartbreak is less sharp, that will mean she's even further away from me.

I've got it bad. I love Keeley. The fact that I fell in love once is a miracle in itself. I don't expect it to ever happen again.

Maybe that explains why my brother turned into such a miserable asshole after Britta.

Frankly, it makes the fact that he's most likely boffing the one woman I can't live without even more infuriating. He knows how terrible having a gaping hole in your heart feels.

I glance at my phone. Nothing. I should stop hoping to hear from her...but I can't. It's not quite six thirty. I'll fill up a few hours with pacing, cursing, wall punching, and regret. But really, what's after that? I'll have to face the bed eventually.

Fresh air. Maybe that will help me not want to slit my wrists with rusty spoons. At least now I know why people write so many songs about breaking up and heartache. They're real and they suck.

The last rays of the day beam through the glass doors leading outside. My lanai beckons, and I head out there.

Immediately, my gaze darts to the beach. I zero in on the rocks where I first had sex with Keeley. Everything was light and fun and easy that night. I wish like fuck I'd taken it—and her—way more seriously before it was too late. Yeah, I could say I'd never come close to really caring about a woman before so I didn't recognize the symptoms. They crept up on me. Love is a sneaky bastard like that.

I want to rewind time to that night—was it really only twenty-two days ago?—and start over.

But I have to stop wanting what I want when I want it. It doesn't do me any good now.

I can only go forward...and I'm not sure how.

I breathe in the fresh air and watch the last rays of light disappear. The moon rises. It's waxing gibbous. Granddad taught me moon phases, along with lots of other fun stuff. Miles Ambrose was good at so many things. He sure did love my grandma before she passed away, too.

Why didn't I make him my role model and ignore my dumbshit father? Come to think of it, Granddad always disregarded Barclay Reed.

I guess I had to reach thirty-three to get half as smart as he was.

If he were here, he wouldn't tell me that feelings were pointless or stupid. He would tell me to feel them...and to figure out how to handle them so I can go about life like a man should—strong, confident, steady. With honor.

I scan the lanai again, absently trying to decide which chair will give me the best view of the sea so I can contemplate. I spot Keeley's yoga mat. She must have accidentally left it behind.

I peer at the purple rubbery thing standing in the corner. I roll it out. She always claimed that yoga centered her. Not precisely sure what that means, but I have a general idea and it sounds helpful.

Except...I'm staring at the mat with no idea what to do. There are poses, I know. I'm simply not sure what they're called or how to get into them.

Reaching for my phone, I open an exercise app I subscribe to. I'm usually doing a weight/cardio mixture for men. Now I click the button for yoga. A few seconds later, a woman in a gray tank and matching spandex pants, hair neatly pulled away from her face, is giving me a too-cordial smile I don't trust. She says her name is Chandra and welcomes me to the beginner's class.

I have this feeling she's going to kill me.

Immediately, she starts talking to me about blocks and blankets —huh?—all while assuring me I can do this. I'm physically fit, so I should be able to.

Still, she scares me.

The background music is both exotic and folksy. She tells me to do the easy pose. Thankfully, the visual lets me know she's sitting cross-legged. Why didn't she just say that? Then she instructs me to roll my shoulders and shake my head. After that, I'm supposed to put my head over my heart, my heart over my pelvis. What? I already have to contort myself? No, just sit up straighter. Okay. I can do that. I'm good...until she says I'm supposed to come into the moment with "integrity." What the fuck does that mean? Sighing in irritation, I decide to skip that part and press on.

Mostly because I can see Keeley doing this, which makes me feel weirdly closer to her.

From there, it's a lot of breathing and a little stretching. I probably need it. I have to admit that the deep inhalations and exhalations are calming my head a little. At least I'm not trying to think about fifty things at once. It's taking most of my mental energy to figure out how to press my palms together in a prayer pose and lift my sternum to my thumbs. It's not so awful...until we shift.

Suddenly, I'm sitting on my knees, back on my heels, and curling my toes under my feet. That doesn't feel good at all. I'm relieved when she instructs me to get into a tabletop position. I follow along, then realize I'm on all fours on my patio, wearing nothing but pajama pants. Any of my neighbors or the vacationers in the unit across the pool can see me round and sway my spine like a cat in heat looking for a good time.

Fuck whatever they think. This is for me. To better understand Keeley.

I'd rather pass on the downward dog stuff. Perched on hands and feet, my body in an inverted V shape, I kinda feel like a canine waiting for some random animal to come sniff my butt. Plus, my shoulders ache from holding up my weight for a few minutes while

I stretch my hamstrings and calves like I'm made of rubber. I'm totally relieved when we switch positions again and finally do some standing shit. Warrior poses are more my thing.

Then after a little more breathing and her telling us to take this grounded center through the rest of our day, it's over. I feel better... and worse. I'm definitely less scattered mentally. But the temporary Zen of focusing on the exercise is fast dissipating. Reality is crashing back in, as is my mental whine about missing Keeley.

With a curse, I roll up the mat and slip inside my condo, grabbing my laptop before I plop on the sofa. Magically, I manage some productivity. I answer a few emails, return a few phone calls to other agents. I even sort through the Stowe presentation for tomorrow morning, adding extra notes and incorporating some of the final research details we received earlier.

I'm as ready as I'll ever be. I'm still not sure I've chosen the right tack. The listing may already be Griff's. But I can't control that. I can only do my best, give the Stowes something to think about, and work my ass off the rest of the year.

I'll go through the motions of this pitch, but I'm not sure I care anymore. For weeks, it's taken my time and stolen my sanity. And it's cost me Keeley. Well, I helped, too, but...

I look at the clock. It's just before eight. Some people go to bed this early. And I'm feeling exhausted. The sofa in my office must have had a former life as a torture rack in a medieval dungeon. I'll be replacing it ASAP. I'm grateful that I'll be sleeping in my bed tonight, except...I still can't decide what to do about the sheets. Change them and get rid of Keeley's scent altogether? Once it's gone, it's gone. But if I sleep on the sheets, I'll likely be torn between crying and fighting the urge to hump the mattress all night.

I feel like I should hand over my man card for even silently making that admission.

My stomach rumbles again, and I raid the last of what Keeley had in the fridge, then come back to my laptop. I'll deal with the great sheet debate later. I click open Facebook out of boredom… then remember that I accepted her friend request last week. Maybe she's posted something.

At the time we became "friends," I was so wrapped up in the Stowe deal that I didn't look through her timeline, but I should be able to see her pictures now. I'd like to see snapshots of Keeley as a kid, of her adventures around Maui. I wonder if she posts her bar crawls with girlfriends, political rants…or her innermost thoughts.

When I click her picture from my friends list, the first thing that pops up is a change in her status. In big letters, a post last night proclaims that she's now in a relationship with Griffin J. Reed. There's a selfie of the two of them somewhere on the beach as the sun sets, his arm wrapped around her waist. My stomach free-falls to my toes—and beyond. Twenty-four hours after their first date, and Keeley is already fucking committing to my brother?

And when did Griff get a personal Facebook account? He hates making his private life public.

In the next instant, my chest implodes. Then a whole slide of symptoms I'm beginning to know well set in. I can't breathe, can't feel my fingers, can't find calm.

I jump to my feet, pace, trying to figure out how all this has happened. I fucked up. I admit it. I've even tried to tell Keeley that. But Griff will be no better. He's the sort of man to walk away from his own son, and she knows that. Why is she willing to be "in a relationship" with him so soon? I was with her for three fucking weeks. I got to know about her, care about her. I even tried yoga for her. And I can't believe she chose him instead.

I also wonder why Griff is suddenly feeling so public about his commitment. He was never a PDA kind of guy, even with Britta, and now he's practically proclaiming his love for a woman he barely knows all over social media?

Of course I wanted my brother to like her. Yeah, I expected him to dig her. But…this?

I want to hit something, strangle him. I already know if I did, it wouldn't be enough to release the valve building pressure inside me. Fuck, it's growing, straining my ability to hold it in. My panic is going to swallow me whole.

Maybe I should blame her or be angry that she's already jumped in my brother's bed. It would be easy, yeah. But I'm the one who sent her out my door. So no matter how much I want to slam my fist into a wall, I'm going to swallow it down, suck it up, and get my shit together.

I guess there's no such thing as a panic attack prevention hotline, and Keeley's not here anymore, so I'm on my own.

What would she tell me to do?

Meditate.

Fuck. At this point, I'll try anything.

I scroll through my apps and come to one that's supposed to boost the selected brain activity. There's specialized music and nature sounds for focused work, which I use during crunch time. There's also a section for deep sleep and naps. And meditation. I tap on the button for the guided tour because what do I know about this shit?

The dude tells me he's going to walk me through an effective technique I can use whenever I feel stressed or overwhelmed. Like now. Good. Can I lie down for twenty minutes? Sure. It's not as if I've got anything better to do now that Keeley isn't coming back. He's asking me to clench and relax each of my muscles systematically to release the tension and increase circulation. All right. Whatever.

More closing my eyes, focusing on my breathing, and looking inward while trying to block out the pain. This guy wants me to think peaceful thoughts. I snort. If I could, I wouldn't be here. But he insists I should be feeling my body let go.

I try to adhere to the spirit of his words. But...my mind drifts. I think about the last time I saw Keeley. I knew something was off. I recount my conversation with Britta on Tuesday night. My assistant is right. Keeley didn't feel valued when I chose the Stowe deal over her. How much better would I feel if I could tell her how untrue her assumption is? Would she listen? Maybe not because those are just words. They're easy to say. But what if I showed her? Would she still be choosing Griff if she really knew how much I love her? I drafted a plan a mere two days ago. I just need to update it a bit, go the extra mile, and implement.

When my "tour guide" calls me back to full alertness, I feel a little better. Meditating didn't necessarily make me feel as if I've had a spiritual awakening or a major hug with peace. The good news is, I'm no longer going to lose my mind and do something stupid like hurl chairs over my balcony...or hunt Keeley down right now and insist she talk to me. But the better news is, I'm dedicated to getting her back. Having a plan makes me feel more in control. I have a lot of action items to put in motion, but that's all right. I have ammo and I have persistence.

I will not rest until I make that woman mine for good.

Suddenly, my phone dings in my pocket. It's probably Britta texting me. Again. For two days, she's been harping about two things: whether I'm ready for tomorrow morning's presentation and whether I know what happened between Griff and Keeley. I don't really want to answer either of those questions. Mostly because I can't.

With a tired sigh, I pull my phone from my pocket. Maybe my assistant wants to make sure I intend to wear clean underwear tomorrow, too. Or have shiny shoes. We're doing this presentation over Skype, so I don't think George and Vivienne Stowe are going to get a good look at my undergarments or loafers.

I'm shocked when I glance down and see Keeley's name on my display. Her message is short and to the point.

You promised to meet your brother at a time and place of my choosing for one hour, no arguments. Tonight. Nine p.m. Merriman's in Lahaina.

I stifle the urge to reiterate via text that I fucked up and I'm sorry. She's heard all that and was unmoved. Instead, I try some-thing new because...well, I have to. `I value you more than my brother ever will. Where are you so I can tell you how I feel in person?`

No reply.

She's a smart, stubborn woman, so I'm not surprised. I'm crushed to know that she's with Griff. Part of me is hoping that she's merely trying to teach me a lesson. A guy can dream, right? Yeah, I know I lost her fair and square. She must already have my brother wrapped around her finger if she's able to convince him to meet with me, something that nothing else—not even finding out he had a son—could accomplish.

The realization hurts like hell. But I'll do my best to move past it, man up, and be better. Someday, somehow, someway, I will win Keeley back, put a ring on her finger, make her Mrs. Maxon Reed, and love her forever.

The screen tells me it's eight thirty. Britta and Rob would disap-prove of me going out now. We agreed to have a calm evening and get a good night's sleep so we'd be crisp and ready to do another practice run first thing in the morning before the real presentation.

Fuck that. Griff knows where Keeley is, what she's doing, how she's feeling... And I need to know because she is way more impor-tant than any listing, any paycheck, any prestige.

I'm going to prove that to her once and for all.

AFTER DRAGGING on a clean shirt and a nice pair of pressed pants, I make my way to Merriman's. It's a classy place on a little peninsula, surrounded by ocean and overlooking Kapalua Bay. Lots of weddings and other special events are held here. When they lived on the island, my parents celebrated their wedding anniversary at this restaurant every year. Mom would always insist we kids come along, probably so she didn't have to be alone with Dad. At the time, I resented her because I would ten times rather have been playing video games or hanging out with friends. Can't say I blame her now. I refuse to be alone with that asshole, too.

I wonder what prompted Griff to pick this place tonight. He never liked it much. Except their pineapple and macadamia nut bread pudding with rum sauce. That was a hit with me, as well.

Technically, their dining room closed half an hour ago. Their sign says they should be locking up now. A native man in a subdued tropical print shirt and beige slacks is waiting for me at the door. He ushers me in, then closes up behind me.

Across the room, near the open doors leading to the deck and the ocean beyond, I spot my brother. He's looking right at me, jaw clenched. Not much has changed except that he looks harder, angrier. Bitter. Closed off.

Why the fuck is he mad? He got the girl—at least for now.

We're the only patrons left in the joint, and Griff stands as I approach. Not out of deference, I realize. He simply doesn't want the psychological height disadvantage of me towering over him any more than I would if our situations were reversed.

"I didn't think you'd come." He gestures to the chair opposite him at the table.

I proceed cautiously to my seat until he does the same. "I promised Keeley I would be here where and whenever she chose. I'm keeping my word. Where is she?"

He won't tell me, I'm sure. But it's worth a shot.

"She doesn't want to see you now."

Those words make confetti out of my heart. Yeah, they hurt that bad. I suck in a breath, try to rein in the pain. Winning Keeley back will be a marathon, not a sprint. I have to remember that. I have to hang tough.

"She left her yoga mat on my lanai. I'd like to give it to her."

Griff raises a dark brow at me, silently asking me if that's the best I've got. "I'll buy her another one."

That grates at me...mostly because he can. Because she's apparently chosen him. "I'll return this one. Tell me where to find her."

"Seriously, she won't see you now," he reiterates, his tone more forceful.

"All I need is five minutes." *Which I can hopefully parlay into the rest of our lives.*

I don't beg my brother. If I thought it would do any good, I would blurt every bit of my regret and love. But I know better.

"Look, Maxon. You're a lot of things. A bastard, a son of a bitch, and a shitty-ass brother. But I know you're not stupid. The answer is no."

I'll put it aside for now, but I'm not giving up.

"Why are we here? Isn't this place closed for the night?"

Griff nods. "I sold the owner a new pad about six months ago. He told me the doors were always open for me. So when Keeley insisted we have a conversation, I figured this was neutral ground. Apparently she thinks an hour is all it will take for us to patch up our differences."

I snort. "Did you tell her that's impossible?"

He reaches for a tumbler of whiskey I hadn't noticed just beside his elbow and cuts a stare at me. "You think it is?"

Griff thinks it isn't? Does he want to make up? That would be a sudden change in tone.

I sit back and study him. But I still can't figure him out. What does he want?

Suddenly, a bartender sets a Grey Goose martini in front of me. My brother remembered my drink of choice? He should, I guess. We drank together for a decade. But it's still unexpectedly nice.

A waitress approaches us next with two dishes of bread pudding and sets one each in front of Griff and me. The haupia ice cream is already beginning to melt and mix with the oozing rum sauce. The bready confection is covered in candy nuts. It smells divine. I remember it as an orgasm for my mouth.

But I'm not particularly interested in dessert right now.

I stare across the table at my brother and drink my vodka concoction. "If you and Keeley are going to be 'in a relationship,' then yes. It's impossible."

He cocks his head, stares. The fucker is dissecting me. He's good at it, too. "She means something to you."

It isn't a question.

I'm not ready to confirm his supposition. I've already given him way too much to use against me.

"Are you only here to make your new girlfriend happy or do you have something else to say?"

Griff's mouth slides into a cynical smile. He doesn't answer for a long minute. I can't tell whether he's enjoying my suspense or he has an outcome in mind and is trying to figure out how to get there.

"Just for grins, let's say Keeley's feelings have nothing to do with my reason for tonight's peace accord."

As he digs into his bread pudding, I ponder his answer. If he's not here for Keeley, I can only think of two other possible reasons why he's come, both equally unlikely. Well, almost equally. "Your pitch today went badly?"

It must have. The even less likely scenario, that he's here strictly to repair his relationship with me, can't possibly be true.

He hesitates for a long minute, his face giving nothing away. Finally, he gives me a slow nod. "Disaster."

I'm shocked he replied at all, much less that he was so honest. "And you want my appointment with the Stowes tomorrow to try again?"

That infuriates the fuck out of me. He used the feelings he must know I have for Keeley to drag me here to steal my hard-won opportunity out from under me. I hustled, I sweated, I thought outside the box, and I prepared like hell.

None of that matters now.

He hasn't confirmed that's what he wants but...

I lean across the table and glare his way. "What are you willing to give me for it?"

I'm hoping like hell he says Keeley. Negotiating for a woman is a bit more underhanded than I'd like, but all Griff can give me is a chance to speak to her. I'll still have to win her back on my own.

"I didn't say I was in the trading mood." He leans closer, too. We're almost nose to nose. He's wearing that amused smirk again that makes me want to rip his face off.

"You didn't say you weren't in the trading mood, either."

"Touché." He shrugs as if conceding the point. "All right. I want something."

But he won't tell me what?

Suddenly, I'm tired of this cat-and-mouse game. Every minute we live out this stupid charade is another moment that Keeley is somewhere else thinking that I love a fat commission check and my big reputation more than I love her. "C'mon, you bastard. Spill it."

"What if you're right? What if I was willing to trade my knowledge of Keeley's whereabouts for your appointment tomorrow?"

I don't hesitate a second. "Done."

And happily. I don't care if Rob quits. I'll figure something out. Britta might still leave me, too. I can handle that. For Keeley, I can handle anything.

As long as I get her back.

My brother raises a brow at me. "You're serious?"

"I've never been more serious in my life. I will trade you my appointment for the chance to explain everything to Keeley. You can have my notes and my goddamn presentation, too. It's better than your verbal pyrotechnic and ticker tape parade crap. They want subtle."

Suddenly, he laughs. "You're right. I didn't see that and I didn't listen."

That's a huge admission for Griff. He *hates* to confront the fact that he's wrong—ever.

On the one hand, it's gratifying to know Keeley and I were right. Not so much because I wanted to beat Griff, although it doesn't hurt. Mostly because I feel like I've learned something about being not only a better Realtor but a better man from this experience. She's helped me so much.

"If you'll arrange for me to meet her tonight, I'll hand everything over to you. Every note, every idea, every slide. It's yours. In return, I expect you to end whatever you've got with her and to fuck off. You don't get to see her again. She's mine. And she's going to stay that way. You will forget every minute of every day—or night—you spent with her." When my brother looks as if he's going to protest, I shut him down. "Look, you asswipe. I'm potentially giving you one point seven million dollars for this privilege *and* the title of the number one agent on the island. So I don't want to hear another fucking word."

"I wasn't going to object. I simply had a few questions."

He probably wants me to paraphrase the presentation so he can be sure it's up to snuff. Fuck him. "It's going to sell the Stowes. Don't worry about that."

"I'm not." He shakes his head. "Do you love her?"

Why is he asking? First, I've already shown my hand in the most obvious way. Second, why the hell does it matter to him? "Do we have a deal?"

"Yes or no, Maxon? Do you? I'm not budging until you answer me."

I chug the rest of my drink and slam the stem on the table. "Yes. Of course I love her. I made a huge mistake the day she disappeared from my life. I know that. I've tried to tell her..." I toss my head back and draw in a deep breath, looking for patience and calm. "I've been a fucking mess since she left."

Griff smiles. It's the first genuine curl of his lips I've seen him wear in...well, years. "I should tell you a story."

What? I just admitted that I'm falling apart and I'm completely in love, and Griff wants to blab out some tale? "Now?"

He holds up a finger. "It's relevant, I promise. You might eat your dessert before it becomes a puddle."

I look down and see that my ice cream is rapidly liquefying. I'm not broken up about it, per se. But the dish is in front of me. Wasting it seems a shame, and Griff is going to pontificate about something, so I might as well keep busy while he does.

The first bite is heaven. The next is no different, just sweeter. I moan. "This shit is good."

Griff laughs, and it's almost like old times, hammering out how we're going to approach a client or a property over a meal. We did it so often when we were business partners. I miss it. I miss him. Even though I've spent the last three years thinking I hate him…I don't. I can't. I don't respect him for being a dick to Britta. And I'm pissed as hell that he even looked twice at Keeley, but that's my fault far more than his.

"Yeah." He finishes another bite of the dessert, then wipes his mouth. "It's the only thing, besides the view, I ever liked about this place."

"Ditto." Too many memories of uncomfortable anniversary dinners here for me, too. "All right. Tell me your story."

My brother sucks in a deep breath and lets it out as if he's gearing up to say something major. "When I left following the secret deal and your split with Tiffanii, I…um, had trouble sleeping and concentrating. Four months later, I started seeing a therapist."

I rear back. Griff stating that is basically an admission he's not perfect—something he's sorely resisted owning up to in the past.

"For the record, now that I have nothing to lose, I didn't stab you in the back over the 'secret deal.'"

Griff rubs at the back of his neck. "I've suspected that for a couple of years."

I can't help it. I stare at him like he's the most ridiculous bastard on the planet. "Why didn't you call me, then?"

"Honestly? I didn't think I could. I'd fucked up so big. I thought you would hate me forever, especially after I compounded one mistake with another by moving Tiffanii in with me. She told me so many lies… That you cheated on her. That you'd been working that secret deal for months and hiding it because you wanted all the glory and profit. That you got her pregnant and threw her out."

That fucking pisses me off. "You believed that? It's utter bullshit!"

He holds up a hand. "I know that. Now."

"Why did you believe her at all?"

"She came up with just enough paperwork to be persuasive. Somehow, she copied the signature page of your listing agreement with that prince, which included the date...but none of the terms about confidentiality. She recorded a video of her pleading with the locksmith who re-keyed your place the day you threw her out. She even had a positive pregnancy test from her doctor. No idea how she manufactured that..." He sighs. "I think at the bottom of all that, I heard Dad's voice telling me that partnering up with the competition wasn't blending forces to make something better, just cooking up my own demise."

Yeah, I've heard that speech of his about ten thousand times myself. I remember fighting the pull of his constant browbeating and brainwashing when Griff and I were kids and during most of our partnership.

"I believed in us," I grind out between clenched teeth. "We were doing great things."

He nods slowly. "Amazing things. But I needed someone to help me get my head on straight."

"So you saw a therapist?"

"Yeah. Dr. Wilson was useless. Couldn't stand her or her leading questions. It seemed like she talked more than she listened. But she had this receptionist... At first, I noticed her because she would send me apologetic glances when I stormed out. Finally, she started talking to me. Small talk at first. But she sounded so compassionate, you know. Eventually, those chats led to longer discussions outside the doctor's office. She asked me questions that really made me think. It wasn't long before I realized that this woman who merely answered the phone was far more helpful than the woman with

PhD after her name. So we started having coffee, walking along the beach. She listened. She played devil's advocate. And she refused to take a dime for helping me."

That's pretty selfless. "So what *did* she want?"

"Nothing. A friend, I guess." He shakes his head as if he's still not sure. "To help. That's who she is. Anyway, she told me I'd been wrong. She's been telling me that for over two years." He laughs at himself. "She's the first beautiful woman I've ever spent hours and hours with and didn't want to nail."

Kind of like me with Britta. "Yeah. Platonic friendships with a woman are a mind blower the first time you have one."

"Totally. This receptionist really opened my eyes. At first, we talked about my anger. Slowly, we started talking about my child-hood. And we talked a lot about you."

I'm suddenly wishing I had another martini. The tone of this conversation has been shockingly positive until now...but I can't stop thinking it can still take a turn for the worse. "What did she conclude?"

He looks up at me, his hazel eyes full of gravity. "That I need my brother in my life."

When Griff looks like he's working hard to tamp down emotion, it grips me in the chest, squeezing everything between my ribs until I can't breathe. My brother has never been emotional. Hell, I never have, either. But his words hit me in the middle like a two-by-four, knocking the breath out of me. "What do *you* think?"

He shrugs, dragging his fork through the remnants of his dessert, as if looking at me is too much to take.

"She's been right about so many other things. She knows people. Really gets them." He finally looks my way, and I see more stark emotion he's barely managing to hold back. "I suspect she's right about this, too. She sure reamed me a new one after I called you the other night about Dad. She told me I was looking at the situation all wrong. In retrospect...I was a stupid hothead. She was right about that, too. She's really helped me get my head screwed on straight in about every facet of my life. She introduced me to healthy food, yoga, and meditation." He looks up at me, brow raised. "Sound familiar?"

It takes me about half a second to make the connection. Once I do, I swear I can barely breathe. "Keeley?"

"Yeah."

His confirmation is a complete bombshell. "She's been your friend for more than two years?"

He nods. "The best."

"So…" She was a plant? A spy? A…what? "Was any of her relationship with me real?"

"Let me finish explaining. Then everything will make sense."

When I nod numbly, I have to resist the urge to hurry him up and put me out of my misery. I can't stand the thought that Keeley doesn't love me a fraction as much as my heart beats for her.

Thankfully, Griff doesn't drag it out.

"I just want you to know that I never have touched Keeley, not even once."

"She said you kissed her the other night."

"On the cheek, like I always do. That's it. I probably would have come apart a long time ago if she wasn't one of the best friends I've ever had. I was never going to muddy that with sex. And she's wanted to meet you forever…"

I think through what he's really saying and the truth whacks me in the face. "It wasn't a coincidence that she was in that bar the night we met. Or that she zeroed in on me."

He shakes his head. "She's been insisting for some time that I wasn't going to be whole until you and I cleared the air. Well, she also thinks I need to resolve things with—" He stops himself, shakes his head. I see agony on his face. "The important thing is, the day you called the Stowes to drum up business, I got fucking furious. I was ready to unleash a shit storm on you. Keeley took me aside—again—to remind me about love and tolerance. Forgiveness. I was trying. But that afternoon, I told her I was going to go to that shitty bar and beat the crap out of you. She tsked at me."

I can actually picture the moment. "She does that a lot."

"Yeah, but she's usually right. She suggested that she should meet you at the little dive instead. I called Gus, the guy who owns the place, and paid him a hundred bucks to let her sing." He drags in a breath. "She wanted us back together…but she wanted to meet you first, get the lay of your land, and see the best way to approach you. When you propositioned her about distracting me, she was worried that you extracting revenge would undo all the progress I'd managed and that if she didn't play along, you'd just find someone else to help you. What she didn't expect was to fall in love with you." He taps his fork against his plate. "Her relationship with you was totally real. You broke her fucking heart, Maxon."

I close my eyes. I'm still reeling from Griff's confession that he and Keeley are friends when he stabs me with the sharpest of his words. I doubt he means to…but that's how it feels. I can only blame myself. I know I'm a fucking wretch—but I'm still not giving up. "Hell, I broke my own heart with that stupid shit. But when Dad came by, then you called… It's no excuse for putting the Stowe listing over her. I just…fell into old hatred."

"That's what I told her when she showed up at my place in tears. Normally, I would suggest that two people in conflict work it out. That's what she's taught me. But before I let you see her again, I needed to know that you really love her."

I frown. "That's what tonight's meeting is about? Me proving that?"

"Yeah. I, um…used her Facebook status as a litmus test, to see if it would matter to you. You never lifted a finger to get Tiff back, so I had to gauge you somehow."

I grip the table. "Tiff was never important. Keeley is everything."

My brother murmurs his agreement. "After everything she's done for me, I put aside my pride, my past, my inability to apologize…" He laughs at himself. "I had to know if you'd changed enough to be worthy of her."

"I have," I swear.

"I see." He nods.

My head is still spinning with everything Griff has told me. But my goal is still completely clear and top of my list. "Good. I want to see her now."

A look of regret passes over his face.

She won't see me, period? It's my first concern. I panic. She can't do this, can't leave me. Well, she can but…no. We can't stay apart. I'll die if I can't see her again, at least one last time. If she can't forgive me, that's on me. But I have to at least tell her how damn sorry I am.

I'm already gathering arguments when Griff holds up his hands. "I'm not saying no. I'm just telling you that she's gone to Phoenix."

The bottom drops out of my stomach before logic sets in again. Okay, I need to get on the first flight out. I won't bother with a suitcase. I can buy shit there. I refuse to have her wondering even an hour longer than necessary how I feel about her and if I value her above all else. "I'm going now. Where can I find her?"

He's already shaking his head before I've finished speaking. "She's gone home to think. Left this morning. She wanted to see her mother and clear her head. She couldn't afford the ticket, and she's never asked me for anything, so I surprised her. She'll be back in a week…unless she decides to stay."

"What? She might not come back." After all, she's been trying to return to the mainland for years. "I can't leave her hurting and miserable. She can't make a decision without knowing how I feel."

"She needs this time," he warns. "You can't rush her, man. I've learned that about her. She sometimes gets upset or has her feelings hurt. You can't talk to her about what's happened or how that makes *you* feel until she's sorted through her stuff."

In some ways, I hate how much my brother seems to know

about my woman that I don't. The old me would have thought he
was lying his ass off to spitefully keep us apart. Now…I get the
feeling he's straight-up right. Getting up in her face would be the
worst mistake I could make. "Fuck."

"You've put her through a lot. She already knows you're sorry.
I'll tell her you gave up the deal. After that…she's got to want to
come back, Maxon."

I really despise how much he's right. "So I just have to sit here
for a week with my dick in my hand? C'mon…"

"If you do, I don't want the details," Griff drawls, then turns
serious again. "Do you know what you want to say if you do see
her again?"

"I think so." It's been solidifying in the back of my head since I
switched off the guided meditation and tuned back into my own
train of thought. "Do you, um…"

Griff raises a brow at me. Getting these words out is going to be
tough.

"Are you and I good?"

He swallows and looks away. "You tell me. I'm the one who
fucked up big."

I nod. Getting used to the idea of not hating my brother again
will take time, but now that we're here and I'm sitting in front of
him and we're talking without shouting? I don't want to give up
having him in my life again.

"Why didn't you even listen to me when I tried to tell you I
wasn't stabbing you in the back?"

He closes his eyes. "I was just so angry back then. Dad was on
me constantly about the fact that I was letting you beat me at everything. I probably could have handled that, but things at home
weren't right, either. Britta was hiding something. She'd closed
herself off. So when I found out about the deal and Tiffanii told me
her lies, I just exploded and…I was stupid. I'm more sorry than
you'll ever know."

For my brother, that's a huge speech. He sounds like he's

changed in a lot of ways. He's not perfect. Then again, neither am I. I'm still pissed at him for what he's done to Britta. But one problem at a time.

I stand and wait until he does the same, then I round the table and drag him into a hug. He crashes against me. We slap backs. It's all manly and shit. But it's also monumental and moving. And yeah, I find myself having to fight back tears.

"We're good," I assure him.

He pulls back, looking like he's trying not to lose his composure, too. "Let's do the Stowe deal together."

I've already promised him my notes, my preso, my appointment. I'm handing him the opportunity on a silver platter. "Are you serious?"

"Yeah. I let a stupid misunderstanding screw up our business. Once I didn't have you as my partner anymore, working with you was one of the things I missed like hell. I vote we do this deal together. If it goes well…maybe we can think about making it permanent again."

I pause. Think. In my head, I can hear our dad saying that I'm number one on the island and I'm demeaning my business to bother with Griff again. Then I remember how fulfilling it used to be. And I hear Keeley whispering that she's happy for us.

But I need him to answer one other question because I don't need history repeating itself. "Are you letting Dad stay with you?"

He recoils at the mere notion. "Fuck no."

"Still talking to him?"

"I'm done. He came storming into my place, all full of himself and ragging on you. I realized a few years ago that he's toxic, so I wasn't going to let him stay anyway. But when he told me about some of his conversation with you, it gave me some hope that you'd realized it, too."

"Totally," I assure him. "Let's do the Stowe deal…and think about resuming business together again." It would feel good. "But I might need one more favor…"

When I outline my plan to convince Keeley how much I love her, he smiles. "It's perfect. She'll be the happiest woman in the world if you do that."

As long as she comes back to Maui.

"I wish…" Griff lets out a rough breath as he sits again. "I wish things could have turned out better for me and Britta."

I don't know what to say. He turned his back on his pregnant girlfriend when she needed him most. Of course, that was then… and this is now.

I'm going to try like hell not to give my brother false hope. Britta says their ship has sailed. Maybe. I know she still has feelings for him…but I don't know if that's enough.

"It's not hopeless. But you've ignored Jamie for almost three years. I don't know if she can forgive that."

He frowns. "Who's Jamie?"

Is he for real? I'm trying to figure out if he's being sarcastic or if there's a chance he really has no idea what his own son's name is. I should answer but I'm only managing to gape at him.

"Who is this guy? I saw her about a month ago at a restaurant with a Hawaiian dude who looks like a banker. They were pretty cozy. I wanted to rip his fucking head off. Is that Jamie?"

Okay, I need to take a step back and challenge all my preconceived notions…like the one where Griff received Britta's letter advising him that he was about to be a father.

I scrub a hand down my face and stare at my brother. Shit. I hope like hell I'm not about to betray Britta, but I think Griff has a right to know.

"Jamie is James Tucker. His birth certificate says he's a Stone. But it should say Reed. He's your son. He'll be three in July." I whip out my phone and scroll through my pictures until I come to the ones I took the other night of him smiling while he played with his toy trucks.

Griff grabs the phone, looking stunned and stricken and so fucking confused.

Goddamn it, I should have known that he wasn't the sort of man to completely ignore his own flesh and blood. Now I really regret not confronting him about this a long time ago. I've done both my brother and my nephew a disservice.

"I… My son?" He's grappling for words, staring at the picture like he still can't fathom what he's seeing, fingers hovering over the screen as if he wants to hold his son badly.

"Yeah. He's adorable. Smart. Stubborn. Loved." I swallow. "Britta tried to tell you, I swear."

"She was pregnant when I walked out?" He closes his eyes and shakes his head, rubbing at his temples and looking as if he's fighting tears again. "I had no idea. Did she?"

"I don't know. She told me about a week after you'd gone."

"I have to talk to her. Now. Where is she? I know she moved after I walked out. I don't know where she went."

"She didn't have a choice. She couldn't afford the apartment you two had," I point out. And I can't help the scolding note creeping into my voice. "Besides, Britta wanted a house with a yard for Jamie. I've been helping her with rent since she found this place."

He stands and throws fifty bucks on the table. "Thanks. I have to go. Where can I find her? Please tell me. I'm helping you with Keeley, man. Don't shut me out."

"This isn't necessarily a *quid pro quo* situation. When you didn't respond to her news—"

"I didn't know," he insists.

"But in her eyes, you just didn't care. You left her to give birth and raise a child alone. She says she's moved on. I don't know this for sure…but I'm pretty sure she got engaged tonight."

Griff slaps his hands on the table between us, looking somewhere between agonized and enraged. "Where. Is. She?"

I think hard. I keep coming back to one conclusion: Britta loves him. And it looks a whole lot as if he still loves her, too. At the very least, a son deserves to know his father and decide for himself whether he wants the man in his life. Besides, if Griff hadn't been willing to come forward to talk to me about Keeley, I'd still be a miserable son of a bitch.

Sighing, I whip out a pen and one of my business cards. I write an address on the back and hand it over. "Go gently. You broke something in her. She's not the same woman. And I doubt she's alone."

Griff snatches the card out of my hand and claps me on the shoulder as he runs for the door. "Thanks. I'll call you early in the morning."

I pick up my phone from the table and pause over my open iMessage. Tell Britta she's got incoming…or not? Give her time to put her defenses up…or let whatever is going to happen between my brother and my assistant unfold naturally?

I slide the phone back into my pocket and head to my condo with a little smile.

I have my brother in my life once more. Soon, I'll be with Keeley, too. And this time, I plan to make sure she never wants to be apart from me again.

CHAPTER SIXTEEN

Keeley

*M*y head knows why I'm back in Maui. My heart still isn't sure.

The weather in Phoenix was sunny, warm, and much less humid. I had *amazing* Mexican food there—a must for me. The visit I shared with my mother did me so much good. She's happy with my stepfather, Phil. She even stopped wearing the locket with my dad's picture. She kept it because she'll always love him. But she also said she had to give her current husband equal devotion. The sentimental part of me wanted to argue with that logic, but I can't. She also said she tucked the locket away for another simple reason.

Living in the past isn't moving forward.

She's right, and that best explains why I decided to leave Phoenix for good.

Oh, I had options to stay. Mom and Phil claimed they were traveled out for a while after their amazing South Pacific trip and

offered to let me live in my childhood bedroom until I got on my
feet. The day I arrived, I was convinced I should. I could be perma-
nently closer to family and my roots. I could even see some friends
from high school. It wasn't as if I'd always planned to live on Maui
for the rest of my life. Since my existing professors were great about
working with me during my absence, I could have easily trans-
ferred my credits to Arizona State University and finished my
degree as a Sun Devil. After that, I'd have been able to get a job in
Phoenix that didn't involve tourism and came with better hours.

Best of all, if I'd stayed, I wouldn't have Maxon Reed around to
break my heart again.

But my mom is right. Living in the past isn't moving forward.

I don't belong in Phoenix anymore. The bittersweet week I
spent there clarified that.

So here I am, back in paradise. Lost.

I'm glad that Maxon and Griff finally made up and decided to
work together on the Stowe estate. They're already marketing the
property jointly to prospective buyers and getting a lot of interest,
according to the younger of the Reed brothers. That's great news.
They will finally be on the road to whole hearts. My work there is
done. Their future is looking up.

Where is mine?

I was really trying to decide that while I was in Phoenix. I
started to miss the ocean and trees and the sultry breeze on my
skin. I missed the incredible Asian food, the lazy pace of the days,
and the quaintness of Maui. I definitely missed Griff—one of the
best friends a girl could have. We talked nearly every day on the
phone…but it wasn't the same.

I didn't want to think about the sheer beauty of my adopted
home—or that tall, infuriatingly ego-driven, looks-like-a-god
Realtor I'm mad for—but I couldn't seem to think of anything else.
I still can't. No matter how I try to shove the memories out, they
creep back in. Maxon kissing me on the beach. Maxon holding my
hand as we toured the amazing plantation-style house with the

endless views, where I swore I could picture our future. Maxon trying to karaoke and leaning on me like a trusted partner and friend. Maxon making love to me on his bed that final, fatal night.

I think he loves me…in his way. But being second to his ambition, to his need to win at all costs, isn't something I can accept. I hope he understands.

I'm disappointed that I haven't heard from him since the night of the brothers' reunion. Griff says Maxon was devastated about our breakup and even volunteered to give up the Stowe listing to prove how much he cares about me. That shocked me…and gave me a glimmer of hope, I admit.

Maybe that's the real reason I decided to return to Maui. No denying how badly I want to be with him. I'm still afraid that I'll surrender myself and he'll break my heart once more. But my future isn't in Phoenix…and the romantic in me can't stop wanting Maxon to love me enough to put me first.

Yes, I know expecting him to change is unrealistic, which is why I'm as confused and conflicted as I was three days ago when I boarded the plane back to Maui. Since landing, I've picked up my phone a million times to call Maxon. And I've put it down again every time. I don't want to be wrong about him. I don't want to be hurt by him. I don't want to know that the magical connection we once shared is gone for good.

I'm not ready to face that.

I glance around the little sports bar, relieved to see the surprisingly thick crowd just before I take the stage. I spot Griff in front. As I peek out from behind the curtain shielding the employees' area, he waves. I wave back. He's sitting alone. I try not to let disappointment overwhelm me.

I guess that means Maxon either can't forgive me for my well-intended lies to reconcile him and his brother or he got over me quickly.

I should stop what-iffing because I can't live in the past. It isn't moving forward. Isn't healthy.

And trying to do it now is killing me.

I don't know what I expected from Maxon. More, I guess. But we were only together twenty-two days. Maybe it didn't mean that much to him after all.

I thought he was the love of my life. My soul mate. Actually, I have a feeling he still is—and always will be.

It's not his fault he didn't feel the same.

I meant well when I came into his life. Yes, I lied to him. I simply wanted to figure out how he felt about his brother and if he might have any forgiveness in his heart. When I got to know Maxon, I liked him. A lot. Of course, he was hot. And cocky. He was also different from anyone I'd ever dated. He made me laugh —usually with him, but sometimes at him. When he propositioned me about coming on to Griff, I realized it was the perfect way to achieve my end. Yes, I was insulted and annoyed at first. But then I saw the beautiful irony of his plan.

Unfortunately, nothing turned out the way I thought it would.

"Aloha, Lahaina. I'm Keeley Sunshine. I'm going to sing you some of my favorite songs, and since I'm a single girl who recently broke up with the man she loves, they'll probably all be about heartache."

After a smattering of applause, the little band behind me starts, and I launch into one of the saddest songs I can think of in this moment, Bonnie Raitt's "I Can't Make You Love Me."

The ballad's melancholy melody fills the space between my ears and hits me right in the heart. Every word is enveloped in a grieving note and seems to tell my story. It's a fight to sing without tears compromising my voice.

I'm not even sure how I'll make it through the end of the song. I try to focus on the subtle intricacies of the tune, my appreciation for the keyboard player Gus brought in to better fill the audial space of tonight's set list—anything but Maxon Reed and his absence.

The applause is somehow subdued and hearty at once. It

preserves the moment. I'm weirdly grateful that the people in the bar seem to understand my mood.

Right now, I have to revel in these small victories until I'm over Maxon and am able to appreciate the bigger ones again.

"This is a song that I've been listening to a lot over the past week. I remember it from high school and didn't quite understand it then. Now I completely comprehend the addiction Michelle Featherstone sang about."

The naked piano provides the sole melody for "Coffee and Cigarettes." The bittersweet notes rake across my senses as I close my eyes and sink into the ballad that totally describes my mood in this moment, where I feel as if I've given up the vices I hoped would make my problems dissipate, but my pain hasn't moved into yesterday, as the lyrics suggest it should.

The second verse is a blur. I know it's something about pouring booze down the kitchen drain. I'm not much of a drinker, much less a smoker, but I feel what she's saying about the loss of something you love...and equating it to someone you miss more than anything, even if they're bad for you. Often, the metaphor is more powerful than the straightforward explanation, so I'm grateful to music for helping me through this difficult spot in my life.

But now we come to the part of the song where I can't avoid admitting that I'm still blue, but I've finally figured out what I must quit.

"*You.*"

Some form of this sentiment repeats two times over, then I'm done with the song. It's already hard to breathe, and holding my emotions back is getting so damn near impossible. Why didn't I sing upbeat stuff? "Walking on Sunshine" or "I Got A Feelin'" or "Happy"?

Probably because I would have cried through those, too. Despite what Maxon may think about my "deception," I'm not a good liar. I only wanted the best for him and Griff. I try to be a good person and help others.

I never imagined in a million years how badly it would mess me up.

The small band begins the intro to the next song. I close my eyes and groan. Why did I ever imagine this was a good idea? Yes, I rasped out in the last song that I was going to quit him. It's logical. But, for better or for worse, I'm a girl who thinks with her heart, and Plumb's "I Want You Here" is a much closer representation of how I really feel.

This is another sad tune with a simple piano melody. Is the keyboard the new plucker of heartstrings?

I already know the song rolls and builds to a wrenching chorus. I doubt I'm going to make it out unscathed.

When the lyrics start, I'm thankful the song isn't really about romantic love. But too much of it echoes the sentiment in my heart, the fact that I can barely breathe because my ache is so deep. I've asked myself if it will ever heal.

In truth, I've spent days pondering that question.

I grip the mic desperately and try to hold on. I already know I have to change the whole next set. Everything I have planned is just sad and sadder. I'm a happy person by nature. I need to realize that this experience with Maxon was still valuable, even if we weren't meant to be. He's not my happily ever after, simply a lesson I needed to learn. I'm not sure what knowledge I was supposed to glean yet, but everything happens for a reason. I'll figure it out someday.

I just have to get through this last song, then I'll fix everything—from my set list to my personal life—and start grieving in private.

Then I sing that I'd waited so long for him to come into my life…and now he's gone. I wasn't prepared. I'm in agony. Maybe it sounds melodramatic, but I feel it.

I'm devastated.

Suddenly, I can't see anything. My whole world is blurry. I feel wetness on my face. Hell, I'm crying in front of the whole audience, actually shedding real tears down my face. Music has always been therapy for me, and it's probably good to get this out, but not in front of people who just want to be entertained.

I suck.

I'll stick to karaoke in the future, only songs that make people smile. Things I can breeze through and not have to feel all this drag-down of pain that's taken root in my soul.

I'm almost done. The end of the song is close. I just have to get through the part that rips me up the most…

I close my eyes and imagine Maxon in front of me as I sing how desperately I want him here, my voice a sorrowful cry.

There's a little bookend to the song that mirrors the beginning and wraps the whole thing up. I can't sing it. I just can't finish these lyrics. I have to get off this stage right now.

"I'm sorry, folks. I'll be back in thirty."

I try to run to the employees' section of the bar. Griff is waiting for me by the back curtain with a hug. I tumble into his solace and hear deafening applause from the audience.

"They liked it?" I choke.

"Yeah. It was real and raw. It was you," he assures with a smile as he drags me into a darker corner. "Even I felt it."

I'm grateful for the semi-privacy. Since the kitchen is right behind my escape drape, there really isn't any way of being alone. So I stay with Griff. "You? But you never feel anything."

That makes him laugh a little. "I know. Right?"

Wrong. Just the way he says it tells me he's feeling something far more than nothing these days.

"Where are you with Britta?" I change the subject.

I'd rather talk about anyone's problems—as long as they aren't mine.

His face shutters up quickly. The smile he wore becomes a grim press of lips. "She and I are going to come to an understanding. We're not there yet, but I intend to make sure we do."

What Griff means is that he has some outcome in mind, that Britta isn't cooperating, and that he's looking for some bargaining chip to ensure that she does. She ought to know that nothing and no one can stop the Reed men once they've set their sights.

On the other hand, Britta doesn't seem like a pushover. Maybe she'll put Griff in his place. God knows he needs it.

"I hope you guys can work it out for the best," I say diplomatically.

"Me, too." He drags me against his chest and hands me a tissue.

"I'm sorry again that I didn't tell you about Jamie when I first found out." I really do feel awful about that.

"You made the right decision. If you'd told me the night Maxon dropped the bomb on you, I would have hunted Britta down and made all sorts of demands. Maxon would have rushed to her defense. He and I would never have patched things up. Waiting another few weeks sucked...but it's better for the long-term big picture."

Relief melts me. Griff wasn't quite so understanding when we first talked about this. "Thanks for listening. I'm glad you understand."

"You've always had my back. Dry your eyes. It's going to be all right. Hey, I think Gus booked another act to liven the place up in between your sets. Want to see?"

"I should go to the ladies' room and try to repair my makeup. I'm sure I'm a mess and—"

"Three minutes," Griff says in a tone that's somewhere between persuasive and implacable.

I open my mouth to argue.

Then I hear the strains of a song I haven't heard in exactly two weeks, since the crazy night I dragged Maxon out for karaoke.

I tense. Freeze. Look up at Griff.

He's smiling, the expression between indulgent and superior. He knows what's up.

"This is for the beautiful woman I stupidly hurt. I could tell her that I love her but those are just words, and she deserves more."

My heart catches. I'd know that voice anywhere—in my sleep, a million miles from civilization, moments from death.

Maxon Reed.

With a gasp, I turn around and see him standing on the stage, holding the mic as the strains of the song continue to bloom in my ears.

He's looking right at me, his face full of apology and adoration and something I've never seen there before.

Love.

My chest heaves. I put my hands over my heart as if I'm afraid it will fall at his feet again. Fresh tears come. Is he really here for me? And is he going to sing?

He is. He does. And his ability to carry a tune is just as terrible as it was the last time, only now he actually knows the words and he doesn't seem to care what anyone else thinks. He's singing his heart out—literally. And he's looking right at me and as he vows that he needs me more than he wants me...and that he will want me—and only me—for all time.

My knees give out. I lose my composure completely.

Griff supports me with strong hands and guides me gently toward his brother. Maxon comes off the stage to meet me and wraps a supportive arm around me before he brushes his thumb over my cheek and wipes away my tears.

As the song's instrumental interlude begins, he relinquishes the mic to the stand. Who cares if anyone sings the rest? All I want is the man in front of me.

I stare up at Maxon's face, his green eyes caressing me with a heartfelt devotion I never thought I'd see from him.

"I'm sorry," he murmurs. "So sorry. What I did was wrong and thoughtless and not at all indicative of the fact that, in my heart, you'll always come first."

Words fail me. I know he means that, not because he's spoken but because he's now shown that he'll sacrifice everything—his career-making deal, his need to best his brother, even his substantial pride—for me.

He loves me.

I sob into his chest.

He crooks a finger beneath my chin. "Hey, I'm here and I'm not going anywhere. Did you see what I'm wearing?"

I'm still hoping all of this means that he wants me back as I send him a watery gaze. "Wearing?"

What does that have to do with anything?

Then he shows me the timepiece on his arm. Black band, white face with Roman numerals. Cartier. "My grandfather's watch. I realized I never wore it because I didn't feel like a man of honor. You changed that. You changed *me*."

I send him a teary smile of hope. I wish I could stop crying, but I'm an emotional girl.

I also admit when I've done something wrong, too. "I'm sorry I didn't tell you the truth about who I was and why I was here when we met. I meant well, I swear. I knew Griff needed you in his life... and I figured you needed him, too."

"You're right." He waves my apology away. "If I had known you'd come for Griff, I wouldn't have listened to any of the important things you had to say about changing my life and embracing love. That man didn't deserve the truth—or you. But I'm going to spend the rest of my life being worthy of you because I love you."

With a kiss on my forehead, he drops to one knee and pulls a box from his pocket, then flips the lid open. It's a simple solitaire winking at me from a thin gold band. It's striking and beautiful and perfect. Everything inside me stops.

He's proposing?

I hold my breath. "Are you serious?"

He nods. "Marry me, sunshine. Please say yes. Nothing will ever again be more important to me than you. I promise."

I know some women might hold out longer, want to make him suffer and squirm. They would want to make sure he learned his lesson thoroughly. But I think he has, and that's not how I roll. I love him. Why would I risk losing him again by saying no? If he screws up, I'll remind him of his priorities.

With a watery nod, I urge him to his feet. "Yes!"

"Oh, thank fuck." He sounds relieved.

I laugh in joy. The audience claps and cheers uproariously. Then I cry again as he slips the ring on. It hugs my finger just right.

"I'm glad you said yes because I have another surprise for you." He whips out a set of keys from his pocket, along with a business card of a hammock on a beach. It reads SUNSHINE COAST BED AND BREAKFAST. The address matches the house we toured together, the one in which I pictured our happy future. It lists the proprietors as Keeley and Maxon Reed.

I gasp as thrilled disbelief courses euphoria through my veins. "You…you bought the house?"

"For you. When we met, you said you wanted to be happy. I'm going to make you delirious." He grins at me. "Is it working so far?"

"Yes." I nod like an idiot because I can't imagine being any happier. "This is perfect."

"Good. We already have our first booking eight weeks from now. It's the beginning of our future." He looks near tears, too. He's holding me close, and I feel so cherished. "Tell me you love me."

The way he searches my eyes for my heart nearly takes me out at the knees again. I have a feeling he'll be doing this every day.

"I love you, Maxon Miles Reed," I vow.

"And I love you, Keeley Sunshine Kent."

I giggle. "That's not my middle name."

"Whatever." He shrugs. "It fits you. Just like you fit me. You're my everything, sunshine."

It hits me in that moment that he's mine to kiss and tease and feed every day. He's mine to laugh with and make love to every night.

I can't imagine a better ending than that. A million emotions pelt me, and I wish I could tell Maxon everything I feel. I guess I could try…but I know a better way.

After a glance at my ring sparkling under the muted lights overhead, I kiss my fiancé—I can't believe I can call Maxon that—then lean over to the band and clue them in.

Then I grab the mic with a sniffle. "Aloha, Lahaina. I'm a red-eyed but very happy Keeley Sunshine. I just have one more song for my groom-to-be, then I'm going to go start the rest of my life with him."

The obliging little band starts the music. Now I'm particularly grateful Gus brought in a keyboard. This song would be lost without it.

As Ruelle's "I Get to Love You" starts, I can't contain my smile or my joy. It's sparkling and sweet and hopeful, just like this moment.

I'm going to cry through this ballad, too. But it's a good cry. The happiest cry.

Because Maxon has made me the happiest woman imaginable.

As the song winds toward its close, I look his way and sing every word to him. I promise to love him and always choose him because I'm forever his and I'll forever say "I do."

The bridge picks up about love being a journey. I can't dispute that at all. I sing the song's title a few times, blinking at the happy tears filling my eyes.

Then he comes forward to wrap me in his arms and meet my gaze with the promise of forever. "I get to love you, too. And I always will, sunshine."

Want to see how Griff fights ruthlessly to claim Britta?
Read More Than Need You **now!**

I discovered my ex's secret. Now I'll do anything to win her back.

MORE THAN NEED YOU
More Than Words, Book 2
By Shayla Black
(available in eBook, print, and audio)

I'm Griffin Reed—cutthroat entrepreneur and competitive bastard. Trust is a four-letter word and everyone is disposable…except Britta Stone. Three years ago, she was my everything before I stupidly threw her away. I thought I'd paid for my sin in misery— until I learned we have a son. Finding out she's engaged to a bore who's rushing her to the altar pisses me off even more. I intend to win her back and raise our boy. I'll have to get ruthless, of course. Luckily, that's one of my most singular talents.

Sixty days. That's what I'm asking the gritty, independent single mother to give me—twenty-four/seven. Under my roof. And if I have my way, in my bed. Britta says she wants nothing to do with me. But her body language and passionate kisses make her a liar. Now all I have to do is coax her into surrendering to the old magic between us. Once I have her right where I want her, I'll do what-ever it takes to prove I more than need her.

EXCERPT

I cup her hand tighter. "I was a bastard. Three years ago, I didn't value you the way I should have. I didn't love you the way I meant to. I…" Finding the right words is harder than I imagined. "I never meant to hurt you. But I know I did."

She's had a long time to lovingly craft creative curses to rain on my head for the shit I did to her. I'm expecting to hear a litany of them. Instead, hurt flashes in her eyes. "What do you want me to say, Griff? What are you looking for? Absolution?"

"Be mad. Yell at me. It's okay. I'll answer your questions. I'll stand here and take your anger. Whatever will prove I'm serious. Whatever you need to feel better."

"I don't feel anything at all." She wriggles free and turns to retrieve another chair.

Liar.

So she doesn't want to talk? Well, some situations call for more than words. They've never been my strong suit anyway.

I take the second chair from her grip and set it in the corner beside the first. Then I wrap my fingers around her elbow and give a gentle tug. She stumbles against me. Our chests collide. She gasps. Her head snaps back. I pull her body closer to mine. Our eyes meet.

"Angel," I whisper as I cradle her cheeks in my hands and drop my head. She barely has time to draw another breath before I settle my lips over hers.

Then I'm kissing Britta again after three long fucking years.

A million sensations hit me at once. I inhale her familiar jasmine scent. I caress the velvet of her face, her nape. I hear her rapid intake of breath. Heat burns my veins. I'm melting. Her touch feels so electric. I'm dying. Holding her again is so stunning. Arousal hammers me—heart pinging, breaths sawing, cock hardening. But my feelings aren't the same as before. Now they're desperate. They're so yearning. So deep.

They're the feelings of a man who finally understands love—and has been given a second chance to give it back.

Touching her is also a comfort, like coming home after a long war. I feel as if I've fought myself and exorcised the demons of my past. I'm unshackled but I'm so chained to her that I'll never be free. I don't want to be.

Memories of the hundreds of times I stripped her bare, physically and sexually, and left her blushing and smiling and panting my name bombard me. I'm haunted by the times she told me she loved me and I said nothing in return.

Against me she's frozen in shock. Her body is tense. Her fingers are splayed wide on my chest where they landed when she tried to catch her balance. She's not moving her lips against mine. And goddamn it, I crave her response. I have to know I'm not the only one willing to give us another try.

With a groan, I brush my lips over Britta's again. If anything, she goes stiffer. I breathe against her and try like hell to coax her. I almost back off. But…she's not yelling at me. She's not shoving me away.

I try one more time, giving her a suede-soft slide of my lips over hers. Then suddenly, she trembles under me. Her fingers begin to curl into my shirt. I sense that she wants to give in…but is trying so hard not to.

"Kiss me." I nudge her mouth open and hover. "Just once. I've missed you like hell."

The still moment hangs, suspended. Then finally she exhales and closes her eyes. Her arms curl around my neck. A little moan escapes the back of her throat as she tilts her head, parts her lips for me…

And she invites me in.

Are you craving a nail-biting, alpha-male seduces good-girl story? Meet One-Mile and Brea.

He's ruthless. She's off-limits. But he's just met his one weakness… Now nothing will stop him from making her his.

WICKED AS SIN
One-Mile and Brea, Part One
Wicked & Devoted, Book 1
by Shayla Black
(available in eBook, print, and audio)

Pierce "One-Mile" Walker has always kept his heart under wraps and his head behind his sniper's scope. Nothing about buttoned-up Brea Bell should appeal to him. But after a single glance at the pretty preacher's daughter, he doesn't care that his past is less than shiny, that he gets paid to end lives…or that she's his teammate's woman. He'll do whatever it takes to steal her heart.

Brea has always been a dutiful daughter and a good girl…until she meets the dangerous warrior. He's everything she shouldn't want, especially after her best friend introduces her to his fellow operative as his girlfriend—to protect her from Pierce. But he's a forbidden temptation she's finding impossible to resist.

Then fate strikes, forcing Brea to beg Pierce to help solve a crisis. But his skills come at a price. When her innocent flirtations run headlong into his obsession, they cross the line into a passion so fiery she can't say no. Soon, his past rears its head and a vendetta calls his name in a mission gone horribly wrong. Will he survive to fight his way back to the woman who claimed his soul?

EXCERPT

Finally, he had her cornered. He intended to tear down every last damn obstacle between him and Brea Bell.

Right now.

For months, she'd succumbed to fears, buried her head in the sand, even lied. He'd tried to be understanding and patient. He'd put her first, backed away, given her space, been the good guy.

Fuck that. Today, she would see the real him.

One-Mile Walker slammed the door of his truck and turned all his focus on the modest white cottage with its vintage blue door. As he marched up the long concrete driveway, his heart pounded. He had a nasty idea how Brea's father would respond when he explained why he'd come. The man would slam the door in his face; no maybe about that. After all, he was the bad boy from a broken home who had defiled Reverend Bell's perfect daughter with unholy glee.

But One-Mile refused to let Brea go again. He'd make her father listen…somehow. Since punching the guy in the face was out of the question, he'd have to quell his brute-force instinct to fight dirty and instead employ polish, tact, and charm—all the qualities he possessed zero of.

Fuck. This was going to be a shit show.

Still, One-Mile refused to give up. He'd known uphill battles his whole life. What was one more?

Through the front window, he spotted the soft doe eyes that had haunted him since last summer. Though Brea was talking to an elderly couple, the moment she saw him approach her porch, her amber eyes went wide with shock.

Determination gripped One-Mile and squeezed his chest. By damned, she was going to listen, too.

He wasn't leaving without making her his.

As he mounted the first step toward her door, his cell phone rang. He would have ignored it if it hadn't been for two critical facts: His job often entailed saving the world as people knew it, and this particular chime he only heard when one of the men he respected most in this fucked-up world needed him during the grimmest of emergencies.

Of all the lousy timing…

He yanked the device from his pocket. "Walker here. Colonel?"

"Yeah."

Colonel Caleb Edgington was a retired, highly decorated military officer and a tough son of a bitch. One thing he wasn't prone to was drama, so that single foreboding syllable told One-Mile that whatever had prompted this call was dire.

He didn't bother with small talk, even though it had been months since they'd spoken, and he wondered how the man was enjoying both his fifties and his new wife, but they'd catch up later. Now, they had no time to waste.

"What can I do for you?" Since he owed Caleb a million times over, whatever the man needed One-Mile would make happen.

Caleb's sons might be his bosses these days…but as far as One-Mile was concerned, the jury was still out on that trio. Speaking of which, why wasn't Caleb calling those badasses?

One-Mile could only think of one answer. It was hardly comforting.

"Or should I just ask who I need to kill?"

A feminine gasp sent his gaze jerking to Brea, who now stood in the doorway, her rosy bow of a mouth gaping open in a perfect little *O*. She'd heard that. *Goddamn it to hell.* Yeah, she knew perfectly well what he was. But he'd managed to shock her repeatedly over the last six months.

"I'm not sure yet." Caleb sounded cautious in his ear. "I'm going to text you an address. Can you meet me there in fifteen minutes?"

For months, he'd been anticipating this exact moment with Brea. "Any chance it can wait an hour?"

"No. Every moment is critical."

Since Caleb would never say such things lightly, One-Mile didn't see that he had an option. "On my way."

He ended the call and pocketed the phone as he climbed onto the porch and gave Brea his full attention. He had so little time with her, but he'd damn sure get his point across before he went.

She stepped outside and shut the door behind her, swallowing nervously as she cast a furtive glance over her shoulder, through the big picture window. Was she hoping her father didn't see them?

"Pierce." Her whisper sounded closer to a hiss. "What are you doing here?"

He hated when anyone else used his given name, but Brea could call him whatever the hell she wanted as long as she let him in her life.

He peered down at her, considering how to answer. He'd had grand plans to lay his cards out on the table and do whatever he had to—talk, coax, hustle, schmooze—until she and her father both came around to his way of thinking. Now he only had time to cut to the chase. "You know what I want, pretty girl. I'm here for you. And when I come back, I won't take no for an answer."

LET'S GET TO KNOW EACH OTHER!

ABOUT ME:
Shayla Black is the *New York Times* and *USA Today* bestselling author of roughly eighty novels. For twenty years, she's written contemporary, erotic, paranormal, and historical romances via traditional, independent, foreign, and audio publishers. Her books have sold millions of copies and been published in a dozen languages.

Raised an only child, Shayla occupied herself with lots of daydreaming, much to the chagrin of her teachers. In college, she found her love for reading and realized that she could have a career publishing the stories spinning in her imagination. Though she graduated with a degree in Marketing/Advertising and embarked on a stint in corporate America to pay the bills, she abandoned all that to be with her characters full-time.

Shayla currently lives in North Texas with her wonderfully supportive husband and daughter, as well as two spoiled tabbies. In her "free" time, she enjoys reality TV, reading, and listening to an eclectic blend of music.

Tell me more about YOU by connecting with me via the links below.
Text Alerts
To receive sale and new release alerts to your phone, text SHAYLA to 24587.
Website http://shaylablack.com
Reading order, Book Boyfriend sorter, FAQs, excerpts, audio clips, and more!
VIP Reader Newsletter http://shayla.link/nwsltr
Exclusive content, new release alerts, cover reveals, free books!

Facebook Book Beauties Chat Group http://shayla.link/FBChat
Interact with me! Wine Wednesday LIVE video weekly. Fun, community, and chatter.
Facebook Author Page http://shayla.link/FBPage
News, teasers, announcements, weekly romance release lists…
BookBub http://shayla.link/BookBub
Be the first to learn about my sales!
Instagram https://instagram.com/ShaylaBlack/
See what I'm up to in pictures!
Goodreads http://shayla.link/goodreads
Keep track of your reads and mark my next book TBR so you don't forget!
Pinterest http://shayla.link/Pinterest
Juicy teasers and other fun about your fave Shayla Black books!
YouTube http://shayla.link/youtube
Book trailers, videos, and more coming…

If you enjoyed this book, please review/recommend it. That means the world to me!

OTHER BOOKS BY SHAYLA BLACK

CONTEMPORARY ROMANCE
MORE THAN WORDS

More Than Want You

More Than Need You

More Than Love You

More Than Crave You

More Than Tempt You

More Than Pleasure You (novella)

Coming Soon:

More Than Dare You (July 28, 2020)

More Than Protect You (novella) (TBD)

WICKED & DEVOTED

Wicked As Sin

Wicked Ever After

THE WICKED LOVERS (Complete Series)

Wicked Ties

Decadent

Delicious

Surrender to Me

Belong to Me

Wicked to Love (novella)

Mine to Hold

Wicked All the Way (novella)

Their Virgin Concubine

Their Virgin Princess

Their Virgin Hostage

Their Virgin Secretary

Their Virgin Mistress

Coming Soon:

Their Virgin Bride (TBD)

DOMS OF HER LIFE

(by Shayla Black, Jenna Jacob, and Isabella LaPearl)

Raine Falling Collection (Complete)

One Dom To Love

The Young And The Submissive

The Bold and The Dominant

The Edge of Dominance

Heavenly Rising Collection

The Choice

The Chase

Coming Soon:

The Commitment (Late 2020/Early 2021)

FORBIDDEN CONFESSIONS (Sexy Shorts)

Seducing the Innocent

Seducing the Bride

Seducing the Stranger

Coming Soon:

Seducing the Enemy (June 25, 2020)

STANDALONE TITLES

Naughty Little Secret

Watch Me

Dirty & Dangerous

Her Fantasy Men (novella)

A Perfect Match

THE MISADVENTURES SERIES

Misadventures of a Backup Bride

Misadventures with My Ex

SEXY CAPERS (Complete Series)

Bound And Determined

Strip Search

Arresting Desire (novella)

HISTORICAL ROMANCE

(as Shelley Bradley)

The Lady And The Dragon

One Wicked Night

Strictly Seduction

Strictly Forbidden

BROTHERS IN ARMS (Complete Medieval Trilogy)

His Lady Bride

His Stolen Bride

His Rebel Bride

CPSIA information can be obtained
at www.ICGtesting.com
Printed in the USA
LVHW052212080321
680888LV00015B/2829